PEG'S Stand

SATAN'S DEVILS #6

MANDA MELLETT

Disclaimer

This is a work of fiction. Names, characters, businesses, places, events and incidents are either the products of the author's imagination or used in a fictitious manner. Any resemblance to actual persons, living or dead, or actual events is purely coincidental.

Warning

This book is dark in places and contains content of a sexual, abusive and violent nature. It is not suitable for persons under the age of 18.

ISBN: 978-1-912288-09-0

AUTHOR'S NOTE

Peg's Stand is the sixth in the Satan's Devils MC series, but can be read as a standalone.

If you're new to MC books you may find there are terms that you haven't heard before, so I've included a glossary to help along the way. I hope you get drawn into this mysterious and dark world in the same way I have done—there will be further books in the Satan's Devils series which I hope you'll want to follow.

If you've picked this book up because, like me, you read anything MC, I hope you'll enjoy it for what it is, a fictional insight into the underground culture of alpha men and their bikes.

GLOSSARY

Motorcycle Club – An official motorcycle club in the U.S. is one which is sanctioned by the American Motorcyclist Association (AMA). The AMA has a set of rules its members must abide by. It is said that ninety-nine percent of motorcyclists in America belong to the AMA

Outlaw Motorcycle Club (MC) – The remaining one percent of motorcycling clubs are historically considered outlaws as they do not wish to be constrained by the rules of the AMA and have their own bylaws. There is no one formula followed by such clubs, but some not only reject the rulings of the AMA, but also that of society, forming tightly knit groups who fiercely protect their chosen ways of life. Outlaw MCs have a reputation for having a criminal element and supporting themselves by less than legal activities, dealing in drugs, gun running or prostitution. The one-percenter clubs are usually run under a strict hierarchy.

Brother – Typically members of the MC refer to themselves as brothers and regard the closely knit MC as their family.

Cage – The name bikers give to cars as they prefer riding their bikes.

Chapter – Some MCs have only one club based in one location. Other MCs have a number of clubs who follow the same bylaws and wear the same patch. Each club is known as a chapter and will normally carry the name of the area where they are based on their patch.

Church – Traditionally the name of the meeting where club business is discussed, either with all members present or with just those holding officer status.

Colours – When a member is wearing (or flying) his colours he will be wearing his cut proudly displaying his patch showing which club he is affiliated with.

Cut – The name given to the jacket or vest which has patches denoting the club that member belongs to.

Enforcer – The member who enforces the rules of the club.

Hang-around – This can apply to men wishing to join the club and who hang-around hoping to be become prospects. It is also used to women who are attracted by bikers and who are happy to make themselves available for sex at biker parties.

Mother Chapter – The founding chapter when a club has more than one chapter.

Patch – The patch or patches on a cut will show the club that member belongs to and other information such as the particular chapter and any role that may be held in the club. There can be a number of other patches with various meanings, including a one-percenter patch. Prospects will not be allowed to wear the club patch until they have been patched-in, instead they will have patches which denote their probationary status.

Patched-in/Patching-in – The term used when a prospect completes his probationary status and becomes a full club member.

President (Prez) – The officer in charge of that particular club or chapter.

Prospect – Anyone wishing to join a club must serve time as a probationer. During this period they have to prove their loyalty to the club. A probationary period can last a year or more. At the end of this period, if they've proved themselves a prospect will be patched-in.

Old Lady – The term given to a woman who enters into a permanent relationship with a biker.

RICO – The Racketeer Influenced and Corrupt Organisations Act primarily deals with organised crime. Under this Act the officers of a club could be held responsible for activities they order members to do and a conviction carries a potential jail service of twenty years as well as a large fine and the seizure of assets.

Road Captain – The road captain is responsible for the safety of the club on a run. He will organise routes and normally ride at the end of the column.

Ronin – A biker who travels alone, sometimes wearing a patch denoting he's Ronin. Not affiliated to any club, but often bearing a token which will help ensure safe passage through territories of different clubs.

Secretary – MCs are run like businesses and this officer will perform the secretarial duties such as recording decisions at meetings.

Sergeant-at-Arms – The sergeant-at-arms is responsible for the safety of the club as a whole and for keeping order.

Sweet Butt – A woman who makes her sexual services available to any member at any time. She may well live on the club premises and be fully supported by the club.

Treasurer – The officer responsible for keeping an eye on the club's money.

Vice President (VP) – The vice president will support the president, stepping into his role in his absence. He may be responsible for making sure the club runs smoothly, overseeing prospects etc.

Brothers protecting their own

CONTENTS

Chapter 1

Peg

As her hands toy with her drink, Lorelei gives me sly glances through her eyelashes while pretending to examine her glass on the table. A glass full of Californication. A concoction of vodka, gin, white rum and tequila topped up with lemon and orange juice, the bartender had explained merrily as he made it after I, feeling awkward and out of place, had blundered through my request for the cocktail. I hadn't missed his smirk at me, a hardened biker being forced to ask for such a girly drink with the suggestive sounding name.

Lorelei might be sneaking looks at me, but I'm subjecting her to equal scrutiny. Being here tonight is scarcely different from being on a blind date, neither of us knowing much about each other, our first time meeting in the flesh.

The Satan's Devils clubhouse is rapidly changing, brothers finding old ladies, fuck, having babies as well. We've even got a room set up as a fucking nursery. Has it made them go soft? Nah, I see even more of an edge around my brothers who've gone from having a different woman in their bed every night to taking that special one to be a permanent fixture in their life. Their desire to keep the women they love safe sharpening them, giving them new balance. A new focus, and a new meaning to the word protection.

It's not been difficult for them to remain faithful to their old ladies. Once each of them found their soulmate, that seems to be it for them and, watching from the side lines, I've no doubt their relationships will last forever. Over the years I'd gotten used to Bullet and Viper being married, but lately the status quo has been turned upside down with Wraith, Drummer, Slick, and Dart in quick succession finding their mates. And even Heart has managed to find happiness for a second time.

My single brothers still don't understand what makes a man want to settle down, each vowing there's more fun to be had making use of readily available sweet butts or the hangarounds who come to our parties, or, for that matter, any female who catches their eye. Me? All I've ever wanted was to find that one woman I could love, who'd give me a place to come home to and reason to live. I've watched with envy as my brothers have settled down.

That's what I want, an old lady and, hopefully, a couple of kids. Now that would make my life complete.

I thought I had it once, but it was an illusion. Sure, being burnt has made me cautious, but since then nothing resembling anything like the right woman has crossed my path. Which brings me to tonight, the result of an impulse to join the twenty-first century and try online dating.

I've not lied to her, she knows exactly who and what I am. We'd spent weeks communicating via instant messaging. Complete disclosure on my part at least, well, as far as I could without discussing club business. I hoped that it had been on hers. I'd been amped up to meet her tonight, neatening my beard, and even, with hopes but no expectation, grooming my man garden. I'm wearing aftershave, something I don't normally bother to do, and under my cut is a crisp white button-up shirt.

She's pretty enough but looks aren't as important as they were when I was younger. She's wearing a nice dress which outlines her curves, ample breasts, slightly rounded stomach, and hips I could hold onto as I fuck her from behind. Her body is topped by a pleasant enough face, sufficient to interest me.

I'm thirty-seven years old, and time's getting on. Perhaps the reason I'm still alone is that I've been too fussy, so rather than allowing her thin lips or slightly overly large nose to put me off, I try and concentrate on the woman underneath, listening to what she says, hoping that nothing she's telling me is a lie.

She's told me about her family. I don't have much to reciprocate, there's nothing to tell about mine. Fuck knows who they are. I ask about her job, her likes and dislikes, and so far, so good, in many of the important ways we seem to be compatible.

"Like another?" I offer, though I hope she says no. I don't like my women drunk. Any offer she might make has to be put forward sober. I won't take advantage unless it's with full and conscious consent.

"No." A quick smile, then, "I've had enough, thank you." *Another point in her favour.*

A glance at my phone shows me it's time to bring this evening to an end. I finish my beer, then stand up. "I'll settle the tab, then take you home."

A nod, another quick smile. As I go to the bar I turn to confirm the burning sensation I feel on my back is indeed, as I suspected, her eyes staring at me. I wink, she blushes, but before she turns away I've seen a spark flare in her eyes.

I'm not too bothered how this night is going to end, in her bed or with just a kiss on the doorstep while we arrange another date. Slow burn, that's the best way. A chance to really get to know each other before we commit. I can be patient. It's been months since I last went with a woman. I avoid the sweet butts in the club, not having much inclination to indulge in meaningless sex just because it's on offer. I want the act to mean something, and to be with a woman who's all mine, not one who's been used by everyone else.

At my age, I know I won't find a virgin, or probably even a woman who hasn't had a committed relationship before. I'm not looking for perfection, just someone who's perfect for me. I know she'll probably have baggage, like Lorelei, who's divorced. I wouldn't even mind if she had a kid.

What I won't compromise on is that spark which must be between us, both in and out of bed. I want to be the man she respects and looks up to. I want her to be my strength, my reason to get up every morning. I want to be her best friend, and her mine. Paying the tab, I turn back to the table, a little uncertain. Tonight's not yet shown whether Lorelei can be any of that for me. Yeah, take this slowly. That would be best.

I hold out my hand and help her out of her chair, then walk her to the door of the restaurant, my hand to the small of her back. I frown at a man who's blocking our way, and that's all it takes before he steps aside with a murmured apology. At my truck I take her around to the passenger side and open her door, helping her step up, then find and pass her the seat belt. Once she's settled comfortably I go around to the driver's side, slipping out of my cut as I do so, not wanting to collect a fine for wearing it in a cage.

I'd picked her up from a location where she'd asked to be met, a friend's house I assume. Now she gives me directions back to her home. A frown plays at my lips, wondering whether I should warn her. She still knows virtually nothing about me. I could have been lying, leading her on, my nefarious purpose to harm her or rob her. Any caution goes unuttered. I'm a man and she's an attractive woman. I keep my mouth shut.

When we arrive, I tell her to stay put until I can help her down. I slide back into my cut, then once she's steady on the ground, hold her hand and walk her to the front door with every expectation she'll turn and wish me a good night. Then I'll leave, possibly after having made arrangements to see each other again.

Instead, she fumbles in her purse, extracts a key, and puts it in the lock. As she opens the door, she says over her shoulder, "Are you coming in?"

I inhale sharply. "If you're sure."

"Oh, I'm sure."

Is she asking me for a drink, or a coffee, or something more? Not wanting to get my hopes up, even though my cock starts to swell—well it has been months since it saw anything other than my hand—I nod as nonchalantly as I can, and step over the threshold.

Once inside, she shrugs off her light jacket, worn more for fashion than for any actual need—it is late spring after all—then turns to look at me.

"I've wanted to say this all evening," she starts in a husky voice. "Thank you for your service."

As her hand comes out to land on my chest, I control the urge to flinch. It's not her touch, it's her words. I didn't put my life on the line with any virtuous thought of serving my country. It started as an offered alternative for prison, for some minor infraction which they went down on me hard being as I was already in the biker life. Believing I was simply swapping one set of brothers for another, I took the escape route and had no regrets. Sure, sometimes it was hard, the conditions rough and demanding, but what young man doesn't like playing with guns and a real-life version of shoot 'em all up? That there was a possibility of dying never crossed my mind, a young man's arrogance that nothing could harm him guiding me. A belief that my team could take on anything and survive.

Until we didn't. I lost friends and received a medical discharge. Had I not, I'd have done a few more tours. I was enjoying myself, simply exchanging one desert for another, one set of rules for a not so different way of life.

No civilian should thank me. I didn't do it for them, and, well, the way that it ended, for my friends that weren't as lucky as me, insincere words so easily uttered aren't nearly enough.

A guilty twinge goes through me, I can't look her in the eye. I'm the man I am now, not the soldier I was then. If she's expecting a hero, she'll be disappointed. I've met women like Lorelei before, in both my lives. Giddy young girls wanting to snag a biker, or older women, disregarding anything else but the fact that I'd served.

In reply I just nod, acknowledging her comment, hoping she's not going to press it. I'm uncertain, not sure whether I can be what she wants me to be, and on the verge of leaving, when fuck me, she turns and says cheekily over her shoulder, "Unzip me?"

My brain might be having second thoughts, but my cock thinks she's made a brilliant suggestion, and my hands start moving of their own volition, as if receiving instruction from the wrong head. Fastening undone, the flimsy material falls to the floor, and now she's standing in front of me naked, except for a lacy bra and matching panties in a pale green. Her skin is unblemished, her ass decent enough.

My hands move automatically, now touching her waist, and turning her to face me, I trail my fingers down her breasts over the material. Her nipples peak and her eyes become lidded, and a little gasp escapes her mouth. *She's moving quickly.* Fuck, we've barely stepped over the threshold. Now I've overcome most limitations, but know only too well where I'm most comfortable, and fucking standing up in the hall isn't it. Especially if I'm auditioning her for a position as my old lady. Our first time shouldn't be frenzied, instead taken slowly and relished.

"Where's your bedroom, sweetheart?"

"This way." A breathy response, and my hands fall as she turns around, her arm reaching back to wrap her fingers around mine as she leads me into her private domain. As she walks off she's swinging those hips, a sight enjoyed by my cock, making it jump in anticipation.

My dick might be leading me, but my brain's weighing mixed feelings. If this is the woman I'll be going to make mine, it feels wrong to jump into bed after just one date. *I should leave now.* She'd be disappointed and feel rejected. *If she's the right one, she'll understand.*

Even if she's not, my cock says persuasively, *take what's on offer.* Placing the heel of my hand to my dick, I attempt to get him to see reason, but as she looks back, and I see her teeth worrying at her lip, taunting me, offering my swollen organ release for the night, my thinking head gets overridden. *If this is just one night, I'll take it.* It's a clear invitation, no need to feel I'm stepping where I'm not wanted. Two adults, no harm, no foul.

After my slight hesitation, I get my feet moving, and for my reward receive a beaming smile as I follow her into a very feminine bedroom.

"I want to see you." Wasting no time, she lies prone on the bed, propped up on her elbows. She sounds eager as she waves her hand from my head to my toe. "I want to see *all* of you."

What man can refuse such an instruction, especially when there's an almost naked woman splayed out on her bed offering up everything?

I smirk, knowing I'm in peak condition, and if it's muscles she's after, that's what she's going to get. I also have no concerns about my endowment. Yeah, I'm not being modest when I say I'm built to impress.

I remove my cut, putting it carefully down on a chair, then slowly unbutton my shirt. If she wants a striptease, I'll give it to her. My smirk widens as I notice her eyes sharpening, and her tongue coming out to lick her lips as I slip my arms out of my sleeves. I work hard in the gym and know I've got a decent six pack, almost an eight, and I don't carry an ounce of fat.

As I turn slightly to put down my shirt, I hear a sharp indrawn breath. "Turn around."

I do. I've only two tattoos; one for my fallen brothers on my arm, and the large Satan's Devils patch on my back.

"Wow."

I grin, that one word showing me she appreciates them.

When I turn back I can see a flush all over her fair skin, and it's not because it's warm in the room. *She likes what she sees.*

Encouraged, I give a suggestive thrust of my hips before tantalisingly lowering the zip. My jeans fall open, but my boxers beneath hide everything except a large bulge. I'm a big man, standing six-foot-five, and every part of my anatomy matches. Her eyes fasten on the clear object of her desire, and once again she moistens her lips. *If she wants a taste, I'm not going to protest.*

I might not have fucked for a while, but I'm no stranger at this. Before going further, I sit down and take off my boots, then stand again, with my back facing her—hey, she's got to wait a minute before she gets a close look at the goods—take off my jeans, then unstrap the prosthesis on my leg. Metal parts and love making don't mix. Now getting to my one remaining foot, I balance easily, hop around, the high bed hiding the part of me that's missing, and put my hands at the waistband of my boxers.

She's lying back, head on the pillows, hands behind her head, staring entranced as I make her wait.

"Go on, then." The encouragement sounds hoarse.

Grinning widely, I slide down my boxers with a flourish and drop my ass on the bed, sliding myself up with the intention to cover her….

She shrieks, covering her mouth with both hands. I'm well endowed, but not that much. As I rear up in confusion, she jumps off the bed and runs to the bathroom.

For a moment, as I hear retching sounds, I can't connect them to anything I've done, my first thought being she's eaten something that's disagreed with her. I'm so used to my body, I don't even think about it nowadays, but, could it be…?

Looking down at my missing leg, I shake my head. Full disclosure, I'd told her what happened to me, carefully explaining what she would be faced with, or rather what she wouldn't if we ever got down to do the deed. My stump completely healed over years ago now, apart from bones and muscles that should be there, and which are missing, there's nothing unpleasant to see. She knew. I'd told her. She said she'd be fine.

My mind's whirring. Whatever, the woman whose body I thought I'd be sliding into is instead throwing up in the next room. With no sex in the cards, I strap back on my prosthesis and pull up my jeans, putting back on my socks and boots. I'm reaching for my shirt when she reappears, her face pale, her hair wet at the edges where she's just washed her face.

I stand, unsure what to do or what to say, but she shakes her head as I try to approach her, her hands held out as if making an invisible barrier.

"I'm sorry. I thought I could do it. Thought I'd be able to ignore it."

It *is* my leg. I roll back my head and close my eyes, fighting to push down my anger. "No need to be sorry," I say in clipped tones. An apology doesn't cut it with me. As far as I'm concerned, I could have fucked her as well as any other man. If she'd been taken by surprise it would have been different, but I'd made sure that I'd explained. Hell, there's been times I'd forgotten to give a warning and the girl I was with had been shocked—now that I could better understand.

Her voice, which I'd thought pleasant earlier, now grates. "But I thought I could do this. You know, fuck you…with your leg like that."

Something hits me. It's more about her tone, a thought niggling at me. Forming my features into my normal expression, the one I wear as sergeant-at-arms for the Satan's Devils MC, the countenance she hasn't yet seen, I take a step towards her. She takes one back, I take another. She tries to mimic me but comes up against the wall.

Placing a hand over her head and leaning my weight on it, I narrow my eyes. "What are you fuckin' sayin'?"

Her eyes flit to my hand as if I'm caging her in. Her lip quivers, and goosebumps rise on her skin, still only covered in that lacy underwear that I now have no difficulty ignoring. Without looking down, her hand indicates my leg. "I wanted to do my bit. You know, you vets need someone to take care of your needs."

A damn pity fuck. She'd had me fooled right up to the last moment.

I stare at her for a second before tearing my eyes away, grabbing my shirt and cut, exit the room and the house before finishing getting dressed. Uncaring what anyone who sees me might think, unable to trust myself to stay in that bitch's vicinity, let alone keep in any words which might have come out of my mouth. I get into my truck, lay my cut on the passenger seat, and button up my shirt with shaking hands.

Does she really think I can't get my needs filled by any number of willing women? I know there are a few women who have fetishes and like to fuck amputees, but at least they're upfront about it, though I'm not particularly keen on being used in that way. Just like I don't want a woman to force herself to be with me only because I've lost half my leg. Pity fuck indeed. She's done more damage tonight than any other woman who might have turned me down.

She's lucky I don't hit women. Ever. If she'd been a man we'd likely have been extending Road's dirt bike track, where all the bodies are buried. She led me on. Not because I was a biker, not because of any prospects I might have had. What she wanted was far more deviant, to fuck a vet with only one leg. *To do her bit.* Well fuck you, Lorelei. I don't need it.

It takes me a minute to calm myself down. I've met women aplenty, women attracted by the cut that I wear, women who like an ex-soldier, and even some of those women who get off on going with an amputee. Never one who was trying to force herself to fuck me despite her delicate sensibilities.

My missing leg doesn't define me. Neither does the fact I ride with the Satan's Devils nor that I did time in service for my country.

I put the truck into gear and pull out into the night, trying to put the fuck-up of an evening out of my mind.

Where am I going to find a woman who likes me simply for me?

The clubhouse is full by the time I return. Jayden must be babysitting, as all the women seem to be here. Sophie's sitting on Wraith's lap, Drummer has Sam lying half across him. Slick's got his arm around Ella, and Heart's fussing over Marcia. Even Viper and Bullet are over at the bar with their old ladies. After the night I've had, I've no desire to join them and have happy couples rubbed in my face.

Before anyone notices my arrival, I turn around, heading up to my suite to swap the keys of my truck for those of my bike. A good ride and hopefully the night air will clear my head and put all thoughts of Lorelei behind me once and for all.

Lorelei. Fuck. What parents name their daughter after a siren that lures sailors to their deaths? Perhaps her name alone should have been enough to warn me off.

Chapter 2

Darcy

You *hit* me." My hand goes to my burning cheek, and my watering eyes open as far as they can. The forceful slap had come completely out of the blue. No one's ever raised their hand to me before.

He's standing in front of me, entirely unrepentant. "You asked for it. How the fuck was I to know where you'd been?"

"Where do you think I was? I was working."

Glancing pointedly at the clock, he shakes his head. "You should have been back hours ago. It's fucking eight o'clock at night."

"I can't just leave. That's not the job that I do." Half of me wonders why I'm even having this conversation, wasting time trying to justify myself. The blow must have been hard enough to stun me. "Look, let's just admit this isn't working out." I ignore his indrawn breath and incredulous look, and my brow creases as I think things through. "We don't have the type of relationship where you have a right to question me. And now you've overstepped the line. It's late. You can sleep here tonight, but I want you gone in the morning."

He stands straight, pulling himself up to his intimidating full height, his face darkening. "What did you say?"

Ignoring his menacing tone, I try to explain. "I know you wanted more from me, but we're not compatible, and I've never looked at you in that way. This was never going to be anything more than a temporary arrangement." When I'd given him a place to crash, I didn't expect it would be for more than a few days. Now it's been weeks, and in that time, he's been lounging around *my* house, eating the food *I* bought, as well as drinking *my* beer. Lots of beer. Probably the reason for his unexpected behaviour tonight, and why I'm not throwing him out right away. I'll give him a chance sober up enough to drive first. Don't want my colleagues to have to deal with another MVC, or motor vehicle crash, as most people know them.

I've underestimated him. He moves quickly, his muscular arms bulging as his hand fists in my hair. "You bitch. Kick a man when he's down, why doncha?"

My generosity had led me to letting him move in after there'd been a fire at his apartment, making it uninhabitable. Normally I'd help put out the fire and leave, but Pete Mercer had been tall, well built, as well as good looking, and with his general thanks to the firefighters came a more personal invitation to take me for a coffee. Once sitting across the table, he'd been so charming as he told me about having nowhere to stay. He didn't ask for anything, the suggestion of my spare room I came up with all by myself, only later wondering why. He'd jumped at my offer, and hadn't hesitated moving in.

He might have had the looks and the type of build I go for, but I quickly realised that alone wasn't enough to attract me. We had nothing in common, and unfortunately, it became clear early on that he thought I was offering more than what I'd put on the table. After a fumbled kiss which left us both embarrassed, and my explanation that the deal was simply board and lodging to help him out while he was setting up a new place to live, he'd thankfully kept his distance. I'd expected him to find alternative accommodation long before now, but it obviously hadn't been on his list of priorities. After tonight's performance, it appears he had an ulterior motive in dragging his heels. *He thinks he's got rights over me.*

Why did I let him stay? As I warily watch this wild-eyed *stranger* in front of me, I can't believe I hadn't seen he was unstable before. I suppose initially I enjoyed having a companion around the house, helping to share the chores, keeping the yard tidy, and doing the jobs that I hated, but that was when he'd been on his best behaviour.

When he'd buttered me up sufficiently, with excuses he had to wait for his insurance to come through, I hadn't put up much of an argument when he asked to extend his stay. That's when he started to change, but so slowly it took a while for me to notice.

I wasn't prepared for the signs he was becoming possessive, or when he expected, after a long and tiring shift, that I'll come home, cook dinner, and tidy up after him.

The yard's now a mess, he hasn't been out there for weeks. Me throwing him out might have been too long in coming, but now he's blown it. I've made up my mind, and nothing he can say will change it.

Looking at him warily, I realise tonight is the first time I've actually been afraid of him, and conscious of the physical disparity between us. *He's a big man.*

The observation makes me keep myself calm. "I'm not kicking you when you're down," I try to say reasonably, stupidly ignoring the fact that he's drunk, and this talk would be better left for the morning. "You knew when you moved in this was only for a short time. And you want something from me that I'm not prepared to give. I clearly don't see you in the same way you see me. You're my housemate, not my boyfriend, and can make no demands on my time, or question where I've been." House-mate? I don't really know how to label him. Renter or boarder doesn't fit. He's not paid me a penny in rent. I put a little more strength in my voice as I add, "You're going to have to move out and find somewhere else to go." *And someone else to sponge off,* I add, but don't say out loud.

He tightens his grip on my hair. "I'm going nowhere. And," he looks disparagingly up and down my body, "you can't make me."

He's got a few inches of height over me, and his muscles, well, he's either dedicated to working out or taking steroids of some sort. I'm not weak by any sense of the word, but he's right, I couldn't get the better of him physically. Realising he must really have tied one on tonight to get in the state he is now, I try not to let him see how much he's scaring me and continue to keep my tone even. "Pete. Be reasonable, will you? This man isn't you, and if this is what I drive you to, it just shows how anything more between us would be wrong…"

The hand not holding me swings for my face again, this time his fist connects with my nose. I'm lucky it's not his right hand, I'm sure he could hit harder, but it's enough to make it bleed.

Even the sight of my blood doesn't give him pause, but he does let me go, by first swinging me around by my hair then dropping me. I hit the wall, then the ground. Stunned, I can only watch in fear as he stares down at me. "I'm going to bed. And that will be the last we'll have of this discussion. I'm going nowhere, *sweetheart.*" After sneering the last word, he does what he says, and I can see he's entering my bedroom, not the guestroom as usual. *Does he expect me to join him in there? Or is he just so drunk he's made a mistake.*

I lie still, stunned and hurting, wondering what the hell just happened. He might have revealed himself as inherently lazy and slovenly, and a bit overbearing at times, but never violent before. I have no idea how to handle it. One thing I do know, even though this might be my house, I've no chance of bodily turning him out, and to stay here could well be inviting worse. *Especially if he gets impatient waiting for me.*

I've a few rest days coming up, and quickly I decide to put them to use. Although it's late, I'll drive to my parents in Phoenix. Perhaps, after he's admonished me for letting such a brute into my home, my dad will have some advice on how to rid myself of my unwanted guest. Or then again, maybe not. At least I'll be out of Pete's reach and somewhere I can plan my next move.

Pausing only to get some tissue to mop up the blood running from my nose, and to gingerly touch it to check it's hopefully not broken, I collect my purse and car keys and leave the house, closing the door quietly. I act fast, not wanting him to come out and demand why I haven't followed him to bed.

I'm not sure which emotion is at the fore, as different ones hit me one after the other. Anger that I've been forced out of my house, disgust with myself for not fighting back, and dismay that I hadn't seen what monster I'd invited into my life. I drive on autopilot, only thankful that the streets are relatively empty this time of night.

I'm tired as hell—it had been a long, trying shift. I'd got home hours after I should have clocked off. But in my job, you don't punch out at a set time, you stay until the job's done. Pete's never understood, never shown me compassion when I've come home tired, bearing the weight of the world on my shoulders.

I should have given him his marching orders a long time ago. Or better still, never have offered him a room.

Worrying how I'm going to get him out of my house, it takes me a moment to notice my car feels wrong. It jumps forwards, then stutters back, the engine noise sick sounding. *Shit, don't let me break down.*

But tonight's really not my night. The engine cuts out, and now I'm coasting onto the hard shoulder. The electrics are fine, the dashboard's lit up, and a red light flashing shows in my panic and pain, I've forgotten one thing. *Pete must have used my car and didn't refuel it.*

I'm stuck on the I10 just outside Tucson. What's worse, when I open my purse I immediately remember, the first thing I did when I got home was to plug my phone into the charger. The charger on my hall table. Resting my head on the steering wheel, I force myself not to cry.

What on earth am I going to do now?

Get out and walk? No, I can't do that. It's almost midnight, and there's dangers being a woman alone on the road. *Spend the night in my car?* That's not much safer. Someone might crash into me, a drunk driver perhaps, not expecting a car to be stopped on the median. Which reminds me, I switch on my hazards.

Shit. What options have I got? Feeling alone and vulnerable —a man's already hurt me tonight—I force myself not to dissolve into those threatened tears, and hit the central locking, making sure all the windows are rolled up. All I can do is wait until morning, then perhaps try to walk back into town when it's light and there's more traffic on the road.

I lean my sore head back on the headrest, turning it to the side to relieve the tender spot on the back where he'd pulled at my hair. Blood's still running down my face, an inconvenience more than a concern. I know a nose can bleed like a bitch, and I've just got to wait until it decides to stop. I dab with my tissue, regretting I've not even got tampons in my purse that I could use to stop the bleeding.

Pulling down the sun visor and switching on the interior light, I'm examining my hands, face, and shirt, which are covered in the red sticky liquid, when I hear a thunderous noise which passes, and then stops a few yards in front. I've switched my headlights off to conserve power, but from the lights and the sound, know it must be a motorcycle. Unknowing whether this could be my saviour or someone out to harm me, I recheck the button to make sure the doors are locked.

In the light coming from inside the car, which I haven't yet turned off, I can just about make out a giant who'd dwarf even Pete, coming toward me. As he draws closer, I can see he's wearing a leather cut. Then, when he's right by my door, see the flash that denotes him as sergeant-at-arms.

Nervously, I keep my eyes on him, remembering the Satan's Devils biker compound is rumoured to be around here some-where, down a side road off this highway. It's a bit of a myth among firefighters, as the original vacation resort now taken over by bikers had been destroyed by a wildfire.

Frozen in place, not knowing what I should do next, I see his mouth move but can't make out the words. He shakes his head, then raps on the window, making a motion with his hand which obviously means he wants me to roll it down. He crouches down by the side of my car, and immediately looks less threatening.

I'm a woman on my own, broken down, the odd car passing but no one stopping except this lone biker. I shiver, unsure what my best move is. He waits patiently while I decide. After a minute or two has gone past, I roll my window down an inch. Enough so we can talk, but insufficient for him to put his hand through.

He's clearly had enough time to examine me, his first words not what I expect, nor is the business-like tone of his voice. "Have you broken down, darlin', or stopped because you're hurtin'?" Unnecessarily, he points to my face where, at last, the blood has stopped flowing freely and is beginning to dry. As he watches, his brow creases, and the light reflected in his eyes appears to darken. "Who did this to you? Nah, scratch that, it doesn't matter for now. You need help. Tell me what I can do."

Mouthing 'thank you', I take a second to think. My confidence in men has been shattered tonight, and I have no idea what to ask for. It seems a bit much to request that he goes to get me some gas.

Again, he doesn't hurry me, or give me cause for concern. I watch him, crouched outside, the odd truck rushing past far too close, but he's completely unmoving, as if sitting exposed by the side of the road isn't unusual at all.

"I was going to Phoenix. But I've run out of gas. Stupid thing to do." I'm annoyed with myself. Mind you, last time I drove my car I had a full tank.

Slowly, he nods. "Long drive when you're hurtin'. You sure you're up to it tonight?"

I shrug. "Doesn't much matter whether I am or not, I haven't an option." Oh, I've got friends I could wake, but something is making me long for the security of my family, if it could ever be described as that. I should have realised the symptoms of being in shock before, but they've been creeping up on me. Phoenix is the last place I should be going. Suddenly the tears I've been holding back start to fall.

The stranger's eyes soften, but without asking me to do anything which I'm not prepared to now, he moves away back toward his bike. Before the darkness swallows him up, I see him take out a phone.

That's what I should have done. Asked to borrow his phone. I will when he comes back. Then I can get gas and be on my way.

CHAPTER 3
Peg

After my disastrous evening, even my ride hadn't put me in a much better mood. I wasn't feeling particularly charitable riding back to the compound but had automatically slowed as I drove past a car with its hazard lights flashing, seeing by the interior light that there was someone inside. As I passed, I could make out it was a woman.

I could have driven on, but something made me stop. Maybe helping someone else might help salve something of this fuck-up of a night—for them, even if it wouldn't do anything for me. I'm handy with engines, maybe getting my head under the hood might give me something else to think about rather than that bitch Lorelei. But as I stepped off my bike and went cautiously back to see her, always aware anyone could be carrying a gun, and let's face it, I'm not the friendliest looking guy around, what I noticed first in the light coming from the interior was the blood. She was covered in it.

Admiring her caution that she didn't want to roll down the window, I was patient, waiting until finally she cracked it so we could talk. At first I was worried she was seriously hurt, but she was making sense, despite looking tired and confused, and surmised her injuries were probably worse than they looked. And it looked bad enough. No stranger to such things, I immediately suspected someone had hit her.

Whether my approach was the right or wrong one, I watched as she started to shake, and those tears came to her eyes. I've seen it before, people carrying on after getting an injury, thinking they're fine and can just work through it, the hows, whys, and wherefores only slowly catching up. I give her some space by going back to my bike and placing a call to Fergus, one of our prospects, uncaring I'm dragging him out in the middle of the night to rescue a damsel in distress. As a prospect he'll do whatever I ask him, even if I instruct him to perform a striptease in the middle of the road to entertain her. *And* he'd do it with a smile on his face. But I won't ask. The sides of my mouth turn up at the thought. The last thing she probably needs to see tonight is a naked man.

Then I frown. What do I know what she needs or doesn't? I've barely seen anything of her, just a face which might be attractive were it unbruised and not covered in blood. I can't even tell how old she is or what shape her body is in. As for conversation, we've had none at all. But I've a strange reluctance to walk away without learning something about her.

No questions asked, the prospect is coming. It won't take long, the compound's only a few miles up the road. Returning to the car, I'm about to inform her, when I suddenly feel stupid. Of course, she's probably already contacted AAA or someone to come and help her, and there's no need for me to stay. Unless she's called that motherfucker who hurt her. If she has, I'll wait and have a few words with that person. With my fists. Men who hit women are scum.

"Sweetheart," I start as I rap on the window again. "You got anyone bringin' gas?"

A shake of her head, and it gets me deep in the gut to see the hurt in those eyes. "I left without my phone."

She must have left fast or been chased out. I wipe my hand over my face. "Got a prospect bringin' some gas for you, darlin'.

Only a gallon can, but it will get you on your way again at least, then you'll need to stop and fill up."

I watch as another tear runs from her eye, and it doesn't take a genius to realise she won't want anyone to see her in the state that she's in, even a gas station attendant. I don't know how, but something tells me she's a strong woman, and whatever happened tonight isn't normal for her. She's not acting cowed and scared like someone used to abuse. *Has she been attacked? Mugged?* Whatever, I have a desire to help. "Our compound's just up the road. Why don't you follow me there? We've got a doc we can call to come have a look at you. Get you sorted and cleaned up, a bed for the night, and you can be on your way in the mornin'."

She gazes at me, her eyes open wide, and I realise she's going to refuse my invitation before she says the words. "I couldn't do that."

It's not that she doesn't want to put anyone to any trouble, it's that she's wary of exactly what I might be offering.

I crouch down again, resting my back against the door, wishing I could comfort her or make a practical suggestion. "What happened, darlin? A man hit you?" As I wait for her answer, I watch the traffic, not too much now, but it's probably not the safest place to be sitting. My leg's protesting the unfamiliar position, my stump resting at the wrong angle on the prosthesis.

"Who says it was a man?"

"Huh." I almost laugh. "Less likely to have been a woman. They tend to slap rather than punch."

"He did that too." Her breath hitches. "He slapped me first. Then he took objection to me asking him to get out of my house…and you're right. He punched me, then threw me to the floor, pulling me around by my hair."

I stay where I am. From this position I'm not able to look at her, nor she at me. Probably the reason she's opening up. "Your house? Who is he? Husband." I frown. "Boyfriend?"

"Friend or, I suppose, housemate, if you want to label it. He moved in a couple of months ago, only for a week supposedly, but then he stayed."

"And now he's outstayed his welcome."

I hear a deep sigh. "I would have given him time to sort another place out, but he's started to get these crazy ideas. I was home late from work—admittedly, very late—and that's when he started on me. But he knows what I do, and that I can't control it, or pick up a phone and say, 'Honey, I'll be late getting home'."

"What do you do?" I'm prepared for anything, doctor, nurse, receptionist, shop assistant. What I'm not primed for is what she tells me.

"I'm a firefighter."

I start. Fuck me. That wasn't what I expected. The woman sitting behind me runs into burning buildings, rescuing people, providing first-hand medical assistance at the scene, wearing heavy clothing and carrying fuck knows how much equipment in the already blazing hot Arizona climate. I take my hat off to any man willing to do that job… A woman? Hell, she must be up there as the bravest and toughest I know.

As I haven't thought of anything to say, she gives me more. "We were on a call, a warehouse fire. You can't simply give up and go home. The next crew came on shift, but they still needed us." She pauses, a takes a deep breath. "There were reports there was a person stuck in one of the offices. We did what we could, kept on trying to reach him, *could hear him screaming for help*, but the fire kept beating us back." Her voice breaks off, but I sense there's more coming. "When we eventually managed to find him, it was too late, and he was dead. His wife was waiting for us to bring him out…but we couldn't, or not alive at least. She was pregnant."

Shit. I thought I'd had a fucked-up evening. Her shit of a friend should have been letting her talk it out, listening to her and giving her a shoulder to lean on. Not fucking going off on her for being late. My fists open and close as I know just what I want to do with them.

Suddenly I stand, placing my elbows on the roof of the car. I lean in and speak through the cracked open window. "Here's what's gonna happen," I speak through gritted teeth. "Prospect will bring enough gas to get you movin'. You'll turn around and I'll follow you home. Get this prick out of your house once and for fuckin' all. He's not a man. Fuck, woman. The job that you do? You deserve someone better than him."

You deserve me. Leaning my head back, I look up at the star-scattered sky. What am I thinking? I don't deserve a heroic citizen like her. I remind myself, apart from her occupation and that she seems to open her home to strays, I know nothing about her.

When I look back down again, her mouth's open in shock. "I can't ask you to do that."

I smile, gentling my features for the first time. "Didn't hear you askin', but I sure offered."

I hear the distinctive sound of a Harley approaching, and step away from the car before she can say anything else, thinking the best thing is to leave her to mull it over it for a moment. She can see what I am, a biker, and, if she's read my cut, an officer and the sergeant-at-arms. She'll have no doubt that I can chuck one motherfucker out of her house but is probably worrying whether she'll end up exchanging him for a devil. A Satan's Devil at that.

Fergus draws up. Without a choice, she passes me the keys and we empty the gallon can into her gas tank, then Fergus waits for further instruction. As I go to hand back her keys, I see her stifling both a yawn and a groan. Her face must hurt, and if she was thrown on the floor, other injuries which I can't see. Now the first rush of adrenalin has worn off, it's clear to see she's had enough.

"Shift over."

"What?"

I dangle her keys in my hand. "You must have had medical training. You should know you're in no state to drive. You're the very picture of exhausted, and from what you told me, in a lot of pain as well. I don't care to think what could happen. What if you took someone else off the road?" She's a firefighter, she must have been called to enough car crashes to know what I'm talking about. I'm playing on the fact she wouldn't want to add to them.

Her eyes widen, and I know I've got her when she says, with a worried look at the second biker standing next to me, "I'm not coming to your compound."

"No. I'm driving you back to Tucson."

"But your bike?" I've found one thing out, she's not selfish. Her glance ahead and the way she worries her lip shows me she's concerned about my expensive Harley being left unattended.

"I'll get Hyde, our other prospect, to bring the crash truck down. They'll get my bike loaded up, then Hyde will come pick me up. Wouldn't want to be in your hair any longer than you want me to be, darlin'."

She gives me a searching look and places one hand to her forehead. As she rubs it, I think I'm right about her pain making itself known. A last glance at me, and then she's sliding across the seat, manoeuvring herself over the handbrake. I give her some time to get set, then turn to Fergus.

"You get all that?"

"Call Hyde, get him here with the crash truck, then come and get you. Got it."

I nod. I've taken to him over the past year and think he may well patch-in soon. Hyde, well, he's doing alright. He's just got to get Slick and Heart's vote to proceed. Which will mean we'll be on the lookout for more prospects. Can't run a club without someone to do the shit jobs. Or who you can call in the middle of the night to help a woman you've only just met.

I heard a clunk before she slid across, and realised she'd popped the locks. As I open the door, I turn back. "I'll text you the address."

Fergus nods as he takes out his phone, and walks off, clearing the way for me to drive off. But first, I place the cut I've just taken off in the rear, then I have to push back the seat. A long way. I notice she's looking at me wryly, so I shrug. "Sorry, I'm a big fella." *Shit, I'm supposed to be reassuring her. I hope she doesn't take that the wrong way.*

But that wasn't what she was worrying about. "I'm Darcy, by the way. As you now appear to be my chauffeur, I think we ought to exchange names."

"Too right." I hold out my hand. "I'm Peg."

"Peg?"

"If you're thinking there's a story there, you'd be correct." But I don't say anymore. It's her who needs taking care of tonight. I'm not getting into a discussion about my missing leg now. Thank fuck, she's got an automatic. Oh, I can drive a stick shift, it just takes me a bit longer to work an unfamiliar clutch, and like any man, even in these circumstances, I want to impress, and who wants to stall in front of a woman they're intrigued by?

She gives me her address, I text it to Fergus. I know the area, so only need to ask for details when we're coming up close. It's a small house, front yard looks like it could do with some work, but I've no doubt doing the physical job that she does, keeping it tidy is probably the last thing she wants to do when she comes off shift. But the fucker I haven't yet met goes further down in my estimation. If he's freeloading off her; surely he could repay her by doing some work around the place?

CHAPTER 4

Darcy

My house is dark and quiet. Pete's must be sleeping off his drunken state. As we draw up out front—I've told Peg not to park on the drive else he'll block Pete's car in—I see my place through Peg's eyes by the light from the streetlamps. It's untidy and looks completely unloved. For a moment I feel ashamed. I didn't mind doing the work on my days off, but thought it wouldn't hurt Pete to provide some labour in exchange for room and board. But even though I'd left it, he hadn't taken the hint.

Why had I been so stupid to let him live here at all?

Why had I done such a crazy thing as letting another imposing strange man, and a biker at that, bring me home? He could have taken me anywhere, dumped my body and stolen my car. *But he hadn't.* My instincts, which have proved so wrong with Pete, seemed more on the right track when it comes to the man at my side. Every vibe he gives off is that he'd use his strength to be a protector, not an aggressor.

"Prospects shouldn't be too far behind. It won't take long to sort your man out, and then we'll see what's what."

I look at him curiously. "What's what?"

He shrugs and points his index finger in the direction of my home. "Man like that, gets his feet under the table, might have got comfortable and not want to leave. If he causes trouble, threats or the like, I'll get the prospect to stay here to make sure he keeps away from you."

Again, my eyes widen. "You'd have a man watching the house? Why on earth would you do that?"

When he places his hand under my chin and raises my head, it's the first time he's touched me, and I notice he does so gently for such a big man. "I don't like seein' women hurt. Don't like men who hurt women. I'll ask him politely, but if he comes back, he might need a lesson to teach him he's got to stay away."

As he lets me go, I look out of the other side window. "Violence, you mean."

"Hey, darlin'. He started this, not you. Wouldn't do him no harm to find out what it's like being on the other end. You gonna argue with that?"

I work with burly firefighters all day, know enough about them to understand they wouldn't be averse to solving arguments with their fists in a similar situation. I'm a woman in a male-dominated career, and up to now I've fought my own battles, have tried to be tough. But Pete's proved too much for me. *I ran, rather than stay and fight.* It wouldn't hurt to leave it to Peg. *No one else need know you didn't sort your problems alone.*

As if he's sensed I've given in, he opens the door. "Stay there, I'll come around."

But I don't wait, pushing my door open, and all but stumbling out when tiredness, worry, and a bump to my head catch up with me.

"Fuckin' told you, Woman." Peg's arms are around me, holding me up, as the lights go on in my house and the front door opens.

It's only a second before the silence is broken. "Bitch! Knew you had another man."

"Pete!" If I had it's no business of his.

Before I can say anything else, the man who'd caused me such pain tumbles out of the door and comes right up in our faces. "What? You thought I'd be gone, so you might as well bring my replacement back?"

I start shaking, with fear and with something akin to embarrassment or shame. The man in front of us is not someone you'd invite into your home. Peg must be wondering what I'd been thinking. But Pete's changed, so much. He didn't use to be this way. *He's dropped his act.*

The big biker lowers his head and speaks quietly into my ear. "He's not just drunk, Darcy, he's strung out." My eyes widen at his explanation, and it makes me pause. *Could he be right?* But Pete's belligerence when faced with the biker who's even bigger than him is certainly a possible indication there's something other than alcohol in his system. *Why hadn't I seen it?*

But I don't continue my self-recrimination, that can come later. Pete's standing close, too close. He sways gently, his head turning as the sound of vehicles fill the night air, huffing when he sees the bike and truck pulling up behind my car. He rolls his shoulders as though getting ready for a fight.

Peg must see the threat too. "Fergus, Hyde." All he does is incline his head toward the man quivering with tension, and immediately the prospects leave their vehicles and come up beside Pete before he can act, each taking a secure hold of an arm. Suddenly restrained, Pete tries to fight them off, but he's no match for them.

"What do you want us to do with him, Peg?" Fergus sounds almost bored, as if they do things like this all the time. *Perhaps they do.*

What are they going to do to him? I want this man out of my life, but I've heard about biker methods of retribution. While I might not like Pete any longer, I wouldn't want to see any man beat up or dead. But it's clear we can't just put him in his truck to drive away, not in the state that he's in. I'm at a loss what to say, but one thing I know. "Don't hurt him, please, Peg."

Peg's eyes meet mine. "He hurt you."

I gaze up intently. "I just want him gone, please." Yes, he hurt me. But two wrongs never add up to a right.

Peg's arm tightens, then he lets out a sigh and pulls me further away. He speaks quietly, as though not wanting to inflame the situation further. "He can't drive," he starts, giving voice to my thoughts. "You know any friends of his where we could take him?"

I shake my head. "I don't know much about him at all. Not that way. He never had friends over or mentioned any family."

I'm tired and hurting. Even though I've only just met him, I'm pleased Peg still has his arm around me, else I'm not sure I could hold myself up. All I want to do is take a shower, wash my blood away, and perhaps get some ice for my face. Painkillers for certain. There's no fight left in me tonight. Now glancing over at Pete, he seems subdued, a sudden mood swing away from his rage. Another sign Peg was right in his assumption about drugs.

Though unsure what I'm dealing with here, I come up with a suggestion. "He's quieted down." Seeing Pete's head is bowed down to his chest and that he's slumped in his captors' hold reinforces my decision. "I'll let him sleep it, whatever it is, off in the guest room, and then send him on his way in the morning."

Peg's arm tenses a fraction, as if he doesn't like what I've said. Confirmed when he starts speaking. "Not sure I like that. He's docile now, but later? Fuck, darlin', not gonna leave you alone with someone in this state. What guarantees have you got that he'll pack his bags and go quietly tomorrow?"

I purse my lips, hating to admit it, but knowing he's right. I'm fit, I must be to do the job that I do. Able to carry a man bigger than myself out of a burning building. But I couldn't hold my own in a brawl or know how to defend myself against a man so much larger. If Pete got rough again, then I'd come off the worst. Especially in my already damaged state.

"You okay if we stay over tonight?" Before I can protest, he puts his finger to my lips. "Here's my idea. Let him sleep it off in your guestroom. Fergus and Hyde will stay with him and make sure he doesn't get out of hand. We'll sort it out for good in the mornin'. Tonight, babe, you need to get your injuries looked at, and then have a good, long sleep."

Okay, I started this night with one man I didn't want in my house. Now he's proposing I add three more? The only thing I know about them is that they're bikers and come with a reputation, and one which means no upstanding citizen like me would want to be associated with them. As my suspicion and unease grow, wondering whether he's any expectation of the type of reward I'm not willing to offer, I ask, "And where will you be staying?"

"You got a couch?" When I nod, he mimics my action. "That'll do for me."

I half pull away and turn, my face staring up into his, needing to know, to understand what's happening. "Why are you doing this, Peg? You don't know me at all."

"Bit of an unusual situation. You're right, I don't, and you don't know me. Or my kind." He pauses, and his hand touches my head, and not for the first time I notice how soft his touch is. "I don't like this, darlin'. Not gonna leave you alone with him. Look, there are two options. Either we take him away and deal with him ourselves, or we stay here where we can keep an eye on him."

"What will you do if you take him?"

A shrug. "Depends on how he behaves."

Biting my lip, I try to think which is the best of the two evils. I never intended things to go as far as they had with Pete. A stupid offer to give him a place to stay for a few days, an even more ridiculous move when I allowed that to turn into weeks. This is my chance to be rid of him.

I don't want to face him alone in the morning, but I can't let him go off with these bikers, not knowing if he'll be facing daylight alive. The rumours I've heard about the Satan's Devils might well be true.

"I know you don't know whether you can trust me, darlin'. And just sayin' the words won't help."

That Peg's given me the option and not pressuring me or trying to persuade me one way or another, and that the only thing he's insisting is I'm not left alone with the man who hurt me, is what helps me come to a decision. Peg stopped by the side of the road when no one else had even slowed to help. Peg had got angry when he'd seen the damage Pete had done to me. Even faced with the man who'd hurt me, he restrained himself from violence at my request.

Maybe I'd have taken another route if I wasn't dead on my feet after pulling what was almost a double shift and hurting, but this way I'll soon be in my bed, and won't have to lie awake worrying. "Thank you. If it's not putting you out, stay."

Fergus and Hyde have overheard our conversation. Not so much Pete, who barely seems awake, and is muttering incoherently to himself and no one in particular.

"Come on," one of the prospects says. "Let's get you inside." I watch, but though they're not giving him a chance to get loose, they're not overly rough with him. Even in my current state I wonder if they're holding themselves back in front of me.

Pulling away from Peg, I show them the way.

Peg glances inside the guestroom. "You assholes stick to him like glue. He's not leavin' this room unless it's to piss, and then you'll be right there beside him." Having barked his instruction and received two nods, Peg looks down at me. "Now, let's get you sorted. Got a first aid kit, babe?"

I wait for a second, seeing Pete drop onto the bed and immediately start to snore. Christ knows why I ever opened my home up to him. Then answering Peg, "Yes. I've got one in the bathroom. I'll bring it into the kitchen." I could argue I can treat myself, but there's something about him that makes me want his company. Just for a few minutes longer, before I take that promised shower and fall into my bed.

When I've collected my first aid kit, I go into the kitchen to find Peg looking so large in the small space. He's been busy in the couple of minutes I've been gone, there's the makings of hot chocolate out and ready. He raises his eyebrow, and I feel the first real smile of the night, wondering how he knows exactly what I need.

"Help yourself to a beer," I offer in return. The slight quirk of his mouth shows me that's what he'd intended. But it's little enough reward after everything he's done for me tonight.

Moving quickly for such a big man, his hands come to my waist, making me jump, but it's only to lift me to place me on the counter, then he steps away and busies himself once again. Then, when a cup of steaming chocolate is placed beside me, he cocks his head to one side, examining me, and at the same time reaching for the first aid container.

Large, but gentle hands sweep the hair away from my face, and then fingers probe, pressing against my tender skin. I flinch as he touches my cheek, and tense when his light touch smooths along the side of my nose. Taking out some antiseptic, he starts to clean the blood away.

I reach out my hand to stop him. "I can do that."

"I can see what I'm doing better. Looks like a ring or something caught you when he hit you." *Motherfucker,* he adds under his breath. "Your nose doesn't seem broken, though it's bled like a bitch." He seems to have already familiarised himself with my kitchen. Looking right at home, he takes a plastic bag and fills it with ice. "Hold that to your face, will help minimise the swellin'." Then turning back to the first aid kit, he finds some Advil and opens the bottle. Tapping two out, he fills a glass with water, and I'm soon swallowing them down.

His hands probe my skull, and when I wince he reaches behind me and, peering around, lifts my hair. "Not that you'd notice it, but, darlin', he must have pulled a chunk of your hair out. That's going to be sore, but it's not too much. Won't show at all." His hands lightly fumble me, and I realise he's removing the band that had held my ponytail, which had become tangled and mostly undone. When he places the elastic beside me, his fingers comb my hair. Again, so gently it causes no pain, just a sensation I let myself enjoy but don't want to analyse.

I take the opportunity to look at his face. His hair on top is short, and he has a long, unkempt beard divided into two and plaited. He has a ring through his eyebrow, and one in his right ear, and reminds me of a pirate. He catches me eyeing him, and smirks. As the corners of his mouth rise into a smile, crease lines draw my attention to his eyes. They're dark and mysterious.

My saviour. My protector. What am I thinking? This man isn't mine. I know nothing about him. I've already been burned by jumping into something so fast, letting another man into my space. A fire smouldering in my house that even I, as a firefighter, hadn't caught in time to put out.

"I'm done in, Peg." My hot chocolate has disappeared, though I don't recall drinking it, but must have, as it's flavour's still on my taste buds.

"Go to bed, darlin'. I'll be here when you wake."

"There's blankets…"

"I can sort myself out. Slept in worst places, I can assure you."

Seeing how easily he found his way around my kitchen, I expect he probably can and has. Unsure how else to show my appreciation, I put my hand to his face. So quickly, as though I've imagined it, he leans into my touch, then pulls away.

"Go. Get some rest." When he smiles, it transforms his face, and I leave him, putting my strange reaction to him down to gratitude.

CHAPTER 5

Peg

I hadn't lied when I told Darcy I'd slept in worse places, but that hasn't been for a very long time. Most of the night I spend tossing and turning, trying to get comfortable on a couch which is probably fine for sitting, but not made for my tall frame to lie stretched out. I either have to contort myself into a fetal position or have my legs hanging over the end, particularly awkward when you're wearing a prosthesis. But I'm not going to remove it and be vulnerable in a place I don't know, and a man I don't trust two doors down the hallway. Even with the prospects watching him.

It doesn't help that my thoughts are racing, thinking about how the evening before had begun and how it had come to an end. Two different women. Darcy, fuck, a firefighter, brave beyond my reckoning. What makes a woman take up such a career? The things she sees must haunt her, like the man she couldn't save on yesterday's shift. How does she deal with all that shit?

She might fight fires, but it's clear going up against another human being is beyond her. But she's got me for that. In the morning I'll deal with the motherfucker who hurt her, give him a lesson so that he never comes back. Yeah, she's got me in her corner…

No, she hasn't. Not beyond tomorrow. I can't take the risk. What if she has the same reaction as Lorelei when she sees I'm disabled?

Earlier this evening I'd decided I'd take the quick fuck that shallow woman was offering, but was already having doubts about going back, even before she came out and said what she had. I'd guessed my longing for a permanent relationship was at odds with her more immediate desire for my cock. Although hurt by her reaction to my disability, it didn't upset me that things wouldn't go further. Apart from the physical, though I'd tried hard to find something, there was nothing between us, no spark.

Not like what I feel toward Darcy.

But she's a firefighter, and any spark there is she's likely to put out. She's a decent woman, wouldn't want to get involved with the likes of a biker. My additional worry being I've no idea how she'd react to my missing limb. I'd rather leave in the morning, remembering her as a ship I passed in the night, never wanting to test her reaction, not wanting that disappointment to play on my mind. If her response was the same as Lorelei's, I'd be ten times as hurt.

A house, a yard, throw a couple of kids into the mix. Am I dreaming when I think that could ever be mine? Turning over again, trying without success to get comfortable, I remember who I am. Peg, sergeant-at-arms. My role in the Satan's Devils is to watch out for the club and keep it safe. Maybe that's all I can ask. I've already got a family, mismatched as they are. More than some people have. Why should I deserve anything beyond that?

Maybe what I've watched my brothers bringing into their lives, old ladies and children, is something that's never meant to be mine. Grouchy Peg with half a leg missing, why would any woman want to tie herself to me?

Tomorrow I'll cancel my online dating accounts, I've had no success with them. This woman who's attracted me tonight? I'll watch from a distance to make sure she's not bothered again, but it's not fair to bring her into my world. She's got a respectable job, and her happy suburban existence. I could only bring chaos into her life.

I've got my brothers behind and beside me, and the sweet butts for when I can't resist the urge. It's time I looked at what I have, not what I haven't, and accept anything else is out of my reach.

Eventually, just as the sky is lightening, I manage to drop off, coming almost instantly awake when a loud crash sounds. In one swift movement, I've got my cut on and my gun in my hand, a few short strides taking me to the hallway. I'm not the only one to have been disturbed.

"Get back inside," I snap at Darcy, who's opened the door to her room. I must have snarled in my typical sergeant-at-arms fashion, as her face falls, but I've no time to baby her. From the sounds of it there's one hell of a struggle going on inside the guestroom, and I want her completely out of harm's way.

Used to being obeyed, I don't wait for her to get back into her bedroom, instead throw open the guest room door and step inside. "What the fuck is going on?"

My loud shout provides enough distraction for Pete to grab a gun out of nowhere, raise it, and aim toward the door, straight in my direction. My fast reactions mean I'm out of the way before he pulls the trigger, but the bullet keeps travelling and hits the woman who, instead of complying with my instruction, is right behind me. As she lets out a scream, my stomach drops. Spinning, I see her slumping against the door jamb, her hand to her arm, and her eyes wild.

"What the fuck have you done now?" Seeing Hyde's quickly placed chop to Pete's arm, making him drop the gun which is now secured in the Fergus's care, Darcy pushes me aside and steps forward. "You could have fucking killed me." Pete backs up as she screams in his face. Glancing at her look of fury, I would have done the same myself. In that moment, she looks like an Amazon. Apart from the sweet butts, I'm not used to hearing a woman swear, but in the circumstances, would definitely give her a pass. I'd go so far as to say it sounds goddamn sexy coming out of her mouth, and my cock starts to lengthen at this most inappropriate time. I remind myself she works closely with men, in fraught situations, so it's not surprising when riled she resorts to profanity. But that doesn't affect the impact. Not at all. Her effect isn't just on me. Pete seems to shrink in front of my eyes.

Still with her hand clenched to her bleeding arm, the sight of the blood immediately deflating my dick, she points at her unwelcome guest, her voice still shrill as she demands, "Where did you get the gun?"

That's what I want to know. Fergus looks sheepish, his eyes meet mine. "He must have had it stashed under the mattress. Sorry, Peg."

I file that away and will deal with him later. *Fucker should have checked everything out.*

"He woke up, Peg. Started striking out." Hyde's ruefully rubbing his chin. "He was trying to get to Darcy."

Darcy's waving her hand. "Pipe down everyone. Peg, can you get my phone please, it should be on the table in the hall."

"Who you going to call?" My immediate reaction is, of course, not to get the authorities involved.

She turns that battered face toward me. "The police, of course." As my head starts to move in a negative action, knowing she's doing what any citizen would, her face widens into a grin. "It must be his gun, I don't own one. I didn't even know he had it. But the facts are quite clear. He's fired at me and injured me.

That together with the damage to my face must be enough to take him in. It gets him out of my life."

"And we're here, because…?" Cops come in, see us…. Nah, I don't like that idea.

Though I can see the merits of her suggestion from her side. It saves him from a beat down by us. I'd like nothing better than to smash his face in, to show this man how it feels to be on the receiving end for once.

"Because you stopped and brought me home after Pete hit me last night and refused to leave my house." She lifts her hand and touches the side of my face. "I know you don't want to get the police involved, Peg, but this is the best way. He shot a fire-fighter in her own house. No way he's getting away with that."

"Bitch. You can't do this. It was a mistake, I was trying to shoot an intruder. I was keeping you safe, Darcy. You can't throw me out, I've nowhere to go…."

"I think the police might be quite accommodating." She turns her attention from him to me. I wait a second, her touch almost mesmerising, making me want to do anything she wants. Even play it her way. I give her a nod. In a moment I'm back with her phone. She calls up a number. "Hey, Grover. I need some help. My housemate just shot me." She pulls her phone away from her ear. "Just a graze, thank God, but he could have killed me."

"Nah, I've got friends here, they've got him restrained." She jerks her chin at me as if the man at the other end can see her.

"Uh huh. Thanks, man." Sighing, she ends the call.

I'm staring at her, she shrugs. "I'm a firefighter. Got lots of friends in the police department. And," she turns to Pete, "they really don't like hearing that someone tried to take a member of any of the rescue services out."

Of course she does. That's another reason why I can't even consider starting anything with this amazing woman. I lift my chin toward Hyde. "Make sure you keep hold of him."

"And don't rough him up," Darcy instructs. "Sorry, but you'll have to stay, as your fingerprints will be on the gun, Fergus, but there'll be gunpowder residue on his."

Fuck, this woman is smart. "Darcy, will you let me take a look at your arm?"

She looks surprised, and then down at her arm as though she's already forgotten it. A grimace crosses her face as she spots more blood running down.

"Need to get our story straight before the cops come," Hyde reminds me.

Darcy creases her eyes as she looks up. "Just tell the truth. Nothing more to say. You rescued me, stayed when you saw I needed help."

I notice Hyde staring at me, and even Fergus is looking bemused. After thinking about it for a moment, I shrug. We've done nothing wrong, and can hardly disappear when fingers might be pointed young Fergus's way. Telling the truth to the law is not the normal way we'd play it, but she's right. It could work. I feel one side of my mouth turn up as my admiration for this woman grows.

When a friend of a cop gets attacked, the police obviously leap into action. Sirens come up the road, cars screech to a halt outside.

Cops rush in screaming, "Hands up, where we can see them!"

Pete takes a chance to run, but he only runs into the waiting arms of the police. He seizes the opportunity. "Those biker scum came in here, attacked and shot my girlfriend."

There's loud voices, and hardly anyone can hear through the din. It's confusion, with the cops following their natural tendencies to put the blame on the men in leather cuts until one voice rings out above them all.

"I'm Darcy Cavanaugh. This is my house. That man who's been staying here as my housemate, Peter Mercer, attacked me last night, refused to leave my house, and it was him who shot me just now."

There's a sudden lull, and one of the cops steps forward, his eyes still alighting on us with suspicion. "Which one's Mercer?"

She points. "The one who's trying to persuade you he's innocent."

A man in plain clothes pushes through the throng. "Cavanaugh." He nods as he greets her. "Would you care to explain?" As he speaks, he motions for her to show him her arm. When he sees blood running freely, he shakes his head and stops her halfway through her explanation. "Fuck, Darcy you need to get checked out." He casts a look my way. "You say these bikers helped you? Stayed here for protection?" I look, knowing it's in vain, but hoping to see appreciation on his face, but his expression is full of suspicion.

Darcy must have noticed it, because she shrugs off his touch and adds, "I think Pete's been taking drugs. I'd like you to search the house. Whatever you find has nothing to do with me." Breaking off, she frowns. "And he obviously had a weapon, and I had no idea. Perhaps there's more? Please make sure anything that shouldn't be here is removed."

The cops take a protesting Pete outside, but some of them remain. As I get a nasty feeling, I send off a quick text to the prez. My phone pings a few seconds later, but I don't bother looking, I know it will be confirmation.

It's not long before the three of us are on our way to the precinct, and Darcy's been taken off to the hospital. She'd mouthed 'sorry' back over her shoulder as Grover led her out, knowing the police were taking advantage of us being on the premises where a firefighter got hurt.

Shortly after, as expected, I'm sitting locked up in a cell, Hyde and Fergus probably equally confined, but out of my sight and hearing to ensure we don't get a chance to confer. It wouldn't matter, our story would be the same even if we had a chance to work on it. They'd tried to question me, but I value my patch far too much to speak to a cop without the club lawyer present. If we were citizens it all would probably be cleared up in no time at all.

At last I'm led to an interview room. I nod to the lawyer, and sit down beside him, then look over the desk. I recognise the detective but can't readily place him.

"Detective Reed." He introduces himself, strangely stretching out his hand for me to shake, which I do automatically. "I'm a friend of Marcia Hannah."

Ah, now I know who he is. He'd been the one who'd warned Heart's old lady that some dirty cops were out to get her. I suppose it's the friendliest face I can expect to see here.

"Marcia doing okay?" he enquiries politely.

I respond in an equally sociable tone, "Apart from being heavily pregnant with twins, she's doing fine."

An easy smile comes to his face. "And doing some excellent work behind the scenes, or so I hear?"

Now that I neither confirm nor deny. No one knows exactly what Marcia's doing when she's holed up with our computer guru, Mouse, but we know they've been getting results.

"Right." He looks down at his notes. "Ok. Fergus and Hyde have already been interviewed. He pauses for the club lawyer to nod to agree he'd been present. Now, Mr Rinter, I'd like you to take me through exactly what happened last night."

I hate the smell of this place and playing it straight down the line will mean I'll be out of here sooner. Taking a breath, I start from the moment I stopped in front of her car, to the moment the police arrived this morning. He's jotting down what I'm saying as well as consulting his notes. A couple of times he checks what I've said but doesn't seem to have a problem.

At the end he looks up. "Right, that all tallies. I think we've got the story straight."

"Will Mercer be let out on bail?"

He gives me a sharp look. "Too early to say. What you thinking, Mr Rinter? Wouldn't advise you to take the law into your own hands."

I pinch the bridge of my nose. "Look, Miss Cavanaugh seems like a decent sort. If this man's got the hots for her, don't want him to get close and hurt her again. I'll get her locks changed and security beefed up."

He takes off his glasses, polishes them, then puts them back on. "You said you just met her last night? Are you going to be a problem for her?"

"What? Me?" I huff. "No way."

Perhaps now the glass he's looking through is cleaner, he leans back on his chair and folds his arms, his chin resting on his chest for a moment. Then he raises his head and nods. "She does need to get her locks changed and for our part, if for some reason this man walks? Then we'll make sure we'll keep a close eye on Miss Cavanaugh. She plays an important part in the community. Brave woman."

"Appreciate that."

CHAPTER 6

Darcy

"Flash! What the fuck happened to you?"

"What does the other one look like?"

"Shit, girl, six days off and you've rearranged your face." Captain Slade comes nearer to get a close look at the damage and adds his comments to those of my other team mates. He tuts loudly and shakes his head. "Should you even be here?"

"Hey, we can use her to scare off the arsonists."

At that, I raise my middle finger toward Hammer. "Shut it, you lot. It's only bruising." Yeah, and doesn't it look great? Two blackened eyes now a nice shade of purple, although not so swollen, my nose is still red, and my cheek has a nice yellow and green tinge. "Would you believe me if I told you I walked into a door?"

"Oldest excuse in the book, girl." Truck, so named as he's as big as one, joins the captain, his eyes narrow as he takes in the damage. "Who hit you? You got mugged or something?"

I inhale sharply. We care about each other on this team, and I don't want to lie to them. I decide to get it over and done with. "It was Pete Mercer. My housemate. Well, he's not that any longer. And yes, before you go on about it, I made some bad decisions, alright?" They'd never understood why I'd taken pity on the man made homeless by a fire. Come to that, neither did I. Mercer had put me in the awkward position where he'd backed me into a corner. I never really understood how he'd done it.

Hammer, our paramedic, still looks concerned. "Is your nose broken?"

"No, thank God. Just bruised. Look, I'm still a little sore, but I can work, okay. And the bullet just skimmed me."

Now three voices shout out in unison. "Bullet? You were fucking shot?"

Sighing, I explain, rubbing at the small bandage on my forearm. "Fucker pulled a gun on me, got off a shot, luckily it went wide and just grazed me."

"Tell me the asshole's in jail," Slade snarls.

I nod. "He is."

"He shouldn't be fucking alive. Bastard should be dead." Truck's almost shaking with rage. "He could have killed you."

As the seriousness of what happened sinks in, I'm surrounded by three concerned men all talking at once, coming up with rather colourful suggestions of how they'd make someone who shot at a firefighter pay. I let their musings wash over me, basking in their concern, which would have been the same on my part had our positions been reversed. Along with doing a job that I love, we're a close-knit team. When we're fighting what nature throws at us, we need to have each other's back and that trust and camaraderie extends to when we're not out on a call.

"Should have called us." Slade's still harping on. Just as I start to wonder how to put into words that I was ashamed and didn't want anyone to know, I hear another voice.

"What's happened to you, Firefighter Cavanaugh?" I sigh. The battalion chief would choose this moment to walk into the station. I give him the brief version all over again. After exchanging a look and a silent conversation with Hammer, he gives me a nod. "Well, okay. As long as you feel you're up to working. But if you're not pulling your weight, you'll have to take a sick day."

"I'm fine, Chief." *The worst pain I'll have to go through is being the subject of jokes during the whole of my twenty-four-hour shift. I know my fellow firefighters too well.*

Another sharp look, then his concern fades. Slade, being the captain and the most senior of us on the shift, informs him, "All quiet at the moment."

Batt Chief Leadson nods. "Let's hope it stays that way and you'll be doing equipment checks today."

I nod at Hammer. As well as our most qualified medic, he's also our driver and engineer, responsible for operating the pump. I'm letting him know I'll work with him. Truck, the youngest and newest member of our team, is nearing the end of his eighteen-month probation period, something I completed five years ago now, after a gruelling four-month para-military training program.

The physical requirements of the job and my level of fitness is one of the reasons I'm still annoyed Pete got the drop on me, and that I didn't fight back. But being able to carry two twelve and a half pound packs while wearing a fifty-pound vest up the stairs of a high-rise building and being able to swing a ten-pound sledgehammer might mean I'm physically strong, but doesn't translate into being mentally equipped to use that strength against a larger and bulkier flesh and blood opponent.

I'll just have to be more selective who I open my home to. But Pete had showed no sign he'd ever be any kind of threat. Sure, he'd begun taking advantage, but to turn violent? I'm still reeling from that.

"You with us, Flash?"

I shake my head to clear it. I'm a woman able to do one of the most physically demanding jobs there is, but deep down inside, Pete's attack has shown I can still be a victim. *Why didn't I fight back?*

"Okay. If we're not dispatched to any incidents, we'll get the equipment checked, then hit the gym." Slade notices my slight grimace. "Flash. Full pack, on the treadmill."

Asshole. But I'll show him I can do it. I raise my chin.

Dispatch calls, and all conversation stops dead. Like a well-oiled machine, we get prepared and out on the engine in under a minute. It's only then Slade informs us it's a two-car vehicle crash with an entrapment.

The rest of the shift goes quickly. A small fire in a house, a medical emergency which is dealt with by Hammer, and then it's back to the station to try and get some rest. Which we don't, of course. There's a good reason why we have twenty-four hours off after a shift, as the work can be tiring and relentless. Even a quiet shift can seem gruelling, as we try to occupy ourselves, snatching some downtime to watch TV or read, or attempting to get a couple of hours of quality sleep in between activities such as running drills, training, and working out. Then, of course, there's maintenance that always needs to be done.

Finally, I'm able to go home, still wondering why people fit fire alarms then don't bother to check they're working, as that simple action might have saved the house we'd been called out to in the early hours of the morning, and which took the rest of the shift to put out.

Home, that place which holds two opposing memories. One I'd rather forget, and one which I'd have liked to explore further. Peg. Oh, I know that an actual relationship between a firefighter and an outlaw biker wouldn't be looked on kindly, but there was something about him that makes me want to see him again. In one night I feel I'd seen the best and worst of humanity, one man taking advantage, another giving me help and asking nothing at all.

Peg's help hadn't ended after he'd left my house. The morning after Pete had been arrested, a locksmith turned up, some kind of security expert who not only changed all my locks and fitted a security system, but when I asked how much it was going to cost, said he'd already received payment. Stunned, I realised it had to have been the biker. The man who I'd last seen being pushed into a police car, treated as though he'd committed the crime rather than being my saviour. Not liking being beholden to anyone, I didn't know what to do.

While I'm happy and far easier in my mind now I have a more secure home to live in, the fact a stranger is responsible for the upgrade niggles at me. The feeling gets worse as the days go on. At first, I expected him to call me to check whether I was okay, or to see if the work he'd obviously had arranged had been done. Then I realised he didn't have my number, and I didn't have his.

Perhaps he'll drop in and see me? But he never did. Clearly the connection I'd felt with him was one-sided.

The worry I'm indebted to someone continues to nag at my mind. I try to forget it, but on one of my rest days find myself driving along the 110 toward Phoenix, where I'd heard the Satan's Devils compound was located. But as I've no idea of the precise location and, seeing no bikers around who I could follow, soon give it up as a fool's errand. I feel a mix of emotions. Relief that I haven't had to put my head into what would certainly be a den of iniquity, frustration I can't thank Peg, and a loss I don't quite understand, when I finally have to accept that I'll probably never see him again.

Apart from time wasted wondering about the man with the strange name, I've been busy tidying up my house and removing every trace of Pete Mercer. His clothes are bagged up and in the back of my closet, and his possessions are packed and stored in my garage. I've thrown his shampoo, toothbrush, and other bathroom items away. It's the best I can do. I've no inkling of the correct procedure when a man who abused you is languishing in a cell. One thing I know is I never want to see him again. Perhaps I should have donated everything he owned to charity? I might still do that.

I've got one more twenty-four-hour shift left to complete my five twenty-four hours on twenty-four hours off shift pattern, then I've got another six days off. People think we have it easy, but the job's so demanding, we need time to recharge. My work days seem to fly by and drag in equal proportions. One day we've barely nothing to do, the next shift we have call after call.

We've just finished another particularly gruelling shift when Slade comes up. "Ready for some breakfast?"

I've been with these men for twenty-four hours, but after the shit we've seen during the past night, would welcome the time, and help, to unwind. The captain knows it, which is why he's keeping us together. No one can understand the stress of the job like another firefighter can. The last call out had been chilling, a vehicle fire we couldn't put out in time, the crash victims had died while we were watching.

Seated in the establishment we habitually frequent for this purpose, we all order a substantial breakfast, and hungry, start digging in. In between a mouthful of eggs, I raise my chin to the man across the table. "How's the baby, Hammer?"

"Teething." His glum face shows he and his wife are having problems with that. "Crying all the time. Seems tuned in to when I want to get some sleep."

"Poor little mite."

His eyes widen. "I'm not little."

I punch him lightly on the arm.

"Hey. Looks like trouble." Slade's pointing to the TV up on the wall.

As one we all get up.

"Turn up the sound," Hammer shouts at the woman behind the counter, who does as asked. She's used to firefighters coming in here.

"Fuck." Truck voices all our thoughts.

"Only fifty or so acres so far." Slade's repeating what the newscaster is saying about the wildfire burning up in the mountains above Tucson.

"Is it contained?" I'm straining to hear, but I must have missed that bit.

"Twenty percent." Okay, sounds like they're getting it under control, but still some ways to go.

Truck's face looks pinched. "What's the weather forecast?"

Getting out my phone, I take a look. "Windy later."

"Shit, I hope they get it out before then." Hammer's face creases in concern.

Truck's still watching. "They're going to get the planes up. They're hitting it hard to stop it from spreading."

I don't envy my colleagues up in the forest, from whatever station they're based. Fighting a wildland fire is challenging work, and dangerous. It's impossible to guess when the wind might change and blow it in your direction.

"I imagine they'll put it out." Slade gives us his professional view. "As long as it's contained and doesn't spread. And there doesn't seem to be any property nearby."

That's good. No Houses, businesses, or people needing to be evacuated. Satisfied our fellow firefighters will be doing all they can to get the smallish fire under control, we return to our table and resume our conversation. Although we are an urban-based station dealing mainly with structural fires, we're also trained wildland firefighters, and have been called on to tackle many a wildfire over the years.

You can sum up a structural fire based on experience, know roughly what you're dealing with, and estimate how long it might take to put out and bring in the correct resources. But a wildfire? There's so many variables that mean you don't know what you're up against, and conditions can change swiftly. They can also be notoriously hard to extinguish.

I cast one last glance up at the TV, but the newscaster's moved onto something else. Hopefully the local crew will contain it. I'm not worried about myself, I'll fight whatever fire I'm asked to. But a wildfire can be dangerous, ravenous, and take far too much.

CHAPTER 7

Peg

"Let's talk prospects." The prez does his usual thing, leaning back in his chair and putting one foot up against the table and wiping his hand over his beard. "Hyde's been here eighteen months or more now. 'Bout time we decided one way or another."

When Wraith and Sophie had their baby, I'd taken over looking out for our recruits. Hence this private discussion between Drummer and myself today. "Prez, Fergus is proving he's a good fit. But I think we should leave it a while before discussing a patch, he hasn't really been tested yet. But Hyde, well, he's been impressing me." My mind goes back to that night when I helped a woman called Darcy. It's been a couple of weeks now, but I still can't get her out of my head.

Drummer sighs. "Slick and Heart will never agree."

"I'll just have to make them. He deserves it, Prez."

"Won't get no argument from me. The fucker's grown on me, and I think he'd make a good brother."

Hyde had made a few mistakes in the past, some of them out of his control, some out of ignorance. We usually patch prospects in after a year or decide they won't make it. But Hyde's been here far longer than that. To get your patch you need the vote from all the patched members. One member voting no and that's final.

"Paladin has it in for Hyde too." Drummer reminds me.

I growl. "Paladin will have to shut the fuck up. It's become too personal for him and Slick, and that shit Hyde did? It's way back in the rearview." These men are still holding a grudge, and for far too long, if I'm asked.

Drum's face shows how hard a job he thinks I'm going to have. But he knows as well as I do that a man can't prospect forever. The time has come that Hyde's either in or he's out. "Okay, Peg, I hear you. You try and work on them, and we'll bring it to Friday night's church."

I agree. Another few days, and while I hate to admit it, if my powers of persuasion don't work, Hyde will be leaving the compound for good. I hope it doesn't come to that.

Drummer levels me with his stare. "What's going on with you, Peg? You seem a bit out of it lately."

Now this is unusual, a personal probe by the prez. He's taken me by surprise. In the pause before I answer, he leans behind him and gets a bottle of whisky and two glasses out of a cupboard. I raise my chin and he pours me a glass.

"Club's changin'," I tell him. Drummer and I go back years, to the days before the Satan's Devils moved to this compound, to the time when Drummer's father, Bastard, ran the club. It was a totally different era then. We were involved in the type of shit I never want to be part of again and, which had in a round-about way, got me enlisting. I'd remained a member, the old clubhouse my home when I was on leave. I'd been there that fateful night when Bastard and most of the old members ended up locked up or dead. Together with Drummer, and some of the others, I'd been arrested during a police raid on our strip club. No charges stuck, so luckily I was able to re-join my regiment.

I went back and forth, easily fitting in with both sets of brothers, returning once on leave to find the club had moved to this new location, a complete step up, and pleased to see we were out of most of the dirty side of life. It was on my very next tour that an IED took part of my leg.

If it wasn't for the club, I don't know what would have happened to me. But they supported me, kept me buoyed up. Built a gym and equipped it so I could build up my strength and get used to wearing a prosthesis. Yeah, Drummer and I go back a very long time.

"Changin' for the better?" His sharp eyes show he's waiting for my answer.

What can I say? For years, apart from Bullet and Viper, who've had old ladies for what seems like forever, and Heart when he was married to Crystal, the rest of us were single, and Amy the only kid in the club. Now we've got a fucking nursery set up, and Heart and his new woman will shortly be adding two more babies to the mix. We've still got the sweet butts, and most brothers remain single, but the atmosphere's changing.

"Bastard would have had a fit. All the kids and ol' ladies?"

Prez barks a laugh. "That he would, Brother, that he would."

"Wouldn't recognise us, Drum. No smoking in the club-room, havin' to watch yer language when the kids are around. Not to mention the fuckin' dog." I smile though—Grunt, having grown into a full-size wolfhound now with whatever other part in his heritage being overshadowed, has fit right in.

"It's a family, Peg. Always been that. Kids and old ladies are part of it, natural progression. Club's growin' up, gettin' older."

Yeah, but sometimes I feel that I'm not moving on like the others. Without my own old lady, I can't help feeling I'm on the outside looking in.

He sits forward and puts his elbows on the desk, watching me carefully. "Are we makin' too many adjustments for the family life? Not caterin' to all the brothers' needs? Single brothers feelin' excluded?"

Quickly I give a shake of my head. "Nah, it's not like that, Prez. Things are different, but not for the worse. With my sergeant-at-arms hat on, it gives us more to protect. The next generation." I pause, trying to brush away the thought that I wish I was personally adding to that. Again, the vision of Darcy comes into my head. *I wonder if she'd adjust to life as an old lady?*

"What you thinkin' about, Peg?"

I'm not going to tell him, he'll think I've gone soft in my old age. *Thirty-seven isn't old.* Probably not, but some days I feel ancient, and as if life's passed me by, that I've lost my chance, just like I lost my leg.

There are some discussions you don't have with your prez. I finish my whisky and stand up. "I've got people to speak to."

His face twists, and it seems like he's issuing a challenge. "You best start straight away. Fuck knows how long it will take you to persuade Slick."

I pull back my shoulder and step into the clubroom only to find neither of the men I need to talk to are there. Frustrated, I exchange chin lifts with those who are present, pat Amy on the head in passing, then go outside. That's where I find one of the brothers I'm after. It's Slick, having a cigarette, but he doesn't notice my approach. He's standing, staring into the distance.

"Slick."

"Peg." Without turning to acknowledge me, he points his hand. Up on the mountains behind the compound, it's possible to see smoke is rising. Part of the Coronado Forest is on fire on the highest slopes of the Catalina Mountains. A common enough sight during the summer months, but one which is always disturbing. No one around here can forget the Aspen Fire and the damage it caused. Nor that shortly after that another smaller fire targeted the vacation resort that became, as a direct result, our compound. Fire, we respect.

"Doesn't look like much."

"Nah, probably no need to worry. No properties up that way that I can think of." He shades his eyes with his hand. "They're droppin' retardant on it from a plane."

"Firefighters know to get on top of that shit fast."

It's far enough away from us that I'm not concerned. Except a fleeting worry for a particular firefighter. *Is she up there right now? Does she tackle wild fires?* Fuck, whether she does or just works in the urban area, it's one hell of a job for a woman. If she was mine, I'd be constantly worrying about her. *Oh, for fuck's sake, she'll never be yours.*

"Makes you think, though."

I am thinking. But probably not along the lines he is. "What's on yer mind, Slick?"

"The fire that swept through here."

I'm not surprised he's thinking the same as I had been. It's automatic to turn around and take another look at the smoke in the distance. It's high up and miles away and doesn't look like much. "Fires usually rise, don't they? Can't think we're under threat here. And certainly not from that one. It's too far away."

My companion nods and finishes his smoke, carefully stubbing out the end on his boot. "You want me for anything, Peg?"

His question reminds me what I've come out here for. "Yeah, need to have words." I take a breath, then dive straight in. "Hyde…"

"Ain't getting my vote." Anticipating my question, Slick replies without pause.

I roll my head back on my shoulders. *Just as I expected.* I make the ramifications clear. "Then he's out."

"Yeah?" Slick's turned around, looking at me straight in the face. "He's out?" He huffs, then turns back to look at the distant fire again. "Good."

We stand in silence for a moment, then I sigh. "He's a good man, Slick. Got a good head on his shoulders. He's grown since he's been here. Takes all the shit and never complains. I think it's time we patch him in."

"Nope."

I knew I wouldn't get all the way in one go, just wanted to give him something to think on. You don't get far arguing with Slick, just makes him dig in harder. I pat him on the shoulder. "Vote's on Friday."

"Won't be changin' my mind."

Yeah, you will. Hyde's given his all to the club for eighteen months. When Slick thinks about it, he'll realise that. Chucking him out now wouldn't be right. Or, at least, I hope that's the conclusion he comes to.

I walk away and go back into the clubroom. When Hyde first came here, he'd made some mistakes—letting the cops onto the compound without a warrant being one of them, but he was as green as shit then, overwhelmed by the cops. Slick's old lady's sister could have been seen when we were trying to keep her out of sight and protected. But that was a long time ago, and while Hyde's fucked up since, it hadn't really been his fault.

A happy scream of 'Daddy' shows me the second person I need to talk to has come into sight. Heart's walking in, his arms around his heavily pregnant old lady, an ex-cop who had to do more than most to prove herself to the club. I wait and watch fondly as he kneels and cuddles his daughter. When he finally stands, I go across.

"Down, Grunt." Slightly staggering as the two enormous paws land on my chest, I push off the attentions of the over-exuberant dog that's never far from Amy. "Heart, a word?"

After kissing Marcia, he places a hand on her stomach, a look of delight tells me the babies are probably kicking. Twins, they're expecting, in just a few weeks. No wonder she's looking as big as a house.

"Beer," he demands of Fergus. I hold a finger in the air, indicating I want one too, then we go to a table in the corner. "What can I do for you, Peg?"

As he sits, he kicks out a chair. I plant myself opposite him, pick up the beer, and start picking at the label. When I raise my eyes, he's looking expectant. "Hyde."

His head rolls back, then down. "What about the fucker?"

"Decision on patchin' him in on Friday."

Both hands go up and brush back his shoulder length blond hair, holding it back for a moment. His blue eyes focus on mine. "Slick's never gonna say yes."

"Not askin' Slick. I'm askin' you."

Heart swivels his head and glances across to his old lady, a soft smile plays on his lips. As I follow the direction of his eyes, the thoughts in my head are that that he's a lucky fucker. *I want me some of that.*

"How long's he been prospectin', Peg?" Heart turns back around, giving me his attention again.

"Eighteen months now."

Heart nods. "Fucker's done his time. He gets his patch or he's gone, right?"

"That's the gist of it."

He sighs. "I trust him. He had Marc's back."

Well that was easier than I thought.

"Ain't gonna get patched in, though. Slick and Paladin will never give him their vote." He grins, drains the bottle, and leaves the empty on the table.

One down. Now I've just got to work harder on Slick. Paladin won't stand out on his own.

CHAPTER 8

Darcy

"Had a briefing with the batt chief and the assistant chiefs."

We all look towards Captain Slade, wondering what's coming next. If he's met with the chief of the battalion and the men reporting to the men at the top, what's coming next needs our full attention.

"That fire the other day, well, we feel that's just the start of it. Tinder box conditions out there. Reminds me of just before Aspen."

"Like that a lot of years. And we always get fires," Hammer comments.

"And put them out," says Truck.

"Sooner or later," Hammer comments dryly.

The captain looks around. "He wants everyone to be prepared. Hopefully when the monsoons start things will get dampened down."

"Cancelling leave?" Truck asks.

"Don't think any of us have got any booked." Slade turns to each one of us, noting the shakes of our heads. "And it goes without saying, we'll be there if there's a need to come in during our rest days." He sighs. "Probably don't need to remind you that the national hot shot crews are all dealing with the wildland fires in California. Something happens here before they're dealt with and we'll be on our own."

Not like we haven't done it before, but it's easier when we've a hot shot crew taking the lead.

There's no predicting where or when a fire might hit. The summer storms can be dry storms bringing lightening with no rain. Then there's our other adversary, fires often started by human hand, either accidentally or deliberately.

"Right. Well I just wanted to catch you before you went off shift."

"We'll be ready." I know I speak for my companions as I reply to Slade.

After the captain's pep talk, I go to my locker to collect my bag. As I take my phone out, I see I've got a couple of missed calls. Eager to catch up on the latest, I return the call.

"Hi. It's Darcy Cavanaugh."

It's Grover. He politely enquires how I am.

"I'm fine, Detective. You?"

But Grover hasn't been calling for chit chat. "What?" My hand goes out and clutches the door of my locker for support. "What do you mean Pete Mercer had another bail hearing? Why wasn't I informed?"

"He's out?"

"Yeah, I know there was nothing you could do. Yeah, thank you for calling. I appreciate the warning."

Having come into the locker room while I was talking, Hammer comes up alongside. Leaning back against the lockers, he folds his arms. "What's up?"

"Bastard who shot me has been let out on bail. His lawyer worked some magic. Some family connection or other." I feel shaky, the thought of that man being free makes my face throb all over again.

"Whassup?" Now Slade's here too.

Quickly Hammer fills him in.

"Well, only one thing for it. You need to get a restraining order, Flash. Make sure he stays away from you."

"Like a piece of paper is going to keep him away. And he doesn't need to get close if he gets his hands on a gun."

"Oh, com'ere, sweetie." Suddenly Hammer's big strong arms come around me, and his meaty hand rubs up and down my back. "You keep a gun?"

"No, I don't like them." I hate the things and won't have them in the house. Well, not knowingly anyway. I frown as I remember how Pete had brought one into my home, and look how that ended. I don't like to think of it, but if that bullet had been a few inches over I might not be here.

Slade's staring at me, but his eyes are shuttered so it's impossible to see what he's thinking. But after a moment he lets me in on his thoughts. "Don't like the idea of you being alone with this fucker running around. Why don't you come and stay with us?"

Him and his wife? Now that would be intruding, and Pete's already interfered with enough of my life. I shake my head. "I can't allow him to push me out of my home. I've got new locks and a good security system now." I frown slightly before adding, "I should be safe." Pete wouldn't be coming straight back to my house. *Would he?* There's no reason for him to, and surely he's got enough sense to stay well away.

"What's going on?" This from Truck. Hammer and Slade quickly update him, and now he looks concerned as well. His brow creases. "You've got a spare room, haven't yer? I could come stay with you. At least for a few days until we know whether he's going to bother you or not."

Let another man into my guest room? Possibly to put down roots like the last one? Knocking the heel of my hand against my forehead, I wonder what's best to do. I know Truck wouldn't take advantage of me like Pete had done. Nevertheless… Eyeing my team, I'm certain if any of them were faced with a comparable situation they wouldn't think of asking for help. Not in the same way. But because I'm a woman they're being overprotective. No, I've got to stand up for myself.

"Truck, thank you. But as soon as I'm inside my house I'll be fine. It's like a fortress now. No one can get in, and if they try, alarms will go off. I'll make sure I always have my phone at hand to call the police." I pause and force a smile. "And there's nothing to say Pete would have the nerve to come back. If he's out on bail, he can't risk getting close. And while he lied and told me he was on his own, he seems to have family enough to raise bail. He'll go to them, I'm sure." Yeah, telling me he had nowhere to go had clearly been a ploy. But for what reason I can't imagine.

My colleagues are still looking worried. I put my hand on Truck's arm, feeling his warm skin under my fingers. As his hand comes down and covers mine, he looks down and raises an eyebrow. I give him my answer. "Thank you, Truck, but I'm sure I'll be fine on my own."

Slade's tapping his hand against his thigh, head tilted to one side. "Can't be a man down when we're on high alert. We've got your back, Flash. Truck, you'll follow her home, make sure the fucker's not hiding out waiting for her. Check it out at least."

"I can't ask you do to that." I'm feeling like a weak little woman the way they're all so willing to help. If I were a man they'd be shrugging their shoulders and wishing me good luck, expecting me to take care of things myself. I frown. I don't want to be treated any differently. I'm able to do this job as well as any of them.

Seeing me looking doubtful, Slade pushes his point. "You're not asking, I'm offering. Well, telling, really. Truck's going your way anyway. Look, Flash, there's no doubt you pull your weight, seen you put even more into it as if you've got something to prove. But while you're equally as strong as a man when it comes to doing your job, from what you said, this Pete's a big fucker, and you know nothing about self-defence."

Shooting my eyes to his, I realise he can read me like a book, knowing exactly what to say to make me feel better. For a second, I bask in the compliments he just paid me.

"Think we could rectify that?" Hammer's looking at me shrewdly. "We spend enough time working out, perhaps we can teach her some moves."

Gently I put my fist to his shoulder. "I'm right here, you know." Then I think about what he's asked. "Perhaps it would be useful. I don't seem to have the best taste in men."

Looking thoughtful, Slade nods his head. "Good idea, Ham. But until you've learned how to protect yourself, we've got your back."

When I first got that phone call, initial thoughts were to panic. But now, having spoken to my teammates, it's put things into perspective. I'm certain I'm right. Pete wouldn't take the risk of causing more trouble, but just in case I'll let Truck help check my place out. If Pete is there waiting, he wouldn't have a chance against the two of us.

My house looks exactly the same as I left it. I park on the driveway, Truck pulls up on the side of the street. I wait for him to come up beside me before putting my key in the lock. Gently he pushes me to one side and walks in. Peering around his huge bulk, nothing seems to be amiss.

"Stay here. Let me check everything out."

Though it's highly unlikely he's managed to get inside without a key, I need to warn Truck. "What if he's armed?" The memory of the bullet hitting my arm causes my healed wound to itch.

"I'll be careful. But I doubt he'll have a gun. He wouldn't be able to get one legally." He pauses, then suggests, "You really ought to have one yourself, you know?"

"No." I shake my head adamantly. "I detest the things and wouldn't know how to use a weapon if I did have one."

"Then it's lucky I do." He slides his out of his pocket and expertly holds it in front of him as he disappears from sight.

I stand, biting my nails and waiting, feeling nervous for once in my life. I'll tackle any fire, run into any burning building, but the thought that what I now know is a violent man might be staked out in my house is chilling. *Perhaps I should move? Go somewhere he can't find me?* But why should I let him chase me out of my home?

Already it's tainted, with memories of him in every room. I thought that time would have erased them, but that's when I thought he'd stay locked up.

How did he get bail?

"I've checked everywhere. Nothing seems to be out of place —you're a tidy freak, ain'cha?" Truck's eyes are twinkling. "No windows look tampered with, and the security system you had installed is excellent. Nothing for you to worry about."

Feeling relieved, I thank him. "Want a coffee or something now you're here?"

"Yeah, could use a beer."

Taking him into the kitchen, I get a couple out of the fridge. As I'm raising the bottle to my lips, I frown.

"What you thinking, Flash?"

"I'm sorry about this, Truck. You know I always pull my weight…"

He steps forward and gets into my face. "Now stop right there, Flashfire. We're a team, you know that. You've been a firefighter for a few years now. Hell, you've got a lot more experience than me. I look up to you just as I do any of the others. You've got nothing to prove, you've done that already. We don't make allowances for your sex, as we don't have to."

But he is, he wouldn't be here otherwise. I go to open my mouth, but I don't get a chance.

"This situation, it's out of the ordinary. And if Hammer had an abusive woman after him, or fuck, if I did, then don't think for a moment we wouldn't be acting the same way. This guy who hurt you, he's irrational. Up against a fire? We know what we're dealing with. Him? Or anyone who threatens one of the team? It's more than one person can take on, male or female."

He pauses to take a gulp of his drink, then points the bottle toward me. "This doesn't mean you're weak, Flash. The way the team stood up to help you? That shows how valued a colleague you are, and that we don't want to lose you."

I hadn't thought of it like that. Slowly my lips curve up, and then tension, and guilt, start to drift away. "Thanks for putting it into perspective, Truck."

He nods. "And for the record, no one thinks you're weak or that you can't look after yourself. The only difference between us is that we've learned to fight back. Just a gap in your knowledge, Flash, and we'll be seeing if we can't rectify that. A few self-defence lessons and you'll know how to handle yourself better."

That's something positive I can work with.

"Hey, I know you don't need me to stay, but I could eat. How about you? Want pizza?"

Pizza? For breakfast? I laugh, then, finding I've got a taste for it too, I readily agree. Truck takes out his phone, I tell him what I want, then disappear to the bathroom while he calls in the order.

After I've freshened up it's not long before there's a loud knock on the front door. Truck indicates I should stay back, then goes and checks who's there. When he returns he's carrying three pizza boxes.

"Three?" My eyes open in disbelief.

"I'm a growing lad."

My eyes widen as I snort a laugh. If he grows much more he won't fit in my house.

Truck's an easy companion. Taking our pizzas into the living room, we sit on the couch. The aroma of food gets my mouth watering, and I devour the half of the one he bought for me, my eyes widening as he manages to make two and a half disappear. I joke I can see how he grew into his name, even though I know his bulk's all muscle. When we've finished he takes the boxes and puts them into the trash.

"You want to talk about it?" he asks when he comes back.

I know what he means. Maybe it will help to open up. "This is going to sound stupid, Truck, but I thought I liked Pete at first. Hell, I hadn't had a good conversation with a man in ages. When he invited me for a coffee, I went like a shot. A man who I'd met when his house was on fire. Crazy, eh?"

"Nothing wrong with that. Fuck, the work that we do? Ain't got no time to meet people the normal way." He rubs his hand over his face. "It's something I sometimes worry about. How do you meet the man or woman you want in your life? Not while we're working, that's for sure. Hardly see people at their best when they've had the shit scared out of them, or they're injured and hurting. Can't date someone on your team, would throw the dynamics right off. And who else do we meet? Cops? Hell, you'd never manage to synchronise your shifts, so you could even date."

It's probably the most he's said at one time. What he has said makes sense and validates what I've come to regret as an unwise decision.

"He seemed normal. Nice." My mind drifts back. "I was cautious. Even though he'd just lost everything he was pretty pragmatic about it. He didn't seem to care about the possessions that had burned, just the fact he was homeless. He even that he tried to brush off. I was apologising that we hadn't managed to save anything. It wasn't what I expected. You know what most people are like."

Truck's meaty hand grasps mine and gives it a squeeze. Man or woman, some of the distress we see can be painful to watch.

"Anyway, so there we were in the coffee shop. Stayed longer than expected." If he hadn't wiped all my good memories away with that first slap to my face, I would have been smiling. "He did everything right, a perfect gentleman. His focus totally on me, I had to dig to get him to tell me much about himself."

"That, right there," Truck interrupts. "He was hiding something."

"I know that now," I agree. "But at the time I thought it was sweet. We stayed longer than I expected, ordered food. Our meal had been entertaining, and he was certainly easy on the eyes."

"Was there a spark?"

I answer honestly. "No, he was a good companion and I told him that. Didn't expect we'd be seeing each other again. But then he offered to pay. That's when it all changed. His wallet and everything had gone. It suddenly got to him, what he'd lost, and he told me he had nowhere to go. It was an off-the-cuff remark that he supposed I didn't have a spare room he could crash for the night...."

"And you said yes?"

I point down the hallway. Why, I'm not sure. "I've got a spare room. It was getting late by then. He would have needed money for a motel or something. Though he wasn't my type, he seemed decent enough. Christ, I'm a bad judge of character, aren't I? Yeah, I said yes."

"And once he'd sorted himself out? You let him stay on?"

"After one night it seemed easy to agree that he could stay for a few days. And then, even longer until he got back on his feet. But he convinced me that was taking more time than it should."

"That doesn't sound right."

"I know, right? But when he was standing in front of me, his excuses sounded plausible."

"Beer?" Standing, Truck waves his empty bottle at me.

"Thanks." All this talking is making my throat dry.

When Truck returns with a couple of beers, I take a swallow and continue. "What you did then, getting me a drink, that's what he did at first. He was so easy to live with. Did all the chores, made himself useful. But then he started hinting he wanted to share my bed." I risk a glance at him to check I wasn't sharing too much information, but Truck just nods for me to go on. "I even considered it. We'd slipped into an easy relationship, but I still didn't see him that way, couldn't force something that wasn't right. But he seemed to accept it, and the company was quite nice. I got used to him being here, having someone to talk to." Looking back now, he'd sucked me in. "I never led him on, Truck. But slowly he started to change, and his mask dropped. He became slovenly, unhelpful. Expecting me to clean up after him."

"Why didn't you show him the door at that point?"

I bite my lip, then admit, "I was going to, but looking back, I think I was nervous of him even then. It was easier to avoid confrontation. But I was trying to pluck up the courage to do it."

"Why the fuck didn't you come to us?"

I stare down at my beer, and then decide to be honest. "It was my problem to solve. I didn't want to be the weak female who needed help."

Truck turns to look at me, his eyes open wide. "You know we'd never measure you by a mess you got into in your private life. Fuck, Flash, it wouldn't have made us think any differently of you." He shakes his head before continuing, "What made him break?"

"I should have seen it. Rather than being supportive, when I started to come home after a long shift he'd talk about you guys. He wanted to know everything about the team. Hammer and Slade, he dismissed as they're married. But you, well, he started asking about you. Were you on that day? Was I working out with you?

"That last evening was day of that fire at the warehouse. It had been a long shift."

Nodding, his eyes look at nothing, as he remembers and adds, "That was a bad one. We stayed late there. Weren't going to give up. I still remember that man's screams, and that we couldn't get to him in time."

"And his poor pregnant wife. I wasn't in a good place, Truck. Hell, I don't need to tell you, I think it got to us all that day. But it was well into the evening by the time I got home."

Truck fills in the blanks. "And he accused you of having an affair."

"More or less, yes. I couldn't understand, tried to reason with him. It wasn't any business of his anyway. The first slap came out of the blue. I was in shock."

"Oh, Flash." His arm comes around me. "You got drawn in by a con."

"I know that now." I want to change the subject, feeling strangely reluctant to explain how bikers came to my aid that night. If Truck believes I make wrong choices, I don't want to compound it by letting what the city thinks are criminals into my house.

CHAPTER 9

Peg

As I sit listening to the normal business being discussed at our Friday night church, I'm mentally preparing for what's coming up on the agenda. Throughout the meeting I've caught the smirks Slick's been throwing my way, and I'm getting more and more worried that today might be the last time we'll be seeing Hyde around the compound. I'm going to miss the fucker. I've always found him to be willing and helpful, and he comes up with intelligent suggestions. Okay, he had problems in the beginning, but he's slowly but surely been learning our ways, and I, for one, wouldn't hesitate in trusting him to have my back.

"So, Peg. What d'you think?"

With a start, I realise I've completely lost track of the meeting. Unusual for me, I make something up, hoping it fits in with what they were discussing. "Sounds okay."

Drummer bangs the gavel. "Okay. That's what we'll do, as we're all in agreement."

Thank fuck no strange looks are being sent my way. But I'd love to know what I just supported.

"Now, Peg. You want the floor?"

I inhale a deep breath. Here goes nothing. "I want to bring the subject of prospects to the table." I wait for that to sink in. Blade has stopped spinning his knife, and Slick sits back, takes out a cigarette, and lights up. His face is impassive, and I still can't read him. It's difficult to see Heart's reaction, he's sitting a couple of seats down from me.

"I'll throw it open in a minute but want to give you my thoughts first. Let's start with Fergus. He's been here getting on for a year, but I'm not recommending we patch him in yet. We need a prospect to do the shit, and while he's probably close to earning his patch, I don't think he's quite ready to bring to the table. Anyone think different?"

"Like the man," Wraith puts in. "But we've not had a chance to see how he responds under threat."

Yeah, one thing I'm happy about. There haven't been any dead bodies to dispose of for a while.

Wraith's observation is echoed around the table and it's not lost on me that while it's not vocalised, my point that we need at least one prospect means whatever happens to Hyde, he won't be a recruit after today.

I take another breath. "Which brings me to Hyde."

Jekyll's hand shoots up, Prez nods. "I'd got a couple of things I'd like to say. I know I'm the newest member at this table, but I worked alongside Hyde for a year. He's hard working and dependable, and I trust him. Don't know if my view counts for anything, but he never turned down even the shittiest of jobs."

"Your views as valid as any other," Prez tells him. "Anyone else got anything to say?"

I have. "Hyde's been prospecting for longer than anyone else. We either patch him in, or part ways." I lean forward, wearing my sergeant-at-arms face. "He's been here eighteen months dealing with all the shit that we've thrown at him." I pause, then slam my fist down on the table. "And never once have I heard him complain. Unlike you, Jekyll."

Jekyll shrugs and gives a quick grin, he can't deny I've said the truth. Though he always did what we asked, he could be a grouchy asshole at times. Paladin, sitting beside him, places a playful punch on his arm.

Prez raises his eyebrow at me, and I shrug. Might as well get this over with. "Right," Drummer starts. "Let's go around the table. And I don't need to remind you, one nay and Hyde leaves the compound tonight."

Shit, that's rough. He'll have nowhere to go, no one beside him. That will hit the man hard. I, at least, don't feel good about that. It's the brotherhood that's attracted him and what's made him put up with whatever's come his way for the last eighteen months.

Wraith nods in my direction and starts us off with a yay. Dollar echoes him. Bullet's quick too, another positive vote. Blade thinks about it, a snide look in my direction, and I know the delay is only to make me squirm, but then he votes the right way too. Now it's Slick's turn.

Slick's staring down at his hands. "Hyde fucked up when my old lady first came here. Fucked up good." He pauses and raises his head, receiving the chin lifts of acknowledgment. Even I jerk my chin in his direction, there's no denying what Hyde had done. "I'll leave Heart to talk about what went on with him." Heart, seated opposite, growls. Then, an unexpected grin comes to Slick's face. "I'll miss givin' the asshole shit, but I'm not adverse to bringin' him to the table. He's got things straight over the past few months. My vote's aye."

One down, two to go. But I can't see Paladin going against Slick. The vote goes quickly around the next few members, Beef, Marvel, Joker, and Lady all giving their assents.

I cock my eyebrow at Paladin and wait for him to speak. "Prospectin"'s hard, it's not far in my rearview, same as for Jekyll here. At the time it's hard to understand all the flack you get thrown at you. But there's a reason for that, as we all know. If we don't have complete trust in a brother, this club's gonna fall."

He breaks off as though pulling his thoughts together. While I'm wondering where he's going with this, I'm also respecting how much he's grown into a man. At nineteen we brought little more than a lad to the table, and that hadn't turned out to be a mistake.

Paladin catches my eye. "Hyde's honest, hardworkin', and he lives for this life and the chance to be patched in. I wouldn't want to deny him. With a dependable man like him, I'd be proud to call him brother. I vote aye."

Thank fuck.

Jekyll shrugs. "I like him, Aye from me."

Viper's quick and says aye. Shooter and Rock don't take much time. Road gives his vote, another plus for Hyde. Then it's Heart's turn.

Leaning forward to look down the table, I see him shaking his head. Damn it. He'll be a no, I'm certain.

Heart clears his throat. "Hyde looked after my old lady. Kept her safe, kept her sane before I came to my senses. I knew what she meant to me, just hadn't admitted it at the time. If I trusted him to look after one of the most important women in my life, I have to trust him to stand up beside me. Sure, there were cock-ups, made me furious at the time. But he got bested by my old lady. Doubt any of us could have done better." That raises a laugh. He leans forward and looks me straight in the face. "I vote aye."

After that it's quick. Mouse doesn't take a minute to give his positive answer, I say mine, and then Prez hesitates. *Oh shit.*

"I don't have a problem with the fucker. Think he'll do good things for the club. It's a unanimous vote, Peg. Let's call him in."

My sigh of relief comes from my heart. Now, this is the bit we all enjoy. Thinking back to my prospecting days, I remember being called to the table, shaking and quivering, not knowing what to expect. Jekyll, his face stern, leaves the room and returns quickly with Hyde in tow.

Drum fixes him with his death stare, and points to a space at the end of the table. "Stand there."

Hyde glances at me, his face drawn. *He knows what this is and expects to be thrown out of the club.* He'll know he'll be unable to put forward any case in his favour. And he isn't stupid. After all the time he's been here, he understands if he doesn't get a patch now, he never will.

He pulls back his shoulders and looks straight at the prez.

The silence seems to last forever. A pin dropping would be louder than any other noise we make. Every brother staring down the table, but to Hyde's credit he takes it, and doesn't look away.

Eventually Drum speaks. "You've been prospecting for us for eighteen months now. Came in with Jekyll, but we gave you longer, as you needed a few second chances."

Hyde doesn't flinch, doesn't show any reaction, doesn't try to defend himself for the mistakes that he made. In the light I see his eyes glisten, the only sign of emotion, but one that signals how devastating it will be if he isn't accepted into the club.

Now prez makes the unusual move. He gestures to Slick. "Slick, you've had problems with Hyde. Anything you want to say?" Briefly he shields his face with his hand, and I guess he's given Slick a wink.

Wraith's passing something to Dollar, who passes it to Blade, and now Slick's fumbling with something under the table. Then he stands up, his hands held down to his sides.

"You cocked up, Prospect. No arguin' with that. Those second chances Prez mentioned, well, you needed them more than once."

Hyde's eyes go to Slick's, but still he doesn't try to stand up for himself, but now his shoulders slump.

Bastard that he is, Slick lets the silence stretch out, then, "You've taken those chances, and proved yourself. Welcome to the table, Brother." With his words, Slick brings out the patches he was holding. The Satan's Devils insignias that Hyde will now be able to sew on his cut and wear with pride as a fully patched member.

Brothers are stamping their feet, banging fists on the table, and hollering. Slick walks around, passes the patches over into Hyde's hands, then puts his arm around his back, slaps it and pulls Hyde briefly to him. Heart's on his feet and giving him a man hug in a similar way. Hyde's not stupid, he knew these were the two he'd have to convince. A smile creeps over my face as I watch. Prez, fucking Prez letting Slick do the honours. He knew exactly what he was doing. Showing Hyde his past crimes have been forgiven.

Now we're all on our feet. Someone yells out, "Patch-in party!"

Hyde's still not cracked a smile, he seems bemused. I wait my turn, then speak to him quietly. "Well done, Brother. You deserve this."

As I look into his face, he wipes away a tear, and then, at last, his face cracks. "Thanks, Peg." Then louder, he calls out, "Thanks everyone. I won't let you down."

"Fuckin' sure you won't." I slap his back, then follow my brothers out, now thirsty. I really hadn't been certain that vote would go the way I wanted it to.

When Hyde comes into the clubroom he's hustled toward the bar. The first thing he does is shake Fergus's hand. Then, with glee, asks the prospect why he hasn't got a drink in his yet. That cracks us all up and breaks any remaining tension.

Marcia, Heart's old lady, heavily pregnant, is waddling over toward him, but I take the opportunity to have a word with him first.

"Heart, thank you."

His eyes, which have been tracking Marcia's progress, turn to me. "It was the right decision, Peg. I know that. Hyde's a good man." Then he leans down and whispers conspiratorially, "And between you and me, Marc would have had my balls if he'd left."

As the woman in question joins us, I point to her swollen belly. "How long is it now, Marcia?"

She frowns. "Technically another five weeks, but could be any day now."

"That okay if they come early?" What do I know about a woman's pregnancy?

"Yeah. They should be okay. There's a higher chance of premature birth with twins, but it's equally possible I could go full term."

The longer those babies keep incubating, the better it will probably be. Suddenly a big grey shape launches itself at me, and as it's unexpected, I'm nearly knocked off my feet.

"Down, Grunt!" Heart snaps out.

But the darn monster of a dog is quite happy licking my face. I push him away, but I can't help chuckling. It amazes me how such a big, clumsy animal seems to be so gentle with Amy and the toddlers.

Maybe I should get a dog. Something to keep me company and ease the emptiness that's in my life.

Grunt soon spies another victim and leaves me alone. Heart and his old lady move away. I stand at the bar, beer in my hand, suddenly crushed by a loneliness that's hard to explain. I've got brothers around me, yet there's a hole in my life. Seeing the kids when they're down in the clubroom, Marcia with her stomach swollen with her old man's seed. *I want that for me.*

"Wouldn't want to be Heart." Beef comes up alongside me, jerking his head where the man in question is walking off.

"Diapers definitely aren't on my horizon. We've got it good, Peg. Never want an ol' lady."

Half listening to Beef as I see Heart taking Marcia out the door, I realise it's getting late. The other old ladies have already gone, and the sweet butts wearing almost nothing are starting to come in.

Beef hasn't noticed I've been distracted. "Look what we've got going for us. Club whores, and there'll be hangarounds from Tucson here in a while. Variety's the spice of life, eh, Peg? This is the life, ain't it? This is what it's really like to be a club member."

Hyde, taking advantage of his new status, is making a beeline for Paige, and is quick in accepting Diva's offer too. With brothers calling and whistling, he flips them off over his shoulder and disappears with both girls out the back to the crash rooms.

I could go with a club whore, get her to keep me company for a while. She'll know the score and won't remark on my missing leg. Even if it disgusts her, she'll ignore it.

But lately I've lost any urge simply to get my rocks off. I must be getting old. I want sex to mean something, to have a woman in my bed who's interested in more than my cock.

Discretely I make my way to the entrance, stepping outside into the night. With my brothers all busy drinking or fucking, or getting dicks sucked, nobody notices me leave.

<h1 style="text-align:center">CHAPTER 10</h1>

Darcy

A week has gone past with no word from Pete, and I'm starting to relax. After our next six rest days I return to work. My co-workers haven't been strangers in the meantime, they've been dropping around, checking I'm doing okay, and that my erstwhile assailant is staying away, each trying to reassure me in their own way that they'd do the same for anyone of our crew who was in difficulty.

Back together at the station, Slade puts on his captain's hat and is wearing a serious expression. He gestures at us to sit down. He doesn't need to tell us we are going to want to hear this.

"While the recent wildfire was contained and put out, we've had reports from State Forestry Service's firewatchers checking the conditions on the mountains," Slade tells us. "They're particularly concerned about the area above the foothills to the south of the Santa Catalina Range."

"Where the Aspen Fire was? Back in 2002?"

As Truck asks, I recall that was a bad one. It took out over three hundred businesses and homes, all but destroyed the town of Summerhaven, and caused untold damage to the infrastructure, phone and electric lines, streets, and sewers. I shudder. It had burned for a month. We deal with smaller fires as a matter of course, but that one left so many homeless it preys on my mind. Before my time, of course, but we'd all heard about it.

"Not so much there, Truck. Further north. We're more worried about the forest that didn't burn that time." Slade wipes his hand over his face. "The forecast is for temperatures to rise, and humidity levels are extremely low. There are a lot of snags, many trees are dead where they stand, and those that are living have moisture levels at the bottom of the scale. Red flag warning has been issued," Slade observes, then thinks. "No large-scale evacuation alert needed though. There's no structures in that part that they're most worried about."

"Infrastructure?" Hammer asks.

"Cell phone tower and power lines," Slade informs him. Then continues, "Extra posters and warnings have been erected. And we've got adverts running on TV."

"Are they going to ban the public from the area?" I wonder aloud.

"Not yet, not unless something sparks. Just hoping they'll take notice of the warnings."

"Can't warn a lightning strike." That's Truck's contribution.

There are many factors we need to keep into consideration, but the likelihood is that area will burn, and we'll be right in there fighting it. A large out of control fire could easily spread to areas where there are people living.

"Obviously dispatch will call us in if and when we need to get involved, but I just wanted to remind you that we'll be the IA for that area." Yeah, we don't really need another reminder that in the absence of the national firefighting teams, we're the initial attack team called in for wildfires in that locality.

Slade nods at the captain. "We're going over strategy and preparedness today. Make sure everyone is up to date."

The shift begins slowly, and Slade has three hours in which to drill the importance and positioning of lookouts, communications, escape routes, and safety zones into us. None of us are bored, and reminders can't hurt when it could be a case of our life or death. Then the speakers blare out and we're being dispatched. Turns out it's to a fire in an apartment, caused by a faulty appliance. We bring that under control, make sure no sparks remain, and then return to the station house. Hammer starts making coffee, but before we can drink it we're being dispatched again. This time to a burning car on the highway.

Twelve hours into our shift, and we get the first reports. A wisp of smoke has been spotted exactly in the area predicted. On high alert, we wait for the updates on the situation. It's being dealt with by the local crews for now, and our assistance isn't needed. There's no breeze to speak of, and they seem to have successfully put the fire out, losing little more than a couple of acres.

After our twenty-four-hour shift, we're able to stand down, relieved that the wildland fire had been easily contained.

"Er, Flash?"

"Yeah, Truck?" I notice he's standing with his phone in his hand.

"A couple of buddies are home on leave and want to know whether I can meet up with them today. It means driving to Phoenix, and I'll need to leave now."

His phrasing makes me grin. "I'm not your mother, Truck. Of course you can go." I laugh. "You don't need to ask my permission."

But he's still frowning. "I won't be able to follow you home."

I sigh. He's been checking out my house after every shift, but as so much time has gone past, I'm convinced Pete's moved on and I really don't need his help.

"For goodness sake, Truck, I don't need a babysitter." I cup my chin in my hand. "There's been no contact from Pete since the day he was arrested, and he's made no move since he was released. I doubt there will be now. I've got my security system, so I'll be fine."

It's the answer he wants, but which he feels guilty receiving. I prod him with my hand in the direction of the entrance. "Just get gone, Truck. Go let your hair down for once."

"What hair?" He laughs, smoothing his hand over his shaved head.

I might have reassured Truck, but as I drive toward my home I start to feel nervous. *Oh, pull yourself together. Pete's not going to be there waiting.* It's early in the morning, and remembering his behaviour, he wouldn't even be awake at seven am. Giving myself a mental shake, I stop off to grab some breakfast before continuing my journey home. Driving up, I park on the driveway, then, food sac in hand, I approach the front door, fumbling in my purse for the front door key. Just as I've found it, a hand grabs at my arm.

My meal ends up on the ground as I give out a very girly squeal and turn to face my nightmare.

"It's just me, Darcy." He looks down at my spoiled breakfast, and then up at my face. He sounds both calm and apologetic. "Darcy, I am so sorry."

His presence puts me on edge, and I don't want to make him angry. I shrug and dismiss it. "It's just food."

He shakes his head. "Wasn't apologising about that. But I'll own that too." He gives me an intense look. "I'm sorry about the way I acted. My head was all fucked up. I really thought there could be something between us, but you kept putting me off. I hated the thought of you being with someone else even though you weren't mine. I got to the point when I had to lash out, and regret so much that that was at you."

"You're on drugs." If he hadn't been, I doubt he'd have tried to shoot me.

For a moment it looks like he might deny it, then shrugs. "I'm clean now." His sincere tone is meant to convince me.

Can someone get clean so fast?

"Look, Darcy, I'm no addict. But I was feeling so low with your rejection, someone offered me something to take the edge off, and it affected me badly. I had such a reaction because I'm not used to taking the stuff." As he sees he's not doing a good job of convincing me, he tries again. "Tell me, honestly, all the time we were together, did you see me take drugs?"

I didn't, but that doesn't mean he hadn't been taking any, just that he hid it well.

"Pete. We were never together. You were a housemate, that was all. If you read anything else into that, well, that's on you. And don't think you're taking a step inside this house. I'm not having you back. You've blown it. I'm sorry."

"I know you've moved on. You've had a whole raft of men going in and out of the house recently." A harshness appears in his voice.

I flinch. *He's been watching me.* "I couldn't *move on,* as anything between us was all in your mind. Not that it's any of your business if I've got a man or not. You blew your chances of staying with me when you raised your hand to me." *Why am I standing here talking to him?* "Pete. There's nothing more I have to say to you. I'd like to go into *my* house, now."

"Let me come in. We should talk."

He's not getting inside. "There's nothing to talk about." I'm feeling very uncomfortable even speaking to him like this. There's an edginess about him that has suddenly appeared, which makes me uncomfortable.

He brushes his hands through his hair and takes a breath, looking like it's an effort to keep himself calm. "You've still got my stuff. My clothes and all that. I've been getting by, but I need to have it back."

He's lucky I never got around to giving it away. "You wait out here. I boxed it up." I glance behind him, but don't see a car.

"Your clothes are in a bag, do you want that now? Take the boxes when you've got a ride?"

A half smile comes to his face. "Clothes will be fine."

"Step back a bit then, I'll go inside and bring them out." I don't want him close enough to barge through the door.

The smile disappears, and his mouth turns down. "I understand. I'll wait at the end of the walkway."

I watch, making sure he's putting sufficient distance between us, and then put the key in the lock and open the door. I stop the alarm beeping. Not wanting to have him on my property one moment longer than necessary, I all but run to the closet where I'd left the garbage sack full of his belongings and take it back out.

As I'm opening the door he's there and pushing inside. Keeping the bundle between us, I try to push him back.

"What the fuck are you doing?" I hiss, my fear rapidly rising. "I don't want you here, Pete."

"Well that's just your bad luck. Here's where I'm staying." It's only now in the light I realise he hasn't given up his habit at all. His pupils are dilated.

The boys have been teaching me some moves, but faced with a real live and large assailant, everything I've learned goes out of my head. *Escape.* I can't run past him as he's blocking the door. But my bathroom's got a lock on it and my phone's in my purse, which is still over my shoulder.

Pushing the trash sack hard in his chest with all my weight behind it, I take that split second of surprise and run for the bathroom. He swings for me, trying to hold me back by the strap of my purse, but only succeeds in ripping it away from me. Then I'm in the bathroom, slamming that door and throwing the lock. That's when I realise the window's too small to climb out of, and having left my purse in Pete's hands, I've no longer got my phone. *Fuck.*

Frantically, I try and think. *The window's alarmed.* I haven't tried it before, but presumably a sound will go off if the glass is broken. I wrap my hand in a towel, grab a bottle, and swing it with all my might against the glass.

Slivers come flying around me, but there's no sound. *Did I switch off the window alarm as well as the doors?*

Shit! I can't remember. Maybe Truck did by mistake. *What the hell do I do now?* Loud banging sounds, and the wooden door bulges against the lock. Pete's trying to kick in the door.

Quickly I look around for a weapon. I've got shampoo bottles, but they're not much use. I search through the cabinet, but there's nothing I can find. Only a bottle of antiseptic, and a small pair of scissors in the first-aid kit. *Could I really stab a man?*

I must do something, else he'll hurt me again and this time he might not stop. For all that he sounded reasonable and contrite, I'm dealing with a deranged man.

That door's going to smash into me if I don't move away. I push myself back until I'm touching the back wall next to the toilet, my meagre weapons in my hands. The frame's cracking, the door's moving. Any moment now…

It burst's open, and Pete's there, his face twisted in fury. I try to throw the antiseptic into his eyes, but my aim's off, and while some reaches its intended target, most covers the bottom of his face.

I hold my scissors in my hands. He sees, and smirks. Yes, he's right, an inch-long scissor blade's not going to cause much damage.

With a cry of rage, incensed that my home's been invaded, I throw myself forwards, aiming a kick into his balls. I hit him, hard, and he goes down. But he's driven by something that's giving him additional strength, and as I go to move over him, his muscular arms come around me, holding me tight. He's panting but overcoming his pain. If I'd been wearing my firefighter's boots I could really have hurt him, but my light sandals I'd worn back from work haven't incapacitated him enough.

I struggle to get out of his grip, but his arms have imprisoned mine. He oomphs as I get in a few kicks, but it doesn't stop this beast of a man from getting to his feet, taking me with him.

I scream, hoping a neighbour will hear and raise the alarm, but there's no sound of anyone coming to my rescue, and my puny attempts to get loose don't deter him. Although I'm not light, his inhuman strength has him half dragging, half carrying me into my bedroom, and he throws me on the bed, covering my body quickly with his.

A heavy slap to my face stuns me, and for a second I see stars. He lifts a little and I don't register what he's doing until he's got a wicked looking sharp knife in his hand.

Is he going to kill me? Try to rape me. "Pete, you don't want to do this."

With a painful grip on my hair, he forces my head back and puts his knife to my neck. "I'm just going to give you what you were begging for all the time I was living here. You asked for this, Darcy. You were flirting with me."

My mouth drops open. "Pete, no. You've got it wrong."

"Then why else did you invite me to stay? Relax, Darcy, and I'll show you what you were missing. After you've had me you'll never want to let me go again."

Oh yes, I will. And he's not having me.

He's lying across my legs, too heavy for me to move, but I haven't stopped struggling. I'm not going to allow him to take this from me. He's laughing at my puny attempts to get him off me.

I'm a fucking firefighter. Muscular and fit. But he, he…. Much larger than me and driven by drugs, it's nothing for Pete to overpower me. I'm at the mercy of a madman, irate and wound up. In direct contrast, my scissors might not have worried him, but the knife that he's holding certainly concerns me.

I try to buck him off, but that blade comes straight back to my neck. "God help me, Darcy. If you don't keep still, I'll cut you."

The look in his eyes shows me he means business. I swallow, unsure what to do as he leans over me, using his weight to keep me down, and he starts to cut off my clothes. I want to struggle, to protest, but I'm wary of that blade slicing my skin.

Talk him down. It's the only thing I can do.

"Pete." My voice comes out too shaky, so I try again. "Pete, you wanted to talk. Let's talk then, shall we?"

He sits back on his heels between my bare legs, a tight grip on my ankles to keep them in place, allowing me to feel the cold steel of the blade he's still gripping against my skin. The last item of clothing he hasn't yet sliced off are my panties, and for now they're a barrier I want to preserve.

"I think we're done with talking, don't you?" He's eyeing me like a piece of meat, licking his lips, and, oh Christ no, having shifted up, his ass now trapping my legs, he puts his free hand over the crotch of his jeans and he's fondling his cock through the denim, his other still waving the knife threateningly.

"You're right, Pete. We could have been good together, I just didn't give you a chance." I lie. "We could try again. You can move back in."

His head cocks to one side. *Am I reeling him in?* But his next words chill me to the bone. "But I'm moving in anyway. Oh, no, pet. I'm not going anywhere again. First I'm going to show you exactly what you've been missing." The knife flashes once again, and the last barrier between us disappears.

"You don't want to do this," I tell him, trying to keep my voice reasonable, while inside I'm screaming. "You've already got a charge for assault with a deadly weapon."

"Oh, my lawyer got me out of that. Said those biker scum friends of yours were lying. The gun wasn't registered, no proof it was mine or that I fired it."

That's not what the forensic evidence shows. He's totally lost it. *But the police released him.*

I try pleading with him. "Look, we were friends. Let me up and we'll talk about this."

"I'm done with talking. Seems I'd do better to show you how good we could be together instead. One taste of my dick and you'll want more. But keep fighting, Darcy, you're making me hard."

Good together? He's delusional. But Jesus, he's opening his zip, and now he's stroking his naked cock, pre-cum leaking out. I close my eyes to shut out the picture, now ignoring the knife, thinking being cut can't be worse that having him violate me, I start struggling.

Suddenly I'm pinned to the bed by his heavy weight and I open my eyes to see him looming over me. I'm still thinking this is it, but he's opening the drawer by the side of the bed.

"No condoms? What woman doesn't keep condoms?"

"This woman." *Will that stop him?*

"Used them all up, more like. With all the men you've had going in and out of this house over the past week or so. Proper little whore, aren't you? Couldn't even stay faithful. I'm going to remind you how much better than them I am. No matter. I'll just take you bare."

Bare? A drug addict who might well use dirty needles.

I breathe in, tensing my muscles, and then push as hard as I can, but my efforts don't even budge him.

He laughs, a high-pitched giggling sound. "Oh, keep moving like that. This is going to feel so good when I'm inside you. I'm going to get the ride of my life, I can tell."

"Nooo!" I scream as loud as I can as he lines himself up.

Chapter 11

Peg

I seem to have taken Hyde under my wing, but fuck it, why not? I happen to think the asshole's okay, and strangely enough he seems to like me—no accounting for tastes. But he could do worse than learn about the club from an old timer. Today I've brought him down to the store we have under what was the second swimming pool of the old resort, and which now looks as though it's been filled in just like the third one. So well disguised it's fooled the police and the feds before now.

It started as our armoury but has more than enough space to store people's treasured possessions too. When we'd had word of a police raid a couple of years back, Drummer stored his precious turntables here, Mouse his laptop and hard drives, and others brought things they didn't want damaged or inspected too closely.

While we've haven't had trouble come knocking recently, it always does to be well prepared, and today I want to see the state of our ammunition. Hyde and I are making an early start to get the job completed. I instruct him to start checking our stock of bullets, aware brothers have a habit of taking them out and leaving empty boxes behind on the shelves.

We've not been at it long when my phone pings with a text. I sigh at the interruption but slide it out of my cut.

Mouse: *Security alert at that firefighter's house.*

Shit!

"Peg?" Hyde's noticed the change in my expression.

I show him the text, thinking rapidly. Fuck it, I'm going to take a look for myself. Could be nothing, but I got that system put in for a reason.

Mouse: *Mercer's out on bail*

That settles it. It may be nothing, but I've got to investigate. *Darcy might be in danger.* Or she might be on a shift and there's a robbery in progress. Whatever, I can't stand by and do nothing. "Gotta run, Hyde."

Without missing a beat, he offers, "I'll come with." And that's why I like the fucker.

Going up the steps we pause only to slide the cover back on, and then race for our rides. Wraith, his hand over his mouth stifling a huge yawn, is just coming out of the clubroom. "Mouse told me you'd probably be following up on his text. Want company?"

As I don't know what I'm going into, it couldn't hurt. "Yeah, Wraith. Might be useful."

Within moments we're mounted and roaring down to the gates. Fergus is there and slides them open, and soon we're away down the track, and finally, out on the open road. I start to curse as we weave our way through the rush hour traffic, desperately hoping we're going to find nothing as I try to recall the way to Darcy's address. I tap my handlebars impatiently when we're caught by a red light.

Finally, our pipes sound loud as they echo around the residential district, and then we're coming up to her house.

Her car's parked in the driveway, no other vehicles in sight. I reach into my cut and take out my key ring, I'd had a key cut for me and had kept it just for situations like this. I knock. There's no answer, so I don't delay, turning the lock and pushing the door open.

A piercing scream comes from the direction of the bedroom.

With Wraith and Hyde hot on my heels, I race down the hallway, kick open the door, and have the man who's attacking her off her and pinned to the wall in what must be little more than a couple of seconds. My hand comes back, and I let fly, punching him in the face, then a second time for good measure. My foot connects with something, and looking down I see it's a long, sharp knife. *He came to hurt her.*

I take hold of his shoulders and shake him. "You never fuckin' learn, do you?"

"Peg, go see to your woman."

Wraith takes over from me, and I fall at Darcy's side. Hyde's already got a sheet on top of her, but I'd seen enough as I ran through the door to know she's naked underneath. With trembling hands, I reach out to her, but she curls up into a ball, holding the sheet tightly around her, and sobbing so hard she's gulping for air.

I don't know what to do, how far he got. Whether it's my right as a strange man to hold her, whether she wants any man's touch right now. *How far did the bastard go?*

Behind me I hear fists slamming into flesh. Wraith knows what it's like, he'd caught Buster trying to rape his woman. He's got no time for motherfuckers who take what's not offered.

Darcy hiccups, and tears are flooding out of her eyes. I can't hold back. Even while knowing I might be taking the worst possible action, I sweep her, in sheet, up into my arms, cradling the back of her head as I hold her to me, rocking her like I would a child. "Hush, shush. It's over. We've got him."

Hyde quietly speaks into my ear. "Got Fergus on his way with the truck."

I nod. *Good man.* Without instruction he's made the right call. The sooner we get this bastard out of her house, and out of the land of the fucking living, the better.

"Hush, hush." I rock her again, feeling my t-shirt getting damp with her tears.

Gradually her hands loosen their hold on the sheet and come up instead to grip my cut. She hiccups again, and her sobs start to slow. Then she looks up, her eyes rimmed red and still watering. "Peg?" she asks, cautiously.

"I'm here, darlin'. I'm here."

Out of the corner of my eye I see Wraith drag an unconscious body out of the doorway. Well, I hope he's just been knocked out. I'm going to be the man who delivers the final retribution. A vow reinforced as my eyes fall on her ruined clothes lying on the floor beside the bed.

I need to hear it. Need to know how slow I'm going to have to take it. "Darlin', did he…?"

I feel the movement of her shaking her head. "No, thank God. Almost. It was close. You got here in time, but…. How the fuck did you know he was here, Peg? Why do you always turn up just when I need you?"

"Not an accident, this time. That security system? Our computer guy has it linked to our set up. A window being broken triggered it, and I came straight down here to see what was up."

"Thank God you did." She voices the words I'm thinking. *If I hadn't responded so fast…. If I hadn't looked at that text…. If I'd stopped to shoot the shit with someone….*

Wraith pops his head around the door. "Fergus is here. We'll get this place cleared for you."

I nod to thank him. The last thing Darcy will want is to lay eyes on her attacker again.

As if she's reading my mind, she asks, "Pete?"

"Gone," I tell her, simply. That's all she'll ever need know. Well, only that he's never going to be able to bother her, or any other woman again.

Her body relaxes in my arms as she hears the front door opening and closing.

"Can I get her anything, Peg?"

She jumps as she hears another voice and then relaxes. "He was here with you, last time, wasn't he?"

"Yup. That's Hyde. Would you like a drink or something, darlin'?"

She bites her lip. "I'd like to get dressed. I, er, feel vulnerable like this."

Of course she would. I must remember, though in my thoughts we've become close, in reality this is only the second time we've met. "I'll give you some space."

I squeeze my arms gently, hugging her for just a second, then get up and leave, closing her bedroom door behind me. I find Hyde in her kitchen, leaning back against the counter.

"She alright? He didn't…?"

"No, thank fuck. But it was a close call. We got here just in time." Hyde and I exchange glances, both of us realising how significant that is. If he'd raped her she'd have far more to recover from.

"Wraith said he'd keep him secured for you."

"Thanks, Hyde. You did good, gettin' Fergus here so fast."

He shrugs off my compliment. "Knew she'd want him out of her sight."

In the background I hear the shower running, she must be washing off the touch of his hands. I don't blame her. Swinging around, I slam both my fists down on the counter. "If we'd taken longer, Hyde. If Mouse hadn't been monitorin' the system…"

"Well we didn't. And he was. And now that fucker's going to be taken out of the equation." I feel a male hand resting on my shoulder. "It's done, Peg. Finished. She's safe now."

Safe. He's right. That's my job's done.

"Is there anything you want me to do, or shall I get back to the compound?"

"Just give it a minute, Brother. I'll check she's okay, and then come with you." I've no right to be here, however much I feel it's my place.

Hyde gives me a strange look. "Peg? I think you should stay. She's had a big shock. She'll need someone with her."

But that person can't be me. I'm not right for her. But everything that I am makes me wish that I was.

"And," Hyde continues, "if you don't speak to her, what's the first thing she'll do?"

Fucking new member's got it in one. *She'll go to the cops.* I've got to make sure she doesn't do that. Would raise too many questions. *Like just where the fucker is now.*

"Knew I did good recommendin' you patched in." It's my way of thanking him. "Yeah, you get back, Hyde. I'll stay here and make sure things stay quiet."

"What things stay quiet?" A gentle voice asks. She still sounds shaky, but stronger than when I'd left her.

Hyde walks to the kitchen doorway and nods toward Darcy. "Glad we could help you. I'm off now, but Peg will stay to make sure you're okay."

Her eyes meet his, and a tentative smile comes to her lips. "Thank you, Hyde. Thanks for…."

"I was glad to be here." His own grin is wide and friendly. Then he half looks over his shoulder and raises his chin toward me and then leaves. Moments later, the roar of his pipes shows that he's gone.

Darcy's dressed in a loose top and a flowing skirt reaching down below her knees. She looks adorable, even though her curves aren't showing. *She doesn't want to encourage me.* She walks over, nudges me out of the way, and reaches into the fridge and pulls out two beers. Opening hers, she downs a good part in one swallow.

She might be acting blasé, but her hands tremble around the bottle. "You look like you could do with something stronger."

She shrugs. "It's all I have." Her red-rimmed eyes focus on mine. "Now, Peg, what exactly needs to stay quiet?"

Rolling my head back on my shoulders, I sigh, knowing this is the difficult part. She's not part of our world, and I can't draw her into it. "I can assure you Pete will never bother you again. I think you'll find he's broken the terms of his bail and skipped the state."

"That's what you'll persuade him?"

"Too right," I confirm.

"Where will he go?"

Now it's my turn to shrug, and it's hard to suppress my grin as I say quite truthfully, "Probably down south." Yup, he'll definitely be going down, but it won't be to Mexico, it will be underground.

She takes another swig of her beer. "You've got a reputation, you know. Oh, not you personally, but your club." The hardening of her face shows she's read between the lines.

"What do you want, Darcy?" I put down my beer, feeling frustrated. "That man was a con man, got himself into your life. How he hid it, I don't know, but he's clearly got a habit. Go to the cops? They may send him to jail for a while, but they let him out last time. And he didn't have the sense to stay away from you. Whatcha think he's gonna do when he gets out again?"

She frowns. "He might get help inside."

"He might just get something to fuel his habit." She doesn't understand how the world works.

Tapping the bottle against her lips, she cocks her head to one side. "Peg, if I keep the cops out of it and leave you to sort it, can I trust you to make sure he goes away and never comes back?" She pauses, then adds, putting emphasis on each word, "But not to kill him."

I close the gap between us. "He ain't never botherin' you again, darlin'. I promise you that. Can't promise you he'll be left breathin'."

"Yes, you can." Her face looks up into mine. "You saved me. Again." Her gaze entraps me. "I've been thinking about you. I'm so glad you've come, and not just because you got me out of a tough situation." As I was thinking she's underestimating what could have happened, she repeats her request. "I can't have his death on my conscience. You have to leave him alive." Taking a deep breath, she raises her hand and touches my cheek. "For me. For…what might be between us." There's a promise in her eyes, and a threat.

What might be between us? Fuck. *Is she saying what I think?* What's certain is without spelling it out she's giving me an ultimatum. I can make him hurt, but not follow through with a final solution. It's not what I want, but I don't want to lose the chance to explore an attraction which doesn't seem to be one-sided. My heart leaps.

I put my bottle down. Right now, for just the chance to be with her, I'd promise her anything. "Okay." It's hard to get the words out which go against everything I am, the desire to solve her problem permanently. "If that's what you want."

"I want." Her hand traces my cheek down to my beard, and with just that one touch I'm a goner. "I'll go to the police station later today. Report he was here this morning…"

Emphatically I shake my head. "They'll want to know why you didn't call 911 immediately."

She shrugs. "Because some friends arrived and saved me. And I'd just come off a twenty-four-hour shift and was dead beat and not thinking straight." She rubs her eyes and yawns, showing she's not far from the truth, then gives me a determined nod. "I have to do this, Peg. Get it on record. Hopefully they'll arrest him again. I'll play the part of a weak woman."

Lifting my hand, I smooth back her hair. "You're not weak, darlin', certainly not that. But if you think you can pull it off, we'll play it your way. Get a restrainin' order too while you're at it if you haven't already. But I promise you this, if he ever comes anywhere near you again, I'll put him in the ground. And nothing you can say will stop it."

"And I'll help you do it." Her vow is just as intense as mine.

I don't like it, don't like it one bit. But I don't want to talk about Pete anymore. I made a mistake when I moved so close to her. My nostrils flare as I inhale a perfume from whatever type of shampoo and body wash she uses, combined with a unique odour of her. It's intoxicating, making me want to lean in further, put my nose to her skin so I can fill my lungs with her scent. I want to strip her naked and lie next to her, holding her so we touch from head to toe, not an inch between us.

My cock jumps, intrigued by the aroma surrounding me, wanting to do nothing more than sink into her warm, sweet depths.

She was almost raped.

I take a step back, turning to hide the obvious swelling in my jeans, trying to think of anything else but the woman standing too near. The woman who's haunted my nights and invaded my daydreams since the first time I'd seen her.

What I wouldn't give to be able to make this woman mine.

I force myself to think of the night I first met her. That evening which had ended so disastrously with Lorelei's clear disgust. That thought that brings my cock back under control. I wouldn't be able to bear it if Darcy's reaction was the same as hers and I haven't had a chance to warn her.

Without allowing myself another look at her beautiful face, I decide to do the only thing I can to retain my sanity. "I have to go," I tell her.

CHAPTER 12

Darcy

I can't understand my reaction to this man standing in front of me. Is it because he's rescued me—not once now, but twice? My own knight in shining armour. Or to put it more accurately, in a worn leather vest.

His face is hardened by riding in the harsh Arizonian sun—and probably what life has thrown at him— but it can soften in an instant when he looks at me. His short hair makes my hands twitch, wanting to run my fingers through it, and his beard—I wasn't sure I liked facial hair before, but his? It's a striking feature, so long, and again today braided in two plaits. *What would it feel like rubbing against my skin?*

He's got a smell that's all his own, a combination of soap, leather, and oil mixed with a slight tinge of sweat, the latter not overwhelming, just letting me know he's all man. It's a concoction that's gone straight to my lady parts, and I feel my underwear dampening under the skirt that I put on for protection.

Pete just tried to rape me. That should mean the last thing I want is another man touching me. But he didn't. This man standing in front of me got here in time. My virtue's intact.

When I'd dressed it was to make myself unattractive, to hide any assets a man might want to take stock of. Now my mind's changing, and I'm starting to wish I'd worn different clothes, something alluring.

Peg's not classically handsome, but there's something about him that makes him extremely attractive. I want to see what he's hiding under the material that covers him. *I want him.*

Is it just a reaction? To take back the control which was stolen from me? To make the decision that I want a man and not have it forced on me? The outline of the cock under his jeans that I'd seen before he turned away shows he isn't immune to me, and is as turned on as I am. If he stays longer, I want him in my bed.

Is it just that he's been so protective? That I'm making assumptions he'd take care of me in all ways?

When he says he has to go, crushing disappointment almost brings me to my knees. The assumed promise that this day would end so much better than it started suddenly taken away. *I don't want him to go.* I put my hand on his arm to physically stop him, and shiver, a tingling sensation alighting every nerve as I touch his warm skin, making the region between my legs throb. Touching him, as I am, I don't miss the tension that runs through his body when I offer up just one word. "No."

He shrugs off my touch. "Darcy," he begins, then turns around to face me. "I…" his hands rise as if to touch me, then flutter and fall to his sides. His sharp eyes must see the desire held in mine. "We can't. *I* can't."

My face falls at his rejection, and my eyes gaze at the floor, unwilling to memorise more details of his face. I must have imagined our mutual attraction.

His fingers are suddenly there, under my chin, raising it up so once again I'm forced to look at him. "You were almost *raped* Darcy. It's not the right time." His other hand taps my forehead. "You've got to get things sorted in there. You're tired. You need sleep."

"I'm not going to rest with thoughts of that bastard invading my head. What if I wanted you to take the thought of what Pete almost did away? Replace it with better memories."

He inhales sharply, and I don't miss the widening of his stance, nor when I look down, the bulge that has reappeared in his groin. "Darcy, you're fuckin' temptin' me. You're playin' with fire."

A surprised laugh comes from me, and my lips curl up. "You could say I'm an expert at that."

I've not heard his mirth before, but now he's chuckling. "Fuck it, Woman." Then he surprises me by letting his hands drop and, stepping away, frowning again suddenly. "You know fuck all about me. You ought to know more before invitin' a man into your bed."

I raise and drop my shoulders. "In our two meetings you've shown me more of the type of man that I want than I've ever found with anyone else. You're kind, you're protective. I don't think you'd hurt me."

"What? Fuck no. I'd never knowingly do that." His hands tug at his beard, playing with the braids. I give him the space to think. "Fuck, Darcy, I need to tell you something." He walks to the door as though he's going to leave.

My eyes narrow as I wonder what he's going to tell me, and I'm holding my breath as I ask, "Are you married?" It hadn't occurred to me, but it would be just my luck if he was. "Is there someone else?"

"Fuck no," he repeats. Though his back is turned toward me, I can tell there's a wealth of emotion in those words. I see his shoulders pull back. "First, you've had a distressin' mornin'. If I take you to bed I want you to want *me*. Not just a cock to take your horrific experience away."

"I want *you*." I take the few steps that are between us and put my hand on his shoulder. "I haven't been able to get you out of my head since that first time that I met you. I tried to find you, to thank you. And," *oh to hell with it*, "to explore a connection that I'd felt." Part of me is screaming, *Why did I make that admission*. Starting something with an outlaw biker is not what I should be doing. But my sensible self is being overruled by the strength of attraction I feel for him. The man who's invaded my thoughts for weeks.

"You tried to find me?"

"Yes. But I didn't have your number, and I couldn't locate your compound."

Another chuckle. "You actually went lookin'?"

"I did. But I only had a vague idea of where it was."

He puts his hand over mine, still resting on his shoulder, and his fingers squeeze gently. "The second thing I have to tell you." There's a pause before he continues. "You think I'm rejectin' you, but when you know, you might reject me. And I tell you this now, Darcy, I couldn't take that from you."

He swings around so suddenly I almost lose my balance, clutching at him to keep myself upright. His eyes crease, and he looks up at the ceiling before bringing his gaze down to meet mine. "Like that you've been thinkin' about me. 'Cause, baby, I haven't been able to get you out of my mind." His hands cup my face, and as he stares it's like he's memorising my features. "I'd rather leave it like this, a dream I can replay in my head, than take the next step and spoil it. I've been rejected before, darlin', and if you did that it would destroy me."

I have no idea what he's talking about.

"You let me into your bed, then I'm in your life, darlin'. I'm not gonna walk away anytime soon. You've already had dealin's with a fuck who wanted to own you, but, babe, you've not even started to see possessive yet."

The thought of a relationship with this intense man has me reeling. Quickly I run through all the reasons why I shouldn't want it. I've obviously got a poor taste in men—and bad judgement. I shouldn't be jumping into this.

"Look, why don't I go and sort business?" He's giving me an out. "Come back when your head's on straight. When you're not dealin' with what Pete did to you. We can talk some, get to know each other, without…" He breaks off.

"Fucking?" I suggest, helpfully.

"Fuck, Woman." He smiles. A genuine smile.

"I take risks every day, Peg. It's what I do." And while we take every precaution, I always know there's a very small chance one day a fire will claim me as a victim. Firefighters give their all on the job and will do what's necessary to try to save lives. It's made me less cautious in my everyday life. When I see something I want, I go after it.

His brow is creased again. "Not sure I like that you put yourself in danger."

I shake my head to reassure him. "I don't. I'm fully trained, remember, and I've been doing this job for a few years now. I've got a team behind me as well, we work together, need to watch each other's backs. But I work with fire, Peg, and that's unpredictable. No one runs into a burning building not expecting to get out, but there's always that chance. Knowing it's there means we're careful. But…"

He rolls his head back. "I'm a biker, darlin'. I live an outlaw life. Oh, we earn our money clean these days, but there's always someone wantin' what we've got."

Now I know what that look was for, because I'm feeling the same emotion. Worried for him.

"I'm sergeant-at-arms, Darcy. Which means my role is to keep the club safe."

I place my hands on his chest, under his leather vest. Firm muscles meet my fingers. *This man keeps himself fit.*

"Darcy, stop that. It's hard enough to resist without your hands on me."

I don't stop, and instead my hands explore more.

Until they're brought to a halt when his cover mine and he tears them away, holding me so my arms are held wide. "You didn't give me a chance to tell you. Babe, what I've been trying to say is I don't want you to have any nasty surprises. I've only got half of one leg."

He's still holding me prisoner, my only reaction is to tilt my head to one side. "So what?"

Examining me carefully, he informs me, "Some women don't like it. It turns them right off."

Actually, I'm intrigued. The way he moves you'd never know it. I glance down at his legs. "You wear a prosthesis?"

He just nods, and I feel stupid. Of course, he does.

"Well, it doesn't bother me." It's other parts of his body I'm more interested in at the moment. I want to see him naked without his clothes, feel his calloused hands roaming my body, feel what I can see is an impressive cock…

"Eyes up here, darlin'."

I feel my face flush as I look back up and see amusement on his face. He lets my hands go, and his own once again cup my face and he stares down intently. "You sure about this?"

Suddenly I know I've never been more certain of anything in my life. "Yes."

His body shudders as though I've broken through his resistance, my easy dismissal of what is obviously a big deal for him being the last straw. He says nothing more and lowers his mouth until it touches mine. I'm fairly tall for a woman at five-foot-nine, and not used to having to crane my neck. I rise on tiptoe and press up against him.

His tongue seeks entry, I open for him, and as he sweeps in and I taste him for the first time. It's captivating. I can't get enough. One of his arms sweeps behind my back, pulling me in close, our bodies flush together, leaving me in no doubt of his arousal, which I can tell by hardness alone clearly matches mine. His size, though. I've never felt anything like it, and a flutter of excitement goes through me. As I whimper into his mouth, my tongue duelling with his, his free hand goes to the back of my head, holding me in place as he completely controls our first kiss.

When eventually we need air, he pulls away and tucks my head into his chest. "Perfect. Fuckin' perfect."

It was just one brief union, a touching of mouths, but it seems almost reverent. As if we've both taken the initial step toward the rest of our lives.

"I want you," he murmurs. I feel the vibration on the top of my head.

"Yes." I don't need to say more.

He turns me around, and instead of leading me into my bedroom as I expected, sweeps aside the empty beer bottles, picks me up and sits me on the kitchen counter, pushing my legs out to the sides, and stepping in between them.

"Don't want you in that bed. Not now."

Not after Pete almost raped me there. I start to worry. Surely for our first time we should be horizontal? Try out the missionary position before attempting anything else? I've not been with men who've been particularly adventurous before. *How do we play this? What should I do with my hands?*

"Stop thinking, darlin'." Peg's head comes down and kisses me again. Another deep kiss, more ravishing than the first. I can feel my lips are swollen when he looks up again. "Fuckin' beautiful." His finger now replaces his mouth, and he traces the swelling he caused, then takes hold of my oversized tee and starts to lift it off. I raise my arms to help him.

He stares in adoration at my plain bra, hands coming out to touch my breasts without removing their covering. He watches his fingers, then looks into my eyes. Such a expressions of devotion I hadn't expected to see. This is no rutting of animals, no quick one and done pairing. This means something to him. *Like it means something to me.*

Then when he expertly undoes the front clasp, I give him space to lower the straps down my arms. Still he holds my eyes, not lowering his yet to see what he's revealed. Then he leans forward, and his voice causes vibrations as he speaks into my ear. "Only have one first time, darlin'. Not gonna rush." His tenderness, so unexpected from such a big man, sends thrills right through me, and I tremble in anticipation.

His hands leave me, and I feel bereft, but then entranced as he slides off his vest. Then in the male way which I swear they must learn in school, grabs the neck of his t-shirt and pulls it right over his head.

Before I can touch those hard muscles I long to trace, or even feast my eyes on his body, he steps forward again and hugs me to him, my chest to his chest, warm skin to warm skin. He holds us together, hearts beating in time. "Dreamed of this. Fuckin' dreamed of holdin' you close."

I moan against him, having a tough time keeping my body still, wanting to writhe against him. "Impatient, aren't you? Feel like a kid at Christmas, but don't want to rush and open everything at once. Wanna make this last. Savour it."

We stay in position for over a minute, then he shifts back, and now his eyes feast on my naked breasts, and as he sees my pierced nipples a wide grin spreads over his face. "Any other surprises?"

"No." I lift my hands, wanting to touch his chest, but he gently bats them away.

But his hands don't stay still, reaching out and smoothing the curves of my breasts, circling around, making the nipples peak, even though he's not touched them.

"Peg," I whine, complaining.

CHAPTER 13

Peg

She's eager, impatient. But I'm not going to rush, instead I give in to my desire to learn her body with my eyes, hands, and mouth. Her little gasps, groans, and whimpers are music to my ears. I know she was surprised I wasn't taking her to bed, but how could I, when it was there she was so recently threatened and almost molested? I'm going to buy her a new bed, burn the old one before I lie with her in her bedroom.

When I first seated her on the kitchen counter she was uncomfortable, but she's going to learn I like sex anywhere. This certainly isn't going to be the one and only time for us. As I've been toying with her, she's slowly been getting out of her head, sexual tension and excitement overtaking any concern.

Now I play with her nipples, pinching those dark peaks, pulling at the rings to make her moan. A quick brush of my lips across her mouth, and now I'm nibbling at her neck as she swivels her head to afford me better access. I suck at her pulse, then trace my lips down, over her collar bone and down to her gorgeous chest.

With my fingers toying with one, and using my mouth on the other, I pull and suck on those nipples, making them peak. I could play with her rings for hours, just lie beside her, my hands amusing themselves, pulling and pushing at those little gold circles. A light tug and she tilts toward me, her back bowed and her head thrown back, eyes closed, completely in the moment.

I can smell her arousal as her body gets ready to take me.

With my mouth still paying attention to her breasts, I fumble around the waistband of her skirt, finding the button and slipping it through the hole, then pulling down the zip. Putting my arm around her waist, I easily lift her to give me the clearance I need to push the material down to the ground.

Seconds later, my hands find her slim, trimmed stomach, and now they slide up and down her muscular legs. She's not built like a bodybuilder, but her strong calf and thigh muscles are tight and well-shaped, paying tribute to the strength she needs in order to do her job. I straighten, and stand with my fingers running along her thighs, first on the outside, then moving in. She jumps as my hands find their way to the sensitive spot between her legs, and her eyes fly open in expectation.

"Put your hands behind you." She obeys. I'd like to rip her panties right off her, but don't want any bad memories to come back into her head. "Lift up." When she raises her hips, I slide them down and off. Then I sink to my knees and just breathe in that perfume that's uniquely her. The musky aroma turns my cock to steel, making me unfasten my zip to give myself space. My head draws closer, I run my nose from her cunt to her clit, appreciating the smooth, shaved surface. Inhaling deeply, I'm aware that my beard is soaking up her essence. She jumps as the hair scratches gently over her sensitive spot.

"Peg, oh Peg."

I can wait any longer to take her. Fastening my mouth like a limpet, I thrust my tongue inside her tight channel, lapping like a cat trying to get the last of the cream. She squirms beneath me, and putting my hands to her hips I hold her still. I slide my tongue to her clit again, circling it gently, then going back for more of that cream.

"Peg, I, oh, there. Just there."

"You like me eating you out, hmm?" The rumbling of my voice causes a full body shudder.

I repeat my actions, the sensations making her produce more of her essence. Now keeping her in place with one hand to her stomach, I use my fingers to circle, then lightly pinch those nerves. Then I exchange mouth for my digits, curling my fingers up inside.

"I, I..."

She's barely able to form words as I continue my slow but steady assault. I feel her muscles tense and know that she's close. Pressure inside, my teeth gently clamping on her clit, and her strong thighs grip my head like a vice as she starts shaking, goes still, then with a scream goes over the top. Her head's thrown back, and she's panting.

When she's at last able to speak, her eyes open in wonder. "Peg, that was, amazing. Incredible." I grin, knowing what she's trying to say. No one can fake a reaction like that.

Putting one hand on the counter to help pull me to my feet and get my prosthesis under me again, I bend forwards and kiss her again. A slight look of surprise as she tastes herself on me, then she's enthusiastically mating her tongue with mine.

Reaching my hand into my pocket, I extract a condom, then slide my jeans off over my hips. She sits up to watch me, her eyes widening as my cock jumps free, and I almost wish I had a camera to record for posterity the look on her face as she first catches sight of me.

"What...?"

I glance down where she's looking, as if I have no idea what she's referring to, then grin at her reaction. "Oh, it's a Jacob's ladder."

"I've never... I'm not sure... Does it hurt?"

I can't help but laugh. "It won't hurt you, and it doesn't hurt me." Hurt like a bitch when I first had the piercings done to please my ex-wife, but now I barely notice I've got it. "You won't get the full effect with a condom, but one day, darlin', when you trust me, and the time is right, I'm gonna take you bare."

She licks her lips as I make her that promise and is still watching as the metal disappears beneath the latex.

My hand now on her chest, I push her gently back down on the counter. "Bend your knees, put your heels on the edge." As she follows my instruction, I take hold of her hips and pull her closer, then position myself at her entrance before taking hold of her once again.

I close my eyes, almost overwhelmed at the feeling, this strange *connection* between us. Even with the woman I married there wasn't this compulsion to make it last, to make it good, to make her never want another man inside her.

And as I slide in, working through her tight channel, I hear her moaning with satisfaction as I slowly fill her, and my piercings roll over her nerve endings. And then, with one last thrust which makes her gasp, I'm fully in. The sight, looking down, of where we are joined, is almost too much. My balls draw up and I throw back my head, screwing up my eyes, willing the feelings to subside. Having regained control, I pull out gently, and then push in again. Slowly, but surely, making sure she's feeling the full effect of the Jacob's Ladder, thankful as fuck I never followed my inclination to take it out. I didn't know it then, but she is the reason I went through that suffering all those years ago.

Her eyes are closed, her head turning from side to side, moans coming almost constantly, though I'd bet she doesn't even know she's making any noise. She squeezes her Kegels rhythmically against my cock, the pressure inciting me, and I quicken my pace. Her sound now is a keening, her hands are clenched, her body covered in a fine sheen of sweat. Her back is bowed, her hips drawing down to meet my onslaught. And now she's screaming again, her head coming up, her mouth wide open, and as her orgasm strangles my cock I lose it.

"Never. Been. So. Fuckin'. Good." I punctuate my words as I pant out my own climax with short pumps into the condom, emptying burst after burst from deep in my balls.

We stayed joined. Our eyes meeting. For a moment we don't need words, just that connection of our sexual organs and sight.

Then she giggles. "You were right. I've never…" Her head turns to the side, and her cheeks turn red.

I swell with pride as I suspect I know what she's trying to say. "You've never come with a cock inside you?"

She giggles again as she turns back. "Yeah, that."

She's got me smiling. "My cock made you come, yeah?"

"Yeah."

I raise my hands until they're at the side of her ribs, and prod gently with my fingers. She jumps. "Ticklish, eh? Well, tell me what made you come. Was it my cock in your pussy?"

She shakes her head. I press in again, making her writhe to escape my probing fingertips. "Peg, stop."

"Not until you tell me."

She tries to evade my hands which torture her, but I've got her pinned tight, tilting my pelvis so she's trapped. As she struggles, my softening cock slips out, breaking our connection. "Tell me." I tickle her mercilessly again.

"Your cock made me come. Your cock in my pussy." She's shouting and laughing all at the same time.

Immediately stopping my torment, I curl my hand around her head to support it and bring her closer, so I can kiss her again. "Never been so fuckin' good." I repeat, "Never. You're mine, Darcy. Not lettin' you get away."

She's still laughing as I make my declaration, and I know she doesn't fully appreciate the implication of what I've just said.

But in my world, if you claim a woman, you're making her your old lady. She's mine for life, she just doesn't know it yet.

"Shower with me." I hold out my hand and help her down off the counter, noticing her kitchen smells of sex.

"I don't know if we'll fit."

"Think we just did, darlin'."

"Babe." She admonishes me with just one word, and fuck if I don't like what she just called me.

"Babe, eh?"

She shrugs, then pulls me in the direction of her small bathroom. I strip off my clothes and take off my prosthesis, using the shower rail to hop in and get my balance on one leg. It's a bit of a tight fit to get under the shower, but we make it, and she takes delight in shampooing my beard, even though I'd rather keep her scent on it. She's fun, we laugh. In fact, I realise I haven't laughed so much since, well, ever.

But as we get out and I wrap a towel around her, she leans her head onto my chest and can't hide her yawn. I can see she's completely exhausted, she's come off a long shift, had to deal with her ex-housemate, and then I, selfish bastard that I am, wore her out. She waits while I strap back on my prosthesis, then I carry her into the living room—don't want her going into the bedroom until I've disposed of that bed—then go and find a t-shirt and sleep shorts in one of her drawers. By the time I'm back with her, her eyes are closed, and she's half asleep. Pulling her forward, I remove the damp towel and pull the tee over her head, and encourage her into the shorts, then sit back on the couch and draw her onto my lap.

She snuggles into me, her arms holding me tight, her grip gradually releasing as she drops off. I settle down for an uncomfortable few hours, but not giving a damn. What could be better than staying awake and watching my old lady asleep in my arms?

Now all I've got to do is get her to realise there'll be no parting us now.

Mid-afternoon I ease out from under her, leaving her sleeping as I place a call.

"Wraith, it's Peg. You got our package still on ice?"

When he gives me the confirmation, I issue him with instruction. "Okay. Well keep it that way. Don't mind if it's damaged, we just ain't discardin' it."

He growls, a response I fully understand. "Yeah, I know. Not my decision, Brother."

When he tells me I've handed over my balls to a woman, rather than my usual snarl, I find myself laughing. "You could well be right."

I listen for a moment then respond. "Yeah." *He's not wrong there either,* I think, as I admit, "It does feel fuckin' good."

The next call I make has Hyde and the prospect knocking at the door a little time later. I let them in quietly, but the swearing and the noise they're making as they try to take her bed apart wakes her.

Darcy sits up, rubs at her eyes, looks at me, then over her shoulder, then gets to her feet.

"Hey." My hand holds her back. "Let them get on with it, eh?"

"Let who get on with what?" Her eyes narrow as Hyde walks past with a headboard. "That's my bed." Shocked, she instructs, "Put it back. I need that."

I slide my arm around her and pull her back, half to remove her from Hyde's path, and half to take the opportunity to enjoy the feel of her ass against my cock. "I'm replacing your bed, darlin'. You don't want those reminders each time you go to bed." She goes stiff in my arms as those exact memories come back to her. So, I nuzzle her ear and add, "And, I'm a big fella. We could do with a larger bed."

Twisting around, she stares in to my face. "You sticking around?"

"If that's okay with you. Won't be movin' in, I wouldn't presume on that. I live at the club. But I won't be a stranger. We've got a lot to work out, darlin'."

Her hand strokes down my face and toys with my beard. "I like the sound of us working out together."

So do I. So do fucking I.

Suddenly I hear someone walking through the door the prospects have left open. I slide my gun out of my cut, and hiss at the large man who's just entered. "Who the fuck are you?"

As she's opening her mouth to explain, her eyes widen in horror at the gun that's appeared in my hand pointing directly at the man striding in bold as fucking brass.

"Who the fuck are *you?*" He throws my own words back at me. Then adds tersely, "Step away from him. I'm here now, Flash."

Hyde and Fergus choose that moment to start walking out with the bedframe.

"What the fuck are you doing with that? Put that down." *He thinks he's got a right to say what happens in Darcy's house?*

Whatever's going on in here, I'm in fucking charge. If he doesn't explain himself, I'm going to be having a fucking conversation using my fists. He takes a step toward me, I take one to him, and Darcy steps in between us, one hand on my chest, one hand on his.

"Shut it, both of you. Truck, meet Peg, he's my, my boyfriend. Peg, meet Truck. He's a firefighter that works with me."

"Boyfriend? If you had a boyfriend, why hasn't he been here with you protecting you?" Truck shouts.

"He was here when it mattered this morning," Darcy fires back.

"This morning? Flash?" Suddenly he must see the bruising on her arms and on her cheek. He glares at me and, ignoring my gun, pushes Darcy aside. "Did you do this?"

Now I'm a big man, but in width Truck has me beat. Even from here I can see he's solid muscle. I'm not even sure I'd be able to take him in a fight, but I'd give it a try.

As I straighten my shoulders, Darcy steps back between us and snaps, "Truck! No, he didn't do anything. Pete did."

"Pete?" His hand covers his mouth, then slides away. "Oh fuck."

"Yeah. Oh fuck. He tried to fuckin' rape her."

Truck's eyes go wide. "Flash, did he…"

"No." Now she turns, and both her hands are on his chest, and I feel a jealous rage start to burn. "The security system Peg had installed alerted his club. They came down and arrived just in time." She points to Hyde and Fergus, who've dropped the frame of the bed, ready to have my back. "That's why I'm replacing the bed. He overpowered me, held me down…." She doesn't say anymore. She's painted him enough of a picture.

The big man's shaking his head, he looks as distraught as he sounds when he says, "How did he get in?"

"Truck, he was waiting for me when I got home." She looks at the other man in dismay as his face falls. "It wasn't your fault, Truck. He could have got me alone anytime. And," Darcy smiles, turns to me and links her arm through mine, and now her hand's on my chest instead, I feel my anger immediately slipping away, "if he hadn't then Peg and I wouldn't have had a chance to sort things out."

Truck looks at me and pays particular attention to my cut, then looks at Hyde and Fergus standing behind me. "You mentioned his club rescuing you. You know what and who he is, Flash?"

There's no point hiding anything. "I ride with the Satan's Devils." I lay it out for him.

His eyes widen. "Satan's Devils? Flash, I hope you know what you're getting into."

Darcy just looks up at me, smiles, then nods. "I know." She repeats, "I know." She touches the leather that had caught Truck's attention, her hand resting just over my heart.

My fingers cover hers, and my eyes sweep to meet those of the other man, recognising the care he has for her, but my head concurring with the feeling in my gut. His concern for her is that of a friend, a fellow firefighter, and not because he's any competition. I'm glad she's got someone like him on her team. Even if he is suspicious about my membership of the club. He's still poised, ready to take me on if need be. To protect my woman.

As my respect grows for the man, I set him straight. "Satan's Devils used to be in some bad shit, got a reputation, for sure. But we run a clean club now." We just live outside citizens' rules.

He studies my face for a moment, and finally nods as something flickers across his face. I believe I see a look of interest there, and file that thought for later. "That your scoot outside?"

"Yeah, man." I tell him. "You ride?"

Now Truck wears a look of contrition. "Did, landed shiny side down when some fucker didn't see me. I got off okay, but my ride was a wreck."

I commiserate for a moment, not failing to notice that Darcy seems pleased we're talking a common language. Even if we're excluding her.

"You staying?"

The huge man looks at Darcy, then at me, and shrugs. "Not if I'm stepping on anyone's toes."

My arm goes around her, hugging her to me, and my hand turns her face toward mine. "Need to check in with the club. But I can be back later." I need to sort out the fucker Pete for a start. Truck's reaction to her injuries firing up my anger all over again.

She gives a little nod, then, "Go do what you need to do, Peg. Truck and I will go shop for a new bed."

"Hell no to that," I snarl. He might not be showing any carnal interest in her, but I'm not going to let him choose the bed where I'm going to be fucking my old lady. *Getting ahead of yourself here, Peg. She hasn't agreed yet.* A thought comes to me. Right now, I need to get back to the compound, deal with Pete, then sit through church, then… There's no better way to see whether she'll fit into the club. "When you back at work, darlin'?"

"Tomorrow morning."

I smooth my hand down my beard, wishing it still smelt of her. "What if Truck takes you down to the police station?" It might be better him than me, and I think she'll feel easier if she has some support. "Then I'll return this evening and, if you're up for it, bring you to the compound."

I hold my breath, waiting to see what she says, knowing I'm suggesting throwing her in with a bunch of bikers.

But her eyes are sparkling. She raises an eyebrow at Truck, who gives her a nod, then looks back at me. "And the day after tomorrow, *we* buy a new bed."

Hopefully she knows she'll be in mine tonight.

"Certainly will, honey. You can bank on that." I take a step toward the door, then turn back, gesturing between the two of them. "What's with him calling you Flash?"

Darcy glances at Truck, then back at me, and laughs.

Truck takes it upon himself to explain. "A flashfire is fast and intense. You should see her jump into action at work. It was said

as a joke, then caught on. So that's what we call her. Flashfire."
He shrugs. "Seemed to fit."

Like a road name. Flashfire. I like it and with her red hair it really does suit her.

I wink at my woman. "See you later, *Flash.*"

CHAPTER 14
Darcy

"A re you sure you're okay with that man?" Truck's staring out the window, watching Peg ride off on his bike, the roar almost shaking the glass. The look of regret on his face reminding me of the accident he'd had the year before. He's still fighting a legal battle against the uninsured driver who shouldn't even have been on the road. As Hyde and the prospect have left to dump the remnants of my bed, I'm alone with my crew member now.

"Miss your motorcycle, Truck?"

"Like you'd miss your fucking arm," he replies, half under his breath, then turns to give his attention to me. "You seem to have gotten pretty cosy in a short time. What do you know about him, Flash?"

Only what I learned in one glorious day. But already I seem to understand more about him than almost anyone else I've ever met. I can't tell Truck Peg already seems a match for my soul, that sounds too far too fast, even to admit to myself. But we'd clicked, that's for sure. Something in him calls to something in me.

In the end I say lamely, "He's a good man, Truck."

It's impossible to read the expression on his face. After a moment he sighs and walks into my kitchen, filling the coffee maker. "So, tell me, what happened this morning? And fuck, Flash, I'm sorry it was today. I couldn't follow you home."

I come up alongside him and wait for him to turn so he can see me emphatically shaking my head. "He must have been watching, Truck. He chose the one time when he saw I had no one with me. You can't stay glued to my side forever. It would have happened eventually." I move so I'm able to place both hands on the counter, and then fill him in on the events of this morning.

Truck's eyes open wide as he realises Peg's foresight in installing a monitored security system saved my sanity, and quite possibly my life. Who knows how far Pete would have gone in his deranged state?

While I've been speaking, he's been making the coffee, automatically pouring two cups. Though it's a warm day, my hands hug around it, needing the comfort as telling the story has made me go cold. Peg coming so quickly, and the events after Pete was taken away, had wiped the worst details from my mind. Now I start shaking as it crashes into me what could have happened if Peg hadn't got here so fast.

Noticing, Truck takes my elbow and steers me back into the living room, positioning me in front of a couch, then pressing on my shoulder to encourage me to sit down.

"I'm alright."

"No, you're not. No one would be. Not after that." He sits beside me and puts an encouraging hand on my arm. "You don't have to be strong all the time, Flash."

Angrily I swipe a rogue tear away.

He gives me a moment, then asks, "What are the bikers going to do to Pete?"

"Have words with him and send him on his way. With a warning should he ever come near me again."

Truck snarls. "I hope they make him hurt."

I say nothing, nor explain how I pleaded for his life. "I'm doing this the right way, Truck. That's why we need to get down to the police station. I need to make a report about what happened."

"And get a restraining order this time." Truck's features set into a frown. "I'll help with that. Least I can do. If I'd been here…"

"He'd have waited for another time." I don't want him feeling guilty.

Truck opens his mouth, but before I can respond my phone rings. I'd left it on the table, so get up to answer it, a smile curving my lips as I see who it is.

"Nicole! Oh my God, I'm sorry, I forgot we had plans tonight." Just as I'm about to tell her I now won't be able to make it, she tells me something that makes me go cold.

"Fuck. Okay. Hey, I've got Truck here. He'll want to hear this." Nicole works for the Forestry Service as a firewatcher looking out for fires. She won't be telling me anything she won't already have reported through official channels, so I press the key that sends it to loudspeaker. Truck's already on his feet and has come up to join me.

"Nicole's spotted some smoke," I explain as he draws closer.

"Hi Nicole, Truck here."

"Hey, Truck. Just called it in. Only a single plume so far, but I don't like the conditions. Temperature is rising, and the forecast is for high winds."

Together with the tinder-dry vegetation that's not good news.

"It's about five miles away from the tower, so I'm going to be trekking out when my relief arrives. Want to check what the fuel is like there. I won't be ending my shift any time soon, that's for sure."

"Is it spreading?"

"Yeah, been monitoring a white plume for a couple of hours." I glance at Truck, knowing if it flares up into something serious we might be called back in. If I go anywhere tonight, it will be with my own transport.

"Where is it?"

"To the north. About half way up the mountain over toward Snake Canyon. She gives the co-ordinates, and Truck's checking them on his phone."

"Wind direction?"

"At the moment it's looking like the fire should go up."

"There's nothing there, no structures if it keeps going that way," Truck interjects.

"Still don't want it to get a good hold. Look, I've got to go now, Darcy. I'll keep you updated when I get closer to it. I can give you a head's up if it looks like your crew will be getting involved. Just thought I'd give you a warning in case."

"Thanks, Nicole. And you take care, you hear me?"

She laughs. "I ain't no fool, Firefighter. I leave the dangerous stuff to you."

I end the call with a smile. Nicole Hudson. One of the first friends I made when I moved here, someone who speaks my language. She spends six months during the warmer months employed by the US Forest Service watching for fires, and the other half of the year writing her books. I've read a few of them, and they even make me blush. Our paths crossed with the first wildland fire I'd fought, and it seemed natural for the two females to team up together.

My admonishment for her to be careful was probably unnecessary. She knows as well as anyone how unpredictable fire can be, how quickly it can change direction. But sometimes in the forest it's difficult to see exactly what's burning, and what type of fuel there is. If there's too much smoke, it's not easy to tell from the air. Having eyes on the ground means the fire crews, such as myself, can be prepared to know what we're going up against. If she thinks it's necessary to see for herself, then it probably is.

"We won't get called in unless it gets a good hold." Truck's pulling at his ear, his tell that he's thinking. "Local crews will have it in hand. If they're even needed."

I nod. We don't necessarily fight all the fires that burn. It can be nature's way of controlling the environment, and if there's no occupied structures to save—businesses or homes—and only a small fire, we'll just check that it's not likely to get out of control, and leave it to burn itself out, or at the most, try to stop it spreading further. But the weather conditions Nicole has reported will put everyone on high alert. If a fire takes hold, then being the nearest city-based crew, we'll be called out under our mutual aid response agreement. Best not to be caught on the back foot when it comes to a blaze which has the potential to destroy lives. I shiver, hoping it doesn't turn into something nasty. With the hot shot crews all in California, we could be short-handed on this one.

But there's nothing to be done at the moment, and Nicole's not stupid, she'll take every precaution. All I can do is get on with my day. Knowing I can't put it off, I place a call and find my friend Detective Grover is at the station today and arrange to go in and see him.

An hour and a half later, after a quick snack—well, a big-bodied man like Truck needs to be kept fuelled—I walk into the precinct, and nod at a few familiar faces I've met when cops attend a fire, and don't have to wait long before I'm shown into an interview room. Hardly a minute passes before Grover walks in carrying a couple of steaming cups, kicking the door shut as he walks in.

He pauses when he sees Truck. "Sorry, I can get another. He nods at the drinks in his hands.

"I'm fine." Truck leans back in his chair, crossing one leg over the other so his ankle rests on his knee. "I'm only here for moral support."

"Not a witness?"

Truck shakes his head. "Sorry."

"Ok." As Grover sits, he pulls a notepad toward him. "What's happened now, Darcy? You mentioned Mercer on the phone."

I draw in a deep breath, and then go over everything once again. As I end my sorry tale I'm shaking. I'd rather put it behind me than keep going over it.

Grover's taking it all in and making notes. I let him scribble it all down, then he looks up and taps his pen against his teeth. "You didn't know the security system was monitored?"

"No."

"Hmm. Could be seen as invasion of privacy."

I put a stop to that fast. "And if it hadn't been, you might have been dealing with a dead body today." I wouldn't have stopped fighting. How far would Pete have taken it? "Or at the very least, a woman who'd been raped." My hand goes to the purple bruise on my swollen face. "As it was, I just got away with this."

"Did they install cameras inside your house?"

"No, they did not." I lean forwards, my fisted hands on the table. "Can we please get back to the real villain of the piece? Peter Mercer? It sounds to me like you've got a hard-on for the Satan's Devils"

He at least has the grace to look sheepish. "Sorry, Darcy. But these are men who think they're above the law. They at least live outside it."

"They run their businesses legit." Half of me wonders whether he'll disclose information that says otherwise.

But he's nodding. "Seems nowadays they do. But it wasn't always that way. Okay, Darcy. I'm sorry, it runs deep with us that we don't like gangs such as them. Now, getting back to Mercer. I'll pull him back in and add on the attempted rape charge and assault from last night. And as long as your biker friends come forward as witnesses, this time he's got no chance of getting bail, never mind who he knows."

Truck uncrosses his legs and speaks for the first time. "Can you guarantee that? He got out pretty fast last time. She's getting an emergency order of protection, but there's nothing to say he won't breach that."

"Locked up is best," I contribute. "Surely the court officer must see he's likely to reoffend."

Grover nods. "We'll try and find him and pick him up today. If he's no longer at the address that he gave us last time he was in, any idea where we might find him?"

I don't. But knowing how angry Peg was that he'd hurt me, and was stopped while he was molesting me, a hospital is my best guess.

That thought I think it's best to keep to myself.

<h1 style="text-align:center">Chapter 15</h1>

Peg

Riding back to the compound, enjoying the wind on my face and the freedom of the asphalt under my wheels, my expression alternates between a smile and a frown. Unable to believe that at last I've found a woman who's exactly right for me, and then wondering how the fuck I'm going to be able to hold myself back when I'm face to face with the man I last saw trying to rape her.

She won't let me kill him. No, my Flashfire's far too sensitive for that. It gives me pause to wonder whether she'll ever fit into my world where we don't bat an eye delivering retribution that's swift and final.

One thing's for certain, even being with me she won't know all that we do. As an old lady she'll be kept far away from that type of shit. My mind runs over Sam, Drummer's old lady, then Wraith's Sophie, a gentle soul from England who ended up with the VP, and finally to Ella, Slick's wife. They've been brought into our life and taken to it fine. Marcia, well, Heart's woman knows the score better than most. Having once been a cop, she knows it from both sides.

How would a firefighter fit in? Well, tonight might provide some clues. *I can't wait to bring her here to meet my brothers.*

It's the smile that's on my face as I ride through the gates, giving a nod to Fergus, our sole prospect now that Hyde's been patched in. Slowing as I come to the clubhouse, I back my bike into my usual slot.

As I throw my leg over the seat, there's a hefty slap on my back. "Christ, Peg. What the fuck's happened?"

My eyes narrow in confusion as I look at the prez. "What?"

"You're fuckin' smilin' is what. Don't rightly recall when I last saw that." His eyes roam over me. "You get fucked?" Then one corner of his mouth turns up. "You fuckin' sly asshole. You did, didn't you?"

I'm usually one who can school their features, but today it's clearly not working. A bit annoyed he can read me so well, I purposefully scowl in response.

He barks a laugh. "Got anything to do with the woman you went after like a bat out of hell earlier? And the fucker Wraith's got on ice up in the store room?"

There's no keeping anything from the prez. Not that I'd want to. "She's that firefighter I met a few weeks back. She had problems with a housemate."

"Know that, Peg."

I look off into the distance, idly noting yet another plume of smoke near the top of the mountain behind the compound, a little bit further over than what I saw a couple of days ago. "Well, the fucker came back. Yesterday. Thank fuck I'd got Mouse to set up security that could be monitored."

"Know that too. What I want to know is why you were out nearly all day, and whether we're now gonna have to bury a body?"

As I said, you can't keep anything from the prez. I turn away from the view and look him straight in the eye. "Might have found my old lady." I give it to him straight.

He sucks in a sharp breath and takes a second to respond. "And that I didn't expect."

While he's digesting that news, I address his other question. "She doesn't want him killed, just scared off."

At that he laughs. "You gave her the choice? Did you hand over your balls?"

My smile reappears as I point out the obvious. "Satan's Devils came to her rescue, and if he disappears, which direction d'you think fingers would be pointin'?"

"There is that." He ponders for a moment, then slaps me on the back again. "Think I want to come see what kind of fucker takes advantage of a woman. Let's get him sorted and dumped, then we'll discuss your other revelation in church."

As he walks beside me up to our storage room, I'm thinking how I can explain my sudden determination to make Darcy my, old lady to my brothers. After I'd perhaps been a bit premature in admitting it to Drum, he's not going to let it drop.

Mercer's been left hanging, his wrists fastened to the struts overhead, giving me the sense of satisfaction that his arms will be hurting just like Darcy's. If he's been hanging all day, as I suspect, his shoulders will be in agony. Wraith's leaning back against a bench, flicking through a magazine, completely ignoring the pleas of the man who's starting to beg.

As I approach, Mercer stops talking and his eyes go wide. "That's it, you fucker. Be scared." I arrange my features into my sergeant-at-arms scowl, the expression that shows I'll have no mercy. "Give me one good reason why I shouldn't remove the filth that you are from the face of the earth."

"I wasn't going to rape her. She was willing. She gives it up all the time. Had a fuck load of men visiting her, started whoring straight after she left my bed. You know bitches like her, never faithful…"

He gets my fist in his gut. "Shut your mouth. Somehow you got her to take pity on you and give you a place to stay, and you're fuckin' lyin', you were never in her bed. And how did you repay her for giving you a room? By giving her a beatin'." As I draw my fist back, his eyes go wild. But this time I move behind him and plant it in his kidney, satisfied the blood in his piss will serve as a reminder for at least a week. He's sobbing as I continue. "You broke in this morning when she came off shift. You dared hit her, you had a knife, you were threatenin' her, stripped her and would have taken an unwillin' woman if I hadn't got there to stop you."

"I didn't, I wouldn't have. I, I don't know what got into me." The words tumble out one after the other. As I walk around him, eyeing him up for my next hit, he continues, "Don't kill me, please. I'll never go near her again."

I choose that moment to at least badly bruise a couple of ribs, following it up with a harsh blow to his stomach that has him gulping for air. "Too fuckin' right you'll never go near her again. If we let you walk you're to leave her completely alone. You see her from a fuckin' mile away, you *run* in the other direction."

Getting control of his breath, he gasps, "Too right. That's what I'll do. I'll leave her alone. I promise you. Please don't kill me."

Tears start to fall, and soon he's blubbering, snot dripping from his nose. The sight offends me. "Wraith, take him down."

Putting down the magazine he appeared so engrossed in, Wraith turns a lever that controls the hoist, and soon Mercer's on the ground, his legs buckling as they fail to support him.

"You mind?" Prez remarks in a disinterested voice.

I give him a be my guest gesture, then watch without emotion as Drum goes behind the man, touching him on the shoulder. Mercer flinches, already in pain from having been strung up so long, the Prez's hand almost appearing sympathetic. Until he takes hold of his arm and twists it back, a pop showing he's dislocated Mercer's shoulder. A piercing scream rings out.

"The bitch scream?" Drum asks conversationally. Then, getting no answer, takes hold of the other arm. "Well?"

"Yes. Please, God no. Don't."

"Don't? Please don't? I'd take a bet that's what she said." But instead of dislocating his other shoulder, takes hold of his hair, forcing his head back. A knife appears in his hand as if by magic, and is now held against Mercer's throat. "We let you go and you're ever seen within sight of her, I'll personally finish you off. Got it? And you'll be prayin' for death."

I get a warm glow inside. This is my life, my prez, and brothers at my back.

Mercer's shaking, a darkening patch on his pants showing he's pissed himself. *Fucking pansy.*

Prez nods to Fergus, who's been standing in the corner just observing. As he steps forward I send a shrewd look his way. The man's fitting in. Won't be too long before we need to go on a recruiting drive. Can't run a club without recruits in the wings. Who the fuck would do all the shit then?

"Throw him in the back of the truck, Fergus. Drop him somewhere discreet in town. If he gives you any trouble, you've got your gun."

Something that sounds suspiciously like, "won't give no trouble," comes from the man on the ground. My take is he just wants to get as far away from us as possible.

"Oh, and just one more thing," Prez says. "Point one finger our way, and we'll find you. You think you're hurtin' now? Give us one reason, and you'll learn this was nothin'."

As Fergus drags Mercer to his feet and leads him away, Prez slaps me on the shoulder and jerks his chin at Wraith. "C'mon. Let's go hear all about Peg's old lady."

From Wraith's smirk he expects me to deny it. I grin back, an expression that has his brows lifting, and then follow them both down the track, noting as I do the plume of smoke has thickened, but seems to have spread further up the mountain if I'm not mistaken.

Sorting out Mercer has delayed proceedings, so we waste no time hurrying into our meeting room and taking our places around the table.

"Okay. Club business first. Dollar?" Dollar reaches into his cut and takes out a spectacle case and extracts a pair of glasses.

"What the fuck?" Blade nudges him and points to his sight aids. "You going blind?"

"He's getting' old." Viper chuckles.

"You should know, old man." Rock laughs. It's lucky he's sitting across from Viper and not beside him, his positioning meaning he only has to avoid being killed by a look.

"Yeah, yeah. Have your fun. It's down to all the numbers you have me lookin' at day after day that's ruined my eyes," Dollar grumbles. "Knew you were going to be assholes about it."

"You can enlarge the spreadsheets on your screen," Mouse offers, helpfully.

"Ain't no good, can't see it all at once then."

"Let's leave Dollar's new fashion item out of things," Prez roars. "Leave the poor asshole alone and let's get this started."

"Takings are up at the Angels and Wheel Inn." As Dollar commences his update, I nod, pleased the strip club and bar and restaurant are doing well. Best thing we did was to start buying up businesses. "As far as construction goes, I've spoken to Viper and Bullet, and they have more work on our hands than they can handle. Got the contract for the new mall in town."

"That's fuckin' good news, brothers." Wraith leans forward so he can nod at both men who're sitting on his side of the table. "Knew you were going for it."

Bullet shrugs. "We've got all the paperwork saying we're up for it, good references too. Might need to take on a few more men."

Shooter's raising his hand. "Want to take on an apprentice?"

"You?" Bullet's raising a quizzical brow.

"Why not? Wouldn't mind learnin' a trade."

Now it's Bullet's turn to lean forward and look toward Viper, who gives a sharp nod. "Talk to us later, Brother."

I glance at the man we used to call Spider, it's a good idea, building work might put some muscle on his bones. He earned his new name Shooter, a couple of years back, when he saved Sophie.

Prez bangs the table. "What's the contract value?"

Dollar runs through some figures, which makes all our eyes open wide. That's some serious shit right there. Now everyone's stamping or banging the table with their hands, or both. This going straight business might be hard work, but here right now is proof. Do it right, and you reap the rewards.

Viper holds up his hand. "Might want to use a bit more of the compound for storin' equipment."

That needs a quick vote, but it's soon agreed, and Heart records it in the book.

"Getting this kick-started might mean a delay with gettin' the new houses built. But we'll try to minimise that. Brothers come first. Yours we'll be handin' over next week, Heart, as planned."

Heart's nodding. He and Marcia have decided to stay here, building a house at the top of the compound, alongside of Drummer's, and by the sounds of it hope to move in before the twins are born. Wraith and Sophie both liked the idea, and piggy-backed on it—and hell, why not? We've got plenty of land. "We'll be tied up soon when the twins are born, so any assistance getting it sorted out will be welcomed."

There's not one brother who doesn't open his mouth, offering this or that to help.

Once the business details have shown we're in a healthy position, Joker raises his hand. As prez gives him a nod, he points toward Hyde. "We're down to one prospect now our new brother's joined us at the table. That's leaving us short. Any plans on what we're going to do about it?"

Drum looks at me, so I update them. "There's a man who's been hanging around at the auto shop. Came in with his bike and has been visiting a lot. Talking about our life here, and indicating he's interested."

"Background?"

I shrug. "Not got that far, but Blade," I nod at our enforcer, "called me down to meet him one day. What I saw, I liked."

"Good guy, from what I can tell," Blade returns.

"Ok. Get his full name and what you can to Mouse, and Mouse, you know what you gotta do."

Yeah, he sure does. He'll use his nefarious skills to make sure the man's genuine, and not a plant. "His name's Matt Gore."

Mouse notes it down. "I'll get Marcia's help too. Well, if she's able." His head tilts to query Heart.

Marcia's old man shrugs. "Better do it soon, or she'll have her hands tied. But sittin' at a computer screen won't tax her none."

Far from continuing to be suspicious, knowing Marcia's one hundred percent on our side, Mouse uses her knowledge to find databases that will be useful, which he then gets into.

Prez bangs the gavel. "Okay. Let's hope we get something sorted. And keep your eyes open for anyone else. We need someone to tend bar. And someone who won't give my whisky away."

Lady waggles his fingers. "Just a thought, Prez. While we usually have a prospect behind the bar, why don't we get one, or all, of the club whores to be bartender? Means we're not a man short all the time."

"'Cause the sweet butts have better things to do with their hands." Joker elbows him in the ribs. I'm not sure how he'd know. I've not seen Joker, or Lady for that matter, with any of the club girls before. It's normally them and me left in the club-room while single brothers go off with their choice for the night.

Prez is stroking his beard, taking a few seconds before slowly nodding. "Sounds a promisin' idea to me. Who wants to find out whether any of them got skills in that direction?"

Beef nods his head. "I can have a word."

Heart records it. To give Lady his due, it *is* a fucking good plan. Means we've freed up another useful pair of hands and with so many brothers getting old ladies, there's not as much call on the sweet butts that there was. 'Bout time they made themselves useful.

But Rock looks dismal. "How we gonna give the prospects shit if they're not behind the bar?"

Hyde nudges Jekyll. "I'm sure you'll find a way." Nope, our two newest patched members won't find that hard to believe.

Prez is staring intently at me. "Movin' on, you got something to say, Peg?"

I look down at my interlinked fingers. "Yeah, I have." Looking up, I glance at each of my brothers, my face fixed as stern as I can. "I've found a woman I'm considerin' of makin' my old lady."

There's uproar. Shouts of pleasure from some, support from others, and an incredulous look from Blade. "Thought you were a confirmed bachelor, Peg." A few others echo Blade's thoughts.

"If it's the firefighter, you've only just met her," Wraith's quick to point out.

I point my index finger at him. "And just how long did it take to know Sophie was the one you wanted?"

He shrugs, and admits, "Less time than it took me to get my head out of my ass and claim her."

"And you, Prez. How long was it with you and Sam?"

"Too damn quick," grumbles Viper. But it's all put on. He's as proud as punch that Drummer's his son-in-law.

"She's a firefighter you say?" Dollar's staring at me. "That gonna cause problems for the club?"

"It's not like she's a cop." I defend her occupation.

"But she's authority. Government."

Prez's eyebrow is raised. "Club business is club business, and we keep it out of sight and hearing of the ol' ladies."

"Not what you said when I brought Marc around." Heart's noticeably upset.

"Cops are different." Drum shrugs. "If they wanted to put a plant in the club, I doubt they'd use a firefighter."

"Can we meet her?"

"Hopefully not in an official capacity." Which I think was quite quick of Paladin.

"Without setting a fire." Blade, catching on, chuckles and points his knife toward our grinning and youngest member.

"I'm collectin' her after this meetin', bringing her to the party tonight."

"Baptism by fire?" Then realising what he's just said, Rock grins and shrugs.

"Yeah, so be on your best behaviour." Another round of laughter echoes as they discuss what the fuck that might mean with each other.

Prez has leaned back in the chair, his foot against the table, his hand stroking his beard, and worryingly, his death stare is focussed on me. I return his gaze steadily, not even flinching. Neither of us blink for a moment. His sudden movement forward has the chair legs smashing to the floor, making some of them jump, but not me. His hand pointing in my direction, he bellows, "I, for one, would like to see who's so special to Peg." Then his stare encompasses everyone sitting around. "None of you fuckers fuck it up for him, you hear me?"

I'm worried enough I won't need any help. With my track record, I'll be the one fucking it up for myself.

CHAPTER 16

Darcy

Truck gave me a list of dos and don'ts for tonight's visit to the compound of the Satan's Devils MC. Mostly involving stuff I already know and practice, such as never leave your drink unattended, watch it being poured, and never drink from a bottle which has already been opened. He warned me of things that I might see, his research being based on a television series he'd watched. But even as he was giving me dire warnings of the violence and drugs he thought I'd be subject to, there was a glimmer in his eyes as though he was vicariously living through me, eliciting a promise that I'd report back to him everything I see, or do, when I'm back on shift tomorrow.

But he's only met Peg once, and that was just briefly. He didn't see the man who stayed that first night to make sure I was safe from Pete, and who'd held me so carefully all this morning, enabling me to have a peaceful sleep even after my ordeal. The person who had installed and paid for the top-notch security system that quite possibly saved my life. The man who deep down something tells me I can trust. Although giving over room in my home to Pete might suggest I have poor taste in men, I always harboured suspicions, and hadn't wanted him as a house guest long term. But Peg. He's completely different, and I want to give this a chance to see where it goes.

Excited and curious about what I can expect, I dress, change, and then look for different clothes. Truck's recollection of what he'd seen on TV being no help at all to figuring out what I should wear. In the end I settle for tight jeans and a cropped T. With the time I spend working out, and the job that I do, my stomach is flat, and I can afford to show it off. As I lean in close to the mirror, I realise It's a shame I can't do much to hide the bruises, hardly a good look to make an impression on Peg's friends. But I can't help that. I look down at what I'm wearing again.

Is it the right thing? Just as I'm wondering about changing again, there's a ring at the door.

Peg's leaning against the door jamb as I open it, his eyes unashamedly looking me over from my head to my toes, his eyes alighting on my high heels. They still do little more than bring me up to the level of his eyes, but the way his mouth shapes itself into a smile lets me know I have his approval.

He's tossing his keys from hand to hand. Looking out of the door, I see he's brought a truck tonight. "You ready?" His hand reaches out and gently grasps my chin, examining the bruise I tried to conceal.

"I am. If you're sure you want your friends to see me like this." His scrutiny makes me feel self-conscious.

"Flash," he admonishes. "My brothers won't give a damn. They all know that bastard hurt you." He steps closer. "To me you're still the most beautiful woman I've ever seen."

It's too much, I grin. "Biased, much?"

"Yeah. I'm biased. So, what?" He smirks.

Feeling more confident, I turn and take my purse from the table, and then pick up my car keys. Seeing his eyes widen, I explain, "Peg, I'm sorry, I'll have to follow you." His eyes crease partly in confusion, partly in dismay. I hurry to tell him the rest. "My friend, she's on fire watch. Maybe nothing at all, but there was a small fire burning earlier, and it's just possible I might get a call. Need to be mobile."

His brow creases. "Yeah, saw some smoke myself. Understand your problem, but I could bring you back if needed."

I'm far too independent. "I'd rather have my own transport if you don't mind."

"Escape route?"

I laugh and put my hand on his. "Don't think I need one of those. And if you think this is a pre-arranged signal to get me out if I'm overwhelmed, it really isn't." Seeing him, smelling the perfume, some kind of aftershave that he uses, makes me think nothing except an out of control burn could separate me from him tonight. "I want this, Peg. I want to see how you live."

His smile widens, and his fingers tighten around mine. "Come on then. You've got a rough idea where you're going, but follow me, okay?"

I drive carefully, keeping him well in sight, but use the time to contact my friend using the handsfree.

"Hi, Nicole. It's Darcy. Just checking if you've got any update?"

"Well, I'm close enough that I can keep an eye on it, but if anything, it's burning itself out. Don't think we need to worry about this one."

I breathe a sigh of relief. "That's great news. I can go out with my conscience clear."

"You're going out? Where? With who?"

I can hear the surprise in her voice, and I smile as I tell her. "I *may* have found a new boyfriend."

A second of silence, then, "Go you! Hey, I'm standing here kicking ash and breathing in smoke. You have a good one for me, you hear? I'll use the force of my will to make sure you don't have any interruptions. And in return, I'll want the juicy rundown when you come back to earth."

"And when you're back in civilisation. Take care, Nicole."

"Always do, babe. Always do."

I end the call, feeling happier. I really didn't want to get called out of Peg's bed and I have absolutely no thoughts except that's where I'll end up tonight. This morning gave me a taste, and I want to explore more. I shift in my seat, suddenly finding it hard to get comfortable as I remember his piercings on his cock and exactly what he can do with them.

Lost in my salacious thoughts, I almost miss Peg indicating and taking a small turnoff. Quickly bringing myself back to the present, I notice it's so innocuous I'm not surprised I never even noticed it before when I was searching for their clubhouse. The road's a bit rutted, so I take notice of where Peg's steering, and follow in his tracks. It's not too far, possibly a mile, then after a few twists and turns, we're coming up to a gate. Peg uses his horn, and soon the gate is sliding open. He pulls up in front of a garage with huge, closed rolling doors, and indicates I should draw alongside.

"We'll walk from here to the clubhouse." He's opened my door and is holding out his hand. Taking my keys out of the ignition, I pick up my purse. After getting out and locking the door, I slide my keys into my pocket.

Linking my arm through his, he leads me up an incline, and I realise the whole compound is nestled in the foothills at the very bottom of the Coronado Forest. I pause for a second and look up ahead, pleased to notice Nicole must have been right. If it was a big fire, I'd see signs of it burning from here.

With my professional hat on, I ask, "What's the setup, here?"

"You know this was an old vacation resort?" At my nod, he continues, "Clubhouse is where the reception areas were, and the kitchen and dining room. Offices are used by some of the brothers, and we've built on crash rooms out the back." He pauses, then hastily moves on. "We've got a gym and a swimming pool."

"Sounds great." I'm genuinely surprised at the facilities they have.

He points to a track that continues past what must be the clubhouse, if the number of bikes parked outside is anything to go by. "We've rebuilt a lot of the suites as our accommodation. There's blocs going up this track and one running parallel. Two suites to a bloc. And at the top of the compound are three houses, and two more the brothers are building."

"Doing the work yourselves?"

"We run a construction company."

That explains why they've been able to get so much done here. I pause and look around. It's a beautiful spot. Although only lit by stars and a half moon, I place it opposite the Tucson Mountains. I remember the co-ordinates of the fire, and while way above, must have been visible from here. "You got a fire break between the houses and the forest?"

"Certainly have. A hundred-foot wide. A lesson we learned when the original resort went up."

I bite my lip. I've seen fires leap four lane highways when driven by wind. Hopefully that will be enough and, even better, that fire doesn't come close enough to put it to the test.

"Seen everything you want?" Turning back to Peg, I notice his eyes are twinkling in the light spilling out of the clubroom we've now reached.

I nod and take my first step into the world of bikers.

At first sight, it's about what I expected. Men wearing the same leather vests as Peg crowd the room, some sitting around tables, lounging on couches, or standing at the bar, and a few scantily clad women, which makes me think the rumours are true, and bikers keep women on tap, but there are also other women who don't look anything like whores. A couple of toddlers running around, and a young child, who looks about four or five, chasing them. A heavily pregnant woman is leaning against who I presume is her man. I hadn't anticipated that.

What I certainly didn't expect when I stepped through the door alongside Peg was for all conversation to stop and eyes turn toward me. *A stranger in their midst?*

"Here, give 'er some fuckin' room to breathe," Peg snarls as he pushes men left and right, clearing space for us to get to the bar. His hand holding tight to mine, he pulls me in his wake until we reach his intended destination. As the silence continues, he indicates a stool for me to sit on, then turns, and I catch a sight of the glare he throws at the mass of bikers we've just walked through, then he swings back around and puts his arm around my shoulder. "Don't pay them no mind, Flash. They're just a bunch of nosy assholes. What do you want to drink?"

I eye the mass of bottles behind the bar, considering I've probably little option. "Beer will be fine." I'll just have one drink and make it last in case I get called into work. Then I realise what he's said. "Flash?"

He grins. "I like it. Suits you." He raps on the counter. "Jill!" he calls, and a scowling woman, one who's dressed in a tiny skirt that would better fit a child, and a short top, under which she's clearly braless, comes across. "Two beers."

I half expect her to snarl *get them yourself*, but with a huff she turns and grabs a couple of bottles and slams them down on the bar. As Peg hands one to me, I pick it up, but just hold it in my hands, conscious I still appear to be the object of everyone's attention.

Peg leans in and says conspiratorially, "New development getting the club women to tend bar." He nods toward Jill, who's leaning back against the shelves, glowering around the room. "She's only just heard about it and, as you can see, doesn't like it that much."

I nod, not really understanding, and more concerned about the looks being thrown my way.

Way to make me feel welcome. Shifting awkwardly, I'm about to ask Peg if his friends are usually this curious about newcomers, when a man comes up alongside us, slapping Peg on the back before turning to me, his eyes roving over me. I survey him in a similar way. He looks to be about forty, he's tall, his hair is dark with signs of grey at the temples, and has a short beard with silver flecks in it. What's most noticeable is his piercing steel-grey eyes. As I meet them, I blink, and though I try not to, I look down, unable to meet his stare, and catch sight of the flash which tells me he's the president. I swallow, unsure whether this is an official examination or not.

"So, you're Darcy." As I dip my head and raise it, I see him move his attention to Peg. "Can see what caught your eye, Brother."

Is that a compliment or not?

Peg just grunts but throws me a wink. He takes a swallow of his beer, then at last says, "Flash, meet Drummer. Drummer's the prez."

At last I find my voice. "Nice to meet you, Drummer. Or should I call you Mr President?" I soften my question with a smile.

He chuckles. "Drummer, or Drum, will do fine." Then he queries Peg. "Flash?"

Peg shrugs and tightens his arm around me. "Flashfire. It's her firefighter name."

"Hey, Sam! Come meet Flash." As Drummer calls out, a pretty woman walks up, holding tight to the hand of a toddler. "This is my ol' lady." He leans toward me as he speaks. "And this little monster here is Eli, our son."

As I smile at the woman, I look down at the child, and need to hide my grin as I see there's no doubting his parentage when cautious grey eyes stare up into mine. "I'm Darcy." I hold out my hand to Sam.

Her eyes fill with warmth, and she waves her hand toward the men and women behind her. "It's good to meet you, Darcy. And don't mind them. They're just curious to see the first woman Peg's ever brought to the compound. You must be one special person."

"She is."

Peg places a kiss to the top of my head, just as a new voice beside me says, "Awh."

Sam chuckles. "This is Sophie, she's the VP's woman." She leans in and says in a stage whisper, "She's from England, but we forgive her for that. If you need a translation of anything she says, just ask me."

Sophie gives her a light-hearted slap on her wrist. "Shut your bloody gob, Sam. Darcy, it's nice to meet you."

"And I'm Wraith. The said VP." Another strikingly good-looking man raises his chin, and I lift mine back in recognition. I remember him being there last night.

Introductions follow quickly. I meet Heart and his enorm-ously pregnant wife, Marcia, Carmen and Bullet, Viper and Sandy, and Slick and Ella. Then Peg takes me around the room, introducing me to all the men, *his brothers*, he calls them. Names become a blur, but far from being suspicious, they're all friendly enough. Gradually it dawns that it wasn't me who was the object of their curiosity, but Peg. *Has he really never brought a woman here before?*

"When you get tired of this asshole, come find me," the one I've been told is called Rock tells me in an exaggerated whisper.

Peg snarls and grabs him by his vest. "Keep your hands to yourself. She's *mine*."

His possessiveness makes me swallow and realise that my panties are damp. Just what is it about this man that turns me on so easily?

At last we get to a table, and Peg sits me down. "Wait here."

I watch as he returns to the bar and leans over, his height making it look easy as he folds himself in half, and I feast my eyes on his amazing ass. He stops the music and puts something else on. As it starts playing I recognise Bruce Springsteen. There's a collective groan, and Peg's mouth twitches as he returns to me.

"Always got time for some of The Boss," I say as Peg takes a seat.

He stares at me then shakes his head. "Fuck, Woman, I knew you were perfect for me."

Another man comes over and drags out a chair, turning it around and straddling it, leaning his elbows on the back. "We've got no chance if you two share the same musical taste."

"Can't help it if we both like the good stuff." Peg offers no apology.

It seems no one argues with him when he puts on his choice of music, but that's okay with me. I sit back and examine him in his natural environment. While outwardly he appears relaxed, he's still slightly on edge, his eyes scanning the room as if looking for trouble. Filing that thought away, I turn to the man who's just joined us. "Sorry, you are?" I try to peer at the name on his vest.

"I'm Dollar. I'm treasurer and look after the club's money."

"Yeah, well go away and count some," Peg grumbles.

Dollar grins and raises his hands. "Okay, okay, keep your hair on, Peg. Just came over to be friendly."

"Well you've outstayed your welcome." Peg's mock bad humour is softened by another wink at me.

Dollar gets up and leaves, and I'm suddenly curious. "What do you actually do for the club, Peg?"

"As you know, I'm an officer, the sergeant-at-arms. It means I watch out for the club, try to make sure nothing's going sneak up and catch us out. I'm responsible for the club's safety, and keep order between the brothers."

I can see how he could do that. His height, for one thing. He must be one of the tallest men here. His explanation clarifies why my safety is so important to him. The urge to protect others must be ingrained in him. "How long have you been in that role?"

He thinks for a moment. "Must be getting on for ten years."

"What's the story behind all the names, Peg?" None of the men seem to use the name they were born with.

He grins. "Best you ask Sophie that. She'll take great delight in tellin' you." My smile fades, and I frown, realising the answer as I ask the question, but wanting to confirm it. "Why are you called Peg?"

He slaps his injured leg. "Peg Leg, in full, darlin'."

I don't know why I hadn't realised it before. My brow creases, and I'm annoyed on his behalf. "That's cruel."

"Just saying it as it is." Well, if it doesn't bother him I won't let it bother me, but I don't like using it. "What's your real name?"

He sighs and places his hand over mine, which looks tiny in comparison. "I'm Peg, it's who I am. I don't mind the handle in the least. My leg ain't gonna grow back, and I'm long past wishing it would. But if you must know, my name's Ronald Rinter. I used to be called Ronnie, or Rint before I left for the Army."

As I look into his face, I realise what he's saying. He *is* Peg, and while I'd rather avoid a moniker with such connotations, I'll keep using it if that's what he wants.

I spot one of the men who helped disassemble my bed and point to him. "Why's he not got a Satan's Devils patch on the back of his vest?"

A laugh bursts from Peg. "First off, it's not called a vest, it's a cut. And Fergus is a prospect. Prospects must earn the brothers' trust before they become members. They do the shit jobs for a year or more until they're ready to get their patch."

I translate that into my language. "They're on probation?"

"Yeah. That."

Though I had my suspicions from the time I walked in, I cast a glance sideways at the women who are barely dressed. The one reluctantly playing bartender isn't the only one. "There's other women here, Peg." I'm inquisitive, as I wasn't introduced to them. "Who are they?"

He looks serious, and takes another sip of his beer, then says cautiously, "They're sweet butts, club women. Whores, if you like." His eyes meet mine for a second as if trying to see what I think of his revelation. "We give them room and board in exchange for their services."

Well, he couldn't put it clearer than that. As I glance around, I see Rock going towards the group and beckoning to one with his finger. She smirks at the girl she'd been talking to, and eagerly gets off her seat. Uncaring she's got an audience, she blatantly places a hand over Rock's cock. He covers her fingers with his and gives a wide grin. But as she licks her lips suggestively, it certainly doesn't look like she's being forced in any way.

I frown. Peg mistakes it, his finger coming up under my chin, forcing me to look at him. "They're here by choice, darlin'."

I admit that isn't what's worrying me. "Do you go…"

"Not for a long time, sweetheart." He answers before I can complete my enquiry. "Been looking for something else, got bored with just fucking. Been waiting for someone who I wanted in my bed, and for more than just sex." He pauses and gives me an intense look full of meaning. "Been waiting for you."

It's so similar to the way I feel about him, it seems too good to be true. I push for more information. "Have there been many women? Women like me?"

Another earnest look. "None like you. Ain't had a woman in my life for a very long time. And when I did, it didn't end well."

My eyebrows rise, and he answers my unspoken question, leaning toward me and speaking quietly as though he doesn't want to be overheard. "You and me? Well, I think we've got something special. So full disclosure, okay?" He pauses and starts to play with his beard. "Fifteen years ago, when I was on leave, a bitch told me she was pregnant, so I married her. I was soon off on another tour." He takes a moment, his face growing dark as he recalls it. "I made sure she had money, had my earn-in's paid into a joint bank account. She was my wife, my ol' lady, and I thought it was forever. I knew I could have done better, should have waited for someone else, but I'd stepped up to do what I thought I should, and having committed, wasn't gonna leave her. Had the piercings done to make her happy. And I'll tell you this, fuck did they hurt." A twisted smile fleetingly comes to his face and disappears just as quickly. "When I came back she told me she'd miscarried. I did my best to make her happy, was as good a husband as I could be. Then I was off on another tour. When I came back injured, she dropped the pretence. Said she couldn't be with me, that my missing leg was disgusting. Made it all about her, as if I'd done it on purpose."

He gazes off into the distance, and his mouth twists. "When I left the hospital, she'd cleared out our bank account. And that's when I found she'd never been faithful. There never had been any baby, miscarried or not, and she'd been fuckin' everyone she could behind my back." He glances up and looks at his brothers, then his eyes return to mine. "Just wanted to snag herself a biker, and so set a trap. I fell right into it."

My hand's been under his, and I now lay mine on top and squeeze gently. "I'm so sorry, Peg."

He slowly nods. "Put me off bitches."

That I can understand. "Who is she, and where can I find her to kill her?" I ask in a conversational tone.

His head had been lowered, he now snaps it back up. A surprised chuckle comes out. "Fuckin' perfect, babe. Fuckin' perfect." Leaning forward, his hand curls around the back of my head and he pulls me to him across the table, his mouth descending and ravishing mine. A kiss of possession.

"For fuck's sake, get a fuckin' room."

I don't know who shouted it, but Peg clearly thinks it's a brilliant suggestion, as suddenly he stands, throwing me over his shoulder in a fireman's lift, slaps my ass, and I'm still laughing as he carries me out of the clubhouse, giggling as I hear Bruce Springsteen's Thunder Road swiftly cut off mid verse.

CHAPTER 17

Peg

This woman was made for me. Nothing I do or say seems to scare her off. She's a perfect fit. *She wants to kill my ex?* Fucking perfection. Now I don't want to waste another minute before feeling our bodies fitting together.

I keep myself in shape, and I can quickly tell she does too—her body is pure muscle, adding to her weight. Though I'd like to make the grand gesture and carry her up to my suite, my stump where it meets the prosthesis is telling me I can't. Outside the clubhouse I slide her back down from my shoulder and rest her feet on the ground, pulling her tightly against me, letting her feel my hardness.

"Fuck, Woman, you turn me on like no one else."

"Fuck, Peg," she parrots, and then stands on tiptoe to whisper. "My panties are wet."

I growl, grab her hand, and drag her up the track, forgetting she's wearing high heels. She stumbles, but I've got her, swinging her around in my arms.

She's laughing so hard she bends double. "Eager or what?"

"I'd fuckin' carry you…"

Now it's her who links her arm through my right one, holding on tight. "Lead on, lover."

Taking her weight on my good leg, wondering if she took the correct side by accident or on purpose, I start walking again, making sure to match my speed to hers, wondering if I can ask her to walk barefoot so we get there faster. My suite seems a fucking long way away, but soon as we pass the other brothers' blocs, two suites in each, we at last come to mine. Opening the door, I push her inside.

We've not pushed for room at the compound, and as no one wanted to share with a grumpy old biker, I've adapted both suites. Got my bedroom one side, and the other's turned into a living area—big screen TV and a music system to rival Drum's. As I don't spend time with the sweet butts, this is my home and a refuge for me.

I don't show her around, but instead, like a cave man, drag her straight into my bedroom.

Her eyes widen as she sees my huge bed. "Not sure something like this would fit in my house." She giggles.

I'm not going to waste time on conversation. I sit on the bed and pull her in front of me between my legs. "Want you naked," I rasp.

Showing she's completely on board with that idea, she takes a step back and raises her top, and with a little enticing wiggle she pulls it off, then blows me a kiss before removing her bra. As I go to reach for her gorgeous tits tipped by those enticing rings, she takes another step back and waggles her finger at me.

If she wants to give me a show, I'll let her. I lean back on my elbows and prepare to enjoy myself.

It's almost as if she's listening to music in her head, moving to a beat I can't hear, but keeping perfect rhythm as she moves those hips side to side. Still swaying in time, she turns her back toward me and reaches down to undo her sandals, able to touch her ankles without bending her knees or crouching. It puts her ass almost in my face, and my palms itch, wondering what it would look like adorned with my hand prints.

Now she's straightening and turning again, shimmying as she pushes her jeans down to the floor, kicking one leg out and then the other. Soon it's just her panties left to go. As she hooks her thumbs in the elastic, my hand starts to stroke my rock-hard cock.

Another slick move and her last garment is gone, and I feast my eyes on the red landing strip leading its way to a taste of heaven. My nostrils flare as I inhale her scent, loving she's enriching the air in my room with that tinge of arousal.

Pushing up on my arms, I begin to get to my feet, but again she gestures and waves me back down. Interested to see what she's going to do, I wait. She wastes no time closing the gap between us, pushing my legs together with her hands, then straddling my lap, her essence rubbing on my jeans, glistening arousal like a snail trail on the denim. *Fuck, she's turned on.*

She pushes aside my cut, slides it off my shoulders, and then puts it carefully on the bedside table. Next, taking the hem of my tee, pulls that over my head. Her eyes flare as they focus on my cut chest, and her hands rest on my shoulders. Again, I go to move, wanting to feel her bare skin touching mine.

"Wait," she demands.

Once more I obey as she shuffles back and folds herself to her knees. A sassy smile appears on her face as she undoes my button and pulls down the zip. A tap on my thigh gets my ass rising, and carefully she pulls my jeans down, removing my boots and taking my pants right off.

She looks at my prosthesis, stares at the strap where it's fastened to my leg. A quick glance to my face, then when I nod, she's working out how to undo it, and taking it off.

Fuck, that's hot. Women have either ignored it or been upset by it, but no one before has treated it in such a matter of fact way, as if it's just as much a part of me as anything else. My cock jumps, bobbing against my stomach, waving as though to catch her attention.

She's viewing my stump with a frown on her face. "It looks red. Is it sore? Have you got anything to put on it?"

A bit. I've been on it a long time today, and carrying her probably didn't help. To test her, I say, "There's cream in the drawer."

Without hesitation, she's opening the drawer and holding up a tube. When I nod to agree she's picked the right one, she squeezes some into her hands and massages the ointment into the reddened skin, her hands so gentle, so competent. To see a woman kneeling, doing something that seems even more intimate than sucking my cock, almost blows my mind, and I suck in a deep breath, rolling my head back as I'm filled with disbelief. *How the fuck did I find her?*

She's running her hands over my thigh, her fingers kneading my muscles as if she instinctively knows the compensatory work they need to do to make up for my inflexible lower leg.

I enjoy her attentions, my breath leaving me on a satisfied sigh. As if I've signalled she's done enough, both hands slide up my inner thighs, heading toward my groin. They advance then retreat, then do it again, gaining a little more ground each time. The hairs on my legs are standing up, every nerve ending in my body seeming alive. Now she's skimming the edge of my balls, and seconds later she's taking them between her hands, rubbing and lightly squeezing.

Soon she's at the root of my cock, and I'm watching everything that she does. My dark pubic hair a contrast to her curtain of red curly locks. A smirk, a wink, then she's licking my shaft, moving her lips tantalisingly slowly up to the head.

Her hands come out and cup my ass, applying a little pressure. Yes, if I move down, fuck, that's it. She takes advantage, her mouth positioned right over my dick and oh, fuck, she's taking me in.

But not far enough. She sucks, and her cheeks hollow. Shit, that feels so damn good. Her lips move up and down, then up again, and her tongue comes out, licking the sensitive spot, then over each of my piercings. Fuck! One hands going under my ass, probing at my most private place.

"Honey, I don't think…"

But she's got other ideas. She sinks her mouth back over my cock, taking me deep until I touch the back of her throat. When she swallows around me, I'm not going to last long. When she does it again I almost explode. "Darlin', pull away…"

She doesn't, her hand leaves my ass, *thank fuck*, but then reappears, and I feel a slickness and realise she's used her own arousal to lubricate her finger, and she's pushing it in. Fuck, there's a burning sensation I don't like, she's got to stop, no one's ever touched, shit, she's humming and swallowing around me I'm on sensual overload. Her finger presses in further and touches my prostrate, and her mouth takes me so deep.

I go off like a rocket blasting into space, my muscles spasming, my body shuddering as I empty my load. I can't shut my eyes, need to see her throat working as she drinks down my cum.

I've been given blow jobs by experts, by a fuck load of talented women, but never, never has it been anything like as good as this.

My deflating cock slips out of her mouth, and she licks around it, cleaning me off, making sure she doesn't miss a drop.

I'm a man who likes to be in control, but she stripped me of it completely, and I don't give one fucking damn.

"Com'ere." I feel drained, and for a moment just want to hold her. As she starts to move for me, I use my abdominal muscles to pull myself up, putting my arms around her and pulling her to me, cradling her head to my still heaving chest.

"What the fuck was that?" I ask, when I can speak properly.

"You like?" I feel her smile against my skin.

"Yeah. I fuckin' like." I agree. *Her finger in my ass?* Yeah, I even liked that.

Now I'm taking charge, turning her over and pushing her onto her back. First, I need to take her mouth, to taste me on her, an incredibly compelling flavour that incites me, and blood once again engorges my cock.

"My turn," I whisper as I plant a last kiss on her lips.

As I move down her body, I take time to worship her breasts, working her pert nipples between my fingers, gently pulling at the rings then pinching until I find just the right pressure, then repeating the same devotion with my mouth and teeth. A mild suck and little nip has her writhing, and I memorise what brings her pleasure. Next, I move lower, stroking her stomach, admiring how taut her muscles are. Leaning forward, I place a gentle kiss above her mound.

Imagining her flat belly swollen with my baby inside, I ask, "Do you ever want kids?" My voice is gruff, rich with emotion as I continue, "Will you have mine?"

Her indrawn breath tells her I've surprised her. I raise my eyes to see she's lifted her head off the pillow, her cheeks flushed, her pupils enlarged. "Peg?"

I don't know if she's using my name as a comment in answer to my question, or an admonishment to get down to the good stuff. Kissing her stomach once again, sucking hard enough to leave my mark there, I follow that landing strip leading me down and, without warning, suck hard on her clit.

Her back bows as she gasps with surprise.

I raise my head, she shudders as though anxious for me to get back to what I was doing. When I'm not quick enough, she prompts me by saying my name again. "Peg?"

Smoothing my hand over her cheek, I make my admission. "I like to be in control, darlin'."

"I can tell that."

"No, *control*," I emphasize, my eyes looking at her seriously. "I want to play, to restrain you. But fuck, after what that fucker did today…"

Her sharp indrawn breath tells me she understands. Taking my hand in hers, she lowers it and pushes on my fingers. "He didn't *do* anything Peg. And that's down to you." She pauses, and her mouth purses. "There's always what might have beens, especially on my job. I won't waste my time worried about something that didn't happen. He's not here, Peg. But you are. And see what you do to me?"

Her cream is drenching my bed. *She wants this.*

She fixes her eyes on mine and smiles. "Go ahead and play, Peg."

I'm unsure, but she's tempting me so much. "Tell me if it's too much," I order. "You want me to stop, I will."

She grins and lifts my hand, offering it to me. I lick her arousal off my fingers, and fuck me, I'm completely lost. *She's mine.* And now she's going to get all of me.

Leaving her briefly, I pull something from under the bed. Flash leans up on her elbows, watching me. "What's that?"

I ignore her question, just proceed with my task, gently fastening one ankle to either side, then ratcheting the device apart, leaving her wide open to me, unable to close her thighs.

"Peg?"

"It's a spreader bar, babe. Does what it says on the tin." Then I'm moving up over her body, taking one hand, then the other, and handcuffing them to the metal swivel ring at the top of my bed.

I sit back on my haunches and admire her. She's captive, and I can do what I like. She tries the bindings holding her, and finding she can't move, a red flush extends from her head to her feet. Suddenly I'm concerned. "You alright? Is this too much?"

"It's perfect." She breathes and jangles the cuffs. "They're lined and so soft." She wriggles as if to test her constraints. "You can do what you want to me, can't you?" Her eyes meet mine again, her pupils dilated and her voice husky as she gives me permission. "Do your worst, Peg."

I'm blown away by how much she trusts me, then get my head back into the game. "Stay still," I say, unnecessarily, as there's really not far she can move.

"Just don't leave me hanging," she replies, making me huff a laugh as I get back to work.

Lifting the spreader bar until it's resting over my shoulders, I take a moment to just admire how open she is to me and she can do nothing about it. I swipe my hands from her clit to her sweet dripping cunt, collecting her essence and licking my fingers clean. Then I do it again, this time with lubricated fingers, continuing down where I circle her tight little rose.

"Christ. Peg."

"Hmm? Just doing what you did to me, darlin'." Fuck did that have an effect I'd never imagined.

"I've never…"

"No?" Seeing how bold she was with me, I'd assume someone had introduced her to ass play before. Fucking ace, something's been saving for me. I continue to play, circling and pushing in a finger. She tenses, so my other hand finds her clit and circles it. Then I put another finger in her ass, scissoring them inside her.

"Peg!" She tries to writhe, but I've got hold of her too tightly. I can't go further today, but soon, very soon.

Unable to resist any longer, I lower my head and sweep my tongue into her channel, lapping up all her cream. Then suck her clit into my mouth, biting down gently. My hand curls up inside her, finding that place that will drive her wild.

She's got my fingers in her ass, my other hand pressing on her g-spot, and my teeth attacking that sensitive bundle of nerves. She stops breathing, holding her breath, then lets it out on a scream as she reaches her peak and soars over the top.

While she's still quaking, I slide out from under the spreader bar, slide on a condom, and utilising the pivot on the ring her handcuffs are attached to, turn her over, her ass in the air. Before she's totally back to herself, I thrust inside her, all the way in one hard push.

She gasps, then pushes that ass back to me. Fulfilling my earlier desire, I slap her hard enough to leave my handprint, and then do the same to the other cheek. The results of my handiwork excites me, and I start hammering in. I'm not being gentle, I'm fucking her like a biker, and she's taking everything I've got.

Her hands are still cuffed to my headboard, the spreader bar keeping her open for me. This brave, independent woman is totally at my mercy, and fuck if my cock can't get any harder.

I slow my pace, a few strokes long and measured, my piercings hitting her in all the right spots. All I can hear is a low keening.

Then I increase my pace and start hammering in once again. Then slow, then stop. She can't learn my rhythm, is just forced to take what I want to give. I feel like the luckiest bastard in the world right now as she starts chanting my name, alternatively encouraging then berating me. Each time I deny her, I'm taking her higher and higher.

Christ, I'm torturing myself. My balls draw up to my body, the tingling in my spine telling me that I'm close. I pinch her clit and hold it, my other hand finding a nipple, tugging at her ring and then applying just the right pressure that I've already learned.

Her muscles clench, release, then clench and hold me, and her orgasm ripples over my cock, causing me to thrust in hard as cum shoots up and out. As I make those few final pumps, I feel her muscles undulating again with another, but weaker orgasm.

Fuck, it's so fucking unbelievable with this woman. *We were made for each other.*

Completely drained and exhausted, I bow my head. My chest rapidly rising and falling, I try to bring air into my tortured lungs.

CHAPTER 18
Darcy

Wow. Just, well, wow. Three orgasms in one session must be the most I've ever had, each one was so powerful it's sapped all my energy and I'm unable to move. I hear harsh breathing behind me, realising he's in no better shape than me. *What he did should have scared me.* But I trusted Peg, I let him tie me up. Had he done it on purpose to wipe every trace of Pete from my mind? Showing being completely under his control, unable to do anything but take what he offered, brought rewards I hadn't even known existed? Whether it had been by design or accident, it worked.

Gradually, as my heart slows to a more normal rhythm, I feel him pull himself up and undo the straps on the spreader bar and massaging my ankles and legs, then moving over me, under the handcuffs, and rubbing hard to bring the feeling back into my hands. It's only when he turns me over that I look to see him staring down at me, his beautiful face shining with sweat, his beard covered in me.

"I've got to go deal with the condom."

As I nod, I see him pick up a crutch I hadn't noticed was placed by the side of the bed, and he expertly hops away into the adjacent bathroom. When he comes back he's got a washcloth and, too exhausted to move, I let him do what he wants to me, relishing the feeling of being taken care of.

He climbs on the bed and puts down the crutch, holding out his hand in invitation. When I snuggle into him, I smell myself on his beard, and start to chuckle.

"What's up?"

I lift his beard so he can see it. "You smell of me!"

"I'm thinking of bottlin' and sellin' it. Make a fuckin' perfume. Eau du Flashfire or some shit like that."

I start to giggle, and then laugh at the thought of anyone wanting to walk around smelling like me. "You're crazy."

"Me?" His eyes open. "I believe it was you who had your finger in my ass. Gotta tell you, babe, that was a new one on me."

"New for me too," I admit softly, still not believing I had the nerve to do it.

"Where the fuck did you learn that then?"

"From a book. I read a lot when we're hanging around waiting for a call out." I don't tell him it was one of Nicole's.

"Hmm." He places a kiss to my forehead. "Anything else in those books you read?"

I feel myself redden before I confess, "Well, it was the first time I've given head."

He lifts my head away from my body and stares in my face. "Honestly?"

I try to look away. "Yeah, I've never wanted to before."

A satisfied smile crosses his face. "And why did I get lucky?"

"It seemed right, Peg. I didn't even know I was going to do it until it was there, waving in front of my face."

As he chuckles I can feel his chest vibrating. "What was waving in your face."

As my cheeks go darker, I don't want to give him another chance to tickle me, so I give him the words he wants to hear. "Your cock."

"Fuckin' love hearin' you talk dirty, darlin'." He considers for a moment. "So, obviously the first time you swallowed. You like my taste?"

I make a face. "Nah, it was actually horrible."

"So, you're not going to do it again?" He sounds disappointed. "I did try and warn you."

Placing my fingers over his mouth, I tell him the truth. "It's you, Peg. And I want all of you. I want to give you pleasure. And as your woman, it's mine to take if I want to, isn't it?"

Suddenly I'm not on top any longer, he's rolled us over so I'm underneath. "Say it again," he says gruffly, and then clarifies which part. "Say you're my woman."

He's so intense, I swallow, realising our conversation's grown serious. Raising my hand, I stroke it over his face, starting at his brow, descending his cheek, and ending up cupping his chin. I don't know what I'm doing here, why everything inside me makes me want to be his. *I barely know him.* But deep down I know he's everything I want. *It's going too fast.* What does that matter? When something feels right, it's right, isn't it?

There's nothing I've got that he needs, he's not using me for anything. Our physical connection is out of this world, and we seem to fit together so well. *Do I take this leap?* I'm a thirty-year-old woman, I'm not getting any younger, and it's not as though I'm committing to marriage or anything. Just be in a relationship with him to see where it goes.

He asked me if I'd have his babies. Is he thinking long term?

"Were you serious, Peg, when you asked if I'd have your baby?"

"Fuck yeah."

His immediate response makes my toes curl, and I swear my womb clenches at the thought of his seed growing there. A man who's already shown how protective he is would be so nurturing toward my, our, child. Shit, is it my biological clock or something that just the idea has me wanting to start now? But that's in the future, when we've explored whether this, whatever this is between us, will work.

Throwing all caution to the wind, I open my mouth and let the words come out. "Yes. Yes, I'm your woman."

He's up and looming over me. Searching my face as if trying to read something there. "One chance, one chance, Darcy. That's all you're getting to change your mind. I want this. I want *you*. You say yes again, and you're mine, you understand me? There'll never be another man in your life, and definitely not in your bed. Just me, forever, babe. You'll wear my property patch to show everyone that you belong to me. I'll get your name tattooed over my heart, babe, and I want my name tattooed on you somewhere. A permanent commitment. And one day, soon, I'm taking you bare and you'll have my baby. Fuck, babies. Our *family*." He pauses, as if struggling. "One chance." His voice is almost hoarse, breaking with emotion. "One chance, that's all I'm giving you. Say yes again, and you've committed."

I gulp, suddenly realising how serious this is to him. He doesn't want me to be his woman *for now*, he is thinking of something long term. I take a moment, knowing I've never been with anyone like him before, but not truly appreciating what this might mean. Can I make him a promise, right here, right now?

I look into his eyes, knowing everything he's asking of me, he'll be giving of him. I'll own him as much as he owns me. How could I give this up without giving it a chance? Raising my hand, I touch his cheek, feeling his bristles against my smooth skin. Never, ever, have I come across someone like him before. I'd be a fool to let this opportunity go. I swallow, then tell him, "Yes." He blinks as his eyes start watering, and I know it's right to throw caution to the wind. "I'm falling in love with you, Peg."

He sweeps me up in his strong arms, holding me tightly as if he's never going to let me go. His voice breaks as he answers,

"Already love you, Darcy, Flashfire, whatever you are to me. I fuckin' love you."

He kisses me, devours me, and I give as good back. His cock is hard between us as he pushes me back down on the bed. After testing I'm wet, he reaches for a condom, slips it on, then slides inside.

This time our fucking isn't hurried, isn't frenzied, and isn't rough. There's only one name for it, we're making love. Another side to my man, and it's just as amazing as anything else I've learned about him.

The alarm goes off early the next morning, giving me enough time to get up and down to the station for my shift. I reach out my hand to the side to find I'm alone, but I hear the sound of the shower coming from the bathroom. I examine the thoughts running through my head, finding I've got zero doubts or self-recriminations. I've done it. I've jumped in with both feet.

So why isn't he with me? Is he the one having second thoughts? Were the declarations something to be left in the dead of the night?

But when the bathroom door opens and he steps out, legless and leaning on that crutch, there's something in his expression that's missing, a guardedness that had always been there before. I look at his eyes, at the shape of his mouth, and realise he looks happy, content, and relaxed. Well apart from his cock, which is up and ready.

"My eyes are up here, darlin'. Keep lookin' at my cock like that and we won't get out of here anytime soon."

I go to sit up and wince. Hell, I got a work out last night and used muscles I don't normally exercise at the gym.

He smirks at my discomfort, then comes across. "You okay?"

"I don't think I'm up for another round, Peg." I grimace, annoyed with myself.

His mouth curves up into a grin. "The truth? I'm a bit on the raw side myself." He stares at me, and suddenly we're both laughing, and when he comes closer, we hold each other as if we've been doing it forever.

"What time's your shift?" He finally asks.

Shit. I almost forgot I had to go back to work. I seem to have been living in a bubble for the past few hours, and now it's about to burst. "Seven," I tell him, for once not enthusiastic about my job.

"That gives us an hour or so. Let's go down to the clubhouse when you're ready, get something to eat. If you're okay with it, I'll see about getting you a new bed while you're at work. I'll get it delivered and set up ready for you later."

I nod. A new bed is the last thing on my mind. "You showered without me," I pout.

"Babe. You, me, in the shower? Wouldn't have been able to keep my hands off."

For a second, I'm worried how I'll get to the bathroom without clothes, and then realise he's been looking at my body all night. So, I stand, naked, unashamed in front of *my man*. Then I frown. "Did I actually agree to getting a tattoo last night?"

Another smirk. "Sure did, darlin'."

I think about it for a moment. Never considered getting one before. "Okay, but you get yours first, alright?"

"How about we go together?"

"Deal."

I shower quickly, taking delight in using Peg's shampoo and body wash, though lamenting that he doesn't have conditioner, which means getting the tangles out of my hair will be a bitch, and then throw on the clothes I was wearing last night. Well, I suppose I didn't have them on very long.

Peg gives me time to get ready, just sits and watches me from the bed. Out of the corner of my eye I see him strapping on his prosthesis, before putting clothes on himself. Once we're ready, I expect him to take me straight down to the clubhouse, but he makes a short detour—very short—into what I'd assumed was another biker's room.

As he pushes open the door, he explains, "I've converted this room into my living area. Got all the comforts you see." I step in. There's another balcony here, just like in his bedroom. It has a wonderful view looking out over the basin and to the Tucson Mountains beyond. "And here," he opens what I expected to be another bathroom, "I've had a small kitchen installed." Small is the operative word—it's tiny. But there's a small stove, microwave, mini fridge, and cupboard space. You wouldn't want to prepare a huge Thanksgiving dinner here, but a simple meal you could easily do.

"It's great, Peg. Like your own apartment." I'm shaking my head, pleasantly surprised at how a biker lives. "Does everyone have rooms like this?"

He snorts. "Nope. Oh, Drum has his own house, Wraith and Heart are building theirs too, but normally there'd be two brothers living here, one in each room."

"Why d'you get so much space?"

"'Cause I'm a miserable asshole and no one wanted to share."

I can't help teasing him. "You should have told me that before you asked me to be your woman."

"Woman. And my ol' lady. And as it's your job to keep me happy, if I revert to being miserable, that's on you."

As I raise my fist to play punch him, he grabs my hand and pulls me in close. Christ, but this man can kiss. When he bunches my hair together to pull my head back, leaning his head down to get access to my throat, gently sucking the pulse points there, I feel weak, as though I could faint at his feet.

When he finally pulls away, I lean my forehead to his chest. "Think I need some recovery time."

Laughing, he takes my hand and leads me outside.

The blast of heat hits me as soon as I leave the air-conditioned building. It's going to be another very hot day. The thought makes me turn to look up at the forest coating the side of the mountain behind the compound. Oh shit.

Peg's stopped beside me and sees what I'm looking at. "We see that a lot this time of year."

I can't be quite as calm as him. "A wildfire can get out of control so easily, Peg." I lift my hand and gesture around me. "It's why you were able to buy up the resort. I heard most of it was destroyed."

He points up to the mountain top. "The fire's miles away. And it tends to burn uphill, doesn't it?"

The first bit of concern enters his voice, so I seek to reassure him. "Never any guarantees, Peg, but yes, it's far away, and," I wet my finger and hold it in the air, "wind's blowing away from here, so nothing to worry about for now. And clearly, you're more prepared this time around, and have the firebreak in place." I gaze at the plume of white smoke again, heading almost straight up in the sky. It's a light wind as well, which will help to contain it. "I'm more concerned about whether the teams on the ground will need extra support." I indicate the top of the mountain. "If it gets worse, might be waving at you from up there later."

Now he does look worried. "Hate to think of you putting yourself in danger."

"Pah. I know what I'm doing."

He takes my hands and turns me to face him. "I know you do, Flash, but it won't stop me worrying about you. Just promise you'll take care."

Going on tiptoe, I can just about reach his cheek. After pressing my lips to his skin, I draw back. "I'm not careless or reckless. And now I've got a reason to be even more careful."

But my eyes return to the smoke billowing up in the air. I'd love to ring Nicole for an update, but she'll be dealing with all manner of communications right now, and while I'd like to know how that fire's behaving, I'll find out what I need to when I go on shift. Hopefully, by then, it will be out. This time, for good.

Chapter 19

Peg

While Flash is at work, I arrange a new bed and get it delivered, and spend hours thinking what a lucky bastard I am, in between having to tamp down the worry about what exactly she might be doing during her working hours.

When she finishes her shift the next morning she gives me a call, and it seems natural to invite her back to the compound. I go to the gate so I can let her in when she arrives. She parks behind the auto shop just like before, and it's only moments before she's in my arms. She smells fresh, obviously having gone home and showered before coming to meet me.

Both breathless when we part, I smile at her. "You tired?"

"No. We weren't called out to the wildfire, and in the end, it was quite a quiet shift. Got my head down for a few last night."

Good. I take her hand and start to lead her up to the clubhouse. She pauses, holding me back and looks up at the mountains. Following her gaze, I see what she's seeing, more smoke blowing up into the air.

"Something to worry about?"

She thinks for a moment. "Nah, not at the moment, Peg." Then she smiles and wipes all thought of the fire out of my head.

There's a lightness in my steps as I walk with my ol' lady into the clubroom, that mirrors the buoyancy in my heart. I've *never* had something like this before. I got married because I thought I should bear the weight of what I thought I had done, but I'd never felt real love for my wife. When I found how she tricked me, well, I cut her right out.

The way my ex, and others, reacted to my disability had damaged something inside. Not that my brothers saw anything except a gruff sergeant-at-arms, intent only on protecting the club. No one knew I was carrying around a big hole where something was missing, just waiting to be filled. As soon as I saw her, I knew Darcy was the part I'd been seeking. Flashfire, the other half of my soul.

I'm the luckiest man in the world that she feels the same way about me. I take her hand, entwining my fingers with hers, unable to keep a smile from my face.

"Fuck, Peg. What the fuck's the matter?"

Darcy and I come to a halt just inside the entrance. I glare at Beef. "What the fuck you talkin' about?"

"Your face is all twisted up. You ill or something?"

Looking around, I see Beef's loud exclamation has caught everyone's attention. Those eating breakfast stop with food halfway to their mouths. I grin wider. Now's as good a time as any, so draping my arm across my woman's shoulders, I let them all know what we had decided the night before last. "Flash has agreed to be my ol' lady."

For a moment there's a stunned silence, as though they hadn't believed such a beautiful woman would look twice at me, and then someone hollers, and others stamp their feet.

"Never thought I'd see the fuckin' day." Rock's shaking his head, but he looks pleased.

"Need to vote on it, Peg." Wraith pours cold water over my head. Yeah, they've agreed in principle, but wanted to meet her before they made it official. As my eyes narrow, his hand claps down on my back. "Can't see a problem though."

"Peg?"

I whisper into her ear, "Formality, darlin'. Ol' ladies need to be voted in by the club."

She smiles up at me. "Then I better be on my best behaviour."

"Peg. There's some breakfast left." Sam's voice rings out clearly, and a glance at Flash's face shows that might be a fucking good idea.

Confirmed when she says quietly, "I could eat. I've had nothing yet."

My arm still around her, I lead her into the kitchen. Now knowing I'm serious, a number of brothers follow us in. But my old lady's not intimidated, not one bit. She fills a plate and takes a seat, kicking out a chair for me beside her.

"So, what do you do, Flash? Drive the engine?"

"No. I'm a firefighter." As Bullet looks confused, she explains, "The engineer, that's the driver, works the ladder and pumps. I'm not trained to do that yet."

"What I can't understand is how a little thing like you can carry people out of burning buildings."

She takes a mouthful of bacon, chews, swallows, then replies to Rock, "It's all technique." She flexes her muscles, a movement so sexy my cock starts to swell. "During out shifts when there's no call outs, we work out." She eyes Rock up. "I'll give you a demonstration if you like."

Everyone laughs as he turns her down, saying that won't be necessary.

As she answers more questions about her job, I listen and watch her. She's not got a lithe slender frame like Sophie or Ella, but she's not fat. She's pure muscle, all over. Perhaps not a figure that would appeal to all men, but she's just right for me. I can appreciate her well-defined triceps, biceps, and fuck, every muscle she has.

"What made you want to be a firefighter, Flash?" This makes my ears perk up. I haven't thought to ask her, so I listen, interested, as she responds to Wraith.

"When I was growing up there was a fire at a neighbour's house. Three kids were trapped inside. I watched as the firefighters fought the flames, couldn't believe they kept going inside, wouldn't give up until they saved all those kids. The image stuck with me."

"Your folks okay with what you do?"

She shakes her head. "Probably no more or less than anything else I could have done. My parents never knew what to do with me. I didn't fit into their mould. Think I was a changeling baby." She sighs. "I moved to a different town, as it made it easier on them and me. I'm not sure they realise what I do in my job, and if they do understand the risks involved, they disregard them."

"She's a brave fuckin' woman." Again, my arm goes over her shoulder, while fear clutches my heart. *She puts herself in danger.*

It's almost like she can read my mind, as she leans into me, raises her face, and speaks quietly in a voice meant only for me. "You're the sergeant-at-arms for a one percenter club. Looks like we both have things we need to come to terms with."

There's one thing I can do to help keep her safe. "After we've eaten, how about we go to the gym and I start teaching you some self-defence moves?"

Her eyes light up. "Sounds good, Peg." She thinks for a moment. "The guys at the station tried to show me some, but when it came to it, Pete overpowered me. He's too fucking big."

Beef snorts. "Yeah, but we can teach you how to fight dirty."

As Flash looks my way I raise my eyebrow, and she grins.

"Still can't understand how a bitch can be as good as a male firefighter." Rock's shaking his head.

I cast a worried glance at Flash, but she's not taking offence. She bites her lip, then suggests, "How about I show you? An arm wrestling match?"

Rock rears back. "No way. You wouldn't have a chance." Raising his forearms, Rock makes his muscles bunch. "You know why I'm called Rock? 'Cause I'm rock hard all over." He finishes up with a suggestive wink, which I don't appreciate at all, and warn him off with a snarl.

Flash doesn't even notice, she's indicating others to move so she can get into position. "Put your money where your mouth is, big fella."

As others mock, she's left him no choice. Either he accepts the challenge or looks like a pussy. I've mixed feelings, not sure how this will go, but trust her to know what she's doing.

In moments their hands are locked, and at first they appear to be evenly matched. Both faces are fixed with concentration, and both arms shake with the effort. Rock looks like he's gaining leeway as her arm moves a fraction, and I feel bad for my old lady. But slowly a smile comes to her face and she's forcing him back. She's now got the upper hand and, while Rock fights it, she's pushing his arm, and now it's flat on the table.

Rock looks around, disbelief on his face. "Best of three," he suggests with a growl.

When she agrees they go at it again. This time Rock's grinning, as though he's worked out how to beat her. But he loses the next two rounds too.

"Fuck, Woman, you're strong." His look is now one of admiration. "Shit, Peg, if I were you I'd rethink your idea to teach her to defend herself."

I shake my head, looking around at my brothers who are laughing at Rock, and looking in awe at Darcy, realising how much she fits in. Knowing it's partly because she works in a mostly male environment, my brothers' antics don't faze her.

She's mine. It doesn't seem possible that this amazing woman who can hold her own against my brothers wants me as much as I want her.

As the good-natured mocking of Rock starts to fade, Darcy's phone rings.

"Yeah, Nicole. What you got?"

Recognising the name of her firewatcher friend, I wave at the others to pipe down.

"Shit. That's not good news. I saw smoke this morning, didn't look like much." She's frowning.

"What's the wind speed now? Still blowing east? So, it's going up." At this she gives me a reassuring nod.

"Yeah. Thanks, Nicole. I know you're busy. Take care, you hear me?"

Ending the call, Darcy looks at me, sucks in a breath and holds it, her cheeks filled with air, then lets it out. "The wind's got up and ignited other areas. There's now multiple fire heads. Nicole's monitoring the hot spot, that's the current most active part of the fire, and trying to predict where it's going to go next." She pauses. "The good news is, it's still going up, and away from any inhabited areas."

"But?" I can tell there is one.

"It's approaching an area rich in ladder fuels. Currently it's burning ground vegetation, perennial grasses, which is the worse type of fuel this time of year, as it burns fast. Now it's nearing trees. We don't want it to move into the canopy."

"You seem worried?"

She nods at me. "I am. Nicole's got a firefighting crew up there with her on standby, but there's some discussion about the let-burn policy. From her experience, this one could turn big, but the conservationists are thinking of just letting it be."

"Surely it's best to put it out?"

She gives a half laugh. "I'm a firefighter, so that's what I'd think. But there's no roads nearby, so it's not in an easy place to get to."

"Will you be called in, Darcy?" Wraith looks interested.

She shakes her head. "Not right now. But it will be all the nearest crews needing to get involved, which includes us, if this one gets a good hold."

"Aren't there hotshots who deal with wildfires?" Anyone but her would be better in my view.

Another shake. "You must have heard about California. They're all occupied with the fires in that state. No, this one will be down to the local crews." As if she's said all she can say on the subject, she changes track. "Right, where's this gym, Peg?"

We spend the rest of the morning in the well-equipped gym that impresses her, and I teach her some moves. She learns easily, already having the strength. It's just a matter of learning how to read an attacker's intentions, and the moves she should make if they come from the front, from behind, or the side. I see her gaining in confidence minute by minute.

At one point she stops and gives a satisfied grin. "Pete wouldn't have got the drop on me had I known this before."

Going back to the suite, we shower to wash off the sweat, and Darcy ruefully puts back on the same clothes.

"Why don't you leave some of your stuff here?" As I say it, I realise how much I want that. To see her clothes hanging next to mine, her toiletries cluttering up my bathroom. I'm lying on my bed, watching her doing her hair, and know I'll miss her when she's gone.

"If I'm going to be here a lot, it makes sense to do that." She walks to the sliding doors leading onto the balcony and looks out. "This is an amazing place, Peg."

"Move in."

"What?"

I shrug. "I want you here."

Her face has gone blank, and I can't read a thing. I'm holding my breath, waiting for all the reasons she can't. *It's too soon. I need my own space.*

"Do you mean it, Peg?" Coming over, she parks her ass on the bed and takes hold of my hand, looking me straight in the eyes. "Me, here, in your space?"

"Nothing I'd like better. If it helps, keep your place, see how we go. But darlin', I'm all in. And that's what I want."

Her teeth worry her lip. "You said I need everyone's vote?"

I sit up, curling my hand around her head. "It's a sure thing, Darcy. This morning showed how well you fit in here."

She's quiet again, looking down at her hands. Then she looks up, and those beautiful green-grey eyes look into mine. "I'll come back after my next shift. And I'll bring some of my stuff."

It's not an agreement to make it a permanent arrangement, but I'll take what I can get. Tightening my fingers into her hair, I pull her to me, my lips meeting hers. My tongue teases her seam and she opens. Fuck, her taste. It gets me every time. My cock lengthens and thickens, my need becoming urgent.

Without breaking the contact of our mouths, she shuffles her body, moving until she's straddling my lap.

We've fucked hard, we've fucked slow. Each time is amazing, and better than the last. We come together in a frenzy, and end both completely sated. She always looks incredible, but with her gorgeous red hair in disarray, spread over my chest, her body covered in a sheen of sweat, her cheeks glowing from exertion, well that's become my most favourite look.

For the rest of the day I show her around the compound—she eyes the pool eagerly, saying she'd like to make use of it sometime—then she eats dinner with my brothers and their old ladies, as if she's been doing it for years. Not taking over conversations, instead joining in and making everyone laugh with a few amusing anecdotes from her work. We spend a pleasant evening in the clubhouse.

By the time we're back at my suite it's clear to see she's exhausted. I help her undress, and then we go to bed. She's quickly asleep. I lie awake for a while, simply enjoying the feel of her in my arms, then I give in and let my body relax. It doesn't seem long before that alarm's sounding, and I hate that it means I've got to let her go and start her long shift.

I walk her down to her car, trying to keep the worry from my voice, but unable to watch her drive away without one final caution. "Take care, Darcy."

"I always do, Peg."

One last kiss, then I indicate Fergus to slide the gates open, and then wait as she disappears down the track, staying until her taillights disappear. It feels like a part of me has left.

"She's a good one."

I nod. "You've got that right, Prospect."

The hours she's away working seem to drag, but I get through the daily grind, and then in the evening return to the clubhouse, and walking in find it crowded. Seeing Prez at the bar, I make my way across, signalling to Allie that I want a beer. She's only just a bit friendlier about it than Jill was, and that's not saying a lot. But having the sweet butts tend bar makes a lot of sense. Someone's obviously set up a schedule.

"What's up, Prez?"

Drummer's eyes crease as they look at me, examining my face. "You look different, relaxed."

"I've been looking for something. Never thought I'd find it, Prez." I take a swallow of beer and check Allie's out of earshot. "Come across enough bitches who were turned off by my fuckin' leg. Never thought I'd find one I'd connect with, and who'd take me just as I am."

"And now you have?"

"Yeah, Prez. I have. Not gonna let this one get away."

Drummer indicates the brothers all milling around. "That's why I called them all in. We should be able to seal this with a quick vote."

"I can't lose her now, Drum. She's it for me. Sounds stupid, I know…"

He huffs a laugh. "No more stupid than with me and Sam. When you find the one, you know it. Unless you fight it like Dart."

I grin. Yeah, Dart nearly lost his old lady because he was stupid. But he came to his senses in time. "I'm not like you were, Drum. Maybe it's because it was more difficult, but I've always looked for a connection, never just wanted sex for the sake of it."

"And now you've found that connection."

I definitely have.

"Church. Now!" Drum bellows out, and I shake my head as his loud voice hurts my ear drums.

With mixed emotions, I follow my brothers into church. *What if someone objects to her?* I take my seat, my customary glare on my face, daring anyone to challenge my choice of woman.

Drum bangs the gavel. "Settle down, you douchebags. We're here for one thing." He pauses and gives a pointed look toward me. "Must admit I didn't see this day comin', but we're here to take a vote on Peg's ol' lady."

"You sure you wanna tie yourself down?" I ignore Beef, who's staring at me and shaking his head. He might not understand, I've no doubt in my mind. It's all I've ever wanted, dreamed of.

"She's good people," says Rock. I give him a chin jerk, acknowledging he's bearing no grudge for losing the arm wrestling match to her.

"I like her." This from Shooter. "She's a good fit."

"Anyone want to raise any objections?"

A welcome silence greets Prez's question, and then the vote follows. Ayes all around. I let out the breath I'd been holding.

"Well, it seems that Peg's got himself an ol' lady." Drummer announces with what for him passes for a wide grin.

"Party!" yells Joker, slapping Lady on the back, his hand lingering a moment longer than necessary. In doing so he draws my attention to him just in time to see a private look exchanged between the pair. I doubt anyone else noticed, but it consolidates some thoughts I've been having lately.

The gavel slams down again, and we all turn to Drummer. "While we're all here, there's something else to discuss. Peg, it's useful you've got an in with a firefighter. Doubt anyone here has missed the fire up on the slopes." He pauses and wipes his hands down his face. "Don't have to remind you all how a wildfire took the original resort here out, damaged it so much we were able to buy it cheap and rebuild. That fire might be miles away, but we all know they can move fast. Anything we need to do, Peg?"

My job is to keep the club safe. From anything. I've been giving it some thought, and now I let them all in on what I've been thinking. "Wind's not blowing it in this direction right now. I ran through the precautions we have here with Flash. The old resort didn't have a firebreak like we do now, and she seemed happy enough with our set up."

"Lightning wouldn't strike twice in the same place..."

Paladin gets a cuff to his head. We all know it does, we have daily thunderstorms all summer, for fuck's sake.

"Well I, for one, ain't relying on folklore." Heart glares at our youngest member. "I've got a pregnant old lady. Any risk I want to know about."

"And I've got my boy," Drummer puts in. "Think we all want to stay on top of this. Peg, you keep us updated with whatever you can find out from your ol' lady. I want to be ahead of anything we got comin' our way." He pauses, then cracks a rare smile. "Okay, let's break for now. I think someone mentioned a fuckin' party?"

The brothers get up and leave, some talking about getting a drink with their old ladies, others joking about which sweet butt to fuck. I stay seated, and after catching the rise of my chin, Drummer does the same. While I'm not anxious to have this conversation with the prez, it does fall under my sergeant-at-arms responsibilities. In truth, I'd rather be out there with my brothers celebrating the fact they've just voted in my old lady. *Fuck. That's something I'd never dared hope would happen.*

Seeing the expression on my face is serious, once the rest have piled out, Drummer opens the drawer under the table and takes out his whisky and two glasses. He pours the amber liquid out and slides one to me, and faces it head on. "What's on yer mind, Peg?"

I jerk my head toward the door, then take a breath. "Joker and Lady."

His brow creases and his hand toys with his beard. "You asking as a brother or sergeant-at-arms?"

My shoulders rise. "Both, I think."

Prez nods his head slowly. "You didn't like Lady at first."

Another shrug. It's true. I took a while to warm to the man. My suspicions immediately aroused by his name. "Lady's Man. Fuckin' wrong handle if ever there was one." I think for a second. "A smokescreen perhaps?"

"Can't dismiss a man 'cause you don't like his handle."

"Not dismissing him, Drum. He's proved himself. Fuck, he went into the sex slave auction unarmed, put himself on the line when we were rescuing those kids. Ain't got no problem havin' him at my back. He might be an asshole, but he's a brave one."

With one eyebrow raised and a hint of a smile curling his lips, Drum observes, "Asshole? Interesting term to use in the circumstances."

Normally I'd shudder, but the memory of what Darcy had done last night comes to my mind. As my cock swells at the recollection, I shift in my seat. Prez misreads my reaction.

"What you sayin', here, Peg? You got a problem with Joker and Lady?"

I stare down into my glass. Club's never been faced with this situation before. Most brothers happy to fuck whores in the open, not being shy about what they do. Never had anyone with a need to hide their sexuality before. While I'm silent, trying to analyse what's niggling at me, Prez fills the void.

"They're not rubbin' it in anyone's faces."

"But they're hidin' it." That's the root of what's bothering me. I raise my head and stare straight at Drummer. "Not sure if everyone's clued up as to what's going on and choosin' to ignore it, but if Joker and Lady feel more for each other than the normal camaraderie of brothers, then we might have a problem if we don't know to look out for it."

Prez, showing his normal mental agility, is quick to realise what I'm getting at. "You're saying they'll have each other's backs more than ours?"

"Could be. Yeah, Prez. Could be. And if we're not expectin' it…"

He nods, completing my sentence for himself. "What if we challenge them and we're wrong?"

I doubt that very much, but he's got a good point. "Look, Drum, I'll admit it. I had a feelin' about Lady when he first came here. Didn't like what I saw, hate to say I felt threatened, not had something like that so close before." I pause and try to explain myself better. "It wasn't so much what I thought he might be, but that he wasn't admittin' it to us. But as I said, he's a good brother. Love him now as much as I do anyone. It wasn't a problem, didn't mind a brother keepin' something personal to himself. Until Joker and him started to get careless."

Prez looks like he wishes we weren't having this conversation. He rubs his beard before stating, "If we expose them, or ask them to come clean, others might not feel the same way as you do. Hate for them to feel they have to leave the club."

Would it really come to that? I suppose it's a risk, but knowing my brothers, it's probably only a small one. "I agree. But they're gettin' to the point they won't be able to hide it anymore." I breathe in deeply, then admit, "Maybe I wouldn't have been so quick to recognise it before I met Flash, but Joker looks at Lady the way I look at my ol' lady, and the way you look at Sam."

"And Lady is the same way with him." Prez drains his whisky and pours another. "Fuck, Peg. Why the hell did you bring this to me? Now I gotta decide what to do." He drags his fingers through his hair, then interlocks them behind his head. "Up to now we've had a don't tell policy. But you're right. If Joker's first thought is going to be to protect Lady, brothers need to know." He glances my way. "They'll have your support?"

I don't have to think about it. "One hundred percent."

Prez closes his eyes, then opens them again. "Okay. Leave it with me and I'll think on it."

Chapter 20

Darcy

I think I've been grinning all the way on the drive from the compound, and I've still got a smile on my face as I walk into the station while mentally preparing for my shift. It's hard to accept or understand how I've apparently become a biker's old lady. Huh, my head's spinning with the speed that everything's happened, but Peg has literally swept me off my feet. But I'd be a fool to let a man like him slip through my fingers. Yesterday it felt so natural and so easy being with him. I hadn't felt so good in a long time, if ever. I suppose other people would say it's happened too quickly, but I'm so wrapped up in Peg it's hard to get grounded.

Sex with him, well, it's like nothing I've experienced before. No wonder bikers have a reputation and women flock to their parties. Strangely, I have no concerns about Peg and the availability of girls around him. I felt gutted on his behalf when he admitted he has to deal with rejection because people can't accept he's lost part of his leg and know my easy acceptance of it makes me more precious in his eyes. But on the flip side, the way he copes with his disability makes him more special to me. He's a brave man, he fought for his country, and is now protecting his club. *And me.*

"So?" Truck comes in, the door of his locker banging as he opens it.

"What?" I reply, innocently.

"That fucking smile on your face. It's the biker that's put it there, isn't it?"

I can't, don't want to deny it. "Yeah, Truck. Things have got pretty heated between us. I'll be going back again after the shift."

He puts stuff away, gets other stuff out, then leans back against the lockers, his eyes sharp and bright. "So, tell me more. What's their compound like? Do they fight? Drink? Do drugs, women?"

I want to quash some of the rumours that abound. "No, yes, no, yes." As his eyebrow rises I continue, "The compound is amazing, Truck. Most brothers—that's what they call them-selves—have a suite to themselves, but Peg's got two together and made himself an apartment. It's in an amazing spot. Beau-tiful views and scenery." I break off, putting it all together. "Some of them have old ladies, wives if you like, and there's several young children around."

"They share their women, don't they?" Now his eyes narrow. "You gonna be part of that?"

"Truck!" I slap at his arm. "That's wrong. They don't share their old ladies." From what I observed, all the taken men are as possessive as Peg. "But there are club whores…" My face twists. "I didn't think much of them. They're there for anyone to go with and get room and board in return for their services." I think back to the almost greedy looks on the whores' faces when the party started to get going last night, and huff a quick laugh. "No one's forced to do anything they don't want to."

As Truck has his head tilted on one side, clearly wanting me to expand, I think of how best to explain it. "Look, Truck, it's like they're one big family, the men, women, and the children. And they have each other's backs, the way we are on shift."

He lifts his head and rests it back, then turns to me with a glint in his eyes and asks something I didn't expect. "How do you get to become a member?"

This I can answer. "Anyone wanting to join has to prospect for a year or more. That means they're not in the inner circle and have to do all the shit jobs." Like breaking my bed up and disposing of it. The memory makes me smile.

"But what about the crimes they commit? Flash, how are you going to reconcile turning a blind eye to things that they do? Shit, you shouldn't be involved in that, you'd lose your job for sure."

"Stop right there, Truck. They run a clean club. Earn their money from their businesses."

He looks doubtful, but as Slade comes in he pushes away from the lockers, a chin lift to the captain, and a puzzled look toward me.

Slade sees I'm not yet ready. "Better get your ass in gear, Flash."

Smartly, I give him a salute.

"Cheeky bitch," I hear from behind me as I exit the room, grinning.

I'm the last to arrive, Hammer is already waiting, Truck's at the coffee machine, and when I wave my hand, starts filling another cup for me. Slade takes a chair and calls us together.

"There's a wildland fire we're watching up in the Coronado Forest. The one over by Snake Canyon has flared up again. Seems to be contained for now. Hopefully we won't be needed." That isn't news for me, as Nicole had already alerted me yesterday. But it could get worse now we're at the start of the likely burning period. Fires tend to spread most rapidly from mid-morning to sunset.

"How much is contained?" I ask. Nicole hadn't been able to tell me that.

"Eighty percent," Slade answers. Which means the fire-fighters already there have it mostly under control. "But I have to remind you all… The NFDRS rating is near its highest level. It's been a dry winter." I think we're all aware of the high possibility of a serious fire as measured by the National Fire Danger Rating System.

"Has it been closed to the public?" I ask.

"It has now, yes. In all the high-risk areas, and some of the other hiking trails where the fuel loads are high." Dead leaves, fallen branches, discarded trash can easily be set alight by a dropped cigarette. Or, as sometimes happens, deliberately fired. Where there's a higher risk it makes sense to keep people away.

Having given his update, Slade reminds us of what we already know—if we're called up on the mountain what we're likely to face. None of us are strangers to fighting a wildfire, but not one of us argues as we go through procedures again. Not only is it a matter of life, death, or injury to any of us, it's vital to save people's homes and businesses, as well as the infrastructure. An out of control fire can result in millions of dollars of damage.

After our meeting we get a call out, quickly followed by another. It's late evening before I have a chance to go to locker and look at my phone. As I hoped, I've got a message.

Peg: *Club voted yes.*

Flash: *Great! :0)*

I've only a moment to digest the good news before the speakers start squawking again. Donning our gear, we roll out to an MVC, a two-car accident at a junction. Hammer goes to work, identifying there's only minor injuries, and all treatable by first aid. As the police arrive and there's nothing to do while our EMT does his stuff, I use the brief downtime to go over the events of the past couple of days in my head. I've been greeted by the attending police officers, two professional services sharing mutual respect, reminding me I can never let my guard down.

Even off duty I'm expected to act with integrity and bring no disrespect either to myself or the service.

Suddenly I remember what Truck said when we came on shift—that I might lose my job. For the first time I start to worry how being associated with the Satan's Devils fits in with me being a firefighter. Peg swept me away, leaving me no time to think. I just reacted purely on emotion and jumped in with both feet. Now that his club has accepted me, my future with Peg, if I want it, is there in my grasp.

What if I can't have both the man that I want and have the career I've worked so hard for? What if I'm forced to make a choice?

I'm so deep in thought, Slade takes me by surprise as he taps me on the shoulder. "All finished up."

I gaze at him while bringing my eyes back into focus. Sharp man that he is, he asks, "You got something on your mind?"

I think for a moment. Either I hide my relationship and risk being caught, or I bring it all out in the open now and deal with it head on. I've never been one to back down or put off something just because it's unpleasant, so I jump straight in. "Actually, Captain, there is. Can I have a word with you when we get back?"

"Certainly, Cavanaugh." His use of my surname and mine of his title serves to let us both know this will be more than an idle chit chat to pass the time.

Back at the station house, Slade wastes no time pointing to the meeting room. I precede him in and sit down. Putting my elbows on the table, I rest my chin on my hands. When he's seated opposite, I respond to his arched brow by laying it straight on the line.

"I've got a boyfriend." It seems a ridiculous title to give to a man such as Peg, but Slade wouldn't understand if I called him my old man.

"And?"

He knows there's more. It's certainly not an unusual statement. Normally I wouldn't dream of discussing my personal life at work. Well, now I've started, I better tell him the rest. "He's the sergeant-at-arms of the Satan's Devils MC."

Slade sits back in his chair and folds his arms across his chest, his eyes viewing me intently, his hand rubbing his mouth. After a moment to digest what I've said, he blinks slowly. "Fuck, Flash." He shakes his head as though he's having difficulty believing what I've just said. Then looks straight at me. "If it wasn't serious, you wouldn't be telling me."

He's got it in one.

I take a deep breath. "I need to know how this fits with me being a firefighter."

He humphs, unfolds his arms, and sits with his hands clasped between his splayed legs. "I take it this is a new relationship and hasn't been going on for long?" When I nod, he continues, "Darcy, you're a great firefighter and team member and a good career ahead of you, maybe promotion in the cards. You've been told that enough in your appraisals, and the fact that you're meeting this head on proves your integrity to me." He sighs. "The easiest thing for me to say is that it carries too much risk, and it's not a commitment that's going to have a positive effect on your position here, or your possible advancement in the service. That you should end it before it gets serious."

I gaze at him over my hands, which have begun to clench. While I expected it, what he's suggesting is not as easy as it sounds. *The thought of not seeing Peg again…* But as I open my mouth, he holds up his hand.

"Tell me more about this man, and what you know of the club."

"His name's Peg, er, Ronnie Rinter. He was a marine, lost part of his leg in service. He's a good man, Captain."

He's nodding. "Ex-Marine? Then I don't doubt it. But what about the club?"

"It's nothing like I expected. They run legitimate businesses in town."

"I know that. They've asked enough times for advice on fire regs and haven't had any problems with us checking things out." He's quiet for a moment, tapping his fingers together. "Trouble is, Flash, they might present themselves as a clean club now, but weren't always that way, and people have long memories. They keep to themselves in the main, which means no one knows exactly what they're up to, but rumours abound." Another pause. "I'm friends with Lieutenant Diaz in the police. Well, he told me one of his top officers, a detective, took up with a man in the club and resigned from her job."

Damn. "Are you saying that's what I've got to do if I want to continue to see Peg?"

"I don't know what I'm saying at the moment," he refutes quickly. "I really don't know what to advise you." His fingers tap again. "Must admit you've caught me off guard. But I'd be wrong to say for definite this wouldn't have any bearing on your career. I do need to consider how it will reflect on the department if it comes out. As you know, Flash, we've got to have the confidence of the public. People get to know who you're seeing? Who knows how they'll react. You have to think very carefully about what's important to you, and while you're doing that, try not to bring attention to yourself."

Have I been stupid? Been blinded by the man without thinking through what the implications of his role in his club might mean to me? *I don't want to give him up.* But neither do I want to leave my job. *Can I give it some time to find out whether this thing with Peg will burn out as fast as it flared?* But deep in my heart, I know that it won't, and it may be best to end it before we both get in any deeper than we already are. The pleasure I'd felt when I started my shift disappears. I look Slade in the eyes. "I won't do anything that's not in the interests of the job. I need to give him up, don't I, Slade." *But how can I do that?*

He looks up sharply. "Don't do anything impulsive. I'm not backing you into a corner here. I'm just asking for space, so I can think what to advise you. It's just a shame the Satan's Devils still have the reputation they earned in the past."

The captain might have said don't do anything for now, but already I feel there's something missing at simply the thought I might have to put an end to this new, intense, relationship. The best one I've had in my entire life.

It would have been easier had the remainder of the shift been busier, but for a Saturday night it's fairly quiet, only a couple of calls to fires which are quickly extinguished. I take the opportunity to grab a couple of hours on my cot. Not that I can sleep, every time I close my eyes I see Peg, and just as he was yesterday, my body throbs as I remember the delicious things he did to me. He's brought me to life, how could I even think of walking away? But is it worth being with him if I'm risking my job? What if I gave everything up, and Peg and I realised we weren't going to work out? How do I know it's worth the risk? Conscious of my teammates trying to sleep, I minimise my tossing and turning, but however hard I try to think of something else, Peg keeps invading my mind. *How could I tell him it's over before it's started?* But isn't it best to end it now before we both get in any deeper?

Typically, I've no sooner dropped off into a restless sleep, when I'm woken when we get a call from dispatch.

Not having undressed, it's a matter of moments before we're all assembled and out on the engine and speeding through Tucson in the early hours of the morning before Slade starts briefing us. "Wildland fire," he states quickly. "Wind's changed direction, blowing it east. Blew up fast, and the team on the ground lost control of it. It's heading downhill, gaining ground all the time. Canyon's like a fucking chimney." He grimaces. "Sorry, no one's going to be going off shift today."

We simply nod. It's as expected. That fire must mean trouble if we're being called in.

Hammer's got a large-scale map and is spreading it out. When Slade points out the location, he studies it. "There's nothing for miles, no dwellings or businesses."

Slade nods at the map and puts his finger on it. "We're meeting with other crews and setting up base here. At the end of this track. We'll meet Firewatcher Hudson and she'll give us the latest as far as she knows it. Can't get the any further until we get the dozers in." He glances at his tablet, where he's getting constant updates. "Planes are ready to go up at first light for a direct attack with retardant. We'll change to indirect attack if we need to."

"What's the wind speed, Captain?"

"Twenty-five miles per hour."

I nod as he gives me the answer. The planes will be able to fly in that, but not if it increases much further. Thirty miles per hour is their limit. Ideally, they'll be dropping their load to try to put out the fire. If that fails and we need to go the indirect route, the retardant will be dropped in front of the fire to try to lessen its progress.

"We'll determine safety zones and escape routes. Make sure you know them." We nod, but really, he doesn't need to remind us of what's vital to our safety. "And I'll liaise with the other crews and post lookouts."

All normal procedures.

"Our radio channel is eight. Got it?"

We all agree that we have. The last thing any of us wants to do is lose communications. It's still dark out there. I shudder.

No firefighter wants to lose contact with his or her teammates with flames rushing toward them.

"What fuels are there?" Truck asks.

"According to Firewatcher Hudson, a mix of heavy and light timber, and dry grass. The terrain is quite steep in places. Be prepared for anything." The captain pauses. "It might not be threatening any structures for now, but there's always the chance this beast may turn and head down toward Tucson."

As we turn off the road and head along the track along an existing firebreak, we're all craning our necks to take our first look at the monster we're determined to beat. A smoke column rises, it's dark and mushroom shaped. I exchange a glance with Truck. It's density more proof of heavy burning fuel and could prove unpredictable in how quickly it spreads and what direction it decides to take.

With temperatures which are predicted to rise later to over one hundred degrees, coupled with the heat from the fire, which we can already feel, wearing protective clothing and carrying equipment, we're heading into a taxing situation. But not one we haven't been faced with before.

CHAPTER 21

Peg

It was a shame that Flash couldn't be here and enjoy the party held in her honour. But happier and more at peace with myself than I'd been for years, I stayed and celebrated on her behalf, but even the amount of alcohol I'd consumed hadn't helped me to sleep. When I returned to my bed it was only to smell her scent all over my pillow and sheets. Although she's only spent a couple of nights in my bed, I miss her.

Feeling like a teenager, I text her again to let her know I'm thinking of her.

Peg: *Miss you*

When I get no response I'm not concerned. She's working after all, and in a job where she must focus all her attention. *She'll contact me in the morning.*

But when I awake, there's still no response. Dragging myself out of bed, I shower, dress, and take a step outside my suite, or, as Flash so aptly named it, my apartment. As my windows face west it's not until I'm outside that I notice the strange tinge to the light and, looking in the other direction, can see the fire up on the mountains has really taken a hold. Smoke's billowing up, covering the sun and turning the sky red. Although it's still some way in the distance, the air's already tainted with smoke.

Shit. The worry I convinced myself I didn't have before rises and almost chokes me. *I hope Flash isn't caught up in that.* But the fact she hasn't made contact suggests that she is. She'd warned me her crew might get called in. I stare at the fire, a cold feeling in my gut, trying to convince myself she knows what she's doing. But the thought of my woman, my old lady, putting herself at risk, drives me crazy. I hate fire. It's one enemy I have no control over, and one that can be so destructive.

I roll my shoulders, coming to terms with the fact I might not see her for a while. Firefighters stay on duty until a fire is beaten. As another waft of smoke drifts to me, I straighten my back. Can't do anything to help her, worrying isn't going to do a thing. Just got to trust she's keeping herself safe.

I glance around at the compound. Our good luck in getting this place was on the back of a fire that blew up fast and wiped the original resort out. Fire takes what it wants when it wants. Instead of worrying, I should be proud it's probably my woman who's, even now, putting herself on the front line, trying to make sure the flames don't reach us again. But it's not easy. I shiver, though the morning is already warm.

Raising my hand to shield my eyes, I try to locate where the fire actually is. It's hard to tell, but it seems a lot further down the mountain than it was the previous day. *Fire doesn't normally burn down, does it?* As the shrubs near me bend in the strong breeze, I correct my own thoughts. *It does if the wind's behind it.*

"Something to worry about?" Drum calls out on his way down from his house, pointing back up at the mountain.

"I hope not." I consider for a moment, realising hope isn't enough. We should be ready for the worst. "Like to get some brothers together to check out the growth that might have sprung up around the boundaries. Get it cleared back if necessary."

"Have you heard anything from your ol' lady?"

My eyes go up to the fire raging on the mountain. "No. Nothing. She should have called when she came off shift, which makes me think she's up there." I jerk my chin toward the flames. "Cell reception is crap, and she'll be doing her job, may not even have her phone with her."

His hand touches my shoulder and gives it an encouraging squeeze. "She knows what she's doing, Peg. She's not a rookie."

"I know, Prez. Would be just my luck to lose my ol' lady as soon as I found her."

He swings me around, both hands now gripping my upper arms, and gives me a little shake. "You ain't gonna do that, Brother. You hear me?"

"Loud and clear, Prez." But again, I'm drawn to watching the smoke billowing up into the air. I swear it's worse every time I look.

Drum turns, and as his eyes narrow I know it's not just my imagination. That fire is taking hold and looks already out of control. Even as I watch I see a plane drop its load of retardant, but it seems to make no difference to the height of the flames.

I exchange looks with the prez and know we're both thinking the same thing. Wildfires in the area aren't uncommon, but in all the years we've been here, we've never seen one that could be heading for us.

Prez doesn't waste time. An hour later and we're sitting around the table. The air outside has thickened with smoke, and the atmosphere inside is sombre. No one has to ask what the meeting's been called for.

Fire. One of nature's most destructive elements. There's not one of us who's going to be taking this lightly.

"We all know the reason we're meeting today," Prez starts without preamble. "I don't want to wait to see if the fire's comin' closer. I want to be prepared in the event it's heading this way. Which means we're gonna do what we can to protect the compound." He points first to Bullet, and then to Viper. "Get any equipment you have off site that we might need back here, like yesterday." Both men raise their chins.

"We've got a couple of bulldozers and an earthmover. We'll get what's on site back here. There's one already up the top of the compound, and we can start using that immediately."

"Thanks Bullet. Peg?"

I sit forward, resting my elbows on the table. "We need to make sure there's a good area around the perimeter that's clear of anything that might burn. There's some scrub taken root that needs to be dug up or stripped back to ground level at least. We've been neglecting it recently."

"'Cause we're not fuckin' gardeners," Slick observes.

Prez isn't going to put up with any shit. "Well today you are." He toys with his beard for a moment. "Might be nothin', but I ain't takin' the risk. This is our home, brothers. Peg, what do we need to do?"

"Remove anything that can burn that's within the hundred-foot boundary." I wave down their protests. "Yeah, I know, we've already done that and taken out the nearest trees. Now we need to remove all that crap, all the grass and shrubs which have self-seeded." I look around the table. "Ideally, we should push back on the tree line, make our no-burn zone bigger."

"My track," Road says glumly.

"Don't give a fuck about your dirt track, Road. It's what's underneath that worries me." I exchange glances with Blade. Yeah, that's where we bury the bodies.

"What would happen if the forest burned there?"

It's something I don't want to think about but must. I wipe my hand over my beard before answering honestly, "Fuck knows. But we buried them deep. Hopefully they won't come to the surface."

"Need to keep the firefighters' diggers away if it comes to it." Prez frowns. "Don't want any of them accidentally dug up."

"From what I know, Prez, the trees have to be cleared back so the firebreak's the width of their height. Shouldn't take much off the dirt track, if any." Bullet's pinching his nose as he thinks. "May help to cut a few of the closest trees down. I'll get a couple of chainsaws brought back for that."

"I'll take charge of the trees." Road nods at Bullet.

I make a decision. "Road, check it out. If need be, take down some of the trees in front of it. We'll extend the firebreak as far as we can without risking exposing any of our activities." Cocking my eyebrow towards Drummer, I silently ask his opinion.

He looks at me, at Road, then nods. "Leave the dirt track well alone. And we'll just have to keep our fingers crossed we've done enough."

For a moment no one speaks, all presumably imagining the horror we'll feel if the fire does come close.

"What about within the compound? Aren't the buildings protected?" Marvel is the first one to break the silence. "Thought someone told me they were when I got here."

Viper nods. "We used fire resistant and/or fire-retardant coatings on all buildings when we restored them. But that only delays fire taking hold. It doesn't stop it."

"But gives us a chance to fight," Drummer says, his hand stroking his beard. "Ain't gonna lose this compound, brothers. Don't want us to be homeless again."

Viper hasn't finished. "Prez's house, the sweet butts', and the empty one we use for visitors have been sorted. And Heart's new house is protected. But Wraith's is just a wooden frame."

At the moment it's just information. I'm crossing my fingers and hoping to fuck we can clear enough undergrowth away, so the fire doesn't come near us. That's if we're unlucky enough to end up in its path. "The shop," I begin.

"Brother. Can't do anything about it." Blade, who manages it, interrupts me and is shaking his head. "It's someway from the clubhouse. If we moved the gas, where the fuck are we going to put it? In the middle of the fuckin' compound where it could go off like a bomb?"

"We're doing all this work probably for nothin'," Beef complains. "Fire might not even be comin' our way."

Drum's hands smash down on the table. "I'm takin' no fuckin' risks with our home or our lives. If this fire doesn't head in our direction, it doesn't mean there won't be another behind it. We've neglected the boundary enough already. Now get the fuck to work and do as I fuckin' say."

All's quiet for a moment. We live in a tinderbox area—whole villages have been burned when they didn't expect it. One by one we nod at the prez. I hope what we're doing is unnecessary, but I'll give it my all to make sure we've done what we can if the worse happens.

"What about Ma Jones?" Dollar asks, his surprising question breaking the silence, and all eyes go to the treasurer.

"She still around?" I haven't heard anything of her in years.

Dollar shrugs as Paladin's brow creases and he asks, "Who's Ma Jones?"

Drum's shaking his head. "She was old when we bought the compound. Not seen or heard of her in ages. Old bitch probably died long ago. She has that place about a quarter of a mile from us, our nearest neighbour you could say. Kicked up a hell of fuss when we moved in. Tried to block the sale."

"Yeah." Viper gives a quick grin. "She didn't want no dirty bikers on her doorstep." For the last he uses his fingers to put it in quotes.

Mouse is tapping away at his keys. "Think she's still there. Got another bitch livin' with her from what I can tell."

How the fuck he gets his info so quickly, I'll never know. "What you thinkin', Dollar?"

"If the fire is coming in our direction, just wonderin' if we ought to be neighbourly and check she's alright."

Prez gives one of his rare grins. "Brave bitch tryin' to take us on. Had some fuckin' admiration for her. If she is in the land of the livin', she must be ninety, at least, by now. Wouldn't hurt to keep an eye on things and check in with her if the fire comes close. Yeah, Viper?"

Having caught the Prez's attention, Viper grins. "Despite the trouble she tried to cause us, I liked the old bitch. Got guts, that's for sure. Would be worth a call if Mouse can get her number. And if we end up in the fire's path, I don't mind trekkin' out to check up on her."

Mouse nods. Yeah, he can do anything.

Drum takes a second, and then nods to Viper. "Okay, we'll leave Ma Jones to you."

As I'm inwardly chuckling at the thought of Viper going up against the woman who's name we coined for her—fuck knows what her real handle is, but Ma Jones suits her—I realise Prez is addressing me.

"Peg. How do you suggest we do this?"

Drumming my fingers on the table, I put together my thoughts. "Compound's basically rectangular. Fire's coming down the hill. If it heads straight for us, it will hit the back of the compound first, or one of the sides if it veers off. So, we concentrate on clearing everything around all sides. We divide into four groups and keep working until we've cleared it."

"Fire might not come anywhere near us," Marvel grumbles.

Prez slams his fist on the table. "I know this will be hard fuckin' work, and hopefully completely unnecessary, but I won't take the risk of losin' this compound." He stares around the table waiting for the chin lifts and nods. "Okay. Let's get to work." Prez bangs the gavel, and brothers start sorting themselves out.

I'm taking the back with Marvel, Joker, Lady, Slick, and Dollar. Drum will be covering the north side with Beef, Jekyll, and Paladin, and Wraith will tackle the south along with Mouse, Beef, and Hyde. Blade, with a vested interest in protecting the shop he manages, will clear around the entrance assisted by Shooter and Rock. Viper and Bullet are off to bring back machinery, and then they'll go where they can help the most. Road goes off to commune with trees or something.

It's a sweltering day, the worst to be outside doing physical work. The air's gradually thickening with smoke, the strong breeze doing nothing to cool us. Brothers work with chainsaws, scythes, shovels, or whatever they can get hold of to cut down or dig up the overgrown shrubs for others to rake away. Mouse has looked it up on the internet, and we need to dig a shallow trench and make sure anything combustible, or fuel for the fire, is clear of it. Some bushes have taken a good hold, and it's fucking arduous work. But as pieces of ash start to float down around us, everyone redoubles their effort, and as it worsens, becoming like black snow, bandanas go up to cover faces.

Complaints this isn't necessary start to trail off as the wind rises and we exchange worried glances. I realise I haven't seen the planes for a while and remember hearing they can't drop retardant in high winds. The smoke becomes thicker, the sun can only just be made out, and I can hear a distant roar.

"Listen up." Drum comes up and my group gather around him. He has to raise his voice to be heard over the sound of the flames. "Just got the text, an evacuation order. Fire's definitely turned and is comin' our way."

"Not leavin'." Viper steps down from the bulldozer.

With a quick grin that doesn't meet his eyes, Drum nods. "Expect that's how everyone feels. We stay here to protect what we've got. But women and children need to go."

"My house," offers Viper, who's got a place in town.

"And mine," says Dollar.

"Yeah, Bullet's already offered his as well."

Drum eyes the work that's been completed. "Think we've done all we can do out here. We're got to start movin' valuables down into storage and get the women and kids out of here."

"Think we've done enough, Prez?"

When his eyes find mine, I find myself answering the question on Drum's behalf. "We can only hope, Blade."

Despite our best intentions, the women don't leave immediately, staying behind to help sort through the stuff we want to keep safe and taking it under the old swimming pool. Slick moves his explosives, and I move the ammunition. Don't want the heat to set them off. Viper uses his digger to make a deep hole, and we bury everything combustible in a metal safe.

I've missed something and immediately act to rectify it. While they're prospects no longer, Jekyll and Hyde make no complaint as I ask them to start clearing the ground around the propane tanks.

When the converted pool's full to bursting with everything from Mouse's computers, my precious hi fi, Drum's turntables, photograph albums, the lot, we close it up and hope, if it comes to it, any fire burns over it quickly. For good measure, Bullet uses the bull dozer and puts an extra layer of sand over the top.

"Paperwork?" Drum checks with Dollar, who's just walked up.

"Fireproof safe," he replies, his face looking worried. "Tried ringing the number Mouse gave us for Ma Jones. It's out of service. Viper's going to take the 4 x 4 and take the direct route over to her. Check she got the evacuation order alright." Viper, standing next to him, jerks his chin in agreement.

I'd taken a moment to ring Flash's station house and got the confirmation it was her crew that was up on the mountain fighting the fire. Having no old lady here to get organised, and now we've done all that we can, if I have time on my hands, I'll only spend it worried about her. It's an easy decision to make. "I'll come with you."

Casting an uneasy glance above, I see the sun has been totally obliterated by the thickening smoke, a weird yellow glow replacing blue sky. It's dark when night isn't anywhere near close as Viper drives the Jeep over the rough ground, saving time by going direct and not taking the long route of going down our track, along the interstate, and then up a parallel, unpaved road to the isolated homestead which I'd forgotten was even there. Ma Jones…well…we'd often prefaced her name with the word fucking. Twelve years or so now and she was threatening to take us to court. But since we've moved in we've seen nothing of her, and presumably have caused her no concerns, despite her dire predictions at the time.

It takes us a while to navigate the direct, but unmade route. As we draw close I swear. "Hope she's already out. Look at that mess." Shrubs and tall trees are up close to the boundary of her yard, and not very far from the timber-frame house. From here, the fire seems closer.

"They've probably already left."

I nod. It's my thought as well that we'll find no one at home, but we've come this far. "Best go check as we're here."

Viper turns onto her rutted driveway and takes the Jeep right up to the house. As soon as he pulls up the handbrake, the front door swings open and a young woman runs out. Viper and I look at each other. This wasn't what we expected. As we open the doors and jump to the ground, I get my first proper look at the frantic woman. She appears to be in her late teens or at the most, early twenties, attractive, but her looks are marred by the tears on her face.

"Oh, thank God you're here. Help us, please!" Her hands wringing, she looks first at me, then to Viper. "My great-grandmother's bedridden, and we should have evacuated, but the phone's out and there's no way I could get help. I can't get her into my car, and the fire's so close…"

"Whoa, hang on there. We've come to help. Where's your gramma?"

She almost staggers with relief. "This way."

We follow her into the house, noting the wooden boards of the veranda look like they're rotting away. Inside, the house is dim and dark.

I try a switch and tell Viper, "Electricity's out." Then take another look at the girl. "What's your name, darlin'?" She's so wound up she's shaking like a leaf, and I'm asking partly to calm her.

"Sarah. I'm Sarah."

"I'm Peg, and this is Viper. Do you need to sit down while we sort Ma Jones out?"

"Ma Jones?" She gives a little giggle at the handle we'd given the old woman. "You better not call her that."

I roll my shoulders, determined I certainly am, and a quick glance at Viper shows he's on board. Amusement or anger, those emotions can damp down the fear. It's easy to see why Sarah was so scared, stuck in this house with no way out, and the fire drawing closer.

She leads us to a bedroom and opens the door, and immediately a crochety voice calls out, "I told you to go, Sarah. Get in the car and go. Leave me here."

"Not leaving you, Gramma, I've already told you that. And I've brought help."

As Viper and I step into the room, Ma Jones makes the effort to sit up. Her eyes open wide, then she points an unsteady finger at us. "Get out of my house. You're those filthy bikers. Sarah, run. Run for your life. They've come to rob us. They'll rape you."

"Now, now." I take a step towards the bed. "We ain't here to rob you, hurt you, or take advantage of you or your granddaughter. We're here to help."

But she's not listening. "Get your phone, Sarah, and call the police."

Sarah walks over to her grandmother and takes her hand. "I told you already, the phones are out. I can't get a signal on my cell. We've no choice but to trust them, Gramma. If we don't, well…" Her head tilts toward the window where the sky's now glowing orange.

Ma Jones looks at her granddaughter. "You're still refusing to leave?"

"Look, Ma." I don't miss how her eyes flare as I call her that. "Sarah's not going anywhere without you. We're takin' you both with us. Now you can come easy, or make it difficult, that's up to you. But we ain't leavin' either of you here. There's too much that's likely to burn around here. If the fire comes this way this place will go up like a tinder box."

The old woman's eyes narrow. "So, it's kidnapping now, is it?" But I don't miss the slight glint in them.

"Com'on. Let's get you up." Viper takes a step toward the bed, throwing a look over his shoulder to the girl. "Pack a bag quickly, anything you need to take get it."

"Already packed," she replies. "We were hoping someone would remember we were here and come get us."

"Can you put your stuff in the back of the Jeep?"

I watch as she nods and goes off.

"Now, Ma, you gonna make this easy or hard?"

"I ain't your ma," she grumbles, and again goes to sit up. Viper helps by putting his arm around her. "I'm heavy," she admits. "Don't know how you're going to move me."

"What's the matter with you?" I ask.

"Me legs have gone." She gives me a sly look. "But my eyes still work. You try and take anything…"

"We're not here to steal from you, Woman. Give it a fuckin' rest."

Viper puts his arm around her and moves her to the edge of the bed, then putting his other arm under her legs sweeps her up into his arms. He grimaces at me, but to her says, "See, light as a feather."

Seeing his muscles straining, I hold the door open wide and then go ahead to clear the way. When we get to the Jeep and he props her up inside, he mouths to me, "Next time you can do the liftin'," and rubs his back as he straightens up.

"Got everything?" I ask Sarah.

"Yes, I've just got to go back and lock up."

"Yeah, because those filthy bikers might come back now they know the place is empty." As Ma complains from the back seat, I turn just in time to see her lips curling slightly.

Sarah's quick, and soon sitting beside her great-grandmother. Viper starts the Jeep, and soon we're on our way. As we turn onto the sand, Ma pipes up. "The road's thatta way."

"Quicker to go direct. Just hang on tight."

There's a few grumbles and moans as we bump over the sand, but they're half-hearted at best. My summation is the old woman's putting on a show, partly to stop Sarah from being scared.

There's no denying it is scary. The slight roar we'd heard earlier is far more audible now. The sky's bright orange as flames are reflected from the smoke that's so thick it's hard to see where we're going. Viper's driving mainly by the compass on the dash. Soon we're getting close to home.

"What the fuck?" he suddenly exclaims.

As I peer in front I can see the compound, and beyond the gate, flames shooting up. How it started, I've no idea.

"The fire's reached us," I shout. "Fuck! Put your foot down, man."

Fire's eating up the ground, and it seems to have come cross from the direction we least expected and hadn't prepared for, cutting off our access to the main road, and the main wildfire is still steadily burning down toward us from the mountain, closer than when we left. We need to hope we've made the compound as safe as we can, as it looks like we'll be surrounded by flames.

Fuck.

CHAPTER 22

Darcy

It's our third day of tackling this fire. The hard, sweaty work broken only by brief cat naps in the engine. So far, the fire's winning, beating us back, forcing us to retreat while we desperately try to place obstacles in its path, planes providing aerial support during daylight hours, dropping retardant. It's on the ground, in the canopy, and burning up fast. Branches crash down, sending sparks shooting. It's fast approaching our fire line.

"Shit!" Truck swears loudly and jumps back, making me swing around to see what's wrong. "Fucking snake. I fucking hate them."

Looking down, I see something slithering across the spot where he was just standing, but not being too bothered myself, knowing my boots will protect me, and harbouring some sympathy for the wildlife simply trying to escape the flames to stay alive. It's a far from uncommon sight when we're fighting a fire such as this.

I laugh and slap my crewmate on the back. "What do you expect, it's the Snake Fire, after all." It certainly isn't the first snake we've seen, but Truck jumps each time, this mountain of a man being driven by a phobia he can't control.

"Fucking baby," shouts Hammer, admonishing him, raising his voice to make himself heard. "Afraid of an overgrown worm." It's a brief moment of mirth. Not much to amuse us about this situation, so we take what we can. Truck takes it good-naturedly. Sometimes I think he exaggerates his reaction on purpose.

"Back." The instruction via the radio brings our humour to a halt. It's not unexpected, having seen our puny attempts are futile, we are already moving backward, toward our previously agreed to escape route.

The wind's got up in the past hour and is now more than thirty miles an hour, forcing the planes to cease flying. It's support we will miss.

Slade comes up. "To me." Retreating a safe distance, our crew gathers around him, straining to hear over the noise of the fire. "The flames are now over four foot, we can't use direct attack any longer. Have to change to indirect. Bat chief agrees, and we're going to move down and build a new fire line, setting up in front of the head." He glances at the monster fast approaching. "Wind's causing it to throw out fingers. We need to get far enough down so it doesn't trap us.

Other crews are getting similar instructions. Radios are passing the information on. The firefighters tackling the flanks are having a similarly challenging task and being pushed back. This fire is growing, and for the moment it's got the upper hand.

"Nicole. What you seeing?" I try to make contact over the radio.

No reply comes back.

"Nicole?" I prompt again, but again get no answer.

Nicole's been checking in every fifteen minutes, but my gut tells me her report is now overdue. Already on the retreat, I run and catch the captain's attention. "I can't get hold of Fire-watcher Hudson."

His eyes widen, and he pinches the bridge of his nose. He knows as well as I do this isn't good news. He tries to get her himself, then shakes his head as he, too, fails to get any response. "Where was she last?" he checks.

"She's in lookout position on the other side of the canyon. Her last report was that the fire had leapt across. She was told to get out of there, fast, but, Slade, I've not heard anything from her since." I'm hoping like fuck she's just dropped the radio or it's malfunctioned. I'm suddenly consumed with fear for my friend. The smoke's so thick it's hard to see further than a few feet, and being alone without communication must be terrifying.

"Flash, I know she is a special friend of yours. It's not been that long, her reports have only just stopped coming in." Though he's trying, that's not much comfort. I don't know what to say, just look at the fire that's drawing ever closer, the ravenous beast consuming everything in its path. He claps his hand down on my shoulder.

"She's part of the team, Captain." Hammer's overhead our conversation. "We don't leave someone behind. You want us to try and find her?"

Try keeping me back.

Slade thinks quickly, then turns slightly away and gets on the radio. After a moment he swings back. "We've got a few other crews going down to set up a new fire line. Bat Chief Leadson's okayed that we redirect our efforts into trying to find her."

His radio sounds again, and this time we all hear it. A report from the crew working the flank who've now themselves been forced to move back over the ravine.

A tinny voice tells us, "We've found an ATV, it's burned up. Looks like it could have been the firewatcher's. No body in it. No sign of Hudson."

I don't know whether I'm glad to hear that or not. She might not be with her vehicle, but I can't understand why she left it. On foot, if she tried to outrun the fast-moving fire, she might not have made it. "How far was it from the cold zone?" That information will help us estimate the chances that she has made it to ground already burned, or out of the way of the flames altogether. But the anonymous voice informs me there's no way of knowing whether she got out before the fire passed through. Right now, we don't know whether we're on a rescue mission, or one to retrieve a dead body. Knowing I've got to remain optimistic, I force my worry for her back down.

Slade looks at me sympathetically, and then he's all business. "Hammer, Truck, Flash. Check your equipment and keep together. If she's alive, we've got to find her."

The Captain, Hammer, Truck, and myself requisition an ATV for ourselves, and skirt around the edge of the fire, having to head down the ravine to find a place to cross, then make our way as fast as possible up the other side as we head as close as we can to the spot where Nicole was last seen. As day turns to night, we're still able to see by the light of the flames, though distance is greatly restricted due to the thick smoke. I keep removing the shroud covering my face to scream out her name. Vegetation is still burning off all around us.

"Keep away from the blaze. If she's in that, she can't be saved, and I'm not losing any more bodies," Slade tells Hammer, who's driving.

"Got it, Captain."

We're in the black now, the area where the fire's already swept through, still smouldering trees reaching into the sky. Hammer pulls the ATV up, and I get off and look at the burned-out vehicle Nicole had been driving. It's up fast against an almost hidden tree stump, giving a clue as to what made her leave it. *She must have crashed and tried to escape on foot.* But which way would she have gone? I concentrate, trying to put myself in her shoes.

Fire burns up. Unless the wind's pushing it down like it is today. But it could quickly change direction if there's sufficient fuel and the wind swings to come from the opposite way. *If the fire was closing in she could have gone up to find the cold spot.* But she knows only too well that what looks like all fuel's been consumed, could easily start burning again.

She wouldn't run down, she knows enough about how fast fire can move, so she wouldn't want to get in front of it.

Sideways. She wouldn't have gone to the left, that would have led her straight into the path of the flames. She'd have gone right. "Captain, I think she would have gone this way."

As I point, Slade nods. "Unless she panicked, you're probably right. You and Hammer go on foot in that direction, Truck you're with me and we'll take the ATV. We'll continue exploring the cold zone. And for fuck's sake, Flash, Hammer, don't the two of you split up. Keep in contact."

"Got it, Captain," Hammer and I say together. I'm happy to search in the direction my gut feels is right. Slade and Truck might well be looking for a body.

I start to move forward, pausing as a heavy and still burning branch crashes at my feet. Hammer gives me a glance and raises his eyebrows. *That was close.* If either of us had been under it, we could have been badly hurt.

Moving carefully, we're nearing the edge of the fire line, unburned forest coming into view, a strange sight with tree trunks singed on one side but not the other. We pause for a moment. *Would Nicole have gone down?*

Smoke's still so thick here, hampering our search.

"What's that way?" Hammer asks. "Any structure, rock that would protect her?"

But all I can do is shake my head. My knowledge of the area is no better than his, anything I say would only be conjecture. Wishing the smoke would clear, but knowing it won't, all I can do is to tell him, that if I was Nicole, I'd be wanting to put as much distance as possible between myself and the fire.

My hopes of finding her alive are fading, horror stories returning to me of firefighters who'd tried to outrun a fire and failed, or who got surrounded and overcome. It seems we're on an impossible task. I call out again, and Hammer adds his loud voice. But around us the fire's roaring so loudly it's hard to even hear ourselves while we're standing next to each other.

Suddenly Hammer's hand tugs me forward urgently. I glance behind and realise that another burning branch has fallen from a crown fire in the canopy, setting the dry grassy ground aflame to our rear, the fire seemingly triumphant it's found easy to consume fuel. Now it's not just a case of locating Nicole, it's getting out of here alive ourselves. Driven now by a sense of self-preservation, all other thoughts leave my mind as I push onward beside Hammer. We both have our Pulaski's in our hands, our specially designed wildland fire-fighting axes that we now use to chop our way through the shrubbery that's preventing us reaching safety. We don't waste time talking, just methodically work our way through as fast as we can, both well aware of the danger we're in. It may be psychological, but I swear I can feel heat pushing at my back when suddenly we burst out into a clearing and we both start running as fast as we can.

You could say it was the fire that took us in the right direction. Putting as much space as possible between us and the rogue flames, suddenly Hammer stops so fast I run into his back. He shoots out my arm to stop my forward movement, and points to a shape lying prone on the ground.

For a moment I don't understand what I'm seeing, then through the smoke the shape in yellow takes form. *It's Nicole.*

Switching into medic mode, Hammer's beside her while I radio it in, checking and giving the co-ordinates of where we've found her. I keep one eye on the fire, whose approach seems to have slowed, and having run out of combustible fuels is starting to change direction, suggesting that at last our luck has turned.

It's now burning away from us and down. I update the captain on the situation. Nicole's just about conscious, but I'm worried about her—she's moaning, and there's no recognition in her eyes.

Slade responds quickly. "They've cleared a helispot at base, and hoping for a lull in the wind to bring a helicopter in. We need to bring her down."

"Can you come by and get us?"

"You in the black?"

"We were," I tell him. "But we've just outrun a blow up. We're now in the dead man zone."

I look over to Hammer, who leans toward the radio and nods grimly. "She needs oxygen, and fast."

"We're on our way."

I eye the fire, knowing we're in unburned ground and that it could change its mind and come after us again. "I'm going to burn a fire line." Without waiting for his nod, which I'm sure would be coming, I light my drip torch and start setting a line of burning fuel between us and the fire, hoping to slow or stop its progress if it starts moving back our way before Slade and Truck manage to swing by and pick us up. All being well, I'll earn us precious moments.

Having had to pick their way carefully, it's some time before the captain and Truck appear with the ATV. Hammer picks Nicole up and passes her to Truck, who cradles her in his arms, then we start taking the best route we can find back to base, having to detour around a couple of hot spots which are still blazing furiously.

At last we leave the fire behind and come to the cleared helispot. The wind drops briefly, allowing the helicopter to land. Medics jump out, already prepared with oxygen, and take over. When Nicole's been transferred into their care, Hammer holds out his arms to me and brings me in for a quick hug. That had been close, for all of us. Relieved everyone's safe, Hammer then pulls Truck to him and slaps him on the back.

As my friend is air-lifted away, I look up into the paramedic's eyes. "What are her chances, Ham?"

"She's breathing, she's still alive. I think she may have taken a blow to the head. She's not got burned but must have inhaled a fuckload of smoke. It depends how much damage has been done to her lungs."

Slade allows us a moment, but not too long. "Ready to get back into it?" It's only then that I notice people packing up around me as he continues, "Fire's moving fast, and we're relocating base. Forecast is for the winds to pick up again."

"They'll need our help setting up a new fire line." The bat chief's joined us. "Your crew good to go, Captain?"

"What we waiting for?" I say cheekily, trying to park my worries for Nicole for the moment. All my concentration is needed for the next phase of us against the fire. There'll be time enough later to worry about things that, for the moment, I can't control.

Even this fire line we've returned to is significantly lower than the one which we left to rescue the firewatcher, and already has to be moved down again. Gradually the fire's beating us back, and we need to do all we can to ensure it's not the inferno that retains the upper hand. As we retreat with the other crews, the roar of the fire sounding like an express train coming down hill almost drowns out the shouts and instructions as firefighters all over are packing up, jumping into vehicles, and making a hasty withdrawal as decisions are taken on the next place where to set up next, quickly analysing wind speed, direction, and the type of fuel in its path. It's frightening how fast the fire's started moving, now quicker than a man can run and straight downhill. Worse, the wind's rapidly picking up again.

As I get moving with the rest of my crew I realise, although it's hard to see through the smoke and if I haven't got disorientated, where the conflagration is heading. Its trajectory is taking it straight toward the Satan's Devils Compound. *And Peg.*

I come up alongside the captain and shout in his ear. "Slade. The fire's heading…"

"Straight for your new friends. We've just been discussing that." He nods over toward the bat chief as we make our way to the engine. "And we've more trouble too. We've had reports that a finger's shot out from the head, found fast burning fuel, and has veered around their compound. It's burning right across their escape route."

"Have they evacuated?" *If they haven't, they're in trouble.*

I'm holding my breath as he tells me gently, "The police have been in radio contact with their president. They didn't get out. Women, children, and bikers are there. They'll be making their own stand."

I gasp. *Stupid. Why didn't they get out while they had the chance?*

"Cavanaugh." The snapped use of my surname brings me back to my senses. When he sees I'm thinking again like a firefighter, he adds, "They've been taking their own precautions. They've got a hundred-foot cleared area around the perimeter. Hopefully sufficient to hold the fire, and one we've decided to utilise. That's going to be our safety zone. We're heading down that way now. The way this fire is moving, it's going to surround us as well. We'll use the compound as our retreat."

I appreciate the time he's taking to explain to me, he knows I've got a vested interest in this. My heart rate, which had finally slowed once Nicole had been safely airlifted out, now starts beating fast again. I'm tired and running on adrenalin. But this fire is giving me no chance to relax. "What about the fire that's already swept around them?"

"Their firebreak seems to be holding for now. New crews have arrived from Phoenix, they'll start tackling the blaze from the road. So far it's burning its way past the compound and heading for the interstate."

Jeez.

Reaching the engine, I hop on and we head down the foothills to the biker compound, making sure we get there in front of the flames. The air is thick with smoke that's being blown in advance of the fire by the strong westerly wind. I hope they've got the sense to stay inside. This air isn't healthy, especially for children, and now the fire has cut off their escape.

As we come below the tree line I can see the back gate to the compound has been opened, and surveying the work that they've done, nod when I see they've done a decent job of clearing all the fuel from around the perimeter. Then my eyes narrow as I see a bunch of what must be a dozen or so bikers standing outside, bandanas pulled up over their faces. They've got a digger, bulldozer, and other machinery including a rotovator that's turning the soil, making sure nothing but earth is in the fire's path.

Captain Slade jumps off the engine as it comes to a stop and marches up to the bikers. He starts gesticulating and talking, but from their stance what he's saying is not what they want to hear.

Unable to contain my curiosity, I go over and join him.

The biker president's facing off against my captain. "Our compound. We will protect it. The firebreak should stop it coming straight through, but we'll be on hand to stop any flare-ups. This is our home."

"All you're going to do is give us more injuries to deal with. You could suffer from smoke inhalation, burns, or injuries and keep our medics tied up."

"Peg," I call out, and see his eyes flare as he recognises me.

"Thank fuck, Flash. You're alright." He pushes past his brothers and comes to give me an awkward hug. Automatically I return it, pleased to see him safe as well, and determined to keep him that way while part of me says I shouldn't encourage him. For three days I've been fighting this fire. Utilising my training with no time for any other thoughts in my mind. Apart from being worried about the people in the club, I've barely had a chance to give a thought to Peg. What happened between us seems a lifetime away, that he called me his woman was in a completely different world. My whole existence is consumed with fighting flames, smoke, and heat. I'm shaking with exhaustion, but beating this fire is the only thing on my mind. *This is my life. This is what I do.*

"Peg." I pull back, unwilling to admit to a relationship that was doomed from the start. Trying to put space between us, I treat him as any other civilian and try to make him understand. "You're the sergeant-at-arms, you need to keep your club safe. We'll be doing everything we can to save the compound, you've done your part clearing the ground. Now let us get on with what we do best. At the end of the day this is just bricks and mortar. The club you should be protecting is the human one, your brothers and your family."

I pause and glance up, and from the expression in his eyes, know I'm getting through to him. "You're not equipped, you've haven't got protective clothing. And you *will* get in the way. Leave this to us. Stay inside the gates. Keep your eyes out for any small fires starting up. That will be the most help to get this fire under control."

"She's got a point, Peg." Drummer walks up, giving me an appreciative nod. "Let your woman and the rest of the fire-fighters get on with what they're trained for. We've done all we can here."

Peg growls, the sound resonating from deep in his throat. He's not happy, I can see that. He'd rather fight by my side, or for me, and doesn't care for me fighting this foe on his behalf. Then his eyes look at me from head to toe, seeing my blackened soot covered uniform, and one side of his mouth turns up in a smile as he leans forward to tell me, "You still look sexy, even in that." His hand comes up to wipe soot from my brow, and I can't help myself flinching away. *Don't touch me, Peg. I'll weaken.*

"Ask her to wear it so you can fuck her in it later, Peg." Beef's comment raises a laugh.

Anxiously, I take a peep at my captain, who's studiously not looking at me but at Drummer. "We sorted?" he asks.

"Sorted," Drummer confirms. Then after a fit of coughing, he straightens and waves his men back inside.

CHAPTER 23

Peg

Earlier

The fire I've seen surrounding the compound scares the shit out of me, and I want to jump out of the Jeep and hurry to see what we're dealing with. But I also feel responsible for Ma Jones, who Viper is carrying into the clubroom and settling down on the couch. Trusting my brothers are doing whatever's necessary, I watch as Viper rubs his muscles and flexes his shoulder, while I give him a rueful grimace. I wish I could have helped him, but wouldn't trust myself to take her weight on my prosthetic leg.

Ma's looking around her with interest, her eyes widening in surprise at the fairly clean surroundings and couches, tables, and chairs only a couple of years old. The décor had refreshed with new paint recently as well, old ladies finding jobs for the prospects even when us men don't see it needs doing.

I see Sophie with Ollie hanging on to her hand, which gives me an idea. Looking at Ma, I ask, "Can you use a wheelchair?"

She tilts her head to one side. "Probably can if someone can lift me in and out. Didn't at home, as I'm too heavy for Sarah."

"'ere. Soph!" Sophie, always curious about strangers, almost runs across. I put her out of her misery before she can ask. "This here's our neighbour, Ma Jones, and her great-granddaughter, Sarah. We brought them here as they couldn't evacuate them-

219

selves. Can you get your wheelchair for Ma? And show them some hospitality?"

"You one of their whores?" Ma's examining her intently.

Sophie bursts out laughing. "No way, Ma. I'm the VP's wife, and this is our daughter, Olivia." Said daughter is currently hiding behind her, sucking her thumb.

"I've got to go and see Drum…"

"They're in church, Peg. Well, those who aren't watching out for the fire." The look of concern she doesn't quite hide shows me they already know no one's getting out of here anytime soon. She shoos me off. "You get along, Peg. I can handle Ma Jones."

As I follow Viper into our meeting room, I grin, wondering if she can. The mirth's soon wiped from my face by the sombre faces greeting us.

"What do we know, Drummer?" I ask, as soon as I sit down.

"Fire has circled around us. Burned down by the track forming a barrier between us and the road. We've no option but to stay and fight here."

"Done any damage?"

"Nah, didn't come close. The firebreak did its job and it just circled around us. Luckily the wind's blowin' it down toward the interstate. Moved fuckin' fast though. Accordin' to the fire-fighters, fire's just unpredictable like that. Went through the grassland as though it was a truck mowing it down. No one expected it to break out at that point. We're just unfortunate I guess. Dollar's taken some brothers to keep the shop dampened down in case anything else flares up. But for now, we're stuck here."

"Well, we were going to stay put in any event." I can't see it makes much difference to our plans.

"Women and kids are still here, Peg."

I nod, frowning at the reminder. That wasn't part of our plan.

"What about the Jeep. We could go cross country…. Evacuate them that way." Slick's looking concerned.

"Have you seen how fuckin' fast that fire's comin' down the hill?" Blade asks sarcastically, pointing with his knife in the general direction of the back of the club. "Too dangerous now. Wind blows up and changes wind direction and even the Jeep won't be able to out run it on uneven ground."

I pull on my beard. We've no other option. "So, we stay and make a stand."

"Only thing we can do." Drummer's hands run through his hair. "Mouse got on the radio and we made contact with the police. There's a hotshot crew on their way to us, and the crews working above us are going to head on down."

"They want to help protect our compound?"

Prez huffs a strangled laugh. "No, they want to piggyback on our fuckin' endeavours. We've made a decent fire break, and they want to use it as a safe zone for them."

"But we're still susceptible to the odd spark or burning ash fallin'. Wind's still blowin' a bitch out there."

As Rock makes his observation, I'm thinking fast. "It's our compound. We do what we can to protect it."

"With you there, Brother." Viper's comment is mimicked around the table, and looking at my brothers my eyes land on Joker, who's face has softened as he shares yet another one of his silent exchanges with Lady. Christ, if they don't want to come out into the open, they better put a stop to their private moments at the table.

"All children to stay inside. And the women. Clubhouse is the safest place, it's in the centre of the compound and slightly away from the blocs." Drum makes the announcement, but his face twists, presumably remembering his house is right at the top. If the fire gets hold it will probably be the first to go.

"My house is most at risk." Wraith's frowning. "Only got the timber frame up."

"We'll damp that down, keep it wet. Will soon dry out, but don't want to feed that fuckin' fire."

"I suggest we get on with it. Damp down anything that might burn." I nod at Drummer as I speak. "That fire's movin' as though the devil's behind it."

Prez scowls. "Well, it's going to find more Devils waiting. Want brothers at all points around the compound. See a fuckin' piece of ash, you stamp it out fast."

"Ride Satan's Devils. Satan's Devils Ride!" The cheer goes up around the table. Invigorated by our battle cry, and ready for the battle ahead, we stand and leave the room.

I take a moment to check on Ma. Sophie's brought her wheelchair down, so I wave Beef over and ask him to move her. As he goes to pick her up, she looks at him and smirks. "Been some time since a sexy young man had his arms around me."

"Ahh, can't be that fuckin' long, can it, Ma?" Beef says with a wink as he lifts her.

Seated in the chair, she bats his hand away. "Mind your language, young man."

Looking suitably chastised, Beef stammers out an apology, looks at me and shrugs, then wanders away.

"Where's Sarah?"

"She's in the kitchen helping Sam get some sandwiches."

"And that's where I'm going if someone will push me." Ma looks at Sophie.

"Nah, Soph. I've got this." I know why she's hesitating. Ma's a big woman, and Sophie's like me, relying on a prosthesis to walk. But as I'm bigger and stronger, it's not the same problem for me.

Ma's obviously used to giving orders. "Why can't you do it, girl?"

Sophie's no longer ashamed of her injury. She pulls up the leg of her pants. I bite back a smile when I realise, for once, Ma looks chastened herself.

I push her into the kitchen, wondering how quickly Ma will try to take charge. There's been a change in her since she arrived. She seems to be invigorated and enjoying herself. It's easy to see why. Fuck knows how long it's been since she's had company other than that of her great-granddaughter.

While I'm wondering how the women will get on, my eyes fall on Marcia. She's got both hands flat on the counter, and her face is red. Her cheeks are hollowed, then bowed as she seems to be puffing air in and out.

"You okay, Marcia?"

She breathes in and out. "Yeah, just give me a moment, Peg."

I may not have experience with pregnant women, but something doesn't seem right. A cold hand clutches at my heart, remembering how we've just been discussing there's no way anyone can leave. Despite my apprehension, I keep my voice calm. "Marcia, come and sit down in the clubroom. I need to go and get Heart."

She tries to wave me away. "I'm fine, Peg. Just these two babies playing games. Think they're determined to try to kick their way out." She pauses, and flushes again, then deliberately straightens and waves her hand. "Heart and you will have enough to do with keeping the fire from the compound. That's the most important thing now."

The important thing is making sure she and the babies are alright. I purse my lips. We've got a raging fire preventing us from getting her off the compound, and another bearing down on us fast. Even though all the doors and windows are shut, smoke's still edging its way into the clubhouse. It can't be good for mother or those unborn kids. As Marcia's eyes flit toward me, I see the flicker of fear she's trying to hide. I bite back my warning words. She's not stupid. She knows exactly what we're facing, and that this will be the worst possible time for those babies to put in an appearance.

I'm the sergeant-at-arms, and it's my job to keep everyone in the club safe. That includes old ladies and children, even those which haven't yet breathed on their own.

Whatever she wants, I'm going to get Heart. He needs to be with his old lady. I've got a strong suspicion that while she's trying to hide, or deny it to herself, she's going into labour.

Fuck.

Stepping smartly out of the kitchen, I make my way up to the top of the compound where some of my brothers are waiting, poised to jump into action, Shooter's driving a rotavator, digging up the ground, and Paladin's moving combustible material onto the opposite side, all eyes watching the relentless orange threat bearing down on us. The fire's drawn so much closer you can feel the heat coming off it now, and the noise is tremendous. Pulling my bandana up over my nose, I squint to see through the billowing smoke.

"Prez." As Drummer turns to me, he must see the look on my face.

"What is it, Peg?"

"Where's Heart? I think Marcia needs him."

I don't need to explain the situation. One look at the serious expression on my face must have alerted him. His eyes open wide. "Not now." He shakes his head. "Not fuckin' now."

I grit my teeth. "'Fraid so. Well, hopefully it's just a false alarm."

Drummer takes off, going to Wraith's timber frame where Heart is manning a hose. He runs up beside him, and I watch as he gesticulates, pointing back down to the clubroom.

Heart's face, reddened by the heat and exertion, seems to go white. I clutch at his arm as he goes past me. "Calm yourself down before you see her, Brother. If this is her time, then she'll be scared witless."

"She's down for a caesarean, Peg. Due to her problems…"

"And she'll know that just as well as you. I know you're worried, Heart, but you've got to keep your concerns to yourself. You've got to be the strong one here, not go off half-cocked." I place my hand around his arm, holding him back. Marcia obviously needs him, but he won't do her any good if she's got to be strong for *him*.

Heart takes as deep a breath as he can, and nods. My brother's quick to anger, but just as quick to calm down. Knowing I've got through to him, I uncurl my fingers and release him.

"What can I tell her, Peg?"

I rack my brains for what I know, which isn't a lot. Really just what I've absorbed from watching films—oh, and the stories that Wraith and Drum have told me about their horrific experiences in the delivery room. "Labour takes a long time, particularly in first pregnancies." Well, it did for Sophie and Sam. "And it could be those things Sam was havin'. You know, the false alarm when Drum lost his shit. She wasn't havin' contractions…it was…what was it called? Braxton Hicks."

Heart's eyes, rimmed red from the smoke, stare at me. "I can't lose her, Peg. Not her, and not the babies."

It's easy to see what's going through his head, after he went off the rails, unable to cope with losing his wife, Crystal. I can't even begin to think how he'd recover if anything happened to his old lady. He knows better than any of us how someone you love can so quickly be taken away. I put all the strength I possess into my voice as I try to reassure him. "You got this, Brother."

He raises his chin and squares his shoulders. "Not got a choice, have I, Peg?" Then he turns and walks off in the direction of the clubhouse.

"Hey!" I call out, and when he pauses and turns, say, "Sparks and Flame. Good names for babies if they come early."

His middle finger raised shows there's no chance he agrees, but the huffed, strangled laugh suggests I may have lightened his mood. Which is what I'd been trying to do. Marcia needs her man strong, someone she can lean on. The last thing she needs is to have to hold him up too.

The heat's getting unbearable. I wave Shooter and Paladin to come back, having assessed we've done about all we can now when I see engines approaching and firefighters appearing. As Drummer goes to greet them, I tag along too. And fuck me, there's Flash. I almost stumble in my relief to see her. While I'm not pleased she's on the front line of this particular fire, I'm happy to see that, so far, she's safe. I school my features to show only my pleasure at seeing her and none of my concern, I approach but can't resist giving her a hug, mindful of her colleagues watching, and knowing she'll want to remain professional.

Like Drum, I was prepared to fight the fire as it approached, but seeing the fire crews are better prepared, we finally agree to do our part inside the compound and leave the firefighters to do what they're trained for. Particularly when I realise they've got a vested interest in keeping the fire at bay—the compound is now their only safe route of retreat.

As Drum and I head back inside, burning ash carried by the wind starts falling around me. Irritated, I brush some off my cut, inhaling the smell of burning leather, then glance back up and check. Already, Flash and her crew have disappeared, swallowed up by the smoke. The fire is fast approaching our cleared area now and has already started burning through the trees where Road's race track is. It's nearing the time when we find out whether we've done enough.

"Drum!" Suddenly I see flames burning, and my fears for Flash have to be put on the back burner, as now I need to fight for the compound. Grabbing a broom, I go to the back of his house where the Prez's veranda is smouldering, but the fireproof paint seems to be doing its stuff. "Bring water. Get all the wood damped down, now!"

A hose appears in Joker's hands, Lady running beside him to help. Drummer's there, one look at his face and I know he's thinking of what he can do to prevent his house from burning to the ground.

Firefighters have started flooding onto the compound, tired looking crews obviously having been working flat out for hours, if not days. Some remain outside, driving dozers to deepen the trench we'd started in front of the line of trees to enforce our firebreak.

As one of the men entering the compound passes, I slap him on the back and mouth my thanks. The roaring of the fire is so loud now, it's hard to communicate using words. He looks up in acknowledgment, then sees the smouldering on Drum's porch and goes over to help.

Leaving them to it, I call Beef and Rock, and we grab another hose and go to the sweet butts' residence. A large fragment of burning material lands on the concrete tile roof, but the roof being resistant to fire, soon burns itself out.

Around us the sound's getting ever louder, as if it's a wild beast hungry for food, and the sky is dark, black tinged with red, the air so thick it's hard to breathe.

"Peg!" Wraith shouts and tears past. I follow as fast as I can, cursing for once my prosthetic leg as the ground's uneven, and while I can do most things, the lack of feeling in my foot means I have to go slower and take care.

As soon as I catch up with the VP, I see where he's pointing. "Fuckin' useless whores!" I berate them in their absence, while knowing the lack of foresight is down to me. *I should have checked.* "Out. Back up, now." There's been bags of garbage left to the rear of their house, garbage which is now merrily burning, right up beside the propane tank.

Wraith grabs Beef and Rock and pulls them back, Jekyll's running up, but gets shoved away.

A firefighter and is talking to Drum. I interrupt them. "There's garbage sacks burning around the," I remember my audience, "girls' house. The propane tank's right next to them."

"Where?" The firefighter says grimly. "Show me."

I take him back, but careful to keep my distance. "Hear that whistling? That's the sound you want to hear. It's venting. The gas is blowing off into the air. It will keep doing that until it runs out of fuel." He places a call on his radio, and suddenly more firefighters appear through the gate and go forward with rakes to pull the burning trash bags away.

Brave men. And somewhere, Darcy's out there, doing the same job as them. Watching them move around, no panic, just putting their trade into practice, carrying all their equipment in this raging heat, without complaint. I'm full of respect all over again for my woman. *Take care of yourself, Flash.*

It's only minutes later that they report the garbage bags have been put out and removed, and they're pretty certain all the gas has been dispelled. Drummer's been swearing up a storm about the laziness of the club whores but turns when he sees his old lady running up the slope.

"Drum. Is there a medic around?"

"What is it, Sam? Who's hurt?"

Fuck no. I hope that feeling in my gut isn't right.

But her next words prove that it is.

"It's Marcia. Looks like the babies are coming."

CHAPTER 24

Darcy

We're right down at the head of the fire, making use of the wide break the bikers had made. Around us the fire's still raging, rearing up into the tree canopy and spreading out on the flanks as it's forward advance here has been halted. The bikers have done well, and we're reinforcing what they've already done, pulling up roots and digging out a dozer line. Fleetingly, I realise it's our job to protect life, whosesoever it might be, but we've also got an interest in keeping the compound fire free. Apart from protecting the bikers, it's going to be our refuge as well. Seeing the fire looping around on either side, there's no other escape route for us now.

Anything combustible is burning, pockets of scrub they were unable to remove keep catching alight, and we attack fast to put those out. Above us, burning ash carried on the fierce winds is heading straight for the compound.

"Hey, Hammer. You're needed." I hear Slade's voice on the radio, and anxiously turn around fast. A call for the EMT normally means someone is hurt.

"Yo, Captain. What is it?" Hammer's immediately on the alert.

Slade appears through the smoke, jerking his head back toward the compound, and for a second I have an irrational fear something's happened to Peg. "One of the women at the bikers' place has gone into labour. We can't get her out, as the fire's got the compound surrounded.

Relieved no one's been hurt, then I realise it must be Marcia, and warn him grimly, "It's twins, Ham."

Hammer puts a hand to his chin as he gives me a sharp look followed by a nod as he digests my additional information. Then he stands straighter. "Christ, I'm no obstetrician. Are we sure we can't get her out? What about a helicopter?"

Slade points to the fire that's surrounding us on all sides. "The wind has increased again. It's well above twenty-five knots." We'd been lucky there'd been a lull to get Nicole out. The captain's shaking his head, showing how little he likes the situation. "You better go too, Flash. If you know her it will do her some good to see someone familiar. And Hammer will need all the help he can get. Bad fucking timing."

That's putting it mildly. I don't even want to think about all the problems we might face.

Hammer rubs his chin again. "I've handled births before, but not a multiple birth. Fuck, I hope it's a false alarm."

We exchange glances, both knowing how much is riding on this, the life of a woman and her two babies. Without having to speak, we waste no more time, pointing our feet in the direction of the compound behind us. As we head through the gate we pass bikers, all looking concerned. I see Peg, and he raises his chin toward me and throws me a weak smile. Sam, who've I met before, is hovering close by with a scarf wrapped around her face. Seeing us, waves us down the slope in the direction of the clubhouse.

Inside we find Marcia, who's breathing heavily. Her man, Heart, has his arm around her and they're surrounded by a group of concerned women. An old woman I don't recognise is barking instructions.

Taking in the scene quickly, Hammer immediately steps up and takes charge. "Can you give us some space, please?"

The women step away, Heart stays where he is. Hammer throws him a nod, then speaks to Marcia. "You're having contractions?"

"I think so, yes." She gasps and clasps her stomach as another one hits.

"Can you do something to help her?" Heart sounds panicked.

Hammer takes hold of Marcia's hand. "We got this, okay?" he tells her in a confident voice. "Not the way you planned it, but we got this."

As the contraction passes, she raises her eyes to meet his and gives a little nod of determination.

"Good girl. Now, can you give me the name of your doctor?"

Heart provides the information on Marcia's behalf. As Hammer steps away, he takes out his phone, frowning when he sees there's no signal.

"Phones are out," another man says, his hair and features giving away he's at least part Native American. "You'll have to use your radio."

"I'll be back in a minute, Marcia. Flash, can you start to time the contractions?"

Nodding, I take out my own phone and select the timer.

After a few minutes, Hammer returns and pulls me to one side, speaking quietly so no one else can hear. "Right. Got good and bad news. The bad is that due to her medical history she was going to have a caesarean. She's got another three and half weeks to go, and the good is that babies should be fine to be delivered now."

"What we looking at here, Hammer?"

He takes a deep breath. "The caesarean was going to be a precaution, but now she's got no choice. Those babies want out, and she'll have to have a natural birth. We treat it as we would normally. After the first baby comes out the second should follow quickly. The doc's going to keep in close contact to talk us through any complications. How far apart are the contractions?" He pauses to smile confidently at Marcia, who, out of earshot, is looking at him, worried.

"Four minutes."

"Shit. It's getting close." He lifts the radio and relays that piece of information, and then we move back to Marcia's side.

Sam's hovering. "What can I do to help?"

Hammer answers immediately. "I need a room. Preferably with a bed. Have you got a plastic sheet?"

Heart overhears. "Got sheeting up in the storeroom." Without missing a beat, he yells out, "Prospect!"

"On it, Heart." Everyone seems to be eavesdropping today.

"We'll also need clean sheets, towels. Whatever you can find."

Sam frowns. "It would be best if we could get her up to her suite."

Hammer shakes his head. "Have you anywhere inside the clubhouse? There's too much smoke outside, and I don't want her breathing more in than she has to, it's already bad enough in here." He's right. The doors and windows are shut, the power's gone off, and the room's stifling, but overheating is better than the poisonous air.

"Then we'll set up one of the crash rooms," Sam says without missing a beat, then beckons to the other women, and they all disappear.

One of them takes the handles of the wheelchair and takes the strange old woman along with them. I see her bending down and saying, "Ma, how about you and I sort out some food. Gonna be a lot of hungry people here soon."

I don't hear a reply, getting back to the matter in hand and seeing Hammer looking at Marcia. "Let's get you up on your feet. Walking around will be better for you."

Heart helps Marcia up, and slowly they start walking around the clubroom. Hammer moves away, and I hear murmuring as he talks to the doctor on the radio. In a very short time the prospect is back, and Heart sends him on back to where the women are preparing a room.

"Room's done." Sam reappears.

"Heart. Can you take Marcia back there, and I'll join you in a moment?" Hammer waits until we're alone, and then looks at me. "The twins each have their own gestational sac, but it looks like they share a placenta."

That's one bit of good news at least. If they were in one sac, there would be a danger of the cords getting tangled during the birth process.

Hammer's on his radio, switching frequencies. "Slade. How's it looking? I'd still rather we get this woman to the hospital."

"Still not possible for the helicopter to land?" When he gets the answer, I can see his hand clenching. "Damn. Okay. We'll do what we can."

Hammer closes his eyes as if summoning up strength for the ordeal ahead, then when he opens them, speaks with new resolve. "Come on. Let's do this."

As he marches away in the direction Marcia had gone, I follow behind, hoping to God we'll not lose either woman or babies today. That we're in for a challenging time is certain. I glance over to where Heart's still encouraging Marcia to stand and keep moving, her face twisting in pain, and sweat running down her face, which isn't all from the heat.

"How are you doing?" Hammer asks in his best bedside manner, but only sounds a little gentler than his gruff firefighter self.

"Like I want all the drugs going." Marcia chokes back a sob. "I'm sorry. It hurts so fucking much."

"Marc…"

"Heart. Don't you fucking say anything."

Hammer ignores her outburst. "Can you lie on the bed, Marcia, and let me take a look at you?"

Moving awkwardly, she does. When Hammer goes to remove her leggings, Heart pushes him out of the way, pulling them off, then stretching her long top down. Hammer covers her lower half with a sheet, then gently moves her tee back up and moves his hands over her stomach, which I can see is rock hard.

Marcia's eyes are wide and worried as she suffers his examination, hardly daring to breathe.

When Hammer looks up, he's smiling. "First baby's head seems to be in the right position. We're going to do this, Marcia, okay? Now, I'm sorry, but I want to examine you to see whereabouts you are." He slips on gloves.

Heart growls when he sees Hammer's intention. "Can't you do this, Darcy?"

I shake my head. "Hammer's got far more expertise than me." I know how possessive these bikers can be, so I lay it on the line for him. "You want your children born safely, Heart. Let Hammer do what he has to."

It's easy to see Heart's torn between watching what Hammer's doing to his woman and being unable to look.

"I can feel the head crowning. These babies want out, Marcia. I know it hurts, but it won't be too long now."

"It shouldn't be this way." Marcia howls, and then as her body goes taut once again, pants through another contraction. After what seems to be a lifetime, it passes.

Hammer keeps in touch with Doctor Cassidy by radio, updating her on how Marcia's doing. We get updates on the fire, which is still burning fiercely, but the efforts of the bikers and firefighters are proving successful in keeping it away from the compound. The woman on the bed is suffering bravely, and as Heart takes her hand I see his turning white as she tries to cope with the pain. From the look of anguish on his face, he'd do anything to be able to suffer for her instead.

An hour passes, and I keep timing those contractions. A particularly strong one has Marcia screaming out.

"How long was that?"

"Two minutes," I tell him.

"Right, Marcia. If you feel the need to push, do."

My heart bleeds for her, she's trying so hard. Beads of sweat run down her face from effort and pain. Heart's wiping her fore-head, speaking words of encouragement, and at last Hammer tells her, "I can see the head crowning. Next contraction I want you to push really hard." He places his hands gently on the baby's head, and I see him checking to make sure the umbilical cord isn't wrapped around it. "Everything's looking good, Marcia. Now, push."

She does, and for the next one, she clenches her fists and grits her teeth.

"Baby's coming. Once again, Marcia, give it all that you've got." Then to me, "There's a scalpel in my bag. Can you get it? And pass me a towel."

As I do, it looks like the baby's covered in cellophane. Hammer quickly breaks the sac and wipes its face.

"Shoulders are out. And baby is too, Marcia."

Hammer wraps it in a towel, but not before telling the exhausted woman, "You've got a boy, Marcia." Holding the baby with his head facing down, he takes the sterile cloth that I'm holding and gently wipes the mucus away. His fingers are resting on the baby boy's chest, then he looks at me and grins.

"Baby's fine, Marcia." The baby screams proving Hammer's right.

Marcia's totally worn out, but the most beautiful smile I've ever seen creeps across her face as she turns to Heart. "We've got a son."

Heart's looking almost as shattered as her. He's shaking his head as if he can't quite believe it. "A son, Marc. We have a son."

Hammer passes the baby to me to hold, who quietens in my hold, and then goes to check on Marcia. "Baby two isn't quite in the right position, Marcia. I'm just going to see if I can move him around." He places his hand on her stomach, and gently manipulates the baby inside while Marcia again clenches her teeth, breathing a sigh of relief when he steps back and tells her, "There, that's it."

"I want to push."

"Go right ahead. Shouldn't take long now, as you're already stretched."

It doesn't. Only fifteen minutes after the first, Marcia gives birth to a baby girl. But she's not breathing. Unfazed, while the worried parents look on and exchange concerned glances, Hammer efficiently gives her mouth to mouth, and then with a cry she starts taking in air all on her own.

Hammer updates the doctor and gets his next instructions. He cuts the umbilical cords, and hands one baby to a stunned Heart, and one he puts into Marcia's arms. "See if they'll latch on and suckle."

She tries, Heart helps her. It seems like he's done this before and knows what he's doing.

Hammer is still watching carefully what's happening, and as Marcia pushes again, the placenta comes out. She's bleeding. It's not unusual, but we have to deal with it.

"I'll go and see if any of the women have a sanitary pad." I go to the door, then turn back. "You want me to tell them the good news?"

Heart's got the biggest stupid grin on his face as he looks up and nods. "Sure, let everyone know."

In the clubroom all the women are waiting around, along with Fergus, the prospect. For the first time today, I've got something uplifting to say as all eyes land on me. "A boy and a girl. Both look okay." When they've digested the news, I ask for what I came out for.

Sam nods. "Marcia's got a hospital bag prepared in her room. I should have thought of it earlier."

"I'll go," Fergus offers. After Sam describes it, he pulls up his bandana and disappears into the smoke-filled air.

"Can we see them?" Sophie asks.

"Let's get her cleaned up and sorted first, okay?"

I return to the room to find Hammer smiling. "The wind's dropped, and they'll be able to get a helicopter here soon. Hear that Marcia? You and the babies will be able to be checked out."

She's trying to get both babies to suckle. Two little mouths are rooting around. She seems so intent on the miracles in her arms that she hardly hears what he's telling her.

Heart does, though, and lets out a deep sigh of relief. He looks over to us and holds out his hand. Hammer shakes it first, then when I go to take it, he pulls me in for a hug. "Thank you, thank you both. I don't know what we'd have fuckin' done without you."

Hammer grins. "This was one of my most pleasurable day's work, man. Don't sweat it man. It's what we do."

A knock at the door, and I take the bag from Fergus. Manoeuvring the babies between us, Heart helps Marcia out of her sweat-laden top and into the nightie she had in her bag. Then I help her with the more intimate products. With Heart's help, Hammer takes the dirty sheets off the bed, and we replace them with the spares Sam had helpfully provided.

"You've got a bunch of eager women out there. Want to let them come in?"

"I think it's too early for that…"

"Heart." With one word, Marcia stops him. "If I'm going to the hospital soon, let them come in for a moment." There's a glow of pride on her exhausted face, and it deserves to be there. She did well.

They must have been hanging around outside. As I open the door, Sophie, Ella, Sam, Carmen, and Sandy come in, immediately crowding the small room. Fergus pushes the old lady in the wheelchair in, then backs away, his head peering around the doorway as if he doesn't feel invited but can't help having a look.

Marcia looks up at them, that proud, beatific smile still on her tired and drawn face. She nods at Heart and says, "Meet Jacob and Isabel." Heart's hand's resting gently on the head of his son as he gives a small nod to his woman.

"They're tiny," gasps Sandy. "What do they weigh?"

"Whoa." Hammer laughs. "We'll let them sort all that out at the hospital."

At that moment, a grey furry bundle pushes past Fergus and comes bounding up to the bed. "Grunt. Down boy." Heart laughs.

"I got him." Sam rests her hand on the dog's collar and pulls him away. "He just wanted to see his new family, didn't you, boy?" Grunt's tail's wagging furiously, and as large as he is, he's getting in everyone's way.

Hammer's quick to notice it's getting too much for the new parents. "Ladies, can we give them some space?"

"You done good, girl." The old woman nods approvingly as Fergus reappears to wheel her out. *I must find out who she is.* But my curiosity will have to wait. Marcia's my priority.

Reluctant to leave, the other women blow kisses at Marcia, and then go, Sam dragging an unwilling Grunt away.

Hammer's back on the radio. He listens to what he's being told, sucks in air, then blows it out, then answers, "Okay." He nods toward Heart and Marcia. "The helicopter's coming in. Should be about twenty minutes. It can't hang about for long. The fire's not as bad as it was, but it's still burning. They're designating a helispot in the area you cleared at the back of the compound. We need to do what we can to protect the babies from inhaling too much smoke."

"Will this do?" I pull out some gauze from his bag.

We fashion some makeshift masks while Heart helps Marcia swing her legs off the bed and slips her feet into some sandals. "I'm a bit underdressed," she tells him.

"You're going to the hospital," he replies. "Not out on the town." His eyes flick to mine. "Will I be able to go with her?"

Hammer answers with a frown. "Depends on the helicopter. They're bringing a medic along in case they need medical attention on the way. I'm sorry, man, but possibly not."

By his expression, Heart doesn't want to be separated from his woman and babies so soon. But it can't be helped. I try to reassure him. "Heart, despite everything today, Marcia's done an amazing job, and the babies look like they're doing well. But it's important she gets to the hospital as soon as she can. I know you don't want to be parted, but hopefully it won't be for long."

He nods. Marcia stumbles as she tries to stand.

"Heart and I will carry the babies," Hammer announces. "You help Marcia along."

But Heart's got other ideas, sweeping her up into his arms and carrying her outside to a Jeep. He carefully puts her in the back seat and takes the baby Hammer carried out and gives her son to her. I sit beside her with her daughter in my arms. As I give her a sideways look, I see her staring down into the bundle she's holding, a look of disbelief on her face.

I nudge her. "You doing okay?"

"I just can't believe they're here. And that they're alright."

"I meant how are you feeling?" I smile.

"Sore, but that doesn't matter. Look what I got for my pain?" She laughs softly. "But I do feel I could sleep for a week."

That's par for the course for any new mother and I suspect a full night's sleep won't be in the cards for a very long time.

As Heart slowly and carefully drives up the compound, I stare at the baby in my arms, feeling a pang inside. I'm not getting any younger and have always expected one day to have a family of my own. A family that I know Peg would be only too happy to give me. Then bite my lip as I realise the chances of that happening now are slim to nothing.

Taking advantage of the moment of peace in the mayhem I've been embroiled in for the past three days, my mind flits over what's happened since I last saw him. The initial call to the fire, sitting in the engine not immediately knowing what we were being dispatched to, but being prepared for anything. Being so scared for Nicole, and the relief when we found her, my own life being at risk when the fire caught up with us, and now the exhilaration that I was able to help Hammer deliver these beautiful babies.

Instead of dampening my enthusiasm for my job, these past few days have enhanced it. I don't want anything to put that at risk. Which, I have to accept, is at odds with a relationship with an outlaw biker.

Especially one who treats the women as he and his brothers do. It hadn't escaped my notice that while I'd be in the clubhouse every woman was staying safe while their men were out protecting the compound from the fire. Cooking up food to provide sustenance, comforting and encouraging them when their men when they came down for a break. If I was here as an old lady, would that be my expected place? Peg's look of concern that I'd been in the midst of the firefighting hadn't escaped me, and neither had I missed his expression of relief and approval that for a time I was going to be out of danger and doing a job more appropriate for a woman. Delivering babies. He hadn't had to say one word, it was all written on his face.

I couldn't be cocooned like the rest of the old ladies, I'd soon suffocate. Peg and I are oceans apart. Coming here today, seeing how the women are corralled and protected, had been an eyeopener for me, and had brought home that being with an overprotective man is not what I want. I want an equal partnership, not one where I'm smothered and kept off the front line.

Fighting this fire has reminded me what I live for. Knowing I'm making a difference, when structures are threatened, saving peoples' homes or livelihoods. A life of being pampered isn't one I'd enjoy, but already knowing what I do about Peg, I'm convinced that's what he'd have lined up for me.

I can imagine his reaction if he knows I might have to give up my job in order to be with him. He'd be delighted. Especially now when he's seen first-hand what I go up against. Could I see Peg happily waving me off each time I go on shift, after having got up close and personal with what I deal with every day? Knowing the danger and risks that we take. For the past three days, I've had no real sleep and no thought of anything but tackling the force of nature in front of me. It put everything else out of my mind. My priority to play my part in stopping its ferocious advance. Now I've an interlude of relative calm, it's put everything into perspective and confirmed what I suspected.

Peg and I have no future. I've got my team around me, people who understand what I do. Much as I might envy Marcia and her babies, I can't see how that can fit into my world. When I realise I won't give up my career for Peg, I also must accept there's no middle ground. I was stupid ever thinking there was. My department would frown on the relationship, and I'd be fighting Peg every day that he believes I'm putting my life at risk.

We're passing through men and going out of the rear gate, coming to a halt as the helicopter appears above us, giving it space to land. The spinning rotor stirs up dust and fans the flames of a small fire, which one of my team runs and puts out. Ash is still falling around us like snow as Heart pulls the Jeep in as close as he can get.

Things move quickly. Marcia's helped inside, then the babies are secured. Hammer has a brief word with the medics, and within minutes the helicopter is taking off again, Heart staring after it until it disappears from sight.

"She'll be fine." I put my hand on his shoulder. "You'll be able to go to her soon." It's clear to see the fire has lost its intensity, with the wind having died down and becoming only a gentle breeze, it's gradually consuming the fuel that's already alight, but no longer such a hungry beast ravenous for more.

"Flash." Slade appears at my side.

"Yeah. Where d'you want me, Captain?" Looking at him is probably like looking into a mirror, bags showing under his red-rimmed eyes, lines etched on his soot-laden forehead, reminding me we've been here more than eighty hours straight, a couple of insufficient naps sleeping in one of the engines, just enough to keep us awake.

"You need some down time. Drummer's offered us the use of his clubroom for firefighters to take a break."

I give myself a shake, trying to rid myself of the overwhelming exhaustion, feeling both mentally and physically drained. "I'm fine to go on, Slade."

"That's an order, Cavanaugh. Hammer, Truck, and I are standing down too. Take a couple of hours, get some food and have a rest."

Actually, that sounds good, as long as I'm not being given preferential treatment. As my crew members come to join me, we walk back through the gate. Heart comes running up. "I've got to get the Jeep moved back anyway. Want a lift?"

As we gratefully agree, Peg appears.

CHAPTER 25

Peg

Flash is dead on her feet. Fuck knows how long she's been out here fighting the fire, and helping Marcia give birth must have been draining. I'm filled with admiration for her, for the job that she does and her willingness to turn her hand to anything necessary. My brave woman, fighting the fire alongside her colleagues, proving herself equal to any man. But now I'm concerned at how drawn she looks.

My intention is to examine her more closely. I reach out my hand, but she takes a step back. I crease my brow, surprised. "Flash?"

"Not now, Peg." She catches my eye before looking down at her feet and shaking her head. "We'll talk later, okay?"

It's the way that she says it, the tone of her voice which has me reeling, suggesting it's *the talk*, the one I'd rather not have. I don't know what's happened since I last saw her, we've had no contact for more than three days. But something's changed. Something that despite the stifling air around us, makes me grow cold. *I haven't found her just to have her walk away.*

She's tired, swaying with exhaustion. Perhaps she's not thinking straight. Seeing Heart waiting to take them down to the clubhouse, I realise some down time might be just what she needs. "Go get some rest, darlin'." It could be she's right not to want to talk now. Something to eat and a nap might put her straight.

I can do nothing but watch as the woman I'd thought I'd claimed as my old lady walks to the Jeep and gets inside. I want nothing more than to be able to hold her. After all my fears when I'd known she was up on the mountain fighting the fire, I wanted her in my arms to reassure myself she was alright.

"Hey. Boy then girl, Heart says. I won the bet." As Beef comes up alongside me, a jealousy burns in my gut at his words. Two more babies on the compound, and neither of them mine.

Shaking off his arm, which he's rested on my shoulder, I leave him shrugging as I step away. Taking up the hose once again, I continue to keep Wraith's wooden frame dampened down. The fire might be losing some of its intensity, but it's still not yet time to celebrate. As I work I keep an eye on the track up from the clubhouse, wondering how long it will be before I see my Flash again.

Two hours later, she reappears, walking alongside her crewmates, still looking tired, but at least smiling again. Talking with them, gesticulating at their surroundings, clearly discussing the fire. Talking animatedly. Until she sees me. Pausing only long enough to utter just one word, "Later," she re-joins her team and gets back on with the job.

Soon I lose sight of her, and that cold feeling becomes icy.

"Peg. You look like fuck, Brother. Go get some rest."

"I'm okay, Prez."

"That's an order, Peg. The fire's under control and fully contained. The fire chief is standin' some of his crews down, so that's what we're going to do to. We've beaten this one, Brother."

As I turn to my, for once smiling, prez, I realise I'd been so lost in my thoughts I hadn't noticed there were no longer shooting flames, just smouldering trees in the distance, and the air which had been so thick with smoke you could hardly see what was in front of you, is now clearing. Ash falling less like a blizzard, now just the odd flurry.

He nods when he sees where I'm looking. "Joker and Lady have volunteered to stay here for a while and keep an eye out for any flare ups. If something happens, they'll let us know and we can come straight back. Don't know about you, Peg, but I'm tired and hungry."

"Which crews?"

"What?"

"Which crews are standin' down?" I snap out. I can't think of food or rest when I'm worried about what my old lady has to say.

"Don't rightly know, except the crew that helped Marcia, Captain Slade's lot, they're already on their way."

As I watch through the clearer air, I see a line of firefighters making their way around the edge of what used to be the tree line, and is now burned-out forest, and over to their engines. Too far away for me to catch up. *She's gone. Without saying goodbye.*

I throw down the hose that I'm holding in disgust. It writhes like a snake and water squirts up, getting Drummer's legs soaked. He leaps back out of range. "What the fuck, Peg?"

But I ignore him, already walking away. She didn't wait to speak to me. Her leaving without a word? Well, that makes it plain what she had to say. She just didn't have the guts to say it to my face.

I stomp down the track, kicking rocks out of my path. Reaching my suite, I open then slam the door shut. As soon as I'm inside I realise it was a mistake. Her perfume, the memory of her is everywhere here. But I can't go to the clubroom, I'm in no mood to be sociable, or to celebrate the birth of Heart's fucking kids.

What's happened? Why did she walk away from me?

Knowing I'm still trapped on this compound, I can't even go after her to get her to explain, nor can I ring her, as the cell tower must still be out of commission. In my living room I eye a cupboard, and while there'll be no answers inside, I've no better suggestion than to drink myself into oblivion and forget her. Though I doubt there's sufficient alcohol in the world which would allow me to do that.

Raising my glass to my lips, I empty it, the spirit burning my throat. Then I repeat. And repeat. And repeat.

My first waking thought is to ask myself why the fuck I hadn't locked my door. "Go away."

"Peg." The man shaking my shoulder is relentless. "Peg. Wake up, Brother."

"Wassup?" Even if the compound was burning down around me I've no inclination to move.

"Come on, man. This isn't like you." Wraith kicks aside the empty bottle that's lying on the couch. "Fuck, man. You didn't even shower last night. You stink, and you're still covered in soot."

I didn't. Didn't have anyone to clean myself up for.

I lean back my head and close my eyes, hoping he'll take the hint.

"How much you have, Peg? Never seen you like this before."

Too much, yet not enough.

"Leave me alone, VP."

"What's happened, Brother?" I feel my legs being moved, then the couch dip as Wraith sits down beside me. "The last few days were fucked up. I'll give you that. But the fire's out, the danger has passed, and the compound survived, everyone's safe. Oh, and Heart's gone to the hospital to be with Marcia and the babies." He pauses for a moment. "Fuckin' good woman he's got there. Delivered those kids in the middle of all that crap."

I sit up, too quickly, and pain blasts through my head, not helping my temper. "For fuck's sake, get out of here, Wraith. Before I do something we both regret." I don't want to hear about my brother or his old lady, and especially not his new babies.

When the VP stands I take it he's going to leave. But he doesn't. He stands a few feet away with a smirk on his face, his hands held out to his sides. "Have at me, then."

With a roar, I get to my feet, a burning sensation telling me I've been wearing my prosthesis too long, but even with a real leg under me I'd still have been unsteady. The room is spinning, and as I take an ineffective swing, I stumble as my fist misses him completely.

"Yeah, just as I thought." As I fall against him, Wraith holds me up, and with an arm around me, starts leading me out of the living area. Feeling ill, I make no protest, and it's lucky he's taking me to the bathroom, as I'm violently sick. *Fuck.* Now I've got vomit on my beard.

The shower starts behind me, and I stand like a child as Wraith strips my clothes off. After closing the lid, he sits me down on the toilet and removes my prosthetic leg, an action he's well practiced with having often performed it for Sophie. He then helps me hop in and waits until I get enough balance to sit on my shower seat, which he's placed into position for me, then hands me soap and shampoo, which I take automatically.

As I wash he folds his arms and leans back against the counter. "What the fuck's got into you, Peg?"

I rub shower gel over my body, realising how dirty I am as black water flows down the drain. As I get the dirt and other unmentionable shit out of my hair and my beard, I begin to sober up and remember in technicolour Flash's dismissal yesterday.

Wraith's still patiently waiting for an answer. He's my friend as well as my brother, so with a sigh, I give him what he wants. "She's gone. And I don't think she's comin' back."

I hear his sharp intake of breath about the same time as I realise it's not just water running down my cheeks. Angrily brushing my tears away, I put them down to the after effects of too much to drink. I can't remember having cried in my life. I suppose I must have, when I was a kid—be unnatural if I didn't. But I've never the fuck cried over a woman. I wash them off under the shower, and hope Wraith hasn't noticed.

He's yet to speak, and turning the shower off, then shaking the water out of my eyes, I risk a look in his direction. He's got his hands over his face, slowly drawing them down. When he takes them away, he looks at me and passes me a towel.

It's only then that he says, "Fuck, Peg. I'm sorry. Are you sure? What happened?"

"I don't know what fuckin' happened," I growl. When she'd left to go on her shift it was the promise of returning, fuck, even bringing some of her clothes and at least making this her home at least on a part time basis. But yesterday she acted as if she didn't want to know me. *What had happened? What had changed?*

He waves his hand between us. "We've been here before, remember? There was a time I got drunk out of my head because Sophie sent me away. You made me pull my head out of my ass. Told me to talk to her." As I pull myself to my foot, he moves out of the way. "So now I'm givin' your advice back to you. Sober up and go speak to your woman." He gives a short laugh. "They're strange fuckin' creatures, you never know what's going on in their heads. Think about it. She'd been fightin' that fire for days. She'd have been tired beyond fuckin' measure. She might not even have been thinkin' straight."

Could it be that?

"I don't know, Wraith. Something's spooked her."

I sit back down on the toilet seat and take out some cream, wiping it into the sore skin of my stump. Wraith's watching carefully. "Looks nasty. Like you shouldn't be wearin' your prosthesis today."

"Just pass it to me, Wraith."

"Even Sophie knows some days she needs to use crutches."

It's okay for her, but I'm the sergeant-at-arms. Ignoring him, I start to rise, and he pushes me back. "Stubborn old fool, ain't you?" But he passes me what I want.

As I strap my leg on I realise I'm sitting here naked. "Get out, Wraith, unless you haven't had enough of seeing my junk."

He smirks again. "Didn't even notice something as small as that."

I grab the towel and flick it at him, and at last he moves away, but pauses in the doorway. "You comin' down to the clubhouse? Drum's called church. That's why I came to get you."

"Yeah. Give me a bit, man." His suggestion that I need to speak to Flash, find out what the fuck's happened and what I can do to fix things between us, has worked to bring me out of my slump. I feel more positive than I had when I watched her walk away. After all that we'd said, there must be something that made her freak out. I've just got to find what it is. Then sort it. As I sit thinking about it, I think of all the shit she'd been through. Things said in the literal heat of the moment might not mean anything at all. Yeah. I'll talk to her. Soon as church is over I'm out of here.

I won't be telling Wraith, but he's right. I should have left my prosthesis off today. But I walk into the clubroom making a concerted effort not to limp—it's not in me to show any weakness. My head's pounding, so I go to the kitchen and take some Advil out of the cupboard. I'm just washing them down with water when I hear a voice behind me.

"Well, don't you look like shit."

Ma. I turn, about to give her hell, when I notice she doesn't look much better. But somehow, I doubt she went on a bender like me. Tilting my head to the side, I ask, "What's up, Ma?" Like me, I doubt it's very often she cries.

She shrugs and tries to look nonchalant. "My house has burned up. Nothing left."

"Fuck, Ma." Not that I didn't expect it, but she must be devastated. Everything she had will have gone up in flames with it.

Another shrug. "Well, now the family will get what they want. Me moved into a retirement home." She looks down, seems to pull herself together, and then wheels the wheelchair around the table. "You haven't eaten, have you? There's probably something I can heat up."

My stomach growls, as though it heard the mention of food. I watch as Ma gets out a plate of leftover something or other and takes it to the microwave, realising I haven't indicated that's what I want. Suspecting she's trying to keep herself busy, I let her get on with it. Soon I've got a plate of a temptingly smelling casserole of some sort put in front of me. Almost automatically, I pick up a fork and start shovelling it into my mouth while watching Ma tidying up and putting things she can reach away.

"You can rebuild," I suggest, if it's independence she wants.

She wheels herself over until she's positioned opposite me. "I could, but I won't. I'm too old, I know that. Can't depend on Sarah to live with me anymore."

"I don't mind, Gramma." The young woman herself walks into the room, leaning over to give the old woman a kiss. A gnarly hand reaches up to pat the one on her shoulder. "And we don't know yet if it's completely destroyed."

"Best to expect the worst. I've lived long enough to know that. And you've got your own life to get on with."

My mind's racing, thinking of the construction company we own, as Sarah says, "I like living in Tucson."

As a man comes in, and Sarah's face lights up, I think I might just know the reason for that. Hyde. Fucking Hyde. From the smile on his face, he's probably getting what I'm not.

Fuck it. I stand up and remember my manners. "Thanks for the food, Ma." I take my plate to the sink, rinse it, then put it in the dishwasher.

"Church, Peg," Hyde reminds me.

Yeah. Church. Then after that my time's my own.

CHAPTER 26

Darcy

We're tired and dirty, but also exhilarated when we arrive back at the station, knowing while it had been hard, we'd successfully fought the Snake Fire, and had come out on top. Eyeing the rest of the crew, I can see we all seem to have fared the same. Exhaustion and tiredness is written all over the faces in front of me and must be reflected in my own. I'm completely drained, no energy to do anything other than strip off my fire-fighter's apparel then run through the shower. After wrapping a towel around me, I lean against the wall. The last few days have been tough, but strangely, enjoyable.

I can't give any of this up, the camaraderie of working as part of the team, skirting the edge of danger. Be the little woman who cowers and lets men take on the battle on her behalf? That won't be me. Ever. *And Slade had dangled that prospect of promotion in front of me.* Even through my tiredness, the thought quickens my heart. *I know I could do it.* Could become a captain, maybe progress event further. Bat Chief Cavanaugh has a nice ring to it.

At least the warm water washed away some of the stench, though the smell of smoke still seems etched into my pores. Deciding I want nothing more than to get home to my bed, I pull on my street clothes, drag my hair into a ponytail, leaving my hair to air dry, and, having worked out when I'm next due on shift, take my leave of my colleagues and friends.

"Drive carefully," Truck warns me as I walk past him to go to my car.

"You too." We're all beat, getting home safe the only thing on our minds.

I take the keys out of my purse and bounce them in my hands as I walk to my car. Not a vehicle I have much love for, but a mode of transport to get me from A to B. As long as it's reliable, that's all that matters. The reason I'm focusing on the vehicle in front of me is to try to keep Peg and my guilt from my mind. As I walked past him without saying a word, I hadn't missed how his eyes had glazed over with pain. *I'm doing the right thing.* Just maybe not the right way.

Now I'm headed home to sleep in the bed Peg had bought. The thought slams into my head, filling me with guilt and regret for the cowardly way that I'd left him. *He deserved more than that.*

I could have held back, my crew would have waited for a bit. But the few short moments they'd have been happy to be kept hanging around wouldn't have been long enough to explain my feelings to Peg. It had been far easier to walk on toward the engine that would be driving us back to the city without even acknowledging that he was there. Sending him a message as clear as day. *We're over.*

That I hadn't given him a reason is bugging me now. I'd been so unfair to the man who wanted me as his old lady. *Should I talk to him and explain my reasons?* Or, if he doesn't contact me, leave it how it is and make it a clean break?

I miss him already.

Opening the car door, I slide into the driver's seat, the thoughts in my head still racing. *What if I've made a dreadful mistake?* My career and future prospects put ahead of the man I've been searching for all of my life.

Tears start to leak from my eyes as I pause before starting the engine, going back over why I acted as I did. Two reasons, and each would stand on their own. First to end it before outside forces would surely push us apart—I won't be giving up my job as a firefighter, and daren't put it at risk because of a whirlwind relationship. The second, even more powerful, I won't be sidelined like the other women, and that's what Peg would want to do. Peg would want to keep me safe and out of danger, while my natural inclination is to rush straight in, fighting alongside the men.

At last I start the car and put it into drive. When I exit the parking lot I see Truck's big truck closing in behind me, his indicator flashing the same way as mine. It seems like once again he intends to follow me home. I give a small smile, in the dark of the night it feels good to have company, even if it's only headlights in my rearview.

I drive on automatic pilot, trying to focus my mind on anything but the man I just left, not wanting to continually double think my decision. Instead I think of Marcia and the delivery of her babies, mentally listing insignificant things like taking some flowers to her and finding out how she is. The I dismiss even that notion. *What if Peg was visiting at the same time?*

It wouldn't take much for me to weaken, and now that my mind's made up, I need to keep to my resolve. One man isn't worth the loss of myself—my identity and what I've worked so hard for. Seeing him again might be too great a temptation.

That bed he bought is going to remind me. Maybe I should spend the night on the couch? But even that holds memories. Peg's presence in my house is going to be hard to eradicate, and while his ghost roams my home, he'll still be haunting my head.

The headlights behind me are flashing, then they flash again more urgently. *Shit. Have I got a light out or something? Why didn't Truck call me?* It's then I realise, my phone, neglected while I was fighting the wildfire, is probably dead.

I'm coming up to a vacant lot where there's some kind of construction work going on, so signal my intention and pull to the side of the road. Truck parks up behind me but doesn't turn his headlights off. I get out, blinded by the glaring light and go to check the back of my car. I hear a door open, but intent on trying to see what's wrong, don't turn around, and just call out.

"Truck? Why did you want me to stop? Are my brake lights not working?" The rear lights seem fine.

It's all I get out before there's a blast of pain in the back of my head.

I regain consciousness to find my hands tied tightly behind my back, rope biting into my wrists, a pounding in my head from where I was hit, my t-shirt rucked up, and my skin stinging where I was presumably dragged across the rough ground. What's worse, someone is taking my pants off and starting to drag my underwear down.

No. Such actions mean whoever it is only has one intention. I move fast. With my jeans bunched around my ankles, effectively immobilising my legs, I've only one weapon in my armoury. I throw my body forward and crack my head against his.

"Fucking bitch," he yells out, and I get a back hander around my face. I freeze as I recognise the voice, my heart beating fast, my fear overcoming the triple sources of pain in my head.

"Pete, what the fuck are you doing?" My words sound shaky, even to myself. *How is he even here? I thought the police were going to arrest him and, this time, keep in him jail.* "Pete, let me go and we won't say anything about this." My eyes flick wildly around, but he's dragged me to the rear of the construction site, and there's nobody around. As I speak I'm desperately kicking at my jeans. I can't loosen the rope binding, me and without the use of my hands, I can't pull them back up, so my best option is to get them off my feet, so I can try to escape. Using one foot, I push my shoe off the other.

"You've made my life hell," he screams at me. "Took a few days for the lawyer to work his magic and set me free. You ever been held in a cell?" He pauses, but I don't respond, too busy concentrating on getting free. For some reason he sits back on his haunches and watches me.

One shoe gone, now for the other. Then just one last kick and I'll be able to run.

"You mucked up all my plans, Darcy. My father's mad at me. You owe me for all the fucking shit you pulled." Suddenly he leans forward, and I can smell his rancid breath. It's as if he's gone feral. "You know what those biker scum did to me? Half-killed me is what. And to top it off, you got me arrested again."

"Pete…" I try to reason with him, keeping him focused on my words and not what I'm doing with my feet. "You hit me, hurt me. Broke in and tried to rape me. What did you expect me to do?"

"You upset all my plans, Darcy. You were meant to fall for me. I'm a good-looking man, you shouldn't have been able to resist. You asked me to move in, thought I had it sorted then. But then you just flirted with me, tempted me, but never gave in."

"I helped you out when you were homeless after that fire burned your house."

He laughs. "Set that up well, didn't I? Set fire to the house, and all I needed to do was come staggering out covered in soot and coughing. Was an easy in with you."

What? "What an earth did you want an in with me for?" I've enough self-confidence to know I wouldn't crack a mirror if I looked into it, but I'd be kidding myself to think I've got the face or figure of a model.

"Plan was, we'd start fucking. Then you'd take me to meet your folks…"

"Whoa. Stop right there. That would never have happened. And why the hell would you want to meet my parents?"

"It's your father, of course."

Good luck trying to speak to him. But despite the negative reaction I know he'd get, I can't understand what he means.

Play him along. "Ok, Pete. Let me up, I'll drive home and get cleaned up. Come around tomorrow, and I'll take you to see my father."

He seems to be having an internal battle with himself. He rocks back and forth, his hand going to his face, and suddenly his eyes blaze with the look of a madman. "You're trying to fool me again. If I let you go, you'll set the bikers and the police on me again."

"I won't, Pete. Look, if it's so important you meet my father…" But something in his expression tells me I'm losing him.

His next words prove I'm right. "You ruined my plans," he tells me again. "And never let me into your bed. Caused me a fuckload of trouble. You should have been grateful that someone like me even looked twice at you."

Someone like him?

I'd come around half naked. He can only intend one thing, and I'm not going to let him have his way. He's still talking, rationalising his behaviour, but I'm not listening. Whatever reasons he had for what he did aren't important now. Escape, however, is. I lurch to my feet and start running, quickly realising it's harder with my hands trapped behind me, in bare feet over uneven ground. As I hear him coming after me, I put on an extra spurt, seeing the outline of a warehouse, knowing he'll easily outrun me, wanting to find somewhere to hide and hopefully outwit him.

The place is under construction, the doorway wide open, and I rush inside, quickly trying to see by the moonlight something I can hide behind, ignoring my feet cut raw by the hard ground. There's a dry wall partition—that will have to do for now.

Racing behind it, I find the skeleton of offices, and stub my toe hard on a metal tool box presumably left behind for workers to return to the next day. The shock makes me gasp.

"I know you're here. There's no escape." He's using a sing-song voice, which makes me think again that he's probably high on something. Wondering why I hadn't noticed when he'd lived with me, knowing now it explains why one minute he was quite normal and even pleasant company, and the next violent and mean.

He knows where I am. Somehow, I've got to get back behind him, go in the direction that he doesn't expect. Self-conscious I'm running around half-naked, I wriggle, trying to shrug my tee down as far as it will go, and then, keeping my back pressed against the wall, start to inch my way to the other end of the newly built room. He comes into sight, looking in front of him, not to the side, but what I see in his hand makes me go cold. *He's got a gun.*

Is he going to shoot me? If I don't have much chance of outrunning him, it's impossible to outrun a bullet.

"Come out. You know what I want. Stop trying to fight me, and I'll make it good for you."

Give in? Never. Hardly daring to breathe, I wait for him to move on, but he's slow, cautious, obviously listening out for the faintest of sounds. I focus on the weapon he's holding, and momentarily the thought being dead might be preferable than being in his hands pops into my head.

I don't know what gives me away, maybe my heart is beating too loudly in my chest, but suddenly he's spinning and looking straight at me. Instinct kicks in, and I turn and prepare to run.

"Stop! I'll shoot." His command and promise make me falter. "Don't think you can outrun a bullet, precious. But I'm game if you want to give it a try." He shrugs. "You don't need both feet working to fuck."

What? What's he talking about? Can he follow through? It's dark, I could weave back and forth. *How good a shot is he? Can he hit a moving target?*

I don't ask it aloud, but it seems he's able to read my mind. "Pop taught me to shoot when I was a boy. Used to take me hunting. I can hit anything, moving or not. Now," his hand goes to his crotch and my eyes follow his movement, "seeing you again is making me hard." He rubs himself through the material. "Ain't no one going to be saving you this time. No bikers charging to your rescue. It's just you and me tonight. I don't really much mind either way, and I promise you, I'd enjoy the hunt. But if you don't want to make things worse for yourself, you'll come to me now."

He's going to rape me. I can't physically fight him, not with my hands fastened behind my back and that gun in his. The only weapons I have to use are words.

"You won't get away with this. They'll know it's you." If he touches me, they'll be some transfer at least.

"I'll take my chances. A girl on her own in the middle of the night. It will only be your word against mine. And what's to say it wouldn't be worth it?"

He's mad. Totally mad.

"Of course my old man will help me out."

This is the second time he's mentioned his father. *Just who is he?* As he'd never spoken about his family before, I'd assumed he hadn't got any. *Who did I get myself involved with? Is he going to kill me?* I vow to fight him, to scratch him with my fingernails somehow, even if it will be hard with my hands tied behind my back. If he leaves me alive he'll know I'll be talking. If I'm dead, I want clues to be left to show what he's done.

Goosebumps come up all over my skin, and my palms feel sweaty. I've never been this scared, even when facing with the worst of the fires I've seen. *But I tackle them on my terms.* This situation is beyond my control.

Run. That's all I can do. Wondering if I've distracted him enough, I set off.

He laughs. "I'll even give you a head start."

Again, without the use of my hands I'm unbalanced, almost bouncing off walls left and right in the newly constructed corridor, trying to ignore the splinters and rough ground under my feet. It's only seconds before I hear the sound of heavy footsteps behind me. *I'm fit. I can do this.* I see stars above as I emerge into the light, and now on open ground speed up, guessing the direction where my car might be. I might not be able to get in and drive, but if I can make my way around to the entrance I can run out onto the road…

I hear a muffled pop and go down heavily on my knees, rolling in agony as blazing pain shoots up my right leg. *He's shot me in the calf.* As the moon comes out from behind a cloud, I watch him walk up. I shuffle back, crab-like, trying to ignore the agonizing wound in my leg. He doesn't even bother to run, each pace of his bringing him closer, however fast I try to drag myself away.

I watch as his hands go to his fly and starts to undo the zip.

"Pete. You don't want to do this. You said you don't want to go back to jail. Just let me go and I'll say the gun went off by accident."

He grins that evil grin again, and I wonder what I saw in him to even let him enter my house. There's certainly nothing that would persuade me to now. "My father's got connections. I won't be going to jail."

Oh yes you will. If I make it the last thing I do. Even if it's only evidence on my body they'll find.

Trying to keep the shaking out of my voice, I try to reason with him. "You're just compounding your crime, even being here. I took a restraining order out…"

"Yes, you did. Think a piece of paper was going to keep me away?"

Well, it obviously didn't. I try again. "Pete, what do you want? What are you hoping to get out of this? You said you wanted to meet my father…" Then my brow creases. *He'd said he and his father had it all planned.* "What is this all about, Pete?"

"You played into my hands, giving me a room when I told you I needed it. In time we would have progressed to a relationship if that fucking biker hadn't interfered." I'm shaking my head, but he hasn't finished. "It was no hardship, I was quite happy to think of getting into your cunt, such a sweet, tempting place. I started to crave it, and not just for business. And now it's not for you to decide. You can't keep me away from what I want."

My eyes open wide as certain words hit chords with me. Again I shake my head as I don't understand. "What do you mean, not just for business? What the hell are you talking about? What do you want from me?" Thinking quickly, I ask, "What was your plan? Maybe I can still help?"

"Too late for that, sweetheart. Now I'm just going to be taking what I should have had all along if you weren't so tight-assed. You're a cold-hearted bitch."

He's still advancing, and my brain goes from trying to work out what all of this means to trying to evade his unwanted attention. The moonlight casting him in silhouette makes him look evil, and that look of hunger in his eyes….

"Please don't rape me."

"Begging?" He drops to his knees. "Oh, I do like to hear a woman beg."

Just give in and let him. Close my eyes and pretend it's Peg. Peg, who's taught me what should happen between the sheets. But there's no sheets tonight, not even a bed, just the cold, hard ground of the construction site.

Could I let him take me? Maybe that's all he wants, and he'll let me live. I can't fight with my hands behind my back, can't run with an injured leg. What choice have I got? Could I pretend? *Flirt with him. Encourage him. Lead him on.* Even as I think it, I know I can't. It's not even that I'm remaining loyal to the man who at this moment probably hates me, it's that I can't bear the thought of Pete's hands touching my skin, moving over the parts which, even now, still belong to another man.

Bile rises in my throat. I swallow it back down, then wonder if puking might put him off. But I doubt it. If he's willing to fuck me when I'm bleeding and in pain, a little vomit would probably do nothing to save me.

He's taken out his cock, smoothing his hands up and down it. *It's going to happen. How can I stop it?* Make him shoot me again. The sound of the gun shot might get someone to call the police. But while I'm no expert, the pop that it made when he fired at my leg shows it's fitted with a silencer. If he shoots me a second time, I could be saying goodbye to my life, and certainly to my job if I end up disabled.

Why the fuck is being a firefighter so important?

Suddenly I realise it's not. Especially if I'm going to die tonight.

I lunge to my feet, trying my right leg, which just bears my weight, and try to run again. He was right. He's fast. A muffled shot and my left foot feels like it's blown to pieces. As my legs shoot out from under me, I crash heavily to the floor in unbelievable pain.

As I lie in agony, he starts to do a strip tease. We're out in the open on a building site, and as he takes off his clothes and carefully folds them, "Don't want blood on me, do I?" he says conversationally. When he removes his jeans, his cock bounces up as though happy to see an unwilling target. The ground feels sticky beneath me, and the metallic smell of blood seems to be turning him on, his breathing quickening as he tugs at his dick.

He makes a move toward me, then stalls and picks up his jeans, taking something out of the pocket. I watch in horror as he opens it up and pulls on a condom.

"Pete. No. Don't." I don't even recognise my own voice. "Don't do this. Please. Look, perhaps I was hasty. Let me up and we'll talk. I'm sorry I mucked up your plan. Tell me what it is, maybe I can help you…" Words are spilling out of my mouth without me knowing what I'm saying. I'll say, do, anything to get him to stop. I tug uselessly at the ropes encircling my wrists, ignoring that they're cutting my skin, and try to get my useless legs to move, but all I can do is to roll like a slug. "You want to meet my father, I'll introduce you."

But he doesn't pause, doesn't stop, and doesn't make conversation. He kneels then crawls toward me, pulling me onto my back and wrenching my legs open. "You know," he starts, "you've been spreading your legs for a biker. Don't think I don't know. Now I'm taking what should have been mine." Without a care for my wounds, he pulls my knees up to give himself easy access. Then he starts.

Tears flow down my cheeks, my humiliation complete. All the reasons I bailed on Peg now seem invalid. Instead of being raped out in the open, I could have been in his safe arms had I not put so much importance on my job and been so adamant I didn't need a man to protect me.

Pete's come armed with three condoms. With periods of rest while he seems content to sit watching me bleeding, yanking on his dick to get himself hard again, I lose track of the time. I don't know how long it takes, but he uses them all.

He's rough. He's hurt me.

At last sated, he puts back on his clothes, and I watch in disbelief as he's almost business like in the way he ties the condoms and pockets them. When he points the gun at me I close my eyes and wait for the end.

"Your cunt's one of the best I've ever had, precious. Shame we won't be doing this again." He places the barrel of the gun to my forehead, and I close my eyes and wait, wondering if I'll hear the final shot, whether there'll be any pain. Then he laughs, a humourless manic sound, and the gun moves away.

I open my eyes. *Has he had second thoughts?* But he's not going to be merciful today. He takes another step back and gives me a wink before taking aim. "Tell you what, I'll give you a chance. If you survive, I'll be back for you again. If not," he shrugs, "there's a certain irony in leaving you here."

The bullet tears through my stomach, the shock making me pass out. Sometime later I come round, wishing he'd shot me in the head after all. At least I wouldn't be feeling such incredible agony. My stomach feels like someone's probing it with a red-hot poker, and I'm lying on the ground made sticky by my own blood.

I'm too weak and woozy, unable to move to try to get help. Turning my head, I look at the sky. Dawn is breaking. *How long until the construction workers turn up? Are they even working here today?* One thing's for certain, no one's going to bother looking for me. I'm not due back on shift for at least thirty-six hours.

CHAPTER 27

Peg

I step into church with Wraith's words going around my head. As he'd reminded me, over two years ago when Sophie first came to the compound, they had things to work out. At first Wraith had done just what I had, stormed off and drunk himself into a stupor. That day, I'd been the one to find him and had taken the time to give him some advice. Same as he's just given to me. *Talk to her.*

Now, as I see the VP chatting to Blade, looking as happy as only a man can with a great old lady and child behind him, I realise it's time to take my own counsel, go to her and listen calmly to what she has to say. Any objection to our relationship I'm certain I'll be able to negate or overcome in one way or another. She's far too important not to fight for. Any decision she made while exhausted can surely be surmounted. Having got my head on straight, after church I'll go hear her out.

Happier now I've decided on positive action, I turn my mind to another subject. Whether there's something we can do for Ma.

As I walk up to my seat at the left hand of the prez, Wraith seated opposite, pauses his conversation, and gives me a pointed look, one brow lifted. As I raise my chin toward him, he gives a quick nod, interpreting correctly that I'm going to follow his advice.

Prez comes in and takes his place at the head of the table. His hand sweeps down his face as he looks around, his eyes narrowing on me for a second, before passing on by. Then he pauses. "Joker, Lady. Thanks for watching out last night."

Stifling a yawn with his hand, Joker replies, "No problem, Prez."

"The fire's completely out, I take it?"

"Bit late to ask, ain't it, Peg?" As prez raises his eyebrow it seems Wraith wasn't the only one who'd noticed I'd been missing.

I feel chastised, having neglected my role in the club while I went on my bender. "Point taken." I jerk my chin at the prez.

Prez looks around the table again. "The firefighters are moppin' up, they'll be stayin' for a while, makin' sure everything's safe. And," he casts another look at me, "we've got most of the compound cleaned up." Now it's me who raises an eyebrow, but Prez shakes his head. "Not your woman's crew, Peg. A fresh lot."

Viper raises his hand. "Prez, got word out to our boys first thing this morning. Stopped them going to the construction site. They're out there now repairin' the asphalt on the track."

"Anyone heard from Heart?" Joker asks.

"Yeah, he got to the hospital no problem," Rock informs us. "Babies and Marcia all doing good."

"The girls want to go visit," Wraith observes.

"Shouldn't be a problem. Sam's been bendin' my ear about going."

Prez is just finishing up when I interrupt him. "Can I ask something?" At his raised chin, I continue. "Does anyone know what happened to Ma's house?"

Beef nods. "Spoke to a firefighter. He said they did their best to protect the property, but most of it burned. It's uninhabitable."

"I'd like to know how much damage was done."

"What you thinkin', Peg?"

"I was wonderin' whether it was possible to rebuild it. She's gutted, it's gone. It was her family home."

Bullet nods at me. "I don't mind going over to take a look. If it's feasible, we can get some men on it." He laughs. "Never thought I'd say this, but I've come like the old girl."

"You didn't get told off for lightin' a smoke," Slick complains. "I wasn't even in the clubhouse. Just standin' outside."

Beef humps his hips forward and back. "Thought you were giving up to give your swimmers a chance."

He shouldn't have made that allusion to Ella, Slick's old lady, not getting pregnant yet while sitting next to the man he's teasing. I wince at the heavy slap he receives to the back of his head.

"Ma told me to take my shoes off before walkin' into the clubroom. Because they were covered in mud and shit. 'Course they fuckin' were. We've been fightin' a fire. What she think we'd been doing?" Rock frowns. "And we've got the prospect to clean that shit up."

Hyde can't hide his grin. Yeah, it wasn't so long ago he'd been stuck with that job.

Dollar's looking thoughtful. "Even if we can save her house, is it right that she goes back to it? She's what, getting on for ninety?"

"Her granddaughter seems happy enough to stay with her." I shoot a look at Hyde, who's looking anywhere but at me at this point.

"Which I suppose brings us to how long they'll be stayin' here for." Prez pinches the bridge of his nose. "Now they can get out, there's no need for us to give them hospitality."

"And no reason why not," Wraith drops in. "We've got the space. We've got the house we keep vacant for visiting officers at the top of the compound. And we've been doing up more blocs."

Dollar nods across to Viper. "We're ahead on the warehouse construction. Won't take that long if we've get the whole crew here. They can easily put in shit that she needs."

Viper's looking thoughtful, as though running things through in his head. "Yeah, could spare them a day or so."

With their construction crew on site, things should move fairly fast.

Prez looks around. "Hold your horses, Viper. Anyone against offerin' Ma and Sarah a place to stay temporarily?"

We all look at each other, but there's nothing more than a few shrugs or shakes of a head.

"Okay. Peg, you seem in with the old lady. Want to make them the offer?"

"Sure, Prez." I'll do that and then I'm out of here. I'm going to see my own old lady, and she sure isn't one like Ma.

At last, Drummer bangs the gavel the final time and I'm free to go.

The track down to the road is still covered with debris from the fire, and the asphalt has melted in parts, so I'm forced to take the Jeep instead of my bike. As I slowly make my way down, I pass Dollar and Viper's construction crew, who've already made a good start on clearing the worst of the wreckage. Driving, a smile comes to my face. Ma had been over the moon when I'd told her she could stay—not that she put it in those words, of course. No, what she actually said was she supposed she'd have to, as she'd got nowhere else to go, and grumbled about the state of the clubhouse. But the light that came into her watery eyes showed the relief that she felt.

She's probably enjoying herself more than she has for years. So many of us 'boys', as she calls us, to bully and order around.

I'm already quite fond of the old girl myself. Maybe it's because she's as grumpy as I can be myself.

It's late afternoon by the time I draw up at Darcy's house, but her car's not on the driveway. The last thing I expected was that she wouldn't be here, having spent the journey over gearing myself up, thinking I'll listen, then, after finding out whatever's bothering her, will come up with a way around it. Having found her, I'm not going to let her get away.

While that might sound a bit stalker like, even to myself, I'd never do anything to hurt her. If she's really got a good reason, I will put her needs first. She means too much for me to force her into a life she doesn't want. Then the corners of my mouth turn up. Who am I kidding? She's such a strong person, I doubt anyone could ever force her to do something she wouldn't want to.

But she's not here. I settle back to wait, expecting her shift won't start until the next morning at the earliest, so she's bound to be home tonight. *Maybe she's shopping.* Whatever she's doing, and however long it takes, I'll be here when she gets back. Not letting her slip through my fingers again.

Leaning my head back on the headrest, feeling a bit like a teenager turning up at a parents' home to take their daughter on a first date, I'm as nervous as hell as I wait.

My phone rings, and I take it out of my pocket. "Yo, Viper."

"Peg. You've got to get to the hospital."

I sit up straight. "What's happened? Who…?"

"It's not one of us, Brother. It's Darcy. Fuck, I'm sorry man. If we'd not pulled the men today…"

"What the fuck's happened?"

"The security guard… I'm gonna fuckin' have his balls for this…"

I thump the steering wheel with the hand not holding the phone. "Just spit it out."

"He was late doing his rounds, didn't go around the back of the site until just now. He found Darcy... She's been shot."

I draw in a breath, and then stop breathing. "She alive?" I whisper.

"Just. Shot multiple times. And Peg? She was mostly naked."

Jesus. I sit, stunned. My heart feels like it's stopped beating. For a moment I can't move, can't speak, can't draw air into my lungs.

"Peg?"

Then everything comes crashing back into life as I hear traffic sounds again and the rushing of blood through my veins.

"I'm on my way."

I start the Jeep and pull out onto the road, knowing I'm going to be speeding to be by her side. *She's in a bad way.* Is she already dying or dead? I can't lose her now, there's no fucking way I'm going to let her go.

Worried as hell about what I'm going to find, I carelessly park and leave the Jeep, not bothering to lock it. Racing inside, I push past people waiting and demand to be told where she is.

The sympathetic glance I'm given does nothing to ease my concern, as I'm told she's in surgery, and where to wait. A man in a uniform I recognise as one of Viper and Bullet's security guards comes over to me. He's holding a cap and wringing it between his hands.

"I'm the one who found her."

My fists clench.

"I'm sorry, man. No one was working today, everything was quiet. The cameras don't cover that area. I toured the warehouse, saw all the tools were okay and nothing touched. Didn't do a proper patrol until later."

I try to control my temper. "How was she when you eventually did do your fuckin' job and found her?"

He takes the seat by my side. A dangerous position. While I've got a rein on my rage now, if I find she died because of his incompetence, he's only got hours, maybe no more than minutes, left to breathe.

"She's been shot in both legs. And," he flicks his eyes to mine, then just as quickly away, "in the stomach."

Fuck! I fold over, finding it hard to breathe as I digest that bit of news. That's one of the worst places to take a bullet. Too many people die from wounds like that.

The security guard continues, as if reliving his ordeal. *His fucking ordeal?*

"I called 911. The operator kept me on the phone. I was describing her symptoms. I watched her breathing, her chest was rising and falling, and then it fucking stopped."

He almost chokes on a sob. "The medics arrived and took over. Somehow got her breathing again… When they moved her, you could see she'd lost so much blood." He breaks off and looks at me. "I only knew who she was because one of the paramedics recognised her. Called it in to Viper and found she's one of yours. I'm so sorry, man. I'm assuming she's your old lady."

"She is," I say tersely. This man watched her die? If she'd been found earlier… "What have they said? What are her chances?" I grit my teeth as I wait to receive information I don't think I can bear to be given.

"I don't know. She's in surgery now." He turns, and this time looks straight at me. Tears running down his cheeks. "Whatever you want to do to me, man. I deserve it. I should have gone out back before."

There'll be time to deliver retribution later. I've never been so scared in my life as I am right at this moment. I'm feeling helpless, knowing there's nothing I can do but sit here and wait.

The door bursts open, a mixture of firefighters and bikers. The security guard fades away as though he only waited to hand the responsibility of her over to me, and now I have to give the only news I have, and none of it is good.

We can do nothing but sit and wait.

Viper is one of the last to arrive. "They found her car," he announces. "She must have pulled up in the construction site. Fuck knows why or how." He looks around. "Where's Bob?"

My eyes crease in confusion.

"Bob, the guard who should have been doing his fuckin' rounds."

It's only then I notice he's left, and from the look on Viper's face, it seems he would have gone after some payback now.

Prez glances up at him and shakes his head. "Viper, put a hold on it. First thing is to make sure she's alright."

But I've got a terrible feeling in my gut that she'll never be alright again.

A shadow falls over me. Looking up, I see it's Truck. He's got stitches in a cut above his eye. "I was following her home last night. I go the same route. Some fucker overtook me, cut in and made me swerve into a lamp post, then he took off pretty fast going the same way Flash was."

My eyes sharpen. "The same man?"

"Look, I've been thinking about it. Only thing that makes sense is that he deliberately got me out of the way. She was tired, we all were. If she'd seen me crash, she would have stopped. If she hadn't noticed, she'd just have kept driving, and was probably still thinking it was me behind her. He might have got her to pull off the road, and she'd have done it, thinking it was me."

It's the only thing that makes sense. A woman like Darcy would never put herself at risk and stop somewhere isolated unless she thought she knew who was following her. She made sure to lock her car and keep her windows drawn up that day I first met her.

"I'd put money on it being that fucker, Pete." Truck's only voicing my thoughts. He leans down and speaks into my ear. "If you're going after him, well, I'd like to get some hits in too. Make sure he can never hurt her again."

He's surprised me. Slowly I nod. Pete's the obvious person, but what has he got to gain from shooting her and leaving her for dead? *But he'd tried to force himself on her before.* And from her lack of clothing when found, I have to deal with the possibility she was raped.

"Did you get a look at who hit you? Was it him?"

Truck sighs loudly. "Fucker had his lights on full when he rammed me. And then sped off fast." His hand touches his wound. "Dazed me a bit. Sorry, Peg, I didn't see a thing."

CHAPTER 28

Darcy

I know that I'm dying, but try to hold on, as I want the man who abused me named and caught. Dawn has come and gone, and the last time I was conscious the sun was high above. I'd expected the construction workers to come on the job early this morning, but no one's arrived. My arms have gone completely numb, and my mouth is dry as I dehydrate in the sun. Slowly I'm giving up hope that anyone will find me.

Peg. I've no right to long for him after how I'd dismissed him, but even my pain doesn't stop me wishing I could see him one last time, and feel his strong, safe arms around me. Then I realise he's going to take this hard, and if I could, I'd do anything to prevent him knowing what happened to me. A strong woman brought low by a man and violated in such a way that it would be hard for someone so possessive like Peg to handle. While I had thought it best that I leave him, I didn't want it to be this way. It's not fair on anyone to know the woman they care about was abused and left alone to die.

In the past hours I've gone through every emotion from anger to despair, and now I've hit rock bottom again.

My body has reached the end of its tolerance, and I feel cold rather than the pain or even the heat of the blazing sun.

Am I dreaming? I can hear a voice speaking. But I can't reply, or even move. But perhaps I'm not dying alone. I've no strength, can't talk, but as I take my last breath, in my head I'm saying goodbye.

I'm floating in a cosy cocoon. *Is this what death's like?* I think people are around me. *Angels or devils. Which way will I have gone?* But isn't that Peg's voice? It must be a dream. *Is there life on the other side?* I strain to hear what people are saying—if there's a heaven and hell, I want to know where I'm heading.

Then the pain registers. Not as bad as it was before, but enough to make me uncomfortable. *It must be hell. Surely in heaven I wouldn't feel anything?* Then there's a strange numbing sensation spreads through my veins, and soon my brain registers nothing at all.

Now I can hear a machine's beeping, a regular annoying sound. It's rhythmic beeps keeping pace with my breathing. My breathing. I'm taking air into lungs I never expected to work again. Experimentally I try a deeper breath—it hurts—but my muscles seem to obey my brain. The beeping speeds up as I struggle to open my eyes, but the light's too harsh, and I have to close them.

"Flash? Darcy?" An anxious voice sounds close to my ear. "Darcy, I'm here, darlin'."

I try to fight to confirm with my eyes that it's Peg talking and not my imagination, but the fog pulls me under once again.

Next time I awake I feel stronger, and this time my eyelids pull all the way back, blinking furiously in the glare from the room. Turning my head to the side, I see Peg sleeping right next to me, leaning on the bed, his head on his hands, which are clasped around one of mine.

"Peg?" My voice sounds hoarse and rusty.

He jumps with a start and stares at me. As I never expected to see anyone mortal again, he's got to be the most beautiful sight in the world. His hand comes out to stroke my cheek. "You're gonna be fine, Darcy."

He reaches up to press a button, and within minutes the room is filled. There are two nurses checking everything they can possibly monitor, and a doctor looking cheerful as he sees me awake.

"What?" I stammer out.

He interprets my one word correctly. "You're going to make it, Darcy. You were lucky, the bullet to your stomach missed everything vital. You'll be sore, as it damaged a muscle, but help got to you just in time. You've got a tear in your calf muscle, but like the wound on your foot, the bullet went straight through. You've lost so much blood you'll feel weak for a while, but with time you'll make a full recovery."

I try to process his words, and then remember what else Pete did and shudder.

The doctor continues, clearly trying to put my mind at rest. "The bullet from your stomach showed the gun was a twenty-two calibre, so your wounds could have been worse. Your foot will need time to heal, as there's a fracture to the bone, but you should be able to walk normally again. Can't deny you gave everyone a scare, and if you hadn't been found when you had, it would be a different story. But you were, you're here, and you're safe."

Experimentally I move my arms. My shoulders are stiff, and bandages circle my wrists. The doctor watches me carefully and gives me a moment to take everything in as one of the nurses gives me an ice cube to suck. Feeling as sore as I do, it's hard to believe I'll recover. I try to concentrate as the nurse shows me how to work the pain pump, and then explains the dressings need to be changed.

Peg's been waiting in the corner, standing out of the way, but now he's being dismissed while they get me cleaned up. I can tell by his face that he doesn't want to leave me, but his chin lift to me promises he'll be back.

When he's gone, the tears start flowing.

"Hey…" The doctor comes and sits on the bed, taking my hand in his own. "You're going to be fine, Darcy. Some recovery time, yeah? Can't promise you'll be without pain for a while, but you're alive, and that's the main thing, okay?"

I look into his kind eyes and swallow. Then my words come out as a sob. "I was raped." I might be able to physically heal, but mentally? "Overpowered and raped," I repeat.

The doctor doesn't flinch. "I know that. We examined you when you came in. I've seen the bruising and bite marks all over your body." He nods towards the drip running into the back of my hand. "The antibiotics are for that as well." His eyes give me a look of concern. "When you're feeling stronger you should talk to a counsellor."

Talk to someone? I shake my head, not sure I want to speak to someone and tell them what Pete had done.

"The police will want to speak to you as soon as you're up to it."

"I don't want to see *anyone* yet." I've got a lot to come to terms with, and the list of people I don't want to see includes Peg. "Peg…" At his lack of understanding, I flick my eyes toward the door. "The man who was here. Ronnie Rinter."

"He's not left your side, Darcy. He told us he was your fiancé, so we let him stay." His eyes narrow. "Is he not someone close to you?" He laughs sharply. "Had to let him in before he broke down the door. He was frantic to see you."

"I can't talk to him." I know I must have worried him, I could see that in his eyes. But if it's even possible, first I've got to come to terms with what Pete did to me. If I'm not strong enough to cope with it, how could I take Peg's reaction to knowing I'd been raped? Would he be able to keep it together? I remember how I longed for him when I lay alone, hurt and thinking I was going to die, how all the reasons I'd pushed him away seemed insignificant. But now, perhaps, it would be him that walks, unable to think of another man taking what he considered was his. I'm scared. Too scared to see him. Too scared to see the disgust in his eyes, when I'm filled disgusted myself.

"You prefer someone else to visit with you?" Again, the doctor laughs as he interrupts my thoughts. "There's a waiting room full of people, firefighters and bikers of all people."

I give a weak shake of my head and repeat, "I don't want to see anyone yet." *I can't.*

I was raped. Violated. Pete was so rough, more like an animal than a human being. *And he left marks.* I need to get right with that in my own head before talking with people who'll either try to ignore it or give me platitudes that everything will be alright, when I can't see a way forward.

I was going to split up with Peg. But my reasons seem so ridiculous now. Why were they? Oh yeah, because a relationship with him might interfere with my job. But even if I heal, will I still be able to be a firefighter? Will my co-workers ever look at me in the same way? Will this have made them realise what I'd worked hard to disguise, that I'm a weak female trying to live in a man's world?

What was the second reason? That Peg would have suffocated me. But if I'd let him look after me, protect me, I wouldn't be in this hospital bed.

Huh, I don't even know why I'm worrying about that, it's the last thing that matters. I feel so dirty I can't imagine a time when I'd want him, or anyone, to touch me intimately again. In fact, I'd like to wipe out the entire male race, anything with a dick. While I know that's not fair, it was Pete who did this, no one else, it doesn't stop my skin crawling at the thought of a man's hands on me. Any man. Even Peg's. I never want to be at the mercy of a man again, never again want to feel overpowered.

I'm destroyed. *I'd like to cut off Pete's dick.*

I don't want to see him ever again, even for that. Just the thought of looking at him over a court room fills me with horror, knowing he'd have a smirk on his face reckoning his fancy lawyers would help him get off. Promising retribution if they succeeded. The machine beeps speed up as I remember his face just before he shot me and left me for dead, and the promise he'd made — if I survived, he would be back.

What I wouldn't do to wipe yesterday from my mind. *But it's not possible.* Unless Pete's locked up, I'll always be looking over my shoulder.

Not if you're with Peg, my traitorous mind suggests. No, that would be using him like a crutch. I can't do that to him. I doubt he'd be interested in a platonic relationship. The thought of even him looking at me, stroking his cock, brings back memories of Pete. *All men are alike.* No, they're not.

"Darcy." An even-sounding voice gets my attention. I look up to see a man I know is called Ralph. He's a paramedic on another crew that I've bumped into on a few shouts. He's not looking at me like a friend, but as a medic. "Open your eyes, Flash. Are you in pain?"

I do, and see him watching the monitors, his hand on the pulse in my wrist. He's looking concerned. "How did you get in here? I said no visitors."

"I have my ways." He winks, and leans over, looking carefully into my eyes. "You not been pumping the pain meds lately? Or has your heartrate increased because you're getting lost in your head?"

His business like, yet still sympathetic bedside manner helps me concentrate on steadying my breathing. A couple of minutes later, he eyes the monitor again. "That's better. You were headed for a panic attack there." He pauses to explain why he's here. "I was the paramedic who was first on the scene. Had to come in and see with my eyes you're alright. You'd stopped breathing, Flash." As his eyes fill with pain, I feel sorry that I put him through that. *No, I didn't. Pete did.*

But it doesn't stop me apologising. "I'm sorry, Ralph. You shouldn't have had to see me that way." I try moving my arm and reach out to touch his hand briefly. "Thank you for bringing me back." Though there's a little voice inside saying if he hadn't, I wouldn't be dealing with what I am now. Would death have been easier?

"There's no need to thank me. I'm just glad I was able to do my job." He straightens stiffly. "And, Flash, the police are outside waiting to speak to you."

I turn my head away. "I can't talk to them now."

"Listen to me, Flash. I don't want a call to pick up anyone else the way I found you. Christ, girl, I thought you'd gone, and for a moment there, you had. This guy needs to be caught, and caught fast. He's got away with…with hurting you." He tactfully avoids referring to my obvious rape. "Now he's got a taste he might do it again. Fuck, you might not even have been his first. Help them to catch him."

He's right. But seeing how quickly Pete got out of jail last time, I've started to have grave doubts in our legal system. But with a slow nod, I agree he can let them in, Pete has to be stopped. *Has he tried something like this before?* It was luck, not judgement, that I'm not dying a slow, painful death. If the bullet in my stomach had been an inch over, I wouldn't have had a chance. It's the second time Pete nearly killed me. *Next time he'll probably succeed.*

Ralph doesn't waste time showing the cops in, and soon his place by my bed is taken by a female detective and, who I assume, is her male partner, neither of whom I recognise. She pulls up a chair and looks on at me sympathetically. *Almost textbook so far. Let the female take the lead in a case of sexual abuse.*

After a period of silence, during which she seems to catalogue my injuries with her eyes, she asks me to tell her what happened.

I tell her everything I remember, which unfortunately is too much. I start by saying how I'd thought it had been another crew member behind me, and I'd pulled off the road. Then Pete overpowered me, raped me, and shot me. I spend a few minutes taking them through everything that he did.

She looks pointedly at my wrists. "You were tied up?"

"Yes. He pistol-whipped me or something, and when I came around my hands were roped together behind my back." An unbidden sob comes to my throat as I admit how he'd taken control. "He shot me like an animal."

"Rope." She seems almost to be ignoring me. "That's what you used?"

What? "Me? *I* didn't use it. Pete did. He trussed me up, so I couldn't move." I try to pull myself into a sitting position, but only succeed in pulling on my damaged stomach muscle and have to lie back down, gritting my teeth against the pain. "What the fuck are you suggesting? That we were playing games? And why the hell was Pete out of jail?"

"While we were waiting for you to come round, we've spoken to Mr Mercer, who you took out a restraining order against. Mr Mercer explained you like rough sex." She says it dismissively. "Said the bikers interrupted one of your games before, and you were too embarrassed to admit it. That construction site where you were picked up belongs to the Satan's Devils. Mr Mercer mentioned you were seeing one of the bikers and thought it could have been one of your sex games gone wrong."

"That's utter crap..." Suddenly, I remember Pete's strange comment about the irony of the location. He must have known who owned the site.

"And so's your story. Mr Mercer has got a cast iron alibi for yesterday evening and night. He was with his father until late."

I don't think I could open my eyes any wider. "Then they're both lying."

Her eyebrow arches. "When he left he went straight to his girlfriend's house and spent the whole night with her. She lying as well? You either convinced yourself you thought you saw him, or you're trying to accuse him of something he didn't do. Maybe to deflect attention from the bikers. There's no evidence to suggest he was there."

"He wore condoms, which he took with him."

"Oh, I agree you had sex with someone. But it could have started off consensual."

I give her an incredulous look. "The bite marks on my body? The bruises?"

"We were told you liked it rough." She repeats her earlier assertion.

Again, I try to sit up, feeling vulnerable in a prone position. I fail and have to make do with pointing down to my stomach. "How do you explain I was shot? Pretty extreme for a sex game, wouldn't you say?"

"Your foot or leg could have been accidental. The other shots when your assailant realised what he'd done. One of those bikers wouldn't hesitate to take someone out. You're playing with fire getting involved with them."

"And conveniently left me to be found on their construction site?"

She shrugs. "They pulled off their crew. Maybe so you wouldn't be found in time to be saved."

She's got it all worked out. A way to keep Pete out of it and dump bikers who no one in the city trusts, right in it. "Who's paying you?" I suddenly feel compelled to ask. "A man rapes me, shoots me, and leaves me for dead. I give you his name and you believe a false alibi without digging deeper. And you have the nerve to suggest the sex was consensual?"

I can't believe this. The detective behind her coughs. "We'll be investigating it, but from the men we've seen outside in the waiting room, you consort with the wrong types."

The memory of how gentle Peg had been with me comes into my head, and the way both men and women acted on the compound. I hadn't even seen one of the club whores with bruises or looking afraid. He couldn't be further from the truth.

"Look, Miss Cavanaugh, I know you were fighting the wild-land fire over the past few days and must have been absolutely exhausted. Maybe that made you make some wrong decisions. Now, tell us the truth and we'll go and pick up the man who hurt you. He has caused grievous bodily harm."

"I nearly died," I interrupt her. "I've already told you who did it. He must have blood on his clothes…"

"And we've been told you've got a grudge against him. You've already tried to set him before. This time," she waves at my broken body, "you went too far. Knowing how injured you are, Mr Mercer isn't going to press charges. But he's taken out a restraining order against you."

"Against me?" Due to my weakened state, my indignant scream comes out more like a squeal from a pig being slaughtered. I can't believe what she's saying.

The detective behind her coughs again. When she turns to look at him, she raises her head, he shakes his. It's obviously some kind of signal as she gets up from her seat. With one last look toward me, she says, "If you remember anything else that would be helpful, you can reach me on this number." She holds out a card, and when I make no move to take it, places it on the table beside me, wedged in between a bottle of water and a glass.

"Hang on." I find the energy to call them back. "You are going to continue to investigate this, aren't you? The bite marks for a start. You can match them to Mercer's teeth…"

She stares back at me. "I'm not going to put Mr Mercer through anymore distress, not when he's proved he couldn't have been there. But I assure you, we'll keep looking to see whether we can find any evidence. When we do, we'll be talking to the bikers again, and if it's anyone's teeth we'll be looking at, I suspect it will be some of theirs." She regains the step she took backward and is at my side once again. "Mr Mercer Senior is a very important person. It's not unlikely someone would try and get to him through his son. Think very carefully about your accusations. It seems it's becoming common to accuse a powerful man in order to get attention."

"What the ever lovin' fuck are you on?" Peg blasts through the door in time to hear the last statement. "Miss Cavanaugh has been badly hurt and you accuse her of lyin'." His eyes fall on me and soften, then harden again as he turns back to the cop. "What's your name?"

"Detective Harper."

Peg smooths his hand over his face. "If you're in the Bureau of Investigations, you probably report to Lieutenant Diaz, don't you?"

"You know him?" She sounds surprised, then smirks. "Oh yeah, well, someone in your position, I expect you do."

A nasty grin spreads across Peg's features. "Oh, you'd be surprised how I know him. He and I will be havin' words."

If I wasn't feeling so poorly, I'd laugh at the look on her face —her features battling to maintain control, while worry widens her eyes. Then I feel despair once again. Whatever sway Peg has with the lieutenant, I suspect Pete's father will have more. *Just who is Mr Mercer Senior, anyway?*

Peg pointedly holds the door open, and the police walk out. He shuts it behind them and comes over. "What the fuck, Flash-fire? What have they been sayin'?"

I'd rather not talk, but I tell him anyway. As I describe the suggestions the detective had come up with, Peg hums with rage. His reaction isn't too much different from my own.

"Darcy, I'll get Mouse onto investigatin' who this Mercer Senior is. I assure you Pete's not going to be gettin' away with it."

Weakly I raise my hand and point to the door. "They think he is."

"They don't have a fuckin' clue," Peg snarls. "You've been attacked and raped. That man had his cock near you once again, which is one time too many."

He knows. My eyes flick to his to see how he's taking it. As his eyes meet mine, I read the hurt in them, but it doesn't stop me telling him the worst. "Three times," I whisper, mentally seeing those used condoms lying on the ground and Pete carefully picking them all up.

"Oh, fuck, Darcy." Peg comes closer, and I put up my hands to ward him away.

"Peg, no. I can't. I don't want…"

He looks crushed. "You don't want me to touch you."

I turn my head so I don't have to see him, but can't block out his words.

"I don't know what to do, what to say. But just know this, nothin' you say or do is going to make me go away. You might not want me in the room with you right now, and that's okay, I'll give you space. I'll just tell you this, Darcy. I love you. And when you're ready, I'll be here."

I keep looking the other way, knowin' I'll break if I see how much he hurts.

"One thing, Darcy. I'm so fuckin' sorry."

"It's not your fault, Peg."

"It is," he contradicts in clipped tones. "We own the construction site. Viper and Bullet pulled their men off to fuckin' help clear the track to the compound. You should have been found so much earlier." His voice breaks. "I can't believe what you went through, lyin' there hurtin' and no one comin'…"

"It's not your fault, Peg," I repeat, unable to come up with anything different to say. I feel weak, I hurt and I just want him to leave.

"I love you, Darcy. I'll be here. I'm not going anywhere. Whatever's happened, we can work through this, okay? I *love* you."

Hearing the door closing, I suspect he's gone out and has at last left me alone. Which is good, I don't know how to respond to his declaration.

"Oh, hello. You must be Darcy's man. I'm Mrs Easton, a social worker. I just want a quick word with Darcy." I groan. It's someone else coming in, not Peg going out. I bite my tongue, not wanting to get into it with Peg, so don't contradict her. "Darcy, the doctor's told me about the tablet you asked for, but I wanted a word with you first to ask that you reconsider."

I realise what she's talking about, the doctor and I had discussed it. "Just tell the nurse to bring it in, please." I go to sit up and again fall back because of the pain. Peg's arm comes around me to help, and once I'm propped against the pillows, immediately pulls away. It wasn't a sexual or even affectionate touch.

"Now you need to think carefully. What might come could be a blessing…"

"I don't want to think about it." I'm adamant. I know Pete used condoms, but they're not infallible. While I'd been fighting the fire, keeping up taking the pill was the last thing on my mind. Pregnancy's probably a tiny risk, but one I don't want to take. Trust me to get a pro-life social worker visit me.

"Can you tell me exactly what you're talkin' about?" Peg's addressing Mrs Easton, there's tension in his shoulders, but any anger is directed her way.

"Well, it's lucky you're here. Miss Cavanaugh has requested the morning after pill…"

"What you fuckin' waitin' for then? Give it to her," Peg snarls.

"But, sir, if you're her man, and she's pregnant, it could be yours."

"Is she pregnant?"

I glance up to see the social worker shaking her head. "Doctor says it's too early to tell."

"Then I don't see what the problem is. If she is, whether it's mine or the motherfucker who raped her, the decision is hers. Her body, her choice. And certainly no business of yours."

The social worker looks stunned and opens her mouth as if to argue, but Peg doesn't give her a chance. "If Darcy doesn't want the slightest chance of there being a lasting reminder of what happened yesterday, then I'm right there with her. You people, I can't understand why you'd interfere with another woman's decision. Look at her." Peg takes her arm and pulls her over to me. "Just look. She was *raped*." His voice has got loud.

"What's going on in here? Nurse Johnson, have you given Miss Cavanaugh the medication I prescribed?"

Both the doctor and nurse have come in, the nurse holding a paper cup.

"No, she hasn't," Peg informs the doctor bitterly. "This woman here's given her a lecture instead."

"I was just waiting until Mrs Easton had finished." The nurse inclines her head toward the social worker.

After a sharp inhale, the doctor snatches away the paper cup in her hand and brings it over to bed. "Mrs Easton, go and wait for me in my office. Nurse Johson, can you escort her, please?" When the door closes behind them, he throws me a look of apology. "I'm sorry."

Peg takes the cup from him and gives it to me. "Your decision," he tells me as he wraps my fingers around it. I glance up at his face and can see nothing but acceptance there. I pause, wishing he wasn't there, hadn't known what I was going to do. Then I swallow the tablet.

CHAPTER 29

Peg

It can't have been easy to make the decision to take that pill, even if the chances that she was pregnant were so slim. But I agree one hundred percent with her decision. Waiting nine months to discover whether a baby was mine or that bastard's? What sane couple would want to do that?

I know she wants to be alone, and appreciate she's got a ton of things to deal with. While I'll respect her wishes for now, that in particular it's me she doesn't want to speak to, I'm not leaving her without company. Especially not when both the police and the medical staff seem to have it in for her today.

Returning to the waiting room, I update her crew, who've been waiting for hours to see her, and arrange that one of my brothers will be here later when they need to go on shift.

I know they're not going to want to hear this, but I'm so annoyed I can't keep it to myself and want others to be warned to stay close if the police come back again. Through clenched teeth I tell them what's just gone on between Flash and the cops in her room.

Slade swears as I update them. "You're fucking joking, aren't you?" One look at my face shows the captain I'm not. "Flash isn't like that."

"No, she's fucking not. She doesn't lie. She's as straight as they come." Truck's looking incensed. "And you, Peg. Might not know much about you, but I know enough to tell you wouldn't treat a woman like that."

Pinching my nose, I look up. "I'm going to find out all I can about this motherfucker, Mercer. His daddy's got some pull, and I need to find what."

Slade grimaces. "Be careful, Peg. Your lot earned the reputation you've got. Something happens to Mercer, you'd be the first place they'd look."

"Earned. As in past tense," I emphasise, my eyes shifting to his. "And don't think I haven't thought of that already. Much as I hate to say it, we're gonna have to play this straight."

"Not that I wouldn't like to see him deep underground for what he did." Slade frowns. "But his daddy sounds well connected."

"*Too* well connected," I agree.

Slade slaps me on the back, and I leave them to keep my woman company. If she doesn't want me near her for now, I'll be doing what I can for her behind the scenes. There's no dissent to my suggestion that someone will be there with her if the police come calling again. Christ, she's got enough to deal with, what with the pain in her body as well as her mind. Doesn't need more shit dumped on her.

It broke me when I thought she nearly died. During the time I was waiting for news I was trying to prepare myself for never seeing her again, I'd made a vow. If she recovers, the rest of her life I'm going to be there to protect her, and there'll be nothing she can do to stop me, even if I can't do it at her side. She's my woman, even being apart won't change that.

I'm standing in the corridor when Heart appears. "Hey, Peg. Glad you're here. Marc's heard about Darcy and wants to know how she is." He's looking tired himself. "We both want to make sure she's okay and thank her for what she did. Breaks my heart to think what's happened to her. Fuckin' hell, I could have lost both my ol' lady *and* the babies if those firefighters hadn't been around."

As he stops, I pull him in for a hug and slap his back. "But they were, and Marcia and the babies are good." I pull away, allowing him to see the hurt in my eyes. "Flash is going to recover physically, but it will take time…"

"Whatever we can do to help, just say, Peg. We've got this." Heart clasps my arm, his squeeze of support undoing me.

Suddenly it all crashes down on me, and I know I'm going to need all the support my brothers can give me. "She was raped, Heart. Fuckin' raped. She was tricked, overpowered, and left helpless. That's going to be so hard for her to deal with."

There are tears in my brother's eyes, and his look of compassion shows he'll be doing anything he can.

I step back, wiping moisture that's escaped and is leaking down my face. I clear my throat and change the subject, unable to process what's happened to my woman. "Marcia and the babies doing well?"

"All doing great. Jacob is being given extra care at the moment, but Marc and Isabel should be able to come home this weekend. We're hoping that my boy will come too."

I want that to be me, Flash bringing my baby—singular, I won't be greedy, and let's face it, I won't even know what to do with one—back to the compound. Instead I had to watch her take that fucking pill because she'd been raped. Life's so unfair at times.

"Can I see Darcy? I'd like to thank her."

"Slade's in with her now. We're not leaving her alone, Heart."

Heart nods. Out of everyone, he knows what it's like to be stuck in a hospital bed. "I'll take my turn, I'm here all the time anyway now."

I thank him. I stand, hesitating, unsure what to do, wondering whether Darcy might change her mind and let me back in to see her. After a while, Slade comes out, and Truck goes in.

Her captain comes over to me, looking downcast. "Peg, I'm sorry, man. Flash is adamant she doesn't want to see you. I've tried talking to her, but her head's in a bad place. Knocked her for six, this has. She's only just tolerating us being around. Don't think she'll be changing her mind anytime today."

I stare at the floor. If that really is the case, I'm wasting my time being here.

"She needs time to cope and to understand it wasn't her fault."

"It wasn't her fuckin' fault," I throw back, incredulously.

Slade shrugs. "She wasn't careful enough when she thought it was Truck behind her. She couldn't get herself loose. She got into whatever fucked up relationship with Mercer in the first place."

"They didn't have a relationship," I contradict, my hands fisting.

"Yeah, I know. He conned her and got himself into her house, then got fixated on her for some reason. Peg, look. You know what it's like. Something happens, and all you can think of is what you could have done to prevent it. She needs to work through that." He pauses, and as he runs his hands down his face, I realise that's exactly what I'd done when I'd lost my leg. Looked for what I could have done different to prevent the men with me dying. My hands uncurl.

Slade nods as he sees me relax. "It's harder for her. She's used to being in control. Must admit, man, I've never seen her so low. She's not in her right mind, so give her some space, yeah? One of us will be here until we go on shift. If there's any change, I'll get straight in contact with you."

He's right. She's very far from being in her right mind—no one would be, given what she's been through. I raise my chin in thanks, grateful he's brought me, at least to my senses, then with one last lingering look at the door separating me from the woman I love, leave the hospital and make my way back to the compound. If space is what she needs for now, that's what I'll give her. But not too much. As I drive I feel I'm leaving a piece of me behind, a big fucking part. My heart.

I knew when I met the right woman I'd fall hard and fast, and if I lose her I'll never find anyone to replace her. I try to convince myself I haven't lost Flash yet, that her reaction to what that bastard did to her was understandable, and that once she's feeling stronger we'll find a way to move forward. Right now, all I want to do is take her in my arms, sink my cock inside her, and remove every memory of him from her mind, though I know she's nowhere near ready for my type of cure.

At the back of my mind, I'm worried there's more to her putting distance between us than yesterday's ordeal. Something wasn't right between us before that. Those dreaded words, *we need to talk*, echo around my head. Something's spooked her, and I've no idea what it is.

It was when she went back to work.

There's a fucking car dawdling along in front of me, and my fists tighten on the steering wheel in my impatience to get past, my rage finding a target in the slow-moving driver. Finally, able to overtake, I start to wonder…she's a firefighter married to her job. Could a relationship with a biker threaten her career? Seeing Heart must have brought that to mind. Heart's woman was forbidden to him until she gave up being a cop. Surely what Darcy does is different than that? As long as she does what she's asked, what does it matter who she's with outside of work? But the coincidence of the timing makes me wonder if I could be on the right track… *I should have asked Slade.*

She's an independent woman. I'd never stop her doing anything she wants, however scared I might feel inside as she puts her life on the line every day. *But have I told her that? Does she think I want her just to keep house for me and raise my kids? Have I been too overbearing, not giving her enough space?* But it's my psyche to protect those I love. Perhaps I pushed too hard and too soon.

I slam my fist against the steering wheel again, this time with determination. If it's something I've done, I can mend it. I have to. I've taken a lifetime to find her, and I'm not giving her up without a fight.

I park the Jeep and unfold my limbs to slide out, then stretch. Fuck, how I hate driving a cage, but from the work that's already been completed on the track, next time I go out I'll be back on my bike. The endeavours of the construction workers I view with mixed feelings. Although Viper and Bullet were doing what they thought was best for the club, withdrawing their men from the construction site had almost caused the death of my woman. My gut clenches again as I think how alone she must have felt, lying injured and bleeding, feeling her life blood seeping away, not knowing if anyone was going to find her in time. Shit, on top of everything else, that must really have fucked with her head.

Give her time.

But I'm not a patient man. *I'll have to be.* I stand by the Jeep, tossing the keys in my hand. I'm not going to give up. I'm going to fight for my old lady. Yeah. That's what I'll do. Give her bit of space, then go on the attack. Resolution made, I allow myself the relief of knowing at least she's alive and still breathing, and go up to the clubhouse, making plans in my head. *I've got this.*

Immediately I take a step inside the clubroom and breathe in an enticing aroma, one which reminds me I haven't eaten all day, and which pulls my feet toward the kitchen that's already jammed with my brothers, their women, and also the sweet butts, everyone drawn by the amazing smell.

Elbowing my way in, my eyes open and, unwittingly, a smirk comes to my face when I see Ma in her wheelchair clearly directing operations, and the old ladies doing her bidding. Trays of meatloaf are emerging from the oven, Sandy and Carmen are mashing potatoes, and there's big dishes of mac and cheese and green beans. But it's the meatloaf that has my mouth watering.

The VP's hovering just inside the doorway. "Darcy going to be alright?"

I take a breath and tell him simply, "She will be." Then add more firmly as if to convince myself. "She will be."

Wraith grins at my news, then nudges me, inclining his head to what's going on inside the room. "Ma's recipe," he informs me. "Can't wait to get a fuckin' plate."

Sophie hears him. "Not long now, Mr Impatient. You'll just have to hold your bloody horses and wait." She smiles at him, then goes back to her task.

No wonder everyone's here, no one wants to miss out. When Sarah announces it's all ready, the vultures descend and start filling their plates. Me? Although I would have said food was the last thing I wanted, I'm suddenly hungry. I shovel down everything in front of me, then go back for seconds.

"Ma," I wave my loaded fork toward her, "this is the best fuckin' meatloaf I've tasted in my life."

"So it should be," she snaps back. But I see the twinkle in her eyes. "Taken me nigh on ninety years to perfect it."

"You're that old?" Ella queries.

"I'm ninety-three," Ma announces proudly. Well, I'll be fucked. I knew she was old, but that's ancient.

"She's got recipes for other dishes we'll be trying." Sophie edges past with another loaded plate for the VP. "She says her fried chicken is the best."

She would. I grin at the elderly lady who seems to have been given a new lease on life. Instead of being bedridden with only her great-granddaughter for company, she's being helped in and out of the wheelchair, and has been adopted by a new family.

"Ma," Joker calls out from somewhere at the back of the pack. "Any more left?"

"Plenty," she replies. "I know how hungry you boys can be. Had five sons myself."

Five sons? So why aren't they looking out for her? "Where are they now?" I ask, interested, wondering what sort of boys she's raised who'd leave an old woman alone.

Her eyes meet mine, and while she gazes at me steadily, I recognise hurt there. "Buried four of them already."

Well, fuck me. But I don't say a useless 'I'm sorry', comprehending sympathy wouldn't go down well. But no parent should have to put their child in the ground.

I feel a hand on my shoulder. Looking around, I see Sarah. "Thank you," she says quietly. "I've been doing what I can, but she was so lonely. Gramma needed this, *needed you.*"

Nodding in understanding, I reassure her, "Seems we've all adopted your gramma now. You both can stay as long as she wants. We'll get you sorted with proper accommodation."

Hyde comes up behind her and gets her attention, but not before she offers another heartfelt thank you to me.

My belly filled, the food seems to have sharpened my mind. I'm no longer consumed by things I have no control over, and instead want to get started on what I can. I look over to Mouse and see his plate is empty.

"Mouse, Brother. Spare a few?"

He nods and rises, and seeing Ma's glare, leans over, picks up, then goes and rinses his plate. Not wanting to be subjected to the evil eye, I do likewise, pause to thank her and the old ladies, then follow him out.

Mouse's cave reeks of marijuana, and as soon as he sits, he starts to roll a joint. Multi-tasking, he glances over his monitor. "What can I do for you, Peg?"

Taking a breath, I lay it on the line. All about Pete Mercer, and the mysterious Mercer Senior and the power he seems to have.

As I suspected, Mouse is intrigued, and immediately starts tapping the keys, his brow creased in concentration as he starts following a trail. He's doing what he likes to do best. We're lucky to have him as a brother. There's not much he can't find. When he puts his mind to it, he's one of the best. What he can't do, he's got the contacts to help.

I wait, silent, giving him space to follow his thoughts. I'm hoping for an easy, quick answer.

Mouse's fingers pause, and he throws me a contemplative glance, then looks back at his screen. "Ok, so Peter, yeah, he's got the same name as his son. Peter Mercer Senior runs a private bank. He's now the sole owner and partner."

Okay. So he's loaded. "What's the name of the bank?"

"Top Loans." Mouse lifts his finger and traces words on the screen. "Started after the big crash in 2008. Seems he invested a lot of his own money in it, and there was a partner at the time, who's since died. All the money went to the company."

"Got any bad smells to it?"

"Might well be. But the official records show it as fairly legit from what I can see. Died in a car accident along with his wife."

Convenient. My brow creases, then I look up. "I haven't heard of the bank before."

"You wouldn't have." My eyes go to Mouse's as I wait for him to explain. "I'll need Cara's help to get into his client list, but they don't provide bankin' services for the likes of you or me. You have to be rich and require a multi-million-dollar loan." Mouse lowers the lid of his laptop and peers at me over the top.

"This kind of set up stinks of being cover for a high-class loan shark."

"I'd like that list of customers." My forefinger and thumb go to the bridge of my nose. "Be interestin' to see whether he's got any judges, politicians, or high-rankin' cops on there."

"I agree. I'll keep workin' on it, okay? Could explain how his slippery son always gets out of jail."

"The police believe Mercer the younger's got a cast-iron alibi for Flash's attack. Can we find out who the girl is that apparently spent the night with him? I know for a fact she's lyin'." Darcy wouldn't get muddled up over who shot and raped her.

Mouse's eyes soften, and he gives a slow shake of his head. "Fuck. Peg, I feel for you. And yeah, I'll keep diggin' 'til I find something. That woman of yours? What she and her colleague did for Heart, means we owe her a lot."

Right place, right time and *I was only doing my job* is what Darcy would say. But we all know they went out of their way to save mother and children. Club's not going to forget that in a hurry.

CHAPTER 30

Darcy

I didn't see the social worker again after she'd given me a lecture, something for which I'm extremely grateful. I'd seen red when she asked Peg's opinion. Whatever the situation, the decision whether to rent out my body for nine months should be mine. I had been pleased when Peg agreed it was completely up to me, a side of him I hadn't expected. Oh, in the circumstances I thought he wouldn't object, raising another man's child is one thing, but not when you're effectively inviting a rapist to share part of your life. But Peg had gone further than that, saying it would be always be my choice. From such a possessive man, it came as a surprise.

Maybe I've been wrong about him? This thing between us burst into flames so fast, we didn't take the time to learn much about each other.

I'm lonely and leaning toward rethinking the decision to cut Peg out of my life. Oh, I haven't been left alone, there's always someone with me except at night when the medical staff throw them out. It's either one of my crew, or, when they're on shift, a biker's normally sitting with me. Heart's been here the most, and Marcia's come along to see me. She's brought tiny Isabel as well—Jacob's not doing as good, and is in an incubator for now, nothing serious, the new parents have been assured that it's normal with twins for one to be slightly less well developed.

Conversations are okay for a while, but those visiting me have brought in books and magazines for themselves as well as me. You can't keep talking every hour of the day, and they seem to appreciate I need time to try to work things through in my head.

"Up for a visitor?"

My eyes open wide at the face peering around the door. "Nicole!" Obviously, I'd asked after her and heard she was doing well, and at the same hospital as myself, and had made plans to track her down once I was mobile. But all the words telling me she was making a good recovery are nothing compared to having her in front of my eyes. "Aren't you a sight for sore eyes. How are you? Yeah, come in."

"I'm better than you, it would seem." She smiles, and then when she coughs, explains, "Smoke inhalation."

I raise the head of the bed so I'm in a sitting position, and shudder as I remember searching for her while the fire was raging. "Tell me everything. What happened to you?"

She knows exactly what I'm asking. Taking the chair by the side of the bed, she sits forward as she starts giving me the details. "The fire flared up, took me by surprise. Crossed the ravine when I wasn't expecting it. I ran for the ATV, but in my hurry to get away, snagged it on a tree stump and turned it over." My eyes open as I listen to her escapade, and I nod for her to continue. Taking a breath, she shakes her head as she remembers, and then shudders. "Thought I was a goner. Fire was coming up fast behind me, so I ran uphill to try and get away from it. Managed to get to some black but inhaled a lot of smoke. Got disorientated and tripped. Hit my head hard."

"Shit." She was lucky we found her. By the look on her face, both of us seem to be considering what might have been. "I'm so very glad you're okay."

She nods, reaches out, and takes my hand. "I'm so glad you found me."

"We weren't going to leave you behind."

We're quiet for a moment as we both think about her narrow escape, then she squeezes my hand. "I only heard you were here when I bumped into Slade in the corridor. What the hell's happened to you, Darce?"

Tears come to my eyes, and I find myself telling her everything. Up to now, apart from Marcia, who I don't know very well, I've had no female company. Somehow the things I left out when talking to the men seem easier to admit. My feelings, the fear that I was going to die alone, and the horror that Pete had taken what I fought so hard not to give.

When I've finished, she's got tears in her eyes. Then she's quiet and thoughtful and it's a few minutes before she speaks. Pulling herself up straight she tells me firmly, "You need to get help, Flash. You can't cope with this on your own. And you can't run from Peg. You need to talk to him."

Moving my head from side to side, I contest her suggestion. "Nicole, Pete took all my choice away from me, stripped me of any control I had. I couldn't escape, I could only take what he gave me. Peg could do the same."

Her eyebrows rise so far, they almost reach her hairline. "You're saying Peg would rape you?"

"No!" I protest immediately. "He'd never do that. But he's sergeant-at-arms for the MC. He's overprotective. I know he wouldn't want me to keep doing my job, it would mess with him. He doesn't want a woman in the kind of career I have. He'd want to control everything I do. I know he would."

She leans back in the chair and folds her arms. "Does he? You know this for a fact?" She waits, and when I don't respond, continues, "Seems to me that you got together pretty fast. You ever actually talked about your expectations? You of him, and he of you? Or is this just conjecture?"

Nicole's picked up on something. No, we haven't spoken. But I *know* that I'm right. "You didn't see it. The men protecting the compound, the women all kept out of harm's way. That's what the bikers expect of their old ladies, and you know I'd never be able to be someone like that."

"But there are some battles you'd like him to fight for you. Helping you deal with the bastard Pete Mercer, for one."

Again, she's right. "But it wouldn't stop there."

"How do you know?" She sits forward again. "Look, Darce, the man you described sounds like what we're all searching for. I don't think you can throw it all away without talking it out. I'm not here to tell you what to do, you've been hurt and abused, and I can't even imagine how hard that is to deal with. All I'm saying is, just don't rush and do something you'll regret later. From what you say, Peg's an understanding man. Why not give him a chance?"

Biting my lip, I take a moment to think, then again shake my head. "Even if we reached a compromise, Nicole, I might have to give him up if I want to have prospect in my career."

She nods slowly. "Only you can work out what's the priority in your life, Darce. No one can else can help you do it."

Her visit leaves me with so many thoughts whirling, I'm not sure how to sort them out. But I can't keep running away, refusing to see Peg. It's not fair to leave him dangling with no answers, without knowing the thoughts going through my mind. Try as I might, on my own I can't resolve them.

I've been here for three days, when the inevitable happens. There's a shift change of my visitors, and it's Peg who puts his head around the door. His eyes examine me, taking in the now yellowing bruising on my face. With a slight grimace that he tries to hide, he asks, "Can I come in, Flash?"

Flash. The name he's called me almost since the moment we met. He liked that I had a handle, and I like, *liked*, him using it. But now I'm not sure I'll ever be that close to him again.

"If you can remember my name's Darcy, yes." I know I sound waspish, but I'm not in the head space where I want to be called by my firefighter name. Getting myself situated right, I raise myself up into a sitting position, feeling less vulnerable that way. Peg's there, immediately, propping the pillows behind me. This close I can see the lines on his face, more I think than he had before. *Have I put those there?* Quickly suppressing my guilt for yet one more thing that can be laid at my door, I incline my head toward the chair. "We need to talk, Peg."

"Darcy." He lifts his hand, it hovers over mine, then he returns it to his side. I'm not sure whether I dread or long for his touch. I'm so confused, I almost miss his mouth twisting. "You've said that before. If you're up for speaking, I'm ready to hear you out." As he pulls back his shoulders, I don't think he knows he looks as if he's preparing for a fight. "I've got some things to tell you, but I'll let you have your say first."

Is that the right way around? If I say what I do, he might just walk out. But it's time, and I can't delay this any longer. I take the deepest breath that my sore ribs will allow and start. "Peg, we rushed into this…whatever this thing is between us." He looks like he's going to speak, so I shake my head. "Let me get this out, Peg. And before you think anything that's happened has caused me to change my mind, I assure you, this is what I should have said the day I left you without a word on the compound."

He gives a deep sigh but keeps silent, allowing me a moment to gather the words.

"I agree there's a strong connection between us, something I've never felt with anyone else. But it's not going to work."

"Tell me why," he demands quickly, his voice not sounding quite right.

"Two things. Firstly, my job." I look down at the cast covering my foot. "The chances are I'm going to get back to full fitness and join my old crew again." I take another deep breath as I search for the right words. "A firefighter's on the job twenty-four hours, seven days of the week, whether on shift or not. We've got to maintain a squeaky-clean reputation. Whatever one of us does reflects on the service as a whole. The public must have complete trust in us." Risking it, I glance at him. He's looking pained. "The Satan's Devils have a reputation, whether earned or not. As a firefighter, I can't afford to be associated with a member, or anything the club does. Particularly if I want to go after a promotion."

He inhales sharply, then waits a moment before letting the air out on a sigh. "I love you, Darcy. It happened fast, agreed. But I've always known I'd recognise my ol' lady soon as I found her." A smile of longing comes my way before he grows serious again. "I thought your job might have something to do with it, so I've been doing some thinkin' myself. I've been in the club for getting on twenty years now, don't know how I'd get on in the citizen world, but if that's all that's stopping us being together, I'll leave the Satan's Devils."

Would he? Could he? Isn't that just as bad as him asking me to stop being a firefighter?

"I couldn't ask you to do that, Peg."

He shrugs. "You're not asking. You wouldn't. But the offer's there on the table, darlin'."

As the endearment slips out, I almost relent, but I haven't addressed the principal issue. "That's not all, Peg. You like to be in control, you're protective, possessive." I clench my hands together, as if to stop myself from reaching for him. "You'll smother me." I'm afraid of losing my identity, of becoming nothing more than Peg's old lady, and not myself anymore. "I've seen how the men treat their old ladies."

He sits back and folds his arms. "Not sure you have. You've seen them in the club with their men, you haven't seen them out working. Take Sam, she's one of the best mechanics we have, keeps the boys in the garage in line. Sandy runs our restaurant and does a fuckin' good job there. Carmen has her own hairdressing business." Now he leans forward. "Yeah, we're protective, we like to keep our women safe, but that doesn't mean we keep them tied to our belts. Our relationship wouldn't be one-sided. Fuck, Darcy, I don't want to take you away from your job. I might not like what you do, but only because it's fuckin' dangerous. But I'd never try to stop you doing what you love. It's part of you, and I don't want to change you."

He doesn't? I go to speak, but he raises his hand in a 'you've had your chance gesture'.

"We jumped straight in without sorting any of this out, didn't we, darlin'? I hear you, but you've got this all wrong." Peg shakes his head. "There's things we need to learn about each other, and maybe slow this thing between us right down. We can take a few steps back, not go all in. But I'd like the chance to show you you're so very far from the truth."

"I gave Pete a chance," I admit, biting my lip, remembering how he conned me into letting him live in my house.

"Don't compare me to that son of a bitch," he snarls.

Immediately, I feel contrite. The two men are nothing alike. "I'm sorry, Peg." I wave my hand down at my body. "Everything that's happened... I just..." I breathe in deeply. "Pete overpowered me, Peg. Made me feel helpless. One blow to my head, my hands tied behind me, and I couldn't defend myself. I don't ever want to feel out of control again." What's in my mind would hurt him, but how can I explain if I don't put it into words? "You're, you're so..."

"Rough in bed," he supplies, his hand resting on his beard. "You're scared of being hurt again."

"Yes, no." I shake my head. "It's not just you, Peg. It's the thought of any man. Pete almost got to me once before, and he hadn't given up. I hate feeling vulnerable." Though I enjoyed it at the time, the thought of allowing Peg to restrain me like he had before makes me shudder. Even though I trusted him and wanted it at the time, now, after what Pete had done…. Peg likes that. Possibly needs it. Now I won't be able to give it to him.

He reaches out his hand, lightly resting it on top of mine, and gives a quick look into my eyes to check I'm alright. As our skin meets, I feel a flicker of electricity shoot up my arm, and it's that that makes me pull away. He misunderstands, and the sides of his mouth turn down. I keep quiet, unable to explain that my traitorous body still reacts when my brain is telling me it's wrong.

I don't explain my reaction, it's easier that way. "I'm sorry, Peg."

He rolls his head on his shoulders. "I'm gonna give you some time." As I go to interrupt him, he puts up his hand. "No, you've had your say. Let me say mine. What happened to you, well, there aren't the words to describe how horrific it was. I'm only just keepin' control here, babe. It shouldn't have happened, and it's destroyin' me thinkin' how I couldn't protect you. You're right, that's what I want to do, but wrong in the way you think I'd do it. Wouldn't want to tie you down, understand you're independent. But, park that for now. Just keep the door cracked open, okay?" Leaning forward, he clasps his hands between his splayed legs. "There's things you need to know. Mouse found out who the Mercers are."

He's got my attention. My brows rise.

"Okay, you ready for this? They're bankers, fundin' high rollers in the city. Politicians, judges, you name it. When they need funds for their gamblin' debts, or for their spouses' over-

-the-top expenses, or even, fuck it, for something legit, they go to Top Loans. Confidentiality assured, backed by temptin' low interest rates." He glances to see how I'm taking it. "We thought they were loan sharks to start with, but they're playin' a different game. You take out a loan from Mercer, and you're in their pockets. Mercer Junior gets into trouble? Mercer Senior does something like wipe out part of the judge's debt, and hey ho, bail hearin' granted."

"So, he's always going to get away with it," I whisper, fear flooding through me that he'll come for me again. *He'll always get off.*

"No." Peg sounds adamant. "But there's a relationship between you and I, can't deny that, darlin', even if you want to believe it's in the past and not the future. Police know that too. They already have a hard-on for us, and you were found on the premises we've got a contract on. We've got to be clever about this. Can't disappear him the way I want, but the alternative is makin' sure we've got the upper hand in the courts."

Again, I'm biting my lip, trying to concentrate on what Peg's saying, and not on the panic that's threatening to rise. "How?"

"That's what we're workin' on. But there is a weak link. The woman who gave him the alibi." He pauses and smirks. "You might not believe this, but I can be quite scary at times."

I believe him. So much so it draws a laugh from me, albeit a bit of a strangled one.

His smirk broadens. "Mouse is workin' to discover who she is, then we'll see what we can dig up on her. Break her down, we'll prove he lied. Then his only alibi is father dearest."

"And what are you going to do about that?"

Peg looks up and meets my eyes. "You let us worry about how we'll do things. But I tell you this, Darcy, I won't do anything that puts our relationship at risk. Satan's Devils are going to stay with clean hands."

But I know the damage has already been done. The residents of Tucson enjoy the perceived threat of having a one percenter club on their doorstep. They're used as a bogeyman to keep little children in line, the roar of their Harleys sending delicious shivers down the spine. While the majority of people have never had dealings with them, there's still a universal distrust.

Some men may envy their way of life, while pretending it disgusts them. Their wives may feign disinterest in the rugged men riding their bikes, while being jealous of the women who ride behind them.

Whatever they do, it will only make things worse, and reinforce my decision that a firefighter has no business being associated with the Satan's Devils.

But what he's told me tears me in two. Peg and his club are the only people on my side, the only ones looking deeper and trying to make a positive case against Pete. If I tell them to stop, from what Peg's said, Pete will once again get away scot free, and may fulfil his promise to finish what he started. But if I turn a blind eye to what they're going to do, the situation can only get worse. The reputation of their club will become even more tarnished.

Knowing I can't lie to Peg, I shake my head and speak softly. "Peg, I'm sorry, but I don't think I can pick up where we left off. You do get that? I can't ask you to do this."

"How often do I have to tell you? I know you're not askin'. I'm just sayin' what's gonna happen. Much as you probably don't believe it, we don't like dirt in our town. None of us like the way Mercer's playin' the odds. We'll do what we can to put a check on him, and that means findin' enough evidence to put Junior away for good."

CHAPTER 31

Peg

My visit to Darcy could have gone better. Or, it could have gone worse. Though she's said her decision's final and that we're over, there's something that gives me just enough hope not to believe her. When my hand rested so briefly on hers, I saw that flicker of desire, that flush that covered her face. I didn't press, it's far too early. She's been raped, for fuck's sake, and any attempt to get back where we were needs to go slowly. What she doesn't understand is I've already waited a lifetime for her, and I'm prepared to wait another one until she's ready. Christ, I've controlled my cock long enough, I'll just have to keep satisfying myself. If she never wants a man that way again, well so be it. I just have to find a way to make her believe just how much fucking time—forever if need be—I'm willing to be satisfied with just being close to her.

But as to her other objection, my only option is to leave the club. If that's what it takes, I'll do all I can to make a life for myself in the civilian world. Get a job working security, maybe. I'll do anything for her. She's *it* for me, and no obstacle is going to be big enough to split us up.

Having timed my return right, I'm back at the clubhouse just as the brothers are walking into church. I follow them in and take my place at Drummer's righthand side. Lady and Joker are missing, and so's Viper, and as we wait, murmured conversations continue. Prez glances up at the clock, then his face relaxes as he sees there's still a couple of minutes to go. They're not late. Yet.

Suddenly Blade speaks, his voice louder than the rest. "What the fuck is up with Ma?"

"Fuck if I know." Beef shakes his head.

My senses sharpen. "What do you mean, Blade?"

Shaking his head, Blade enlightens me. "She's been fuckin' smilin' all day."

"She has that," confirms Rock.

"She's up to something."

Having got to know her, Road's probably right.

"Maybe she's got a new recipe to try."

"Fuck yeah." Jekyll's not the only one to agree with Road's suggestion.

The old ladies aren't terrible in the kitchen, but since Ma has been here we've been better fed than we have for years. It's an unlikely arrangement, but bringing Ma here has brought benefits for both her and us.

"I've got a soft spot for the old bitch," Prez observes. "Fuck knows why. She's always tellin' me off. Makes me feel like I'm ten years old."

Which sets us off laughing, chuckles still going around as Joker and Lady walk in, a sly glance exchanged between them, which doesn't go unnoticed. Blade narrows his eyes, and as I glance at Drum, I see him nod. *It's time.*

When Viper comes in and takes his seat, Prez bangs the gavel.

It's our normal Friday church. We go through the motions discussing the businesses, then with that out of the way, get onto other matters. Mouse is still trying to find more info on the Mercers, so we park that for now, but he's come up with the name of the woman who gave Mercer Junior his alibi.

"Cherry Orchard? You've got to be fuckin' kiddin' me." My head's moving to and fro, thinking that's a fuck of a name. "She a whore?"

"No, man. It's actually the name she was given at birth. Parents must have been fuckin' hippies or something."

"Or on something," Blade suggests to Mouse.

"You going to handle it?" Prez asks me. "Want someone with you?"

That would be for the best. Someone to temper my anger if she doesn't come clean. I look around the table, my eyes landing on Hyde. Yeah, he's got a way with the ladies. "Fancy doing a good guy/bad guy routine, Hyde?"

"Yeah, Peg, I'm in."

"That's settled then." The gavel bangs down. "Take care, Peg. Don't want to make things worse."

I know that already. Prez doesn't need to tell me that, nor does he know the half of it as to why that's so important. Satan's Devils have got to clean up their rep in town, but what's taken decades to achieve isn't going to be turned around in five minutes. *I* know that. As I look around the table, I feel dread in my heart that I might have to turn my back on my brothers. I'd give my life for any of them, as they would do for me, but I'm not prepared to give up the love of my life. Somehow, I've got to find a way to keep both.

"...turn the witness, then if Mouse gets more info, discuss how to sweep away this dirt."

As Prez finishes speaking, I realise I've *yet again* missed part of the conversation in church, but this time I can fill in the gaps. I raise my chin to show I agree.

Now we're on to other business. Everyone's chaffing at the bit to go get a drink and get the party started, fidgeting, and no one raising their hand to speak. I glance at Drum, who's staring down the end of the table. He's leaning back in his chair, his arms deceptively casually folded across his chest.

"Before we get partying," he starts, "just want to remind everyone that old ladies need to be voted into the club. Ain't much of a stretch to say that goes for any partner."

Everyone's looking mystified. Blade, noticing where the prez's eyes have settled, catches on fast, that knife he's always twirling suddenly spins on the table, and he stops it when it's pointing at the two members who'd transferred in from Vegas. Seems a long time ago now, but while they're brothers, they've mostly kept to themselves and have not become particularly close to anyone in the Tucson chapter.

Joker shifts uneasily in his chair. He tries to return Drummer's stare, but looks away quickly, pretending to look as confused as everyone else. Lady seems to find great interest in inspecting his hands, which are resting on the table.

Prez gives it a moment, then his steely gaze becomes more menacing. "Got something to say, brothers?"

Now everyone follows his line of sight. There's no doubt who he's targeting. Slick looks awkward, as though he wishes he wasn't here. Wraith's looking resigned. Beef, Rock, and Marvel have sly grins on their faces, Jekyll, Hyde, and Road just look puzzled. Dollar's nodding his head, and Blade and Bullet are giving their own probing stares to the pair. Viper, Shooter, and Mouse look like they haven't a clue what's going on or couldn't care less if they have. From the various expressions on their faces, it's hard to tell how this is going to go down. I flex my mental muscles, ready to back Prez up.

Joker and Lady exchange glances, meeting each other's eyes for a few seconds. Then as Lady shrugs, Joker puts his hands on the table, palms facing upwards and open. "Lady and I are together."

"And?"

Marvel punches Shooter on the arm, then says, adding emphasis, "They're *together.*"

Shooter's mouth opens into an O.

Drummer bangs the gavel and gets our attention. "Joker, Lady. Thank you for being straight with us."

I can't help it, I laugh, and my head falls onto the table. Peering around I see others are outright chortling or have their hands to their mouths.

Drum snarls. "I'll fuckin' rephrase that. Thank you for being upfront. Now could you fuckin' leave us for a moment, as we've got things to discuss."

Lady hesitates looks like he wants to say something, but Joker takes his arm and as he tugs him out of his chair, gives an encouraging nod. Without a word, both men exit through the door.

As the mirth dies down and a wave of conversation starts up, Drummer bangs the gavel again. "I didn't send them out so we could discuss whether they're in the club or not. As far as I'm concerned, they're both members. They prospected, did their time, and have proved themselves time and again." He pauses and lets his words sink in.

"So, what do you want, Prez?"

"VP, what I want is that if anyone's got anything to say, lets thrash it out. And without puttin' our two brothers through any shit they won't want to hear."

Slick raises his hand. "You said it all, Prez. Lady's a fuckin' brave man when he went into that auction. Could easily have been killed. But he volunteered and did it just the same."

"Joker's had my back a time or two," Rock agrees. "Don't see it as a problem."

Blade's nodding his head. "Saw it comin' a mile off. Only thing that surprises me is that you want it brought out in the open, Prez."

I step in. "You ain't got an old lady, Blade. But those of us who have," I pause as I wonder whether I'm right to number myself with the rest, "wouldn't want to have to hide the relationship we have with our partners. Or for others to understand why we put them first." I point to the closed door. "Joker and Lady must have one hell of a job trying to keep what they feel for each other under wraps. They've been here for two years now, and I doubt they've only just got together. My assumption is that it goes back a ways, and they came here to have a fresh start. We need to get their relationship out in the open. Allow them to be who they are."

"Think there was some difficulty in Red's club?" Rock asks.

"Can't know that. Doubt it was Red but could be other brothers that made their lives difficult."

"Whatever, they don't think they'll be accepted else they'd have come clean before." Dollar's looking pained. "You think they think so little of us?"

The prez shakes his head. "Don't think they wanted to risk it. But since Lady put his life on the line, I think it's been harder for Joker to hold back."

Seeing Shooter's frown, I brace myself for what's coming, but he says something I don't expect. "Can't see it matters one way or another. Each to their own and all that."

Wraith's fingers tap on the table, then he points to me. "What you're thinkin' is where their loyalties lie." He looks around the table, at Heart, at Dollar, Viper, me, and then the prez. "If my old lady's in danger, I'll protect her. I'll still have my brothers' backs, but Sophie and Olivia will always come first."

I nod. *That's* the point.

Prez also is dipping his head. "And that's what we need to agree and accept."

There's a brief period of silence, a few shrugs, a few eyes going to the ceiling, but in the end, it's a series of nods.

Then the corners of Drummer's mouth turn up, and he pushes his chair back from the table, resting his foot against the edge. "Now we've got to vote in an old lady." He grins at each one of us. "Just got to find out which one it is."

The tension is broken. It starts us all laughing again and slamming our hands on the table. Predictably, Beef starts a book and sees if he's got any takers. But no one takes him up on it. I guess we've already got our own ideas.

Prez waves at us to be quiet, and the pair come back in and stand before Drum points them to their seats. When they've sat down, he commences. "You've probably had thoughts on why I sent you out of the room, but what you're thinkin' is wrong. You're members of the Satan's Devils Tucson chapter, and whatever your personal inclinations are they have fuck all to do with that."

Joker and Lady exchange relieved glances, which confirms that was what had them worried.

"Now," Prez continues, "we always vote in ol' ladies. What we need to know is which of you will be wearing a property patch."

Air's sucked into lungs all around the room. Lady's face goes completely white. Blade can't hold it together and his head collapses to the table as he starts laughing again. Shooter's wiping tears from his eyes.

Rock points at Lady. "I guess that look on your face shows you're the bottom in this relationship."

Beef screeches through his belly laughs. "Bottom!" Did you need to say that?"

"I guess you're the taker not the giver." Slick's trying to hold back his mirth and failing.

Joker's frowning, guess he doesn't like all the humour at the expense of his old lady, but I discover I'm wrong when he puts in, "You're all wrong. We take it in turns."

"Oh fuck, man. We didn't need to be given that visual." Marvel's shaking his head, and the wicked grin and wink Joker gives to Lady shows he knows just what he's doing.

Mouse is looking confused. "Thought your full handle was Lady's Man." It's a statement posed as a question.

Lady shrugs. "I'm bi. Or at least I was, before I met Joker." And fuck me if he doesn't take Joker's hand and squeeze it right there at the table.

I'll be fucked if that doesn't look right. In fact, it looks like a weight's been lifted from both men. I'm not the only one to have seen it. Marvel slaps Lady on the back, and Shooter does the same to Joker. A family, that's what we fucking are. A dysfunctional one, maybe, but a family.

Drummer bangs the gavel. "Guess this calls for a party."

No one needs to vote on that.

As we go out I overhear Lady hiss to Joker, "I'm not fuckin' wearin' a property patch."

CHAPTER 32

Peg

Pulling up in front of a large, well-appointed house, I reflect how good it feels to be back on my bike, fresh air rushing around me rather than the recycled shit of the air con in the truck. It's helped raise my mood. While Flash is still lost inside her head, I'll have to content myself doing whatever I can to make sure the fucker who hurt her is taken out for good.

Kicking down my stand, I get off, and after removing my sunglasses and sliding them into my cut, go to stand by Hyde. "Ready to do this?"

"Uh huh." Hyde's studying the house we've arrived at. He waves his hand left to right, then up and down. "There's money there. With a name like hers, I expected her to be whorin' herself out for a livin'."

"Might still be, Hyde. Might still be." What did her parents think they were setting her up for, giving her a name like they had? *Cherry Orchard.* I shake my head in disbelief, hoping I'll be able to keep my face straight when I meet her.

Slapping Hyde on the back, we walk toward the front door. I press the doorbell, hoping she'll be in on a Saturday morning. Seeing how large the sprawling house is, I give her time to get to the door.

I'm almost ready to cut my losses when the door eventually opens, and a stunning blond beauty opens it. Seeing two intimidating bikers standing outside, she immediately tries to shut it again, but I'm ready, and have my foot in the doorway.

"Cherry Orchard?"

"Who wants to know?"

It's her, I can tell by the guarded expression on her face. "We need to talk to you. Can we come in?" I might have posed it as a question, but I'm already pushing past, Hyde hot on my heels.

She stands with her hand holding the door, even though we're already inside. Various expressions cross her face, as if she's considering making a run for it. I put my hand on her arm and tighten my grip. As I pull her away from the doorway, Hyde shuts the door. It closes, and the lock engages with a satisfying clunk.

"What do you want?" Her voice sounds shaky, and I can feel her trembling through my fingers wrapped around her bicep. "I'm expecting my boyfriend, he'll be here soon." *So that's why she opened the door so carelessly.* She was expecting somebody else.

It's clear she's going to offer us no hospitality, so I waste no time, conscious my interrogation might be interrupted. "Pete Mercer."

Her eyes widen, and I feel her body tense. "What about him?"

"He your boyfriend?" Hyde makes the mental leap before I do. *He can't be.* But perhaps someone as moneyed as this moves in the same circles.

"What if he is?"

Then you're totally mad, Woman. While I don't say that aloud, the vision of Darcy in the hospital bed comes into my mind. *Should I warn her?* Nah, if she's in a relationship with him, she'd never believe me.

I get straight to the point. "You gave him an alibi for the other night. And I happen to know you're lyin'. You need to correct that fuckin' story you concocted for the police."

She stiffens. "I told the truth."

"You may have been mistaken about the day," Hyde says gently. "That would be an understandable mistake."

"Or you may just be fuckin' lyin'," I snarl.

Her body leans slightly away from me, toward Hyde, and I smile inwardly inside as she directs her answer to him, while shrugging off my hand. "I don't lie." But as her eyes flick to the side, I not only know that she does, but at this moment she most definitely is.

Hyde's shaking his head with a sad expression on his face. "Thing is, Cherry, Pete Mercer hurt a friend of ours. Raped her, shot her, and left her for dead. That's what he was doing when he asked you to cover for him."

Her hand covers her mouth. "Pete wouldn't do that," she protests. But again, I read the signs she's not being honest.

After Hyde carefully examines her with his eyes, he gives a slight chin lift to me, and I allow him to continue taking the floor. "I think you know that he would, sweetheart. Did he threaten you to say you were with him?" Hyde takes a pace toward her, and keeping his tone gentle, continues, "Did he hurt you?"

"He didn't hurt me." She refutes Hyde's suggestion and I think this time she's maybe telling the truth.

"Thing is, darlin'," Hyde keeps with his reasonable tone, "we *know* you weren't with him. And our friend who was hurt? Well, she's Peg's," he points at me, "ol' lady. And Peg is a man you don't want to cross."

Now she turns to me, her eyes meeting mine before quickly moving away. She inhales sharply as she catches the expression on my face. Unlike Hyde, I'm not in the mood to be friendly.

"Will your…old lady be okay?"

Ignoring the way she struggles with the parlance, I shake my head and say fiercely, "She was fuckin' raped, Woman. What the fuck do you think?"

She moves toward the nearest chair and sinks down. With her head in her hands, it's hard to hear what she's saying. "I didn't know it was something like that. I had no idea."

"What did he tell you he needed an alibi for?"

"I didn't ask, and he didn't say." She swallows a couple of times and seems to slump further. "He frightens me."

Hyde goes over and crouches in front of her. "How does he frighten you, Cherry? Does he use his fists?"

A shake of her head, then she looks up with determination. "I can't change my story."

Hyde and I exchange glances. After a second, I offer, "You set the police right, and Mercer will be taken into custody and out of your way. Until then, we can provide you with protection."

She stands, Hyde mimicking her action. She's faced with two tall, muscular bikers, and still she's not going to bend. "I'm sorry, you've wasted your time. I won't be talking to the police. I *can't.*"

"We can promise he won't touch you again."

For the first time she looks directly in my eyes. "I'm not worried about *me.*" Her voice is harsh.

"What's he got over you, Cherry."

While Hyde's asked the question, she's still focused on me. "Nothing on me. It's my dad."

"Your dad?" I snap.

She nods sadly. "He got into a bit of debt and got a loan from the Top Loans. Low interest rate. Pete told me they'd raise that to a level he couldn't afford to pay if I didn't help him out."

"Fuck, Woman. And you're still callin' him your boyfriend?"

Now she looks down at the floor, unable to meet my eyes as she admits, "The other part of the bargain was me. He said we needed to behave as though we were in a relationship to make the story stick."

"So, you're givin' him your body because your father's in debt? Fuck, Woman." As I wipe my hand over my face, I think perhaps I was right and she's what her name suggests. A *whore*.

"It didn't start that way." She begins to justify herself. "I met him last week. He took me out on a date. Seemed nice. He was a gentleman. Saw him the next day, and things progressed, and he came home with me that night." She breaks off, and a shadow flits across her face. "After that he disappeared for a few days, I didn't know where he'd gone. Then he turned up, early in the morning. That's when he told me I had to say I was with him the previous night."

I place my finger under her chin. "You were okay with coverin' for him?"

A shake of her head. "No, and that's what I told him." Her eyes glaze over as she recalls the conversation. "Pete changed, no longer the pleasant man I'd first brought home. He said he knew about my father's loan, that it was with *his* father's bank, and said the bank would make my father's life impossible, that he'd lose *everything* if I didn't do what he asked." Now she's looking at me again, her face full of determination. "It was my fault letting Pete get close. It's on me to make things right. I've been trying to get him a loan somewhere else, but already the other banks seem to have been warned about lending to him. I've been trying so hard…"

So that's how Mercer managed to get himself an alibi. By a threat. Feeling more sympathetic than I had before, I offer, "Come with us to the police. We'll protect you and see if we can get your father out of this mess."

A rise of her head, a straightening of her back. "I can't. And I won't. Not until I get my father in the clear." Then a worried look cast at Hyde and then me. "Dad doesn't know any of this, and can't. Not until I've sorted things out. It would destroy him knowing someone was using him to get to me. He's not well, and I don't want to worry him.

"Now you have to leave. I can't have Pete seeing you here. He's taking me on a date so we can be seen together in public." There's a pleading look in her eyes as she looks up at me. "I'm sorry I can't help you, but if I can get someone else to take on Dad's debt, I'll tell the police I got muddled about which night."

I glance at Hyde, he's jerking his chin at the door. Fucker probably wants me out of here before Mercer arrives. He's got a point, I'll probably kill him. Even now my fists are clenching in anticipation.

"Let's take this back to Mouse."

Hyde's right. If flags have been raised against Cherry's father's name, Mouse can probably remove them. If her dad gets a new loan elsewhere, she'll have no reason to keep to her story.

While part of me wants to stay and give Mercer the lesson of his life, if he turns up and sees our bikes, he might just take off, and will be warned we're trying to break his alibi.

Reluctantly, with no other option, we leave. But I will be coming back. We've found the weak link in the chain, and now we've just got to break it. However much I want to deal with the fucker who's hurt my woman so badly, now is not the right time. But soon, I promise myself. Soon.

With my mind replaying the conversation we've just had with Cherry, the ride back to the compound seems normal enough, the day heating up the asphalt under my tires. But any sense of normality goes out of the window when we arrive at the gate and find a commotion. An elderly man is standing outside, screaming at Fergus, telling him to open up and let him in. An expensive car is idling and empty.

Exchanging glances, Hyde and I leave our bikes. As we get closer, I see the man's hands wrapped around the bars of the gates, his knuckles white. Then take in the words he's spitting at the prospect.

"You've got my mother here, you despicable pieces of shit. Holding her captive."

His mother? The grey-haired fucker must be sixty if he's a day, and the only woman old enough to have birthed him would be… Ma.

"Whoa, there." I put my hand on his shoulder, and he shrugs it off, but my gesture's got his attention away from Fergus, who, I'm pleased to note, has been standing his ground.

"I demand to see her. I'm here to take her away… If you don't let me in, I'll go to the police and you'll be charged with kidnapping."

I've had enough of this. There's one quick way to clear this up. "Prospect. Open up."

Fergus looks relieved that someone's taken charge, and soon the gate's sliding open. Now that he's free to step inside, it appears it's suddenly become the last thing Ma's son wants to do.

His watery eyes turn to me, his face suddenly pale. "People know where I am, you know. The police will come running if I don't come back out."

I huff a laugh. "Old man, we've got no beef with you. Or with your ma, who's here of her own volition, I assure you. Follow me, and I'll take you to see for yourself."

I go back to my bike and start the engine, mounting up to ride the short distance to the clubhouse. The expensive car follows me and parks diagonally, blocking in several bikes, without a care he might be causing disruption.

"Where is she then?" He wastes no time asking when he gets out.

"This way." I stride off to the clubroom door and step inside, pausing for a second, as once again a spectacular aroma is wafting through from the kitchen. My mouth starts to water as I wonder what we'll be getting tonight. It also tells me my assumption was right and I know exactly where I'm going to find this man's mother.

With the elderly man in my wake, I make my way to where the women have congregated. They look satisfied with themselves and are in the process of clearing up. Wraith's hovering around Sophie as normal, and seeing me, nods toward the stove. "Pot roast," he mouths.

Mmm mm. For a second, I forget the man behind me.

"Samuel!" Ma's sharp eyes have spotted her one remaining son. "What on earth are you doing here?"

Samuel's face sneers as he looks around the room. "More to the point, what are you doing here? I've come to take you away from this den of iniquity."

I bristle at that. But Ma's got it under control. "Are you indeed? You've come now? Where were you when my house was burning down around me? Tell me that, Son?"

Samuel takes a step back, and I feel like retreating myself. The expression on his face is blank as he explains, "I had a business deal."

"Pfft. Just like you. Putting business before your old mother. Why are you here, Samuel? Why did you even bother to come?"

Now he's moving forward again. "Because I heard a rumour you've taken up with this scum. Have you any idea what that would do to my reputation? I'll be a laughing stock. I can't have you staying here. I'm taking you away. I've made other arrangements…"

"Yeah?" Ma spits out. "And what might these arrangements be?"

He pulls back his shoulders. "A nice retirement home that I've picked out. They'll have nurses to look after you." He waves at the wheelchair. "And you shouldn't be in that. You should be in bed, resting." His eyes narrow as he looks around the room. "You're making my mother slave for you. Don't think I don't recognise the smell of her hot pot cooking. She's not well enough…"

"Hold your tongue!"

Fuck me! I thought Drummer's voice could sound like thunder, but Ma's got him beat. I hide my smile behind my hand.

"This *scum*, as you call them, are treating me better than you've ever done. If your brothers were alive…"

"But they're dead and gone, Mother. All you've got is me. And now I'm going to be looking after you." Ma's changed since she's been here, it's clear she's been enjoying herself. But the arrival of her son has drawn all the emotion from her face.

"The only way you'll be looking after me is to dump me in a home, and never visit. I know you, Samuel, remember? I gave birth to you and watched you grow up. And I'll tell you now, every one of these men here act like a better son to me than you've ever done." She leans back in the wheelchair, and for a moment she looks exactly what she is, a tired old woman. Then she seems to come back to herself. "Get out of here, Samuel, and leave me alone. You know what? I don't give a fuck about your business or your reputation. If you'd shown any compassion for me over the years, maybe I'd place myself under your care. But as long as this *scum* here will have me, then I'm staying. And that's the last word I'll say on the matter. Peg?"

I start, surprised to hear my name.

"Show him the way out, will you?"

"This isn't finished, Mother."

"Just get out of here, *Son*." She spits the last word.

Samuel's face is red, and his brow furrows as he looks around, clearly considering whether he can take her by force, then realises with the likes of Wraith, Hyde, and myself, the odds are against him. With a huff and a sneer, he turns and strides out. I follow, making sure he gets in his car, then wait, watching as he drives to the gate and leaves.

When I return, Sam's got her arms around Ma. I hear a sniffling, a blowing of a nose, and then a strong old woman is looking straight at me. "What you looking at, boy? And there's no point hanging around. Dinner won't be ready for hours."

I grin. She's alright. "Sorry, Ma, but that sure smells good. Look forward to eating later."

Ain't that the truth? Already my mouth's watering.

CHAPTER 33

Darcy

How you feeling, Flash?" Truck nods to Slade, who's just said his goodbyes to me. I know their intentions are good but keeping me company throughout every day is getting wearing.

I pull myself up in the bed. "Getting easier all the time. I'll probably be able to go home by the weekend."

"Hmm." He looks thoughtful for a moment. "Don't like the idea of you being on your own. Not with that fucker still walking free. Now don't take this the wrong way, Flash, but you're still injured and hurting. What about if I came to stay with you? It's an offer I'd make for any of the crew." He adds the last hurriedly.

Truck? Stay with me? The idea of going home alone hadn't been inviting, especially not with Pete still walking free. Sure, I want to get out of this place, but my confidence has been shaken, and even if I was up to full strength, I'd still question my ability to look out for myself. My nights are plagued with constant nightmares about Pete coming back to finish what he started. As I look at my crewmate, seeing the resolve in his eyes, I don't take long to decide. "I don't want to put you out, Truck, but if you don't mind, I would appreciate the company. Thank you."

My traitorous mind would prefer it to be Peg watching out for me. However much I try not to think of him, he's never been far from my mind. Telling him a final goodbye and successfully eradicating him from my head are two separate things. In the dark of the night I've been lying awake, wondering whether I was right to put my occupation above the only relationship with a man that ever felt right. *He told me I was it for him. What if he was my one too?* Have I thrown away my only chance at happiness? Would my job really compensate when I'm a lonely old maid?

He told me he'd leave the club. But how would he cope? Would it be enough? His reputation might follow him. Even if it didn't, would he come to resent me? Just like I'd begrudge him if he was the reason I lost my job.

I'm not blind. A very big part of Peg is the role he performs for the Satan's Devils. He lives for his brothers. Would he shrink in front of my eyes if that was taken away? A man whose very purpose for living is to take care of so many, suddenly cast adrift without back up or camaraderie. I worry he wouldn't survive.

The Satan's Devils may live outside the law, but they don't deserve the reputation they have. Maybe I can convince my superiors that being in a relationship with their sergeant-at-arms won't reflect badly on the service. Maybe there is a way to have my cake and eat it too. Slade didn't completely shut that door. Maybe I can still push it open.

I want Peg. Tears prick at my eyes as I realise how much I miss him. Perhaps I haven't tried enough to make our relationship work. I start to smile. There must be a way to have something we both want so much.

"What the fuck?" Truck's exclamation and incredulous laugh catches my attention.

"What, Truck?"

He'd come in carrying a folded newspaper, and now has it in his hands and is staring at the front page. Without a word he passes it to me, and my so recent optimism disappears in an instant as the headlines shout at me.

SATAN'S DEVILS KIDNAPPED MY MOTHER

Prominent businessman Samuel Jones, 64, who owns a shoe factory in Phoenix, has today told this reporter that the outlaw Satan's Devils MC in Tucson have kidnapped his mother, Mary Jones, 93, and are holding her against her will.

Mary was forcibly removed from her home, which subsequently burned in the recent Snake Fire. Instead of releasing her into his care, they are forcing her to work in their kitchen. Mary should be in a proper facility to receive the attention she needs. Instead this frail old lady is being used as slave labor at the biker compound.

When contacted, Drummer, President of the Satan's Devils, assured our reporter she was not being held captive. But Samuel Jones swears he saw her with his own eyes.

"I could see she wanted to leave with me," says Jones. "She was pleading me with her eyes. But those bikers wouldn't let her, and physically stopped me from taking her away."

Jones admits he wasn't hurt in the altercation, but was given instructions to leave and not to come back.

The matter has now been reported to the police.

The motorcycle gang, which prefers to be known as a club, has made their home in Tucson since the early seventies. Known to the police as criminals for their involvement in drug and gun running, they have a reputation for keeping girls on the compound, but the age of the woman in this case is surprising, and what use she can possibly be to them remains a mystery.

We hope the police can quickly rescue her, and Mary Jones will be returned to her loving son, who only wants to ensure she's properly cared for in her twilight days.

Samuel Jones' factory makes shoes which are sold at the Toe and Heel outlet…

As the article becomes an advert for Jones' business, I stop reading. Stunned, I hand the paper back to Truck and collapse back on the pillows, closing my eyes, hoping to prevent the tell-tale tear escaping. The article made it sound like they were still dealing in the gun and drug trade, and that they regularly kidnapped women.

"What a load of crap." Truck's shaking his head. "You see this Mary when you were at the compound?"

One side of my mouth turns up. "I did, Truck. And while I did wonder who she was and what she was doing there, from the little I saw, I can confidently say no one could make that old lady do anything she didn't want to."

There's a knock at my door. It opens before I can call out permission, and Marcia stomps in. She's waving a paper in her hands, her eyes wide. "Have you freaking seen this, Darcy?" At my nod, she exclaims indignantly, "What a load of garbage. I've just had a nurse ask me whether it's safe to take my babies home."

Truck stands and offers her his seat. "You ladies like coffee?" When we both agree we do, he makes a strategic retreat.

I hadn't thought about the article causing trouble for her. "Are you going to have problems?"

She bites her lip. "I hope not, but mud sticks, you know? Hopefully they'll speak to Ma and find out her son's speaking out of his ass. I don't know what he's trying to get out of it. I'm supposed to be going home in a couple of days, taking Isabel with me. Jacob's being assessed later as to whether he can come home too." She tosses back her long hair. "Now, you know? I'm worried they'll get social services involved. The nurse said they might want to check up on the status at home. As if I'm not a fit mother, just because my old man's one of the Devils." I hold out my hand, she clutches it in hers. "I'm sorry to offload on you, Darcy, but I knew you'd understand."

Only too well. The door which Peg had asked me to keep cracked open slams firmly shut. Even if I decided a man was more important than my job, would I want to be tainted by their reputation? If I had a baby, would I be questioned like Marcia is, threatened with having my home situation inspected, all because I was associated with their club? One thing's for certain, people have long memories in Tucson, and this article will have renewed their bad feelings. It wouldn't be an easy life being a biker's old lady, and I'm not sure I'm strong enough.

"Huh," Marcia exclaims. "I think they're worried the club might steal my babies. If only they knew." She glances at me. "It's how I met them, when I was a cop. They helped solve who was abducting children from Tucson. They were alongside the police when we rescued them."

I suck in a breath. Her words have put a completely different slant on things. "Can't we get that story out? Make people see they're good guys now?"

"I shouldn't have told you that, Darcy. But I trust you. And the police don't want that information released. I had to sign a non-disclosure agreement when I left, and part of that was keeping the details to myself. Heart and Drummer didn't care, they don't want recognition for what they did. Or, at the time, they didn't think they needed it."

"What will this write-up do to their businesses?" I wonder aloud.

Marcia laughs. "I expect some people will go all righteous and avoid them, but others might want a walk on the wild side."

At that moment, Truck returns, the aroma of coffee proceeding him.

Marcia gets to her feet, takes a cup he's holding out to her, and then waves at the door. "Well, I better get back. The twins are due for another feed. I just wanted to talk with someone who understands."

"Thanks, Marcia." I'm pleased she choose to come to me. I needed someone else's assurance that the article was ridiculous. But whether it was or not, the damage has surely been done.

With one look at me, Truck settles down and picks up a magazine. I rest my head back, but my thoughts are reeling. It's the unfairness that gets to me. Why does Ma's son want to take her away? She seemed happy enough when I saw her. Part of the article rings true, that Peg's club had been saved from the fire that destroyed her house. Where had this apparently caring son been? Why has he crawled out of the woodwork now? From what Marcia said *and* what I've seen, Satan's Devils are trying hard to stay on the straight and narrow, and with a few ill placed words, he's destroyed all the good work they've done.

This article has stirred everything up again, I doubt there's any chance the service would want one of their firefighters associated with the likes of the club given the way it had been described in the paper. *If* I want to go back to work, I must stay firm on my resolve not to go back to Peg. If I want Peg, I'll need to leave my career behind. *Am I prepared to do that?* I feel myself weaken, just wanting to hear his voice.

"Truck?" My eyes snap open. "Can you pass me my phone. And can you…"

"Give you some privacy? Sure."

I call up a contact.

"Yo."

"Peg?"

"*Darcy?*"

"Yeah. It's me." Somehow I manage to reveal this is no happy make-up call by the tone of my voice.

"You've heard, I take it?" he snarls.

"Yeah. Why, Peg? What was that report about?"

"Her fuckin' son thinks her being here with us will affect his business."

"His shoe business. Yes, I read about that. The article was half advert for him."

"And he got front page." I understand Peg's anger.

"Peg." I take a breath, and then a leap into the unknown. "I'm sorry I sent you away. I should have talked, should have explained. You deserve that."

"Babe. I love you. I'm not changin' my mind. It's up to you to decide what you want."

"I'm having a tough time doing that," I admit, holding the phone tightly in my hand. "I know what I *want*, Peg. I just don't see a way it can work."

"Because of the fuckin' newspaper?"

I'm silent for a moment, biting my lip. "In part, but it's more than that. Your club's had a bad rep for years."

Rather than pushing me, he changes tack. "How are you feelin'?"

"Better. I'm getting out this weekend. Truck's offered to come and stay with me."

There's silence, then, "Truck's a good man. But I'd rather you were here with me."

"I couldn't, Peg. Even if I thought we could pick up where we left off, it's too soon." I still don't know that I wouldn't freak out if he tried to touch me. *Damn Pete.*

He understands immediately. "I know, babe. I wouldn't rush you. Fuck, I'd wait forever if that's what it takes."

His quick answer surprises me. *How do I deserve such a man?* But I still can't give him the words that he wants.

"Want me to come in and see you? Must admit, darlin', it's difficult stayin' away."

If I saw him I'd weaken. "I just need some space, Peg. I've got so many things to work through. I can't see what is best for me to do."

I hear a deep sigh, then, "I love you, Flash. Can't switch that off. And I'll be here when you're ready." I hear the sound of footsteps, and then he quietly says, "Meant what I said about leavin' the club. If that's what it takes. Not prepared to give up what's between us."

But would he still be the same man without his brothers beside him?

"Take care, Peg." I end the call, knowing I'm no closer to an answer than I was before, not knowing if I've gained anything from hearing his voice other than make myself question even more what's most important to me.

CHAPTER 34

Peg

uckin' piece of shit." I pick up the newspaper and read the article once more.

"Hey, that's my son you're talking about." I swing around to offer an insincere apology to Ma, to find her face set and taut. "In the circumstances I happen to agree with you. Where's that president of yours?"

"You want him, Ma?"

"Why d'you think I asked for him? Of course I want to speak to him. Now run along and get him."

My feet are walking in the direction of Drummer's office before I realise I've obeyed her as fast as if I was still in the services and had been given a command by a senior officer. Wryly laughing at myself, I knock on Drum's door and enter.

"Peg," Drum acknowledges, then turns back to Wraith. "Puts us back fuckin' years. The Wheel Inn's been makin' a tidy profit. Sandy's telling me people are already cancellin' their reservations."

"Viper's worried about the construction business. He's not heard anything yet, but if the suggestion gets out we're using our businesses to launder money, we might lose some lucrative contracts. And while we've been told we've got it, the paperwork for the new mall hasn't been signed."

Prez slams the newspaper down on the desk. "We've got to put this right. Christ. What a thing to happen. Do a fuckin' good deed and it blows up in our faces."

I stiffen. "Couldn't have left her there to die in the fire."

"Of course not, Peg. But we should have sent her on her way."

Instead of waiting for me to return, the door behind pushes open, and Ma wheels herself in. She's puffing with the effort. "And I'd be off in a flash if I thought that would solve this mess out." She glares at Drummer. "But the damage has been done, hasn't it? I apologise for the fuck-up of my son. He's always been hot-headed and selfish."

"Ma…"

"You let me sort this out. My son isn't the only one who can speak to the press. I'll make them do a retraction."

"Ma…" Prez's voice softens. "Appreciate that, but what's done is done. We've worked hard for years to clean up the club, but that article stirred old memories again. It'll take time for us to recover."

"I'm sorry, Ma," the VP puts in, "but I think you need to leave. The club ain't no place for a lady such as yourself, and once you're set up with your son, at least everyone will know we're not forcin' you to stay."

"I disagree," Ma replies soundly. "I think here is where I should be. Oh, yes, I've got a vested interest. You boys remind me of my other sons. They say the good die young. *They* wouldn't have put me into a home and left me to rot. And they'd have died laughing to know I living in a biker club." She frowns slightly at her choice of words. "I feel useful, and that's something I haven't felt for years. Don't expect I've got much time left, but if you'll have me, here's where I want to stay."

I go to refute that her days are numbered, but one glare and I shut my mouth.

"I've already called the police. You should be getting visitors right about…"

Drummer's phone rings.

"Now," she finishes, a triumphant look on her face, trumping the fierce one on Prez's, which confirms she's right. We've got visitors at the gate.

Drum gets them escorted up to his office, and when they arrive, well, fuck me if it isn't Detective Harper, the cop who gave Darcy such a hard time. Immediately I tense.

There's a fake smile plastered on her face as she goes and sinks to her haunches in front of the wheelchair. "Now, Gramma. Your son's very worried about you. But don't worry, I'll have you out of here in no time."

"Ain't your gramma. You treat me with respect, young lady. I'm Mrs Jones to you." The vehemence in her voice has the detective rearing back. As the detective stands, Ma continues, "I want that son of mine arrested and charged with slander. What he told that newspaper is a bagful of lies."

"I can't arrest your son. He's worried about you."

"Well, he's got no need to worry. These boys put their own lives at risk to rescue me. More than that, knowing I've got no home to go back to, they've given me and my great-grand-daughter accommodation here."

"But they're making you work."

The look Ma throws her could kill. Drummer's studying her carefully, as though trying to memorise it. "You think anyone could make *me* do anything?"

"You do the cooking…"

"I'm sharing my old recipes, fool. You always believe everything you read? Fake news. Ever hear of that?"

She's still not backing down. "Your son…"

"My son cares only for himself and his freaking reputation." As Ma wheels the chair forward, the detective steps back. "I was looking out for myself when you were in diapers, and I'm still doing it now. I suppose you're the sort of person who'd put your own mother in an anonymous retirement home just to get her out of sight. Oh, yeah. You'd be the type."

"I, no, I…"

"I suggest you get out of here and go do what you can to put this mess right. And while you're doing that, put some effort into putting this man's woman's rapist behind bars."

My eyes widen. Ma certainly has her ear to the ground. A small smile comes over my face as I realise she's got my back.

"My son isn't the only one who can talk to the press. *I'll* be giving an interview myself. And while I'm at it, I'll suggest the police are holding back in young Darcy's case because they're in the pocket of Mercer."

Wraith, Drum, and I exchange sharp glances. Ma huffs a laugh. "I've known Mercer since he was a snivelling brat. Never had a clean handkerchief on him, that boy. Always wanted more than he was prepared to work for. Nasty piece of work, then and now. Looks like his son's turned out the same way, taking things he hasn't earned or deserves."

"Mrs Jones, there's no proof he was the man who assaulted Ms Cavanaugh…"

"I suggest you look harder," Ma snaps. "Volunteer for this job, did you? Easy work, taking an old lady off the compound. I figure you're a lazy one, and the press might like that story as well. How the police don't investigate the attack on a brave fire-fighter. Yes, I think they'd like to hear that."

The detective starts sputtering, but Ma overrides her again. "Your boss will appreciate knowing you're not going after the man responsible."

"There's no proof."

"Then I suggest you find some. You know who the culprit is. Do your job and go catch him. Now, I think we're finished here.

I've got phone calls to make." Ma turns the chair around, presenting her back to the cops. Giving me a wink, she wheels herself out.

Drum lifts his chin at them and waits.

Without a word, knowing they've been dismissed, they turn and leave. After checking the prospect's outside to escort them down to the gates, I return to the office and shut the door.

Wraith's staring at Drum, Prez looks bemused. They both look at me, and suddenly we all start to laugh.

"Think we should patch her in, Prez," Wraith suggests.

"Don't know about that, VP. I'm rather partial to wearing the president's patch. And she," he waves his hand toward the door, "could probably give me a run for it."

I shake my head. "Wonder what the fuck she was like in her younger days?"

Prez grins. "Too much for you to handle, SAA."

"Too right," I don't hesitate to agree. "Too fuckin' right."

"Take a seat, Peg." He waits until I sit down. "What's the word on your woman?"

My hand toys with my beard. "She's hopefully gettin' out of the hospital this weekend. Truck's going to be stayin' with her, as that fucker Mercer's still walkin' free."

As Drum throws me a look of sympathy, I know he's hearing the words I haven't said. But he focuses on the practical solution. "We need to get Mercer taken off the street."

"We do that." I go cold at the thought of that bastard getting near Darcy again. "Might have to deal with him myself."

"You're too close, Peg. He disappears, you'd be the first place they look."

"With Flash getting out, need to get this fixed as fast as we can." I brush my hand down my beard. "I threatened Harper I'd go over her head to her lieutenant. It's Diaz."

Drum lifts his chin. "I can do that. Figure if I talk to him, and Ma has her say, Harper will definitely be getting a kick up her ass."

I nod my thanks. "We need to get Cherry Orchard," fuck it, I can't say the name without smirking, "to retract her statement. I'll go see Mouse and see if he's found anything more."

Drum raises his chin in dismissal, and I take myself next door to the darkened office Mouse holes up in, walking as usual into what seems to be a solid wall of smoke.

Our computer guru looks up and nods. "You were right." He gets straight into it. "Someone's put a flag on Orchard's name, makin' it impossible for him to get any financin'."

"Has Cherry's father ever had trouble before?"

"Nah, his financial report says no. Don't know why he went to Mercer's in the first place."

"Cherry suggested he got low interest rates."

"Hmm…" Mouse takes a tin out of a drawer and starts rolling another joint. "They may be targetin' people who they want to keep in hand. Then, when they want to use them, raise the interest rates. It was probably in the small print, which no one ever reads. Hey, found something out that's interestin'. Mercer Senior's a member of a prestigious golf club. Orchard's also a member. So's the judge that heard Mercer Junior's bail case…"

I inhale deeply and then sigh. "You think that's how he does it? Makes friends, then coaxes them in with a friend's benefits deal, then they find it hadn't been so friendly."

"Would make sense. I'm looking at other members."

I nod. "See if any are cops. They're not putting the effort into putting Mercer away like they should."

"I'll dig out who the members are and look at their occupations." Mouse sweeps his long hair behind his ears to stop it flopping over his eyes. "It's a private club, not big. And with the sky-high membership fees, I doubt there's many that can afford to join."

"And Mercer will be there to offer his help if anyone needs a loan. Stockin' up favours he can call on for the future. Like keeping his son out of jail."

Mouse offers me a drag on his joint, and accepting, I inhale deeply before passing it back. "What was going on in there?" He jerks his head toward the wall connecting his office with Drummer's.

I laugh, feeling more relaxed than at any time since reading the fucking news article. "Ma's going to give the newspaper a piece of her mind. And she let the cops have it too. Tore them a new one for not going after Mercer." I break off, narrowing my eyes. "How the fuck she knew about him, I don't know."

"Has she not had a chat with you yet?" Mouse looks surprised as I shake my head. "I wouldn't be surprised if she's had a past in interrogation. Let's see, she's learned of my childhood on the reservation—and you know I never speak about that—and I believe I may have told her the name of my first girlfriend in school. I did manage to head her off on the date of my first fuck."

I'm roaring with laughter now.

"Saw her havin' a word with Wraith yesterday. Poor asshole probably doesn't even know how much he told her."

Ma's special recipe fried chicken is on the menu tonight, and it's a full house. Even Slick and Ella, who are now living off the compound, stay around to eat. Having had those words with Mouse, I steer clear and try not to be alone with the old woman, turning away to hide my grin when I see her cornering Drum.

The next morning a reporter arrives early.

CHAPTER 35

Darcy

They get you up early in the hospital. Waking you even if you're asleep. I've no idea why. Surely rest helps while you're healing? But no, they seem to work to a different time frame than everybody else.

The physiotherapist has just left me, when there's a knock on my door. I open my mouth but don't have time to get out any words before Peg comes barrelling in. He's got a huge great grin on his face and, crossing to my bed, thrusts a newspaper at me which my hands take automatically.

Too impatient to wait, he takes it from me again, turning it so it's the right way, then hands it back with the front page facing up.

SATAN'S DEVILS ADOPT OLD LADY – REPORTS OF KIDNAPPING FAKE NEWS

A few days ago, based on information from Samuel Jones, 64, we published a report of the kidnapping and forced imprisonment of his mother, Mary Jones, 93, by the Satan's Devils Motorcycle Club. To tell her side of the story, Mary Jones invited this reporter to visit her at the compound.

As the recent Snake Fire swept down the mountains, Mary Jones was alone with her great-granddaughter, Sarah Jones, 21. Sarah had been staying, looking after Mary, who was bedridden, but was unable to get her in and out of a wheelchair. When the phones went out, they couldn't leave and had no way of summoning help. Sarah refused to leave her great-grandmother, and both were in the direct path of the fire.

Forgotten by the authorities and by her son, Samuel Jones, who lives in Phoenix, the women were all on their own. Remembered only by members of the Satan's Devils MC. Twelve years ago, Mary had complained bitterly about their presence when they first arrived at their compound, expecting drugs, guns, murder, and mayhem to become rife in the area. In fact, she'd heard nothing untoward from the compound during those twelve years. Until they decided to check on their neighbour to make sure she had evacuated.

On finding Mary and Sarah helpless and trapped in the direct path of the fire, the bikers came to their rescue, taking them to their compound. Mary soon found (as I did when I visited) that it was nothing like she had imagined. Families with children were present—in fact, twins were delivered in the height of the fire by firefighters. The bikers used bad language but were always polite around her and her great-granddaughter. There were a few scantily-clad women, but none held by force. Mary rewarded their generosity by sharing her favourite recipes with them. After years of being bedridden, these strong men had no difficulty helping her use the wheelchair, and, as Mary says, can't do enough to help her.

When word came that her house had been burned to the ground, the bikers offered her and Sarah a permanent home, which she accepted, preferring the young company instead of going, as her son had suggested, to a retirement home. In Mary's words, it was her son who wanted to force her to live somewhere she didn't want to, not the Satan's Devils MC.

Mary hasn't seen stocks of weapons, drugs, or any nefarious behaviour and has become affectionately known as 'Ma'.

Take a second to rethink of your opinion of one of Tucson's most notorious biker clubs and compare it with their neighbourly behaviour. The Satan's Devils MC admit they've got a past they're working hard to convince people they've left far behind, and part of that proof comes in the form of their hospitality shown to Mary Jones. I think after hearing her story, we'd all like the Satan's Devils looking out for us.

I, for one, was grateful to be allowed a glimpse into the life of a real-life MC. If it wasn't for the fact I don't ride a motorcycle, would think of joining them myself.

Samuel Jones was not available for comment.

I put the paper down, staring at the headline, then look up at Peg. "Wow," I say, shaking my head. "When that old lady goes to bat she doesn't hold back, does she? She's dropped her selfish son right in it."

"She has," he agrees. "That she has."

After a quick glance at him, I look down at the paper again. A flicker of hope burns in my heart. "This might change everything."

When I look at him again, a pained look crosses his face, and suddenly I feel guilty. He told me he'd leave his club, but I never reciprocated by saying he was more important to me than my job. Now I feel the need to explain. "Peg. If you left the club, you wouldn't be the same person. And if I left the fire service, I'd feel a part of me was missing. We might make it work, but it's one hell of a risk. We could end up hating each other."

My head still turned down, I peer through my eyelashes to see him slowly nodding his head. "I can see why you think you're right. But for my part, what I feel about you trumps anything about where we live and our jobs."

But there's more to it than just our careers. "I might never be the same again, Peg. After Pete..." I don't need to elucidate.

"I'll help you to try. We'll work on everything together, darlin'. If you just give us a chance."

From the moment he'd walked into the room, I'd felt protected, the continual fear at the back of my mind that Pete might try to get to me, even here, disappearing. A calm I don't feel with other people, even Truck. *Peg would give his life to keep me safe.* As his words wash over me, his resonant voice breaks my resolve. "What do you want me to say, Peg?" I whisper.

"I want you to say that you'll give up on the idea of fuckin' Truck stayin' with you. I want you to come back to the club when you're released from here. I want to know you're okay and protected twenty-four hours a day so that motherfucker can't get anywhere near you. I want to hold you in my arms at night, to know you're alright." His words, the tone he uses, are almost hypnotic. The picture he's painting is sounding so attractive.

Biting my lip to stop myself blurting out, *yes*, I try to make him understand. "Pete *hurt* me."

He immediately knows I don't mean the pain that came from getting shot. "I know that, darlin'. And trust me, I'll take it so easy. I'll never go further than what you want. You're in charge, and if you're never ready, well, that'll be alright, as I'll have the woman I love beside me, in my life and, when you've healed fully, on the back of my bike."

A half smile plays at my lips. "On your bike, eh?"

"Back of my bike," he corrects.

"Oh yeah? And what if I wanted one for myself?"

He takes a step closer and touches my hand. When I don't flinch away, he wraps his fingers around mine. "Flash, babe, you must know by now, I'll do what I can to give you the moon, if that's what you'd fuckin' like."

Deep down, I know that. I can't give up someone who thinks so much of me and I know I can believe him when he says he'll wait. "Peg?"

"What darlin'?"

"Will, will you hold me?"

He perches on the side of the bed, and carefully, oh so gently, puts first one arm across me, curling behind my left shoulder. Then his other hand curls without tightening around the back of my neck, then he rests his head down to touch mine. It's not suffocating, it doesn't feel like a trap springing shut. He seems to know just how much I can take. "I'll always hold you, darlin'. I'll always be there when you need me. I hate that I wasn't there when it mattered…"

"It was my fault, Peg. I should have stayed and talked. It wouldn't have happened if I hadn't left."

His hand moves from my shoulder, and his fingertips push my chin up. "The days you spent fighting the fire, the birth of the twins. It all added up. I don't blame you for leavin', and the only person whose fault this all is, is Mercer."

"Are the police going to get him, Peg?"

"That was the other thing I had to tell you. His alibi was false, and I'm trying to persuade the woman who said he was with her to come forward."

"You won't hurt her, will you?"

"Nah, sweetheart. In fact, we're doing something to help her. She's caught in one of Pete's traps too."

"Peg?"

"What, darlin'?"

I search my mind, but already know I'm doing the right thing when I tell him, "I'll come back to the compound."

His head goes back, and he closes his eyes. Tiny changes in the way he's holding himself show the tension leaving his body. His physical reaction to the news more stunning than his words. "Flash, I'm going to make it my life's work to ensure you never regret it."

Saturday morning sees me being wheeled in a chair to the hospital entrance with my man walking alongside me. It's strange to be out in the big wide world again after being cooped up for so long, and the wide-open space of the parking lot suddenly makes me feel exposed. I hang onto Peg's arm. He pats my hand reassuringly, knowing without me telling him how vulnerable I feel. His touch immediately reassures me. *Pete won't get near me if Peg's here.*

The journey back to the compound makes me grit my teeth. However carefully Peg's driving, the slightest turn or bump pulls at the tender, only just starting to heal muscle in my stomach. The doctors have warned me, getting a muscle to knit back together can take longer than the healing of a broken bone. My foot will be out of the cast within the next month, but my other bullet wound just needs care and time.

The track to the compound is the worst, and I'm unable to suppress the gasp which comes out of my mouth.

"Almost there, sweetheart."

At last we arrive. As Peg stops the truck in front of the club-house, I lean my head back with relief and wait for the pain to subside, remembering last time I was here smoke was billowing around and fire raging down from the mountains. Now all's quiet except for a Harley engine being revved at their auto shop down at the entrance.

"Swing your legs out."

As I do what Peg suggests, his strong arms hold me until my feet are on the ground.

"Want to go to the clubhouse, or up to the suite for a while?"

"Clubroom," I say with determination. I've had enough of lying down and being treated like an invalid.

To my surprise, as I hop with my crutch through the door Peg's holding open for me, I see a banner stretched over the bar, and remember that Heart's even now collecting Marcia and the babies and bringing them back today. The 'Welcome Home' banner must be for them. That explains the bikers and old ladies milling around, clearly waiting to greet them. But to my surprise, they all stop what they're doing, the room goes silent as conversations cease, and suddenly, everyone's looking at me. There, at the end of the bar, I see familiar faces. Slade, Hammer, and Truck. I acknowledge them with a little bemused wave of my hand.

I'm still stunned when Drummer steps forward, the president himself. "Welcome home, Darcy."

I go wide-eyed. *Surely the welcome hasn't been arranged for me?*

He sees my confusion. "You're a bit of a hero here. Fightin' the fire and deliverin' Marcia's babies."

I don't feel heroic in the least. Not after what happened with Pete. "I didn't do any of it alone. I only helped…" I wave toward my crew. "Hammer did most with Marcia's delivery, and we were all out there fighting the fire."

"You're a fuckin' brave woman." Peg dismisses my objections. "And everyone here wants to say thank you."

"I doubt you're up to a full-on party." Sam comes to stand by Drummer's side. "But we've got food made up if you're hungry. And my old man's right, we feel we owe a lot to you, and your crew."

Murmurs of agreement come from all corners of the room, and a few of the bikers shout various things, like, 'Welcome home, Flash' and 'Too fuckin' right'.

My eyes are watering, I put it down to still being weak.

"Hey, come sit down." Peg disengages from me as Sam takes my hand and leads me across to a couch. "Shall I get you a plate?"

Mouth-watering smells are coming from the kitchen, and having greeted me, the bikers have wandered off and are returning with filled plates. "Please, Sam. But not too much."

Peg comes and sits beside me, and as the couch dips under his weight, the action pulls at my stomach muscles again. Reaching into his cut, he pulls out my painkillers and passes them to me, then hails Fergus and asks him to get me a soda.

Slade comes over and pulls up a chair. "Glad to be out of the hospital, Flash?"

"Absolutely. And I can't wait to get back to work."

"Don't rush it," he warns. "Make sure you're one hundred percent before you come back. 'Cause I won't be taking it easy on you just because you got shot."

That makes me laugh, as it was supposed to and suddenly the world rights itself. When Hammer joins us, I ask about the calls they've been on, talking shop with Peg's arm casually lying over my shoulder. He's not contributing, just showing an interest in what's been going on.

I'm surprised Truck hasn't come to talk to me but looking across the room I see him deep in conversation with Wraith and Drummer. But I don't have long to wonder what they have to discuss as the clubroom door opens, and Marcia and Heart enter, each carrying one of their twins. Hammer looks at me and grins, and we enjoy a shared moment, flashbacks to when those children were born.

CHAPTER 36

Peg

I t's been two weeks now, Prez." I thump the table, frustrated. "Flash is recoverin' physically, but I can't keep her locked down forever. While Mercer's on the loose, she's terrified of leaving the compound."

"He needs to be put away." Wraith agrees from across the table.

"We need to get Cherry to come forward and change her story." That's a big part of what's annoying me. If she does, Pete Mercer has no alibi, except for the one his father had given him, which, under the circumstance, must be suspect. Cherry's withdrawal of support would surely make the cops at least question him again.

The lines on Drummer's face show he's sharing my vexation. "I've spoken to Lieutenant Diaz, but Mercer's still got his father saying he was at home the night Flash was attacked. To us, it's a dubious alibi, but Mercer Senior's an upstanding citizen until we can prove different, and an important businessman in this town." He catches the expression on my face. "What you thinkin', Peg?"

"I'm thinkin' I want to do what I wanted to do all along. Get up close and personal with Mercer Junior, make him suffer and finish him once and for all."

"Our original plan was to get him locked up, then call in a favour and get him killed in prison. Still prefer to go that route." Yeah, we might be a clean club, but we've still got contacts.

"If the police aren't movin' in on him, it's gonna come to me takin' care of it myself." I give Drum fair warning. I'm not putting my old lady in danger again.

Drummer strokes his beard and seems to be ignoring the comments coming to me in all directions. Flash is well respected here, but all of us have seen the changes in her since she's come back. She jumps at the slightest noise, avoids any man's touch—even mine she'll only just about tolerate. Yesterday, Beef came up intent on his phone, not looking where he was going and bumped into her. She screamed.

When the clubroom gets crowded, she tries to hide it, but I've watched the blood drain from her face, and taking her hand, feel her pulse racing. She might be healing physically, but mentally she's got a long way to go.

Prez raps the table. "Mouse, what's the latest?"

"As you know, Mercer's bank loan agreement has a tiny clause buried in the small print. While the initial interest rate is low, sometimes zero percent, at the discretion of the bank this can be changed to that nearer of a payday loan, over twelve-hundred percent."

"And on the size of the loans he's dishin' out, that would be cripplin' to anyone."

Mouse nods at me. "Exactly. Imagine the interest on a million-dollar deal."

"Is it legal?"

"Yeah, Beef. Perfectly legal. I've checked with Alex, and she went over it with a fine-tooth comb." Alex is taking on more and more duties as our club lawyer. Married to Dart, the VP of our San Diego chapter, Alex is halfway through getting her law degree, which is being paid for by the club. "It's like anything, it's an agreement. Once you've signed it you've agreed to the terms. What is unusual is that the bank don't need a reason to increase the interest."

"Who the fuck would sign that?"

Mouse shrugs. "Rock, it's Mercer's golfing buddies. Deals are often done on the green with little more than a handshake."

"And they say there's no honour among thieves." Shooter looks amazed.

"Mercer must be rakin' it in."

I shake my head and nod to Mouse to let him know I've got this covered. "The top interest rate is rarely applied, or if it is, it's reversed. It's there as a threat, and only pointed out when Mercer needs a favour."

"But it can't always work, can it?"

"No, Road." I tell him what Mouse has already told me. "You're right. Remember that prominent politician's suicide? It was all over the news, as him takin' his own life didn't make sense. He was happily married and had a staunch reputation. It was concluded he must have been suffering depression that he was hidin'."

"But," Mouse takes over, "I've found he'd taken out a loan to cover his mortgage. With Mercer's bank. There's no proof, but it makes sense Mercer would want a politician in his pocket, particularly one who everyone from all political parties agrees on that he's straight."

"You say there's no proof? But if you're right, Mercer must have approached him."

"Not everything's kept on computers," Mouse reminds Drum. "A handwritten estimate of what he'd be payin' would work just as well. Or printed from a computer not connected to the web."

"Mercer must have documents somewhere," Blade observes, his knife spinning as normal.

Dollar cracks his knuckles. "What if we find that proof? We can discredit Mercer and anyone who's been sucked into his control." He throws a snide smile toward the prez. "Think an MC would be handy to Mercer?"

Well, fuck me. "Muscle," I breathe out.

Drum's staring at Dollar, and I watch as what passes for a smile for the prez spreads over his face. "Fuckin' good idea, Dollar. If it doesn't work, we just pay the money back. No harm, no foul."

"And if it does?" Jekyll's looking confused. "We get landed with a bill we can't pay. Even a day's interest at that level would break us."

"Not if it didn't get applied." Dollar takes the floor back. "But I'm guessing it won't be a lowly clerk who'd discuss the hidden clause. It would be Mercer himself."

"Giving us the opportunity to see how he does it."

"It could take a long time before he calls on us." That's my only objection.

"It's worth a try," Drummer says, then smirks. "Right, assholes, what do we need a couple of million for?"

After dismissing some of the inaner suggestions, we settle on expanding our construction company, with the new contract for the mall coming up that would be seen as legit. Although run by Viper and Bullet, all our businesses are owned jointly by the club.

While I was worried that we'd have to play a waiting game, as it turns out, Mercer takes the bait surprisingly quickly. Drummer puts in a request for a meeting on the Monday following Friday night's church and gets an appointment to see the man himself the following day.

"That was fast, Prez." I wave to Pussy, who's taking her turn behind the bar. To give her her due, she seems to enjoy it more than the other sweet butts, and gives me my beer with a smile.

Taking his whisky from Pussy, lines etch his forehead as Drummer replies, "You might have been onto something, Peg. There's no one else on his books who could provide the kind of services he probably thinks he could get from us."

"I'd like to be a fly on that wall."

"You know why you can't, Peg."

Yeah, I do. While I'd have loved to go to the meeting and see the man who sired my woman's nemesis, it makes more sense if the prez and our treasurer go instead.

With time on my hands while Prez and Dollar go to meet Mercer, I spend it with Flash, worried she's clearly struggling to cope. Obviously, she's not able to do any strenuous activity for another few weeks, and I wouldn't even dream of trying to fuck her until I get the okay that she's healed. But I want to touch her, kiss her, show those signs of affection which demonstrate how deeply I feel for her. But apart from allowing me to hold her hand and lightly put my arm around her, she evades all further intimacy.

At night she lies in my bed, but if I try to hold her, she pulls away. *At least she's here.* I'd rather have her with me, where I know she's safe, than out of my sight. Her lack of progress worries me, and every time I see her start at the slightest sound, it makes me wish all over again that Pete Mercer was dead.

I've spoken to Slick, taking advice from him as to how he helped Ella recover from her own ordeal, a multiple rape at the hands of what was then a rival MC. At his suggestion I decide to ask Ella to speak with her. I can only hope she has some success.

Noting the time, I leave her taking a nap and am back in the clubhouse when Prez returns. His raised chin lets me know they'd been successful as he passes over a copy of the contract he's signed to Mouse, and then goes to the bar. I go stand alongside him as he indicates to Allie he wants his whisky from the top shelf.

"Celebratin' being two million dollars richer?"

His mouth twists wryly. "Would buy a decent few bikes." He takes a sip of his drink, ice cubes rattling around. "Had to put the compound up as collateral. Not touchin' a fuckin' cent."

"What's the interest rate?"

"Well, we weren't offered zero, but a fair enough point five percent."

As I'm about to probe further, Mouse reappears, a frown on his face. "This isn't right. It's a standard contract. I've scanned it and been through it line by fuckin' line, and there's nothing about raising the interest rate."

Disturbed, I look at him, then toward Prez. *Mercer's being straight with us?* Shit. That idea didn't work, and now we've got two million dollars in the bank that we don't need. I don't understand how we could have got it so wrong, but trust Mouse to have checked the contract, and compared it to the one with the high interest rate. If he says it is, that clause is definitely missing.

Prez checks for himself and reaches the same conclusion. The three of us exchange worried looks. Why the fuck has Mercer given us such a large loan and played it straight? We were so sure we were on the right track.

We don't often get casual callers to the compound, so the next afternoon, when an unknown person appears at the gate, it's unusual. When Fergus calls up asking for instruction, Wraith and I happen to be in Drummer's office at the time.

"Fergus. Yeah, who is it?"

"Is it now?" Wraith and I tilt our heads, something in Drummer's tone having caught our attention.

"Bring him up."

At my raised eyebrow, Drummer ends the call and gives that half grin of his. "There's a clerk from Mercer's bank here."

"They bring the money in person?" Wraith laughs.

"Nah, that's already in our bank account. Dollar has checked."

A buzz of excitement comes over me. *We were right.*

"Something's going on, Prez."

"Yeah, Peg. And soon we'll find out what it is."

A man who couldn't look less threatening if he tried is shown in to Drummer's office. I stand and wave him to my seat. But the clerk who can be no taller than five-foot-six, and who's built as though he'd be blown over in a strong breeze, shakes his head.

"This shouldn't take long. Are you Rick Felix?"

I haven't heard Drummer's real name mentioned for a couple of years, but realise he must have had to use it to sign the official document.

"Yeah."

"Well, sir, I'm sorry, the contract you signed with Top Loans yesterday was the wrong version. I do apologise on behalf of the company that you were given an old contract to sign. I've come with a replacement that I'd like to ask you to put your signature to."

Drummer's eyes sharpen, and he successfully resists looking at me. I try to keep my face impassive, noticing Wraith studying the floor intently. "Any change I'll have to get my lawyer to look at."

"Oh, there's no need for that." The clerk sounds confident. "It's a minor error. There's a spelling mistake on page three. Look." Taking the wad of papers out of his briefcase, he flicks over the first couple of pages, and then points to a word near the top of the third page. "Contact should be contract. That's all it is. But we don't like to look unprofessional. So, if you wouldn't mind signing this one, everything will be hunky dory."

Hunky fucking dory? Who the hell speaks like that? *Someone who's trying to pull the wool over our eyes, that's who.* A quick glance at Wraith shows he's thinking exactly the same as me. The clerk even helpfully provides a pen for the prez to use.

Drummer's no fool. He flicks through the rest of the contract, skimming it with his eyes, probably giving it the same cursory glance everybody else must have done. He gives nothing away, but picks up his own pen, and scrawls his name at the bottom. Then at the clerk's request, initials every page. "You got a copy for me?"

"Of course, sir." The clerk gets another one out of his briefcase. It looks identical to the one Drummer has signed. To prove it, the clerk goes through the business of pointing out the corrected error again. "And to keep things tidy, could I please have the original back? We don't like incorrect documents hanging around."

Drummer doesn't argue, just opens the drawer of his desk, takes out the paperwork, and hands it back. The clerk nods and disappears it into his bag. Then he thanks us for our time and opens the door to leave. Fergus is waiting outside.

Once he's gone, I raise my brow.

Drum shakes his head. "I couldn't fuckin' see it. Get Mouse in."

Mouse knows exactly what he's looking for, turns to a page near the end, covered in very small print, and points it out. "They've been crafty. It's written in words, not numbers. If it was written as 1200% you'd have probably noticed it, but look, here it is written out, *the bank may increase the rate at their discretion to a sum of at least one-thousand, two-hundred percent.*" We all look at it, the tiny font they've used making it hard to read, and it's buried deep in a multitude of legalistic phrases.

"Fuck me. So that's how they do it." Drum's mouth turns up at the corners. "We've been screwed, brothers." He laughs. "Think it's time for a celebration." Reaching behind him, he opens a cupboard, takes out his special single malt, and pours four glasses. "Here's to becoming muscle for hire."

It still worries me. I'm a man of action, and I don't want to sit back and wait, preferring to be the one with my hand on the throttle. But now that's all we can do. Accepting we're left hanging until Mercer makes his move and starts making demands on us.

"Don't look so miserable, Peg. Mercer took the bait fast. It could be we won't have to wait very long. He might already have something in the works."

Wraith's leaning forward, rolling his glass between his hands. "Or we could report him to the feds. Surely that's the logical step for anyone who finds out what he's done?"

Drummer taps the paper, a copy of which he's just signed. "That's a legal document, and my fucking signature. Hard to prove. And he took the original, so nothing to compare."

"Would everyone just have given him the original like that?"

"His golfin' friends? Yeah. They'd trust him. And us? Well, we're just ignorant bikers."

"So the feds wouldn't have anything to work with. But surely they'd smell something off?"

"He'd come up with some excuse for that clause. Something about protecting the bank. A man like that would be well prepared with answers."

Drummer slowly shakes his head. "Nah, Peg, nothing to do but wait for him to make contact. My bet is the way he does it is to ask for something simple at first. Something small. But enough to dirty a man's hands. A favour, but not big enough to raise red flags. But something he could hold over their heads."

"Mercer is a clever man," Wraith observes.

But it remains to be seen, is he cleverer than us? He's under-estimated us, that's for sure. *We found both him and his game out.*

CHAPTER 37

Darcy

While it's good to get off the compound, I hate this bone-deep fear that invades my body almost as soon as we turn onto the interstate. Today Hyde's driving me to the hospital, and then to the occupational therapist the fire service uses. I'd been excited making my plans, nervous about leaving my place of safety, but knowing I need to get back out into the world.

After the therapist I'll go to the fire house and see if any of my crew are around. I miss their company and the camaraderie that comes with being part of a team. Last night I was thrilled with the thought of seeing them again, but now that I'm actually doing this, I'm starting to regret the arrangements I had made. I hadn't realised going back into Tucson would affect me so much.

My palms are sweaty, and every time the vehicle stops at a light or a junction, I anxiously look around, unable to forget how Pete ran Truck off the road. He could try something like that again, incapacitate Hyde and then take me. *In broad daylight? Don't be stupid.* But all the rationalisation in the world doesn't calm me. *Last time he just watched for the fire crews to get back, then it was easy for him to follow me.* This time he couldn't possibly know when I'd be leaving the compound. *He could have found out about the appointments I've got set up.* He could be waiting in the hospital, or OT's office.

"Hyde, will you come in with me?" I ask, my voice unsteady.

"Peg's told me not to leave you alone." Hyde's comforting voice calms me a fraction, but not much.

"Thank you, I'm…"

"You're scared. We all get that. Fuckin' cops still haven't made a move on Mercer." Hyde pauses as he concentrates on getting into the right lane. "But don't worry, Darcy, I'm not going to let him, or anyone for that matter, get close to you."

I bite my fingernails, a habit I thought I'd grown out of years ago, but today I can't help it. I've faced fires, run into burning buildings, but never have I felt such soul-destroying fear like this.

Despite my concerns, we get to the hospital without problem, and the doctor is pleased with my physical progress, issuing instructions to continue to take it easy for another couple of weeks. The confirmation that I'm healing well only serves to increase my anxiety. How much longer will Peg be happy to wait? I can't put him off forever, but I can't even bear to have him kiss me. While he says he understands, I know it hurts him when I keep pushing him away.

If Pete was locked up, maybe I'd be able to start moving on and begin taking my life back. But knowing he's walking around a free man, nothing can convince me he won't pounce again and this time, finish the job. *He told me he was a hunter* and I'm his prey.

My next appointment, and I talk to the occupational therapist about returning to work, which obviously won't be very soon. I miss being active and working with my crew. That again isn't helping my sanity. Pete's taken so much away from me. *I hate him. I wish I could kill him myself.*

Back in the car, I give voice to my thoughts, the words coming out. "I wish he was dead."

Hyde throws a sharp look at me, his eyes full of compassion. "I'm sure you do."

Another short drive, then we're walking into the fire station, and I feel useless all over again. I wanted to see the people I work with, but as Truck approaches with a huge grin on his face, I can't help but wish I was working alongside him.

"Hey, stranger. How you doing?" As he talks to me, Truck exchanges chin lifts with Hyde.

"Flash!" Now Captain Slade's appeared, and he's walking alongside Bat Chief Leadson. "How are you doing? Got a moment to chat?"

I leave Hyde talking to Truck and follow them into the break room where I update them on my physical condition and apologise for leaving them short. It doesn't help that someone's been transferred in from another crew to take my place. *That's my job he's doing.* I don't miss the glances they exchange with each other, and hate that I'm appearing weak in front of them. I knew this would happen. I absently nod as the bat chief leaves, knowing I'd been right and that they see me differently after what I've been through. A woman too weak to fight for herself. My self-pity brings a tear to my eye, and as I wipe it away, Slade gives me a hug.

A. Hug. To comfort a weak woman. I cringe, immediately making him back off.

Hammer comes in, and his sharp and trained eyes must read the situation. Instead of asking me the same questions everyone else has, he tells me about the call-outs they've been dispatched to. Making me laugh as he tells me about the man who'd threw out his back and got stuck in a car in a compromising position. It had been the woman's car, and how she'd explain to her husband why the roof had to be cut off he didn't know. As we throw around possible plausible excuses, the tears in my eyes are finally from amusement, not sorrow.

And then there's a call from dispatch, and they have to go out. Hyde stands beside me, interested in how quickly they get their kit together, on the engine, and go.

"Fuck, I only thought it happened like that on films and TV."

"No. It's real life. A second wasted could mean a person's life." My eyes follow the truck until it's out of sight, and I sigh with envy and regret.

"They didn't even know what they were going out for." Hyde seems impressed.

"They'll get briefed in the truck."

I'm still looking after it longingly, Hyde tries to comfort me. "You'll be back soon."

But will I be the same?

When I return to the compound, Peg's waiting for me, and there's a look of relief on his face that he's not quite able to hide. After having one of those strange man to man silent conversations over my head, he takes a look at my face then leads me up to the suite. I shake my head as he indicates the bedroom. I'm tired, but I don't want to rest. Don't want these thoughts to keep going around and around my head. I just want everything to stop, to go back to the woman I was before I ever met Pete.

As my thoughts accelerate and start racing through my brain, I feel tears rise, and all of a sudden, I'm swamped with emotion. Pushing past Peg, I go into what he's turned into the living room, and throw myself on a couch, beating my hands against the cushions.

Suddenly there's warm hands stroking my back, and a voice murmuring in my ear. "It's alright, it's going to be alright. I'm here. I'm never going to let anything happen to you."

I turn my head to face him, wiping my nose with the back of my hand. "I can't go on like this, Peg. I can't cope with the feeling he's going to get me again, however much you try to protect me. And I hate feeling like this. He's taken so much away. I want to hold you, to love you. But when you're near me, all I can see is him. When you touch me, I want to push you away, as my skin starts to crawl as my brain thinks it's him. When am I ever going to be normal again, Peg? Will I ever get there?"

"All I want to do is hold you, tell you everything's going to be fine. But fuck, babe, I don't know what to do or say. And I'm scared of doing or sayin' the wrong thing."

"It's so fucking unfair. I want to kill him myself. Want to make him suffer for what he's done to me." I'm wailing but can't help it.

Peg stands, his eyes never leaving me. He runs his hands through his hair, considering me carefully. "You want I should take him out? Would that really make you happy, knowin' he was dead? And that I did it? Fuck, Darcy, I'd do anything for you. And it's not like I haven't done it before, never tried to hide that. But, babe, could you live with that knowledge?"

I shake my head. Put like that, I don't know. What if Peg gets caught? What I couldn't live with is knowing he was locked away because of what Pete had done to me. One more thing that bastard would have taken away.

Rolling his head back on his shoulders, Peg pauses, his eyes on the ceiling for a moment, then he looks down and steps toward me. Gesturing with his hands, I translate he wants me to move over and give him some space to sit down. When he does, he bends his good leg and rests his knee on the couch, turning to face me.

"I'm going to tell you club business, because I think you need to know. It's makin' you crazy not knowin' if anything's being done. Assure you, babe. We're not sitting on our asses." He gives me an intense look. "Anything I say stays here in this room."

As he regards me intently, I nod, curiosity piquing.

"If Pete goes to prison, he won't be comin' out."

"Huh. He could get a light sentence…"

"Listen to me. He *won't* be comin' out." The forceful stare he gives me allows me to interpret his meaning.

"Oh." I purse my lips. "Even if he is arrested, if he gets the same judge, and uses that clever lawyer, he might not even go inside."

Peg sighs and doesn't seem comfortable. "We've got a plan. Mouse's diggin' turned some stuff up. Mercer Senior has the judge and a senior cop in his pocket. And that's who we're going after."

"The judge?"

A mirthless laugh. "No, Mercer, Pete's father." A pause, as though he's struggling with telling me stuff usually not shared outside of the brothers. A quick nod, as though he's sealing his resolve, then he starts with the serious stuff. "Okay, here it is. Mercer cons people into signing loan agreements with a hidden clause that can be invoked any time. Allows him to charge interest at well over a thousand percent."

Wow. "That's a huge amount."

"He also flags them up as a credit risk, and they can't get a loan anywhere else. That's what happened to Cherry Orchard, the witness who came forward for Pete. Her father had taken out a loan with him, and Mercer threatened to raise the rates. Mouse has done his magic and got the flags removed, and Cherry's father got a new loan and will be able to pay off the one with Mercer's bank. When he does so, Cherry is willin' to change her story."

"And tell the police all about them?" That would get rid of both Mercers.

Peg sighs. "Maybe. But there's nothing in writing. A verbal suggestion from Pete Mercer to Cherry." Peg's eyes stare off into the distance for a moment. "Orchard was furious when he found out, but has agreed not to approach Mercer Senior for now, to give us time to dig up more dirt. And at least he can breathe easy knowin' there's no longer a threat being held over his, or his daughter's head."

Suddenly my hand goes over my mouth. "Pete will be furious. He might hurt Cherry…"

Peg's attention is firmly on me again. "Don't you think we've thought of that? That's why we're holding back on Cherry changin' her story. If we wrap this up ourselves, she won't get into trouble for lyin' to the police. For now, Pete doesn't know anything about it."

Now I'm curious. "How are you going to wrap this up?"

"We've taken out a loan."

"You?" I can't for the life of me see how that's going to help.

"Yeah, well, the club. It was too easy. We think Mercer might have use of some of what he thinks are services the club offers. In fact, it's moving faster than we hoped. Prez has been invited to the golf club he goes to. It was phrased as some new customer welcome bullshit, but I figure Drummer's going to be given a choice. Pay extortionate interest or do the work Mercer wants."

"But you've only just taken out the loan. You could simply repay it."

"Mouse has fixed it so it looks like we've already spent the money."

"But isn't it risky? If Drummer goes to meet him and is threatened, it's only his word against his, surely?"

"Drummer's going in with a wire. Everything Mercer says will be recorded. And that's the info we can take to the police. Anyone awarded a loan from Mercer's bank will be suspect. Cherry will testify, and Pete will be up in front of an independent judge. There'll be no chance for him then."

Suddenly something hits me. "Pete… He mentioned I'd mucked up his plans, that I never took him to meet my family.

Is that anything to do with this?" Perhaps if I can find some explanation for his behaviour, it would all make sense. I could never understand why Pete had targeted me in the first place.

"Your dad owns a pharmaceutical company, doesn't he?"

I give a half-hearted smile. "Mouse checked me out."

Peg doesn't bother to confirm or deny it. "An in with that sort of business might open up opportunities for Mercer."

"You mean drugs." Vehemently I shake my head. "My father would never agree to anything like that."

"With ruination hanging over his head? Or is he so straight he'd prefer to lose his company? His livelihood? His house? No one knows what they'd do until they were tested."

Who am I to say? I might have lived with him for the first eighteen years of my life, but I don't know my father at all. Or my mother, come to that.

"Do you really think your plan will work and solve everything?" I stand and walk over to the balcony door, seeing, but not taking in the fabulous view.

"It will solve it in that Pete's not walkin' around anymore and won't be able to hurt you." I hear footsteps behind, then Peg's slowly turning me around to face him. "What I can't guarantee it will settle, is how you're feelin' in there." His thumb gently soothes across my forehead.

"I don't know what to do," I admit.

Again, his grey eyes regard me intently. "I want you to go to counsellin'."

Make me go through my ordeal again? Explain it to another person? Bring my weakness out into the open? "Talking to someone wouldn't do any good."

He bobs his head up and down. "Yes, it will. Look, Slick's spoken to Jayden and Ella, and they're both happy to talk to you. If you can get Jayden on her own without Paladin that is."

"Why Ella and Jayden?"

"Ella was gang raped, and Jayden was groomed and forced to provide sexual services to men."

Once again, my hand covers my mouth. "But Jayden's so young!" She's such a sweet girl, I can't bear the thought anything like that happened to her.

"At the time she was only fourteen." Peg's lips purse.

I can't believe it. Ella's always happy and smiling, and Jayden's just like any teenage girl. "But they're so strong. You wouldn't know anything had happened to them."

"They went to counsellin', babe. And Slick says it helped. Let's give it a try for you, okay?"

I think for a moment. If counselling helped them, should I try it? Rather than talking about it, I'd much rather forget. *Yeah, and you're doing a fantastic job on that. Nightmares every night reliving what Pete did.*

Peg waits patiently while I have my internal battle. I make a decision after a few moments. "Okay," I say softly.

"Okay? I'll set it up? Find out who Ella recommends?"

"On one condition." When he raises that quizzical brow I continue, "That you take me, Peg. Hyde did what he could to make me feel safe, but I'll be happier if you're there." I tug on the edges of his cut. "My very own sergeant-at-arms to protect me. You wouldn't let Pete get anywhere close."

"Too fuckin' right."

CHAPTER 38

Peg

Drum's invitation is for two people.

"You need your sergeant-at-arms by your side," I state, fixing my eyes on him.

"Uh oh, VP." Wraith points at himself.

"Treasurer. You'll be talkin' money after all."

The prez wipes his hand over his beard and shakes his head towards Blade, who was clearly going to offer to attend as enforcer. "Peg," He says decisively, pointing straight at me. As a wave of protests begin, Drummer bangs the gavel. "Shut up and let me speak." His glare encompasses us all. "It's Peg's old lady that Mercer's son's been targetin', Peg's got a right to meet the man face to face. And I've got a right to have protection with me."

As I sit back, feeling relieved, Drum allows some time for his thoughts to settle in.

"Peg's too close. He might lose his temper."

"Wraith, I'm just going to be sittin' back lettin' Mercer drop himself in it." I point my finger at the VP. "Ain't gonna be sayin' a word out of place." Though it will be hard not to reach over the table and throttle him with my bare hands.

"How d'you intend to play it, Prez?"

"We'll play it by ear. Figure I can bluff my way if I have to." Drum changes the subject. "How's Ma settlin' in?"

That makes me smile. "She's doing great. Viper and Bullet's crew have worked hard, set up a hoist over her bed so Sarah can get her in and out of the wheelchair. Adapted the bathroom as well, got ramps everywhere and handrails." I laugh. "She told them 'it'll do', which I translate that she's overjoyed with it."

"Fuckin' good food we've been gettin'."

Wraith's certainly not wrong there. I don't know how the old lady does it but telling the women to use an herb here or a spice there has made a fuckload of difference.

Dollar frowns. "She told me I shouldn't need to use a calculator. That in her day everyone did sums in their heads."

Yup. She always has a caustic comment for everyone. But I can't forget that favour she did me, going to the press and giving us some mark of respectability.

Two days later, Drummer and I park our bikes beside Jags and Ferraris and walk into the golf club's restaurant. Our only nod at their fancy dress code is to wear clean jeans and button-down shirts under our cuts. Mercer must have prepared them to expect us, as apart from curious looks the members can't hide, the staff don't bat an eyelid at our approach, and simply take us directly to a private room.

Mercer's already waiting, and I take a moment to scrutinise the man who, by concocting the plan with his son, is indirectly responsible for causing my woman so much suffering. I already know he's sixty, and he looks every year of his age. His cheeks reddened not by the sun, but by broken veins, suggesting an overindulgence in food and drink. A rounded face, and the way his jacket stretches around the button that he's fastened as he stands, shrieks evidence of gluttony.

In the same way I'm inspecting him, he's observing me, and while his smile is supposed to be welcoming, there's a calculating sharpness he can't hide in the depth of his eyes. He reminds me of a shark I once saw in an aquarium.

"Drummer. Glad you could make it." He comes over and shakes Prez's hand, then holds his out to me. "And you are?"

"Peg."

"Peg." He glances at my cut and sees my position. "Ah, sergeant-at-arms." If my role bothers him, he gives no sign. "Well, now, both of you, please come and take a seat. I've ordered a taster menu for us, I hope that's alright?"

Dubiously eyeing up the amount of cutlery sitting either side of the plates, I'm wondering whether I'll disgrace myself, though couldn't really give a fuck either way. I've not come for food, as the tape tugging a little uncomfortably at my chest hair and pulling as I bend to take my seat reminds me.

When we're both sitting, servers appear, silently placing a plate with a tiny portion of something in front of me. I pick it up and finish it in one bite. If this is gourmet food, it isn't for me. Such a small amount, I barely tasted it.

"Drummer," Mercer starts, licking his lips and fingers, showing how much he appreciated the delicate offering. "I hear you've signed the construction contract to build the new mall. Congratulations. This really puts you in the big league."

Hmm. Mouse has done his work well. He's been laying a fake trail for Mercer to follow.

Drummer doesn't miss a beat. "Yeah, it's the biggest building contract we've taken on. And we've already committed to buying the extra machinery that we'll need."

"Payment in advance?"

Prez nods. "Cash up front, yeah. We haven't exactly got the best credit rating. Had no need for banks before."

A small smile plays at Mercer's lips, but it's only fleeting, and had I not been fully focused on him, I might have missed it. Another course is delivered, this one a tiny bowl of green soup. Only a couple of spoonful's, and I'm starting to wonder whether Mercer got this meal cheap.

Having loaded a soup spoon that's already emptied half of the contents, Drummer has just put the revolting coloured liquid into his mouth, and I'm watching his reaction before sampling mine, when Mercer starts speaking.

"Yes, your credit rating. My board has looked at your loan once again. And I'm afraid we've got to raise your interest rate."

Drummer's got his napkin to his mouth in time to catch the soup that's spluttered out of his mouth. Mercer might think it's because of his words, but I know it's because the banker's approached it so soon. Prez's eyes narrow, but then his features relax. "We signed a contract. Agreed on an interest rate. Put both our signatures on it. You can't raise it now."

"Oh, but I can, Drummer. Oh look, you'll like this one." He waits for the servers to swap soup plates for something that at least looks like meat, the tiniest bird you could ever imagine, surrounded by a couple of leaves. "Thank you, the consommé was delicious," he compliments them politely. "Yes, Drummer, there's a clause in the contract that allows us to increase the percentage we're charging." He looks up and his nose twitches, though I don't think it's the aromatic food he's smelling, but what he thinks is fear in Drummer's eyes.

If this was a normal situation, a businessman having worked out his bottom line based on calculations of a contract he thought he'd bought into, that man would be quickly running through estimates in his head of precisely what level of inflated rate he could afford.

"I had my lawyers look over it." At last prez speaks. "It's water-tight as far as they could see." With knife and fork he starts picking away at the small bird, showing he's confident he's got nothing to worry about.

I do likewise, wishing I could pick the darn thing up and tear what little flesh there is off with my teeth. I quickly give up. Mercer's got that smile back on his face as the servers come back. I tense imperceptibly as I notice behind them, three men have come in, and position themselves around the room. *Here it comes.*

Picking up a briefcase, Mercer reaches inside, pulling out what I expect will be the contract we signed. "This is the contract we made?" He shows Drummer the page at the end, and flicks through the rest where every page is initialled.

"It seems to be."

Mercer takes out a pen and highlights some words, then passes the contract to the prez.

Drummer should get an Oscar. His eyes open wide, he stands up, the plate and the next course goes flying. Hardly a loss, or much for the servers to clear up. "What the fuck is this?" He leans over the table, getting right in Mercer's face. A hand lands on his shoulder, which he tries to shrug off, but the gun cocked in his ear has him quickly retaking his seat.

Mercer grins. "Your new interest rate. One-thousand-and-two-hundred percent, give or take."

"I didn't sign that."

"Yes, you did. Must admit I made a slight amendment to the contract the courier brought to your club."

"You motherfucker," Drum spits out.

Mercer shrugs. "Doesn't matter what you call me or think of me. The fact is, I've got your signature on a legal document, and you've agreed to the terms. I repeat, we've increased the rate to the highest amount written there. You might not be a busi-nessman, Drummer, and I'm happy for you to consult your lawyer again. But you'll just be wasting time. Every day, what you owe to my bank increases."

"We'll pay the loan back," Drummer throws out.

"You've just told me it's already tied up in plant, machinery you've already purchased."

Tapping his fingers on the table, glancing up at the man who's now pointing the gun to the back of his head, Drummer shakes his head. "We've not got that kind of money."

The banker doesn't seem bothered. "You could sell the compound."

Prez looks up sharply. "Is that what you want? All this to get the Satan's Devils out of Tucson?"

Barking a laugh, Mercer shakes his head. Then it's his turn to lean forward, pushing aside the plate of food he now seems to have no interest in. "I like you right where you are. And, as of now, the Satan's Devils are working for me."

"What the fuck do you mean?" Again, Drummer tries to stand, and once more he's pushed down.

Not seeming upset in any way, Mercer continues, "I'll reduce your interest rate, maybe even to zero. As long as you do whatever I say when I ask it."

"And what might be the kind of things you'd ask us to do?" Oh, Drummer deserves an Oscar at least, as he manages to look like a man grasping at straws.

Another shrug from Mercer. "Oh, things you'd be quite expert in. Putting pressure on people by roughing them up. Hell, I don't know all your skills. Setting fires, blowing stuff up. The point is, Drummer, you'll do whatever I want you to do, or I'll ruin your club."

"This little game work for you?"

"My game? A game you call it?" Mercer sits back. "Well, yes, I suppose it could be called that. And you've no idea how many people just gloss over a contract which they've already signed. I knew I could get it past ignorant bikers." He folds his arms over his chest. "You're in *my* pocket now, Drummer. Or I'll destroy you."

"We could go to the cops."

Now he laughs aloud. "A *biker* club? And with what? A legally signed contract? You think they'd believe your word over mine?"

"You've made us your enemy."

He chuckles again. "Isn't the first time I've heard that." He points to the men holding guns on us. "Doubt you'd be able to get close. And, take me out? I've got a board of directors and someone lined up to follow in my footsteps. No, you're trapped, Drummer. And you better come to your senses and admit it. Time's moving along, and with your new high interest rate, every second counts."

Drummer looks at me and raises his brow a fraction of an inch.

For the first time I speak. "Judge Chambers. He happen to take a loan out with your bank?"

As I've been assessing him, I think Mercer's a man who likes to boast. If I'm right, we could get the evidence we need.

"Chambers? God, yes."

Can I get him to admit more? Deciding to give it a try, I attempt to sound impressed. "So that's how your son got out of jail."

"Of course. And now I've got you working for me as well."

Ignoring the man holding the gun, Drummer gets to his feet and throws his napkin on his plate. "I'll have to take this to the table, you understand? Needs a club vote."

Mercer's now forced to look up. "Sure." He waves his hand. "You run back to your little club. But I already know what your answer will be. *Has* to be. You understand me?"

"Oh, I'm hearin' you loud and fuckin' clear."

I stand up alongside my prez, not at all surprised when we're escorted out by the men holding guns. They wait as we get on our bikes. As I put my key in my ignition, I say quietly, "Hope you got all that, Mouse."

Then, engines started, we ride away.

Parking outside the clubhouse, backing into our usual spots, before I get off I reach up under my t-shirt and rip the sticky tape holding the tiny microphone off, taking some chest hair with it. I notice Drummer doin the same. Fuck, I'm glad to get that off.

Drum is waiting for me. "Don't know about you, Peg, but I'm fuckin' starvin'."

My answer is a grin and a slap to his back as I follow him into the clubhouse, heading straight for the kitchen.

"Looks like we've got two hungry boys here, ladies." Ma wheels herself across. "Fill a couple of plates."

"Always hungry for your food, Ma." I nod at Sophie, who's put a laden plate in front of me. *Now this is more like it.* "Never been fed as well since you've been here."

Sandy huffs and puts her hands on her hips. "That's all the gratitude we get? You never complained when you were shovelling our food in your mouth."

Drum gives a little shake of his head, and I respond by raising my chin. Not worth arguing. But there's no doubt Ma knows her stuff.

There's a whoosh and a grey streak as another hungry mouth appears. "Grunt. Get down," Heart shouts as he comes in with his old lady. They're carrying a baby each, and Amy's skipping alongside. My appetite flees as I'm consumed by envy. I'd thought that was in my reach, but Mercer took it away.

I push away my uneaten food. "I'm off to see Mouse."

Drum stands. Unlike me, he's bringing his plate. "Yeah," he says simply, but the fact he's not wasting time shows he's as eager as me to put an end to it.

Mouse just nods to the chairs in front of his desk as we enter his office. It looks like he's been expecting us. "Got everything." He gets straight down to it, as though answering the question I'd asked when I left the golf club. "I've passed it to Devil. He's going to take it to the feds."

Devil's the Englishman who is some kind of a security consultant with useful links in the FBI. Having worked with him a time or two before, I know he's clearly the best man to take this on. He's got the credibility that we haven't. Marcia and Mouse have kept up their contact with him, conducting investigations on his behalf.

"Good move, Brother. I'd have suggested that myself." Drum shows no sign that he's bothered Mouse took it upon himself to contact Devil directly.

"Any idea what's going to happen next?"

A grin slowly spreads over Mouse's face. "I'd watch this space. Obviously the two of you weren't undertakin' surveillance on any official basis, but when they investigate, the facts will speak for themselves. Can't see anyone throwin' this out, and I expect to see Mercer in cuffs before too long. Oh, and how was lunch?"

Drum and I just look at each other and laugh. "Not a patch on Ma's," Drummer responds.

Mouse turns out to be right. The next morning the TV screens are alight with pictures of Mercer being removed from his bank and handcuffed, being put into a police car. The news reports speak of collusion and bribery at the top, and the bank's assets are frozen during the investigation.

CHAPTER 39

Darcy

Seeing Mercer brought low almost took my mind off my appointment today with the counsellor Ella had recommended. Almost. My anxiety at what I know will be a difficult interview for me to sit through translates into me being completely indecisive today. At first it was choosing what to wear. I've still only a limited wardrobe here, and after going through everything, trying to find something smart, decide I'm being ridiculous, and settle for my usual off-shift uniform of jeans and a tee. Both black.

Peg's waiting for me to collect my purse, bouncing the keys to the truck in his hands. He's not being impatient or hurrying me, just watching me with that look of sadness in his eyes I don't think he knows is there. Despite me being here and spending every night in his bed, I'm unable to let him close. While he's pinning his hopes on therapy, I can't see how talking to someone is going to make me feel like my old self again. I've been through too much, am simply a shadow of what I used to be.

He walks by my side as we go down to the shop where the truck is parked, making no move to take my hand. Any physical contact can make me feel trapped and trigger a panic attack, and today, he seems to know it would be even the touch of his fingers around mine.

"I know I suggested this, Flash. But if you're not feelin' up to it…?"

I could easily take the way out he's offered. But what if I do? Nothing else has helped. While I don't set much hope on getting an instant result, there's enough of me left to want to try anything which might help me through. "Can't deny that sounds tempting, Peg. But I think you're right. This is something I need to do." I risk a glance at him, looking into his kind but hurting eyes. "I don't know what you'll be bringing back."

Instead of putting Pete's unwelcome invasion of my body to the back of my mind, today I'm going to be forced to bring it to the forefront. I'm expecting it to be devastating.

Peg starts the engine, the prospect slides open the gates, and now we're driving down the track, past the desolate burned-out scenery. My surroundings seem apt for my state of mind. Like the ground that had everything growing stolen by the fire, Pete's taken away everything.

We're a few minutes early, and I fidget as I wait, unable to concentrate on a magazine.

Peg tries to help. "They'll soon find out about the judge, bring Pete back in. And Cherry will know it's safe to change her story."

I'm tapping my fingertips together. "Wish I was as certain of that."

"Mercer Senior's alibi won't hold up any longer. It will be discredited along with him."

That's all I can hope for. Even today with Peg driving I kept looking around, worrying that Pete was out there somewhere. I hate being scared all the time. My eyes flit to the clock on the wall.

The second hand's just ticked its way past the hour when an office door opens, and a pleasant-looking woman looks out into the room. "Darcy Cavanaugh?"

I get to my feet, and she stands back to allow me to precede her into the room.

I'd expected a doctor's office, but it's nothing like what I thought it would be. Two comfortable chairs are casually placed around a small table. As she waves at one, inviting me to sit down, my hand goes to my stomach muscles protectively.

Concerned eyes watch me. "You're still sore?"

Shaking my head, I explain, "I think it's become habit now. No, I'm more or less healed."

Sitting herself opposite, she leans back to her desk and picks up a tablet. For a second, she reads through some notes.

"Tell me a bit about yourself, Darcy."

"I'm a firefighter." I'm not sure what she wants.

"I'm aware of that. But tell me more about *you*, not your job. Let's go back a bit. How would you describe yourself as a little girl growing up?"

I feel a reprieve that she's not starting by wanting me to describe what Pete did to me, but am confused. Why does she want to know that? I try to answer her question as honestly as I can.

"Hmm. So, I'd be right in thinking your parents were quite controlling? And you spent a lot of time rebelling?" she surmises after I've been talking for a few minutes.

"Yeah. They tried to push me into the science subjects, but I was more into sports."

"Did they put much pressure on you to do what they wanted?"

"Not so much pressure, just disappointment, you know?" I smile. "In the end, we both decided it was best for me to go my own way. They couldn't understand me. Instead of fighting, we agreed to disagree. It was a way of avoiding confrontation."

The doctor smiles. "Would you describe yourself as knowing your own mind and being determined enough to follow it from an early age?"

I smirk. "Well, it was difficult for my parents to push me into doing things I didn't want to do."

"And what's your relationship like with your family now?"

I purse my lips, thinking how to describe it. "We're not close. Don't see each other enough. But we're still family, you know?"

"And do they know you were shot?"

"No. Oh, they'd be there if I needed them, but I don't." As I see her eyes narrow, I try to explain. "When I was young they let me go my own way. They didn't prevent it, but didn't help either. I got to where I am now on my own. Without their support."

"Or their encouragement?"

I think back. They didn't actively encourage or discourage me. In the end I shrug, not sure how to answer.

"Have you ever relied on anyone else, Darcy? Or ever wanted to?"

Her question brings to mind Peg and the reason I'm pushing him away. "It's hard for me. I've always demanded the freedom to do everything for myself. There's a man…"

"A man?" She leans back in her chair, folds her arms, and crosses her legs at the ankles.

Now I'm not sure why I mentioned him. "Oh, that's Peg. The man waiting outside. He wants a relationship with me, but he's a controlling man. Would want to be in charge of every situation."

"And he makes the wrong choices?" she taunts.

"No, no he doesn't. He's usually right."

"But doesn't see things the same way as you?"

Again, I refute that. "We think surprisingly alike."

"But sometimes you clash? Your views, opinions?"

Biting my lip, I admit, "We've never clashed." I remember we even share the same taste in music.

Unfolding her arms, she sits forward again. "Have you ever wanted a family of your own?"

"What woman doesn't?"

"And the man you would want is someone weaker than you, someone who leaves all the decisions to you…"

"Certainly not." I could never see myself with a wimp.

A smile appears as though she's scored a point. "You don't want to be controlled or do the controlling. You want a partner. Seems what you've got to work out is whether you've already found it." She hardly pauses before she changes track. "So, I know a bit more about you now, about what makes you tick. Now, this is getting to what I expect you think is the hard part. What you're going to do, Darcy, is to tell me in exact detail what happened to you."

"I can't."

She waves her hand around the office, drawing my attention to how light it is, the soothing scenic pictures on the wall. "This is a safe place, Darcy. What's going to happen in these sessions is that, yes, you'll be facing the trauma you went through, but by getting it out in this environment it can help you shape different memories about that night. I know you want to lock it away and not think about it, but you're just bottling it up. Take a breath, Darcy. And take me through that night step by step."

I've let down my guard, got side-tracked, and now she brings it up. The details I don't want to think about, let alone put it into words. As she instructed, I inhale deeply and start. "I thought Truck, another firefighter, was driving behind me. When he flashed his lights, I pulled over. I couldn't see who it was, got out of my car, and was knocked out. When I came to I was tied up. I ran. He caught me. He incapacitated me. He raped me then shot me again. I reported him, but he had a false alibi and got away with it."

There. I've got it out. I wait to see the shock and sympathy on her face.

But her expression doesn't change, though she's watching me carefully. "That's the abridged version. Now let's fill in the blanks. Take it from the beginning. What did you do? Remember, this is a safe place, Darcy." Her voice is calm, matter of fact.

My breath hitches, her question taking me back to the panic I'd felt. Feeling my hands tied behind me, my desperate run through the construction site as I tried to find somewhere to hide. Knowing what slim chance I had of escape, Pete behind, stalking me. I was helpless. I try to find the words to relive it all over again. She probes each time, bringing raw emotion to the fore as I recognise I was seeking to take back control of the situation—power that Pete had stolen.

"You realise you haven't dealt with any of this? Have you mentioned how you're feeling to anyone before?"

I shake my head.

"Because you don't want to admit to any weakness."

"I'm a woman." I'm sobbing now. "I work in a man's world."

"Ah." She picks up her tablet and jots something on it. Then her sharp eyes look up. "Tell me, Darcy. Your Peg, I couldn't help but notice how big he is. Would you describe him as a strong man?"

There wouldn't be many people who'd be foolish enough to take him on. "Yes. Nothing would bother him."

"Hmm." She purses her lips. "Picture Peg. Now hold an image in your head of him unarmed, his hands fastened behind him, and a man was chasing him with a gun? Do you think he'd be bothered then? What could he have done that you didn't do?"

I stare at her, my eyes open wide. In the end I shake my head as I've no answer. *Could Peg have escaped? Could he have fought back?*

"Seems to me no woman or man could have done more than you did."

"But I was raped."

She raises her shoulders to her ears. "Men can be raped too. And they're not immune to bullets. Sex doesn't come into it."

"I'm a firefighter. I should have been stronger." I break off and continue in a whisper. "I don't even know if I can go back to my job."

"Will you be physically fit enough?"

I nod.

"The men you work with, they threaten you? Make you worry they'd overpower…"

"God no. Of course they wouldn't. But they know what's happened to me…"

"And why would they think any the worse of you for it? We've just established even that tall, strong man waiting for you outside couldn't have done different."

I don't have an answer. She gives me space to think, then asks, "Are you up for carrying on?"

I know exactly where she's going to go next. But there's no point putting it off. The inclination of my head gives her the answer.

"The man who attacked and then raped you. I believe you knew him. Had you had sexual relations with him before?"

Looking down at my hands, I see they're shaking. "No." I barely recognise my own voice. "I know now he wanted to start a relationship with me, and not for the usual reasons. I was someone to get close to, someone he wanted to control. He wanted to use me to get to my parents."

"And that was never going to work, was it?"

"No." She's ignoring my reactions, not offering false sympathy. For some reason that's helping. "That's how I met Peg. That night Pete had slapped me, and I ran. I don't know why, it didn't occur to me to stay and fight."

"Flight or fight. It's an instantaneous decision."

"I'd been fooled into letting him stay in my house."

"Interesting use of words. Fooled? Or fed a line many people would have fallen for?"

"What does it matter?"

"Why do you think it would matter?"

She keeps challenging me. Like a school kid, I don't want to fail to come up with an answer. Racking my brains, I say, "Because it would affect the amount of guilt I take on myself?"

She smiles as if I've performed a clever trick. "Moving on. Let's go back to the construction site and what happened that night. Tell me more about that."

"He caught me and shot me in the foot to stop me escaping again. It was at that point he told me what he intended to do." I shudder as I remember.

"Did he want to impress you with his physical prowess and ask you to give him another chance?"

My shudder continues, my body now shaking. "Partly, I think, yes. But he was high on something, and the situation excited him. First he said it was to show me what I'd been missing, but all along I don't think he intended for me to live. I was lucky to be found still alive."

She looks at the clock. "We're going to have to leave it here for today, but I'd like to see you again on Friday." As she stands, she tilts her head on one side. "Think about what we've spoken about. Think what you could have done differently. Don't blame yourself for not getting away, put any guilt in the right place. You didn't let something happen to you, Darcy, none of this was your fault. And it didn't happen because you sat back and let it because you were weak. You fought."

As I stand, I realise I did. Perhaps, just perhaps, I hadn't given myself enough credit for it. But what could I change? Not being taken in by a sob story in the first place? Doing more to check someone out rather than taking them as they appeared on the surface? Like Peg, meeting his friends, knowing his status in the club, asking about his background, understanding his life. Because Pete had never mattered to me, he was just a house-mate, I never bothered to find out. That had been my mistake. That's what I can learn from.

"Did it help?"

My feet have carried me automatically out into the waiting room and, distracted, I look at Peg, and after a sigh, reply to his hesitant question with one of my own. "If you'd been in my position, Peg, running with your hands tied, trying to keep out of sight. What would you have done differently?"

He looks at me thoughtfully. "Hands tied? No weapon? Minimal places to hide? Darlin', I couldn't have done more than you. Is that what's been playing on your mind?"

CHAPTER 40

Peg

As I walk Darcy out of the therapist's office and back down to the truck, the question she just asked me makes so many things fall into place. Her reluctance to talk about returning to her job, the confidence that she's lost. She's been thinking she should have tried harder to escape, that someone else would have managed to get free, when under the circumstances, neither I, my brothers, nor her firefighting crew would have been able to do anything more than she did. *He shot her in the leg for fuck's sake.* Unless someone had been wearing magical bullet deflecting jeans at the time, no one could run with an injury like that. She hadn't just let herself be taken and raped, she'd tried her best to escape.

I drive us through Tucson, then out onto the freeway, my mind racing with what I could do to convince her it wasn't her fault, and nothing she had done could have prevented what followed. All the blame lies with Mercer, and certainly none with her.

Mindful of her torn stomach muscles only just healed, I drive slowly and carefully, minimising as far as I can any bumps. Cars and trucks are passing me in the outside lane. I might have a way to go to get Darcy back in my life and my bed, but the counselling today seems like it might have helped. Glancing at her, I see her teeth biting her lip, and stay silent as she works through things that she's heard.

The turnoff to the compound is coming up. I indicate and then swing the wheel around. *Home.* Not far away now, a place where I can at last relax.

Loud pops and the truck violently shudders, and I lose the fight to keep it on the track. *A stinger.* Sharp spikes have shredded my front wheels. The truck's going nowhere.

In one smooth motion I open my door, sliding my gun out of the holster. "Lock your door, Flash, and keep your head down."

Expecting her to obey, I slide out, my eyes looking left and right for danger. Getting my phone out of my cut, I place a call. "Need help. Entrance to the track."

That's all I waste my breath saying, knowing my brothers will already be mounting up. *Who took us off the road?* I sidle around the truck, my head swivelling as I look left, right, forward, and back trying to find our attacker. A spike strip hadn't just appeared by accident.

A shot from the opposite side. *Shit.* Forgetting discretion, I run. My suspicions were right, it's Pete Mercer, and he's shot the lock, and though she's kicking and fighting, he's dragging Darcy out, his arm around her neck, and using her like a shield.

"Get back." He waves his gun at me. "It's just the bitch I want."

I aim my gun even though I can't take a shot. Darcy's a tall woman and he's not much got that much over her in height. Right now her face is reddening as he tightens his arm around her neck, and her panicked eyes stare into mine.

I take a step forward, he drags her a step back.

"I'm warning you, biker. I just want her. No need for you to get involved. I deserve payback, as she's fucked up my plans."

I make another move to close the gap.

He aims, Darcy elbows his arm, the shot goes wide. I look behind him, and now see a Jeep camouflaged by burned scrub he's managed to pile up. *I can't let him get her to that.*

"Let her go and you might live." Now I issue a warning of my own. "You'll have a dozen bikers here any second."

He moves the gun back to her head. "Then she's dead."

She will be anyway if she goes with him. I try to instruct her with imperceptible moves of my head, but her airway's being constricted, and she's gasping for breath.

He steps back again, a little stumble, but rights himself and his burden. I'm not going to let him take her away.

Darcy, fight, I try to tell her. An almost imperceptible tightening of my features trying to convey my instructions.

I see the light dawning. As he moves backward again, she raises her leg and curls it around his. It's enough, and this time he loses his footing and goes down, hard, taking Darcy with him, but his gun hand is flung out to save him.

I take my shot, shooting straight through his wrist. He howls and releases the other arm around Darcy's neck.

Throwing herself forward, she runs to me, and I swing her around and behind me, and then advance. *This fucker is dead.* First, I kick his gun away, then pick it up, handing it and my own to my woman, not wanting to take the chance of him arming himself again. I hear the roar of bikes getting closer, like angry animals hungry for food, but I no longer need help.

Mercer's moving like a crab, trying to escape me. He gets his feet under him, but my fist to his face makes him fall once again. He squeals like a stuck pig. *Just like a bully.* He can dish it out but can't take it. *Oh, I'm going to have fun with him.*

I feel a presence behind me. "Darcy, keep back."

"He's mine, Peg." Suddenly she's launching herself at the prone man, directing a kick straight into his balls. "I'm going to fucking hurt him. Just like he hurt me."

As he screams again and curls up, Darcy plants her foot in his face, and I hear a bone crack. Once started, it seems she can't stop, and I'm proud as fuck of my woman, standing back and watching her work. She's out of her mind with rage and fury, until she stops, breathing hard, her arms wrapped around her stomach.

I hadn't been aware of our audience arriving, but as her eyes meet mine, Drum walks around us and stares at the groaning body.

Mercer's face is so distorted the prez has difficulty recognising him. "This the fucker that's been after you, Flash?"

She nods, and now the tears start. Still fixed upon me, she pleads, "I don't want him to escape. I can't trust this to the courts, Peg."

Stepping closer, I put my arms around her, tucking her head under my chin. It's the first time in weeks she's so readily accepted my comfort.

"Want us to take him to the storage room?"

It's an idea. We could make him really suffer there. But something tells me I need to finish it for Darcy here. "Nah, Blade. He's not worth the effort." I take my gun out of the holster, and holding her face to my chest, take aim at his head…

"No, Peg." She rears back.

"No?" She doesn't want me to finish him off? "Flash…"

Her hand reaches for my weapon, I move it away from her. She jumps up and grabs my wrist. "Peg, let me. Let me end this."

She wants to shoot him?

"Have you ever fired a gun?" I feel as much as see her shake her head. I breathe out a sigh. "Then if you're certain this is what you want, we'll do it together." I turn her to face him, put the gun in her hand, and help her to steady it on her target. After her brutal attack, Mercer's barely conscious. "You sure about this?" I ask softly.

Her answer is simple and succinct. "Yes."

I look into her eyes and see the determination there. I squeeze her hand, the bullet flies fast, and Mercer has taken his last breath.

She's killed a man, and now her body is trembling. She collapses back on me, and I need to hold her up. She's sobbing, but is it regret or relief?

"Sent Fergus back for a cage." Wraith nods at the stricken woman in my arms.

"Thanks, VP."

Drummer slaps my back. "We'll handle the clean-up. Road will want his race track cleared of debris in any event."

I grin into Darcy's hair. The forest around it might be badly burned, but the bodies hidden underneath have kept silent, and now they'll have someone else to keep them company.

Joker and Lady suggest they'll dispose of the Jeep and disappear, Lady driving and Joker following on his bike. Despite the circumstances, I suddenly get the urge to laugh as an amusing thought occurs to me—when they come back Lady will be riding bitch.

Fergus arrives back with the cage, and Hyde appears with a truck. As I half carry, half lead Darcy over to our transport, I see my brother's wrapping Mercer's body in plastic, preparing to transport it to its final resting place.

It's over. She's free. But how will it affect her?

Darcy doesn't say a word when I sit her in the passenger seat, and nothing passes her lips as we complete our journey so rudely interrupted. When I park up, she gets out mechanically and comes without protest up to my suite.

Her silence is worrying. Once inside, I turn her to face me. "Darcy, speak to me. Tell me how you're feeling."

Her hands come out and grab the sides of my cut, but still she says nothing, and is looking down at the floor. I place my hand gently under her chin and try to get her to look up. A bad feeling is churning in my gut, that I shouldn't have let her take any responsibility for ending him. She resists, continuing to look down, and I let her, just wrapping my arms around her back, pulling her close. Worried for her, but on my part, I'm relishing that now she's safe and that bastard will never get near her again.

"What's that?" I heard her mumble something but couldn't understand what she said.

"I did it, didn't I, Peg?"

"You did it." I'm not quite sure which part she's referring to, but Darcy darn near saved herself and killed the man who made her life hell.

"*I* brought him down so you could take the shot. *I* made him hurt. And *I* killed him."

Worried that knowledge that might come back to haunt her, I realise she's taking ownership of everything. But why? To increase the guilt, or to make herself feel better? Torn between two options, I go for the latter. "Sure did, darlin'. Fuck I'm proud of you. You saved me from a bullet, Flash. Don't forget about that."

"We're a team, Peg. Couldn't have done it without you."

A *team*. Fuck me, but I like the sound of that. "A team," I echo.

Her hands grip my cut tighter. "Peg, will you…will…"

"Whatever you want darlin'. Whatever you fuckin' want."

Her arms are suddenly around me, trying to hold me close. "Will you make love to me, Peg? Take those memories of him being inside me away."

"Fuck, darlin'. If that's what you want." I'd like nothing more, and my cock perks up, very interested. "But are you sure? Are you ready? And doesn't your stomach still hurt?" The last thing I want to do is to cause her injury.

She huffs a small laugh. "Kicking him probably didn't do me much good, but I want, *need*, you, Peg."

Knowing I'll have to be gentle, I again put my fingers to her face. This time she leans into them and lets me lift her head up. Her eyes are full of emotion, pupils dilated in desire. *She's taken back control.* Now she knows what, who, she wants and, fuck it, the lucky man is me.

Without delaying any longer, I lower my lips to hers. At first a soft touch, a gentle glide of our mouths moving against each other. Then she opens for me, and my tongue toys with hers. My hands come up to cup her face, the strands of her hair tickling my fingers. I angle her head for better access. Her taste affects me like a man drinking water after being lost in the desert. My own legs feel shaky as emotion swells inside me, and as I tangle my fingers in her hair I vow I'm never going to give her cause to leave me, ever again.

Reluctantly I withdraw my mouth from hers and pull her to me, resting my chin on the top of her head, noting she's a perfect fit for me. I pause for a moment, then ask once more, "Are you sure about this?"

"I'm sure."

But she's not quite healed, and I'll need to keep my beast chained for now. That won't be a hardship, just the opportunity to slide inside her, when I thought I'd lost that chance for good. I let her go, then placing my hand to the small of her back, encourage her inside my bedroom.

When she's standing in front of my bed, with my hands on her shoulders, I turn her to face me, then brush my lips against hers one more time. We both keep our eyes open, gazing at each other. There's no question, no hesitation in hers, and certainly no doubt in mine. Slowly I run my hands up and down her arms, my touch light, my fingers relearning the feel of her skin, I repeat the action until I feel goosebumps starting to rise and hear the hitch in her breathing.

Gently I take hold of the bottom of her tee, my eyes seeking permission. At her nod, ease it up over her head. *I've got my old lady back.* The thought breaks something inside of me, melting my heart, causing my hands to tremble as I reach around to undo her bra, sliding the straps down her arms and letting it drop to the floor.

As I reach out and cup her mounds in my hands, I could almost cry with relief. Though I'd hoped one day this would happen, part of me thought that day would never come, that I'd never be touching her this way again. As my thumbs pass over her peaks, she moans. Moving one hand to her back, I lower my head and pay attention to those gorgeous nipples with their golden rings, feeling them hardening as I play with them using my teeth, lips, and tongue. As if no longer under her control, her body starts grinding against me. The physical sign that she wants me too.

My cock throbs, but I ignore it. This is for her. *All for her.* Knowing the only way of taking Mercer's invasion away is to make this completely different, I focus just on bringing her pleasure. If her torn muscles are still too sore, if it's going to bring back bad memories, my dick will stay where it is, in my pants. I'll get my enjoyment from watching her take her pleasure.

"Peg." She squirms against me, signalling she wants more.

Carefully lifting her, I place her on the bed, my fingers going to the button of her jeans, and my eyes searching her face, making sure I've got full consent. Her little nod gives me the go-ahead to proceed. I remove her shoes, then undo the zip and slowly take down her pants, relishing how I'm revealing her, inch by glorious inch.

I watch her again as my fingers tuck into the elastic of her panties, seeing nothing but desire. As I slide them down, the beautiful aroma of her arousal fills the air.

Her scar on her stomach is puckered, red and angry, and I bite back the rage that that motherfucker caused her so much pain. "Are you certain you're okay?" I need the words, I don't want to hurt her. "If you're in pain, tell me and I'll stop."

"Peg, please. I…I need you."

She needs me, needs this. But whether she can handle it is another question.

"Please, take away the memory of his touch."

I know what she means, and what she's saying. Determined to imprint myself on her brain so all she can remember is *my* hands and *my* cock, I start stroking her inner thighs, then my mouth follows the path my palms have taken, kissing her legs from her knees to that wonderful place, the part of her no other man will ever see or feel again.

She's mine, and I'll give all that I am to keep her.

Her hands come down and she twists her fingers in my hair, pressing my head to get me where she wants me. But I'm taking it slowly, infuriating her on purpose. I need her desperate and writhing. After a few torturous moments, I comply, lowering my head and sweeping my tongue around her sweet cunt. She's glistening with arousal, and her taste, oh, her taste. It's as sweet as I remember, swelling my cock to an unbelievable size. *Have I ever been this hard, this insane for a woman before?* I'd remember, and the answer is I've not.

I lap at her cream, then lick my way to her clit, another gasp and a moan, and her hands fist the sheets, crumbling them up. When my fingers push into her, she freezes, and I suppress my swear word, making sure I only think it in my head.

"It's me, Peg. Open your eyes and watch me, darlin'."

As she does, she relaxes, and starts to welcome my touch, her internal walls clamping on my fingers, another rush of arousal dampening the bed.

I toy with her mercilessly, my tongue circling her clit, then biting down gently while my hand curls so I can reach that special spot inside. As her body tautens, her palms cover her stomach.

"Is it too much?" I rumble, the vibration of my voice making her shiver.

"No. Don't stop. Don't you dare stop."

Realising she's supporting her weak muscles, I go back to my task, relishing every second of the attentions I'm lavishing on her. She's close, I can feel it, her thighs tightening around me. She almost stops breathing as she works her way to her peak.

I press hard on her clit, and at the same time massage her inside, and she comes with a scream. After easing her down, I lift my head. Her skin has turned red and is covered with a sheen of sweat. She's the most beautiful sight I've ever seen in my bed.

"Are you alright?"

"Yes." The word is gasped out as she struggles to get her breath. "I need you, Peg. I need you."

Briefly I break our contact to dispense of my jeans, boxers, and prosthesis, and then I'm back on the bed, one hand supporting me, the other guiding my engorged cock to her slit. "Tell me if it's too much."

"It won't be. I *need* this. Need you."

But as the bulbous mushroom head breeches her, she tenses up, and I freeze. "Am I hurting you?"

She shakes her head, and a tear leaks down her face. "Just do it, Peg. Please."

Rocking my body, I ease gently back and forth. "Stay with me, Flash. Open your eyes and see *me*."

Straightening her head, she does what I asked, and as her eyes lock with mine I feel her relaxing. I gain more ground, gritting my teeth, ignoring my impulse to grind myself into her.

Taking it more slowly than I ever have in my life, I gently thrust forward and back until she's taken all of me. Then I stop. Her eyes have widened, her breaths are coming fast, and that flush has become an even deeper red as her muscles tighten around my cock.

I'm not going to last long, but she's going to have to come with me. I slide out, and then back in, so slowly. I'm torturing us both, using teasing glides, making sure my piercings touch her in all the right places. She pants and flexes her muscles, trying to get me to speed up, but I continue my sedate pace. I'm making love, not fucking.

She might want me to go faster, but gradually I'm bringing her there, my Jacob's Ladder massaging her G-spot with every pass. When I see her take a deep breath and hold it, and her muscles clamp down, I know she's almost there. I shift my body so I'm hitting her clit, see her hands clench, and a ripple goes through her body. Her head rolls back and she closes her eyes as her mouth opens.

"Peg…" It's a wail, and now she's convulsing, her back bowed as she comes.

I push in hard, the undulations of her cunt enough to stimulate my cock, and with just a couple of pumps I'm emptying myself into her.

No condom. Fuck. I wanted to show her how much I love her, and now I feel I've taken advantage of her just like that fucker Mercer.

As my cock softens and drops out, although I'm a bastard, I can't suppress the Neanderthal feelings that come over me, watching our combined juices run out, and my palm automatically covers her slit, as though wanting to keep my cum inside her. *What if we've just made a child?*

"Darcy."

She opens her eyes, a beautiful satisfied look on her face, and looks down to where my hand's lying. She then glances at my face, and must see my brow creased in concern, and then she covers my hand with her palm.

"I love you, Peg."

I'm not sure what she's thinking as her warmth seeps into my skin, but the words from her mouth are the best fucking ones I've ever heard. Hardly daring to move, I raise my eyes and put every ounce of sincerity in my voice as I respond. "I love *you*, Darcy."

Placing her free hand on the bed, she pushes herself up, and suddenly my arms are around her, and I'm holding her tight. This woman that I'd almost given up hope of ever holding like this again. My woman. The one I've been searching for all my life.

"I love you, Peg," she repeats, but then carries on. "I want what you're offering. To be your wife, your old lady. *And* to have your babies." She pulls back and looks into my face, her hand coming up and smoothing over my beard. "But perhaps not this soon…"

"Fuck, Flash, I didn't mean it. I just forgot."

"Shush, Peg. You didn't do anything that I didn't want. Whatever happens, we'll deal with it. You took the bad memories away. It will be your touch I remember. And," she pauses and bites her lip, "I don't want you thinking about the man who's been there."

"Don't you fuckin' worry about that. It's the last thing on my mind, darlin'. You're mine, you always were. Hate that you went through what you did, but it doesn't change anything. You were mine then as well, I know that, here." I cover my heart with my hand.

"And he's dead." Again her teeth worry her lip, and her eyes look down, and for a second, and not for the first time, I'm worrying how she'll cope with what we, *she*, did.

But when she looks up again, there's a grin on her face. "Never knew killing a man could be an aphrodisiac."

I stare at her incredulously, then bark a laugh. "It's not my normal one of choice, babe."

CHAPTER 41
Darcy

I would never have described myself as a violent person, would have laughed in anyone's face had they suggested I'd ever take a man's life. Heck, my job is saving people, whoever they are, running into burning buildings to pull anyone living out, be it righteous citizens, drug addicts, or criminals. But pulling that trigger proved to be cathartic. I couldn't live with the thought that Pete might have got away, might have continued to stalk me. He was just waiting to kill me, and all because I didn't give him what he wanted.

He was an evil man, and now he's dead.

With Mercer Senior arrested, and knowing his son was complicit in his activities, the police have a search warrant out for him, thinking he's disappeared out of state, or over the border. They're looking for a man on the run, not a body. *But they'll never find him.* The Satan's Devils took care of that.

I've continued seeing the therapist, she's been great, but really it was the control *I* took back when I made sure Pete would never come after me again that was my cure—obviously that I kept to myself. And Peg? Well, what can I say? He's been great. My fears he would overwhelm my own identity was groundless.

During the past four weeks, I couldn't ask for more. We fit together like hand and glove. I've stayed at the compound, getting to know the other women better, playing with the toddlers and babies. When I help Marcia with the twins, I have a pang deep inside, and hope that one day in the not too distant future I'll be holding my own. Well, not twins. One at a time would be better for me. Peg's used a condom since that night, but I haven't wanted to go back on the pill, preferring to leave my options open.

Last night, as we were curled up on his sofa, listening to Bob Seger play, our taste in music as similar as everything else, Peg had awkwardly got down on one knee and had proposed. I'm already wearing his property patch, but soon I'll have a wedding ring on my finger, which today is sporting a beautiful engagement ring. Even Ma cracked a smile when she saw it.

Coming up to the station, I realise I couldn't be happier. The last few weeks have made me re-examine what I want out of life. While I'm excited and eager to get back on the job, being a firefighter no longer defines my existence. I'm Darcy, property of Peg, and soon to be his wife, not a twenty-four-hour, seven day a week Firefighter Flash Cavanaugh.

I squeeze my hands around Peg's waist as he pulls up outside, loving the feeling of being on the back of his bike. As the engine ticks, he covers my hands with his. Then I get off and hand him the cut with my property patch proudly displayed on the back and my helmet, then putting my hands around his face, kiss him. The next twenty-four hours will be the longest we've been apart in four weeks.

When I pull away, his brow creases. "You take care, okay?"

I slap his arm gently. "We've been over this, Peg." Yeah, long conversations where I've described all the safety precautions we take, our equipment that's meant to keep us alive. He gets it, I know that. But knowing it in his head and his heart are two different things.

"You have a good shift, you hear?" Though he worries, he's never once suggested I give my job up. If it was possible to love him more, that omission would have done it.

"And you take care, Peg."

With one last lingering look, I turn and walk into the station, entering the door at the same time as Truck.

"Hey, stranger." As he passes me he slaps me on the back. "Long time, no see."

Punching his arm, I laugh. "Yeah, long time since breakfast." I'd quickly found the reason that Truck seemed to spend so much time talking to the bikers. He's a prospect now, the club balancing their needs against his job. He's fit right in. It was only an hour ago I saw him stuffing his face in the kitchen. Oh, and talking to Sam. She's helping him rebuild his shattered bike.

As we walk into the station together, Slade's already there. "Flash. Good as fuck to have you back."

"How did my replacement do?" I can't help but wonder whether they preferred working with another man.

"Rather have you here," the captain informs me. No, he wouldn't badmouth another firefighter, but the slight grimace on his face speaks volumes. *They really have missed me.* I try to suppress my smile.

The speakers blare, and Hammer and Truck appear as if by magic, and in seconds we're out on the engine. *It's good to be back.*

I'm still thinking that twenty-four hours later when I stagger out to the parking lot. It's been a long shift, and perhaps I should have eased myself into it instead of diving into what was an incredibly busy stint with little down time. Walking across to Peg's bike, I feel exhausted.

Taking one look at my face, he pats the seat behind him. "Looking at you, I'm glad I've got that sissy bar fitted."

I glance down and give a tired but thankful grin. While I've been working he's made a mod to the bike, and now I won't be frightened I'm going to slide off the back. He's so thoughtful, always doing little things for my comfort. He offers me my cut, and I proudly put it on, then take his offered hand and just about manage to throw my tired leg over the seat, then put my arms around him, leaning my cheek on his cut, breathing in the smell of leather and him. *Home.*

He squeezes my hands, then starts the engine. When we get back to the compound he takes me straight to his room, gently stripping me and putting me in the shower and joining me, after taking off his clothes and prosthesis.

"How can you do that so easily?" I ask, amazed as always at how Peg copes with his disability.

As he uses a strategically placed rail to hop into the shower, he grins. "Practice, babe." I roll my head back as he shampoos my hair, balancing on one leg. After he rinses it, he lathers up the sponge. His large, but surprisingly gentle hands, smooth the soap over me, and the warmth of the water and his massaging touch slowly remove both lingering odours of smoke and dirt away from me. As he slowly administers to me, my tiredness seeps away, seeming to combine with the dirty water running down the drain. Peg's cock stands proud from his body, adorned by those piercings which glint in the bright overhead light. As I look down, I lick my lips.

"Like what you see?"

"Hmm."

"You're exhausted babe."

"I think you missed a bit." Brazenly, I move his hand to the place he's so far evaded.

He groans loudly. "Fuck, darlin', you're soaked."

Without needing more invitation, his fingers start sliding in and out, and he braces himself with one hand against the wall. "Fuckin' missed you, babe. Missed *this.*"

"Missed you too." Over the last month we've learned each other's bodies, and he knows exactly how to make me last until

I'm burning up with frustration or bring me to the boil fast. Tonight, thank God, he's not teasing me, and I'm fast at the point of no return. His body leans against me, his hard cock pushed against my ass, I'm surrounded by my man as my muscles tense, my legs squeezing his hand between them, but he doesn't stop moving, just twists his hand so his thumbs rubbing over my clit, and I'm gone.

"Peg! Jesus!" I swear each time I come it's better than the last.

As he takes his weight off me, I reach around and take hold of his dick. "Your turn."

"Want me inside you, do you?"

"Yeah." My legs are still shaking, but I can't wait. I want to feel him. All of him. Now his hands are braced on the wall either side of my head, caging me in. I know what to do, and place his cock at my entrance, then he does the rest. Sliding in fast, then hammering in, giving it to me just the way I need it tonight. A hard, fast fucking.

"Touch yourself, babe. I'm not gonna last."

My fingers start working, feeling the studs moving over my hand as he pulls out then pushes back in. Knowing they're touching my internal walls excites me.

"Fuck, darlin'. Fuck, you feel so good. Your cunt's trying to strangle my cock."

Oh yeah, love his dirty talk. I rub faster.

"You nearly there, babe? 'Cause, fuck, my balls are getting tight."

Words escape me, but my change in tempo signals I'm close, then I'm wailing as I go over, and then my hands shoot out, palms flat to the wall as I need to brace myself. His movements become erratic just as I realise we forgot the condom *again*, but he pulls out, his cum splashing on my back before the shower water washes it away.

After rinsing me off, he reverses his previous action, grabbing the rail and hopping out, then sitting down on the toilet lid and passing me a towel. Wrapping it around me, I kneel in front of him, and he takes another and carefully dries my hair, just something we've made our routine. I love him playing with my long tresses, so let him comb it out.

"Want me to dry it?"

I'm so tired, I just want to sleep. "I'll leave it and sort it out when I wake up." Then I stand, pick up our clothes, and carry the prosthesis into the bedroom, returning with his crutch. Another action that's become second nature.

Then I lay my head on the pillow, only vaguely aware of the brief kiss to my head, and knowing nothing more until I wake around lunchtime.

"Hey, Prospect." I can't resist teasing Truck as I walk into the clubhouse. Holding a trash bag in one hand, Truck turns and grins. "Your man's in the kitchen if you're looking for him."

"Thanks." The smell of food would lure me on its own, but the thought of seeing Peg, as always, makes my heart skip a beat. Honestly, I can't get enough of this man.

As I walk in, he gets up, comes over and gives me a kiss. I close my eyes as my arms go up and my fingers link behind his head. When he pulls away, he studies my face, then his lips curl. "Afternoon, babe. Let you sleep in."

"I needed it. Forgot how draining these shifts can be."

"Ma wants to speak to you."

I nod at the woman in the wheelchair and go to take a seat by her side while Peg goes off to get me something to eat. "What can I do for you, Ma?"

She opens an old folder and taps on a page. "Wedding cake. Something like this do you?"

I stare at the picture, it's perfect. Not too fussy. "I love it, Ma." I still can't believe Peg and I are officially tying the knot the weekend after next, which coincides with the start of my six days off. "But you know we're not doing anything special." Our plan had been to go down to city hall on our own, and then perhaps have a nice meal out.

"Nonsense. Not missing out when one of my boys gets hitched." Ma glares at me, easily staring me down. "You're doing this right. We're having a reception here at the club-house."

"And when was that decided?" I look around at the other old ladies, who look quickly away.

Sophie's not so fast, and when she catches my eye, she just shrugs. "Yesterday. Well, Ma announced it."

Peg's grinning as he leans over and puts a plate in front of me, and whispers in my ear, "Go with the flow." He nods Ma's way. "Let her do this." Then raises his voice. "Arranging it will keep Ma out of mischief."

"None of your cheek, boy." Ma's fast to reprimand him. I bite my tongue to hold back my laugh.

"Want to invite your parents, Darcy? Or your brother?"

I think about it for a second. I'm not ashamed of where I've ended up, or who my future husband will be. But having my parents here will just put a damper on things. "Nah. It's alright."

Ma shoots me a look. "They wouldn't want to be here for you? Or know about it first?"

I shrug. "I doubt it."

Peg pulls out a chair and sits down beside me. "How about we give them the choice? Go over there and speak to them? Maybe the day after tomorrow?"

I purse my lips and think for a moment. I suppose it's something I ought to do. A little hesitantly, I agree.

CHAPTER 42

Peg

I didn't know what to expect when I went with Darcy to meet her parents. We arrive in Phoenix on the bike, but minus our cuts as we've come out of the Satan's Devils area. It's immediately clear that she's nothing like her mom, who answers the door dressed to the nines with full makeup on. The woman I'll be marrying in just a few days has on jeans and a tee, her hair windblown from the ride, and her face bare and natural. As I squeeze her hand I think yet again she's the most beautiful woman I've ever seen in my life.

"Darcy." Her mom looks surprised to see her, and her eyes widen as she looks at me. "Well, don't stand on the doorstep, come on in. Pops?" she calls out, and a man in his sixties comes into view.

"Darcy." Like his wife, he doesn't seem able to do much more than utter her name. Then he half turns. "George, come and see what the cat's dragged in."

"Dad." Darcy holds out her hand and he shakes it. It strikes me how little emotion seems to be involved.

Another man comes into view. This must be her older brother. The one who followed in her dad's footsteps. It's a bit awkward, and suddenly her mom realises it. "Come on through," she invites.

I've always envied people who were brought up in a family, going myself from one foster home to another, thinking that anyone who had parents was experiencing the loving affection I never got, but even after a couple of minutes I can see how wrong I was. Darcy's parents don't seem to know how to speak to her, and I wonder how she's developed into such a loving woman when brought up in a cold environment like this.

"So, Darcy," her dad starts after we're seated, me perched on the edge of a posh looking sofa. "To what do we owe this pleasure?"

Darcy takes my hand and smiles into my eyes. "This is Peg. Peg and I are getting married."

"Peg?" Her mom focuses on my name, not her daughter's announcement.

I roll up my trouser leg. "Peg," I repeat. "Lost it in the services. Picked up the nickname and it kinda stuck."

Her mom covers her mouth with her hand, her dad looks a little impressed and just nods.

"But what's your real name?"

Shaking her head, Darcy gives a little laugh. "That doesn't matter. We're getting married, Mom, just wanted you and Pops to know."

Her brother frowns. "And what do you do for a living, er, Peg?"

"I'm a businessman," I tell them. "I'm sergeant-at-arms for the Satan's Devils Motorcycle Club in Tucson. We own a number of businesses, and I make sure everything's running as it should." Darcy and I had agreed we weren't going to sugar-coat anything.

Three mouths drop open. "A criminal club?"

"Pops, no. Not like that at all."

"Well, I suppose you know what you're doing. You've always looked out for yourself and done what you wanted to do." Her mother doesn't seem particularly bothered.

"I've come to let you know, and invite you to the wedding if you want to come? It's next Saturday."

"I'm sorry." George frowns. "But I'll be out of town then."

"Pops, we've got that do at the Wilkinsons'."

"That's right, Mother. We have."

Three pairs of eyes look at Darcy, who shrugs. It was as she expected.

Her father stands up and goes to a cabinet, opens a drawer and pulls something out. He stands, tapping it against the palm of his hand, while giving me an assessing look. "I'll give you a wedding present." It's then I realise he's holding a check book.

Darcy stands and goes over to him, placing her hand on his arm. "There's no need to do that. I've still got my trust fund, which I haven't touched."

His eyes go sharply to me, and I just stare back. "Darcy won't want for anything married to me."

"Are you going to do a prenup?" her brother asks with a frown.

"No," Darcy says simply. "What's mine is his."

"Yes," I say almost at the same time, earning me a glare from my wife-to-be.

Then she turns back to her folks. "Whether we do or not is our business, and none of yours."

Her mom stands up. "Well, it's been nice seeing you, Darcy. And you…Peg. I hope you'll be very happy together."

Just like that, we're dismissed. As I climb on the bike, holding my hand for Darcy to get on and put on my sunglasses before I take it off the stand, I look over my shoulder, seeing the front door already shut.

"I did warn you." Darcy speaks before I do.

"You alright, babe?"

"Peg, this is the way I was brought up. I'm nothing more than a nuisance. They're probably glad you're taking me off their hands."

"Fuck, darlin'. You amaze me."

Her arms surround me, and her hands squeeze my waist. "Why?"

"Because of the wonderful, carin', lovin' woman you turned out to be." I switch on the ignition, then shout over my shoulder, "Thank fuck you didn't turn out like your mother." I shift down into first, then move off.

I'd be the first to admit I would have preferred Flash not to have returned to work, but wasn't going to try to dissuade her. It's going to take some time for me to get used to seeing her leave, not knowing what dangers she might be heading into. After that first day, she's driven herself, never able to promise her shift will end on time. Each time she leaves me for twenty-four hours I miss her like hell.

But I'm marrying her *tomorrow*. I'll be taking all of her, which encompasses her passion for life, and that includes her job. As I walk into church, knowing a few hours after this shift ends she'll be my wife, I've got a smile on my face.

"Oh oh. What's up with Peg?"

"Fucker's face is all wrong."

"Yeah, it's all twisted up."

"Anyone would think the asshole's gettin' married tomorrow."

As comments are thrown at me, I still don't let it take my visible pleasure off my face, just cuff Rock and Jekyll around the head as I walk past to take my seat, then watch as the rest of the brothers trail in.

Seeing Joker arrive with his arm around Lady, Blade points his knife toward them. "I suppose you fuckers will be next."

"What?" Joker's arm drops, and he looks confused.

"Getting hitched."

As Lady cocks an eyebrow at Joker, we all crack up at the resultant expression on Joker's face.

"Okay, let's get started." Prez shuts us up even before his ass hits the seat. "Peg's stag starts after church."

Hoot and hollers sound, but they're not getting me drunk. I want to enjoy my wedding tomorrow. I won't see my old lady again until we meet up to get married. When she comes off shift at seven in the morning, she's going to be catching a few hours' sleep up at Sam and Drummer's. Some stupid shit about it being bad luck to see her before the wedding. Oh yeah, our plans of just sneaking out to city hall had got all fucked up. The whole load of them are coming along, brothers, old ladies, and even the sweet butts. None of them wanted to miss out.

"You with us, Peg?"

"Nah, he's plotting how to get out of this."

"Marc will loan you her rat bike if you want to make a run for it."

I snarl at Heart. Nothing will get me on that Jap bike of hers. If I did want to get away, and I certainly don't, the Suzuki 7/11 would be the last ride I'd have chosen and the fucker knows it.

While I've zoned out they've run through our finances, and we're on to the next subject that is now a regular one on our agenda. The construction at the compound.

"So, Peg, had any more thoughts about your house?"

"Don't know why we're bothering restoring more blocks. Brothers are falling like flies and want houses," Bullet grumbles. But he's got a point. Darcy and I are also taking advantage of the spare land, building a house up alongside Wraith and Heart's.

"Glad mine's finished. Your boys did good there." Heart nods at the brothers responsible. "Was getting cramped with the twins and Amy in our unit, not to mention the fuckin' dog." There had been some fire damage which had delayed Heart and his new family moving in for a few weeks, but they're all settled now.

Prez wipes his hand over his face and says something you wouldn't expect a hardened MC prez to say. "Viper, Bullet, can we get a playground set up? At the top of the compound? Fenced in to keep Grunt and his shit out."

Now we're discussing swings, slides, and play equipment. Fuck me, only a couple of years ago I would never have expected to be discussing matters like this in church.

"Found Grunt taking a dump outside my room," Rock grumbles. "Do something about that, will you, Heart?"

"Yeah, I'll get you some shit bags." Heart's unrepentant. "What d'you expect me to do? Put a diaper on him?"

"Well you should be able to. You're gettin' enough practice."

My mouth twitches, then the corners turn up. I fucking love my life. Love my brothers, and in just a few hours, I'll be marrying the woman I love and who means more to me than life itself.

Mouse is the only one not joining in the repartee, not unusually tapping away on his laptop instead. Suddenly he exclaims, "Oh, fuck."

It's loud enough to get all our attention. "What is it, Mouse?"

The part Native American sends a dark-eyed gaze my way. "Just got a news flash up on my screen. There's been an explosion at a fire." He pauses before adding. "Several firefighters have been hurt."

My gut drops. I swear my heart stops beating. "Out of which station? Does it say?"

Mouse shakes his head, but it's apologetic, full of sympathy, as he says the one word I don't want to hear pass his lips.

I stand so fast my chair falls over backward. It's Flash's station, and her crew is on shift. I wipe my hands through my hair. I don't know what to do. Don't know what to say. Just have agonising pains shooting through me, far worse than when I lost my leg. My mouth opens and shuts, but no words come out.

Suddenly, I feel a presence beside me, and arm around my back. "Peg, she'll be okay."

"She has to be, Prez. Fucking has to be."

I pat my pocket. In the initial moment of panic, I'd forgotten we leave our phones outside the room. Pushing past Mouse, Rock, and Hyde in my impatience to get out, I scrabble through the box until I find my cell. Picking it up I find a couple of missed calls and a message from Truck.

Deciding it's quicker to call him back than listen to voice-mail, I press the button and wait impatiently to be connected.

"Truck, it's Peg."

As he speaks my legs feel weak, and I reach out my hand to the wall, needing its support to keep me standing. "Where is she?"

"On my way."

I slide my phone into my pocket and take a moment to get breath into my lungs. My forehead falls against the wall.

"Peg? What's happened?"

"She was in the building. They brought...they brought her out." I swing around, my head shaking wildly from side to side. "She's fuckin' unconscious. That's all Truck knows."

"You know where she is?"

"Yeah."

"Come on then." Prez wastes no time, calling out to Sam that tomorrow's plans might have changed.

Other brothers come and get on their bikes, I don't even see who they are, but ride after Prez down into Tucson, riding on auto-pilot, hardly aware of where we are, thankful he's in the lead so all I need do is follow him. Tears blur my eyes before the wind blows them away. *I should be enjoying my stag night, not heading to my fiancée's hospital bed.* Fuck, but she's got to be alright. I can't lose her, not now. Not ever. Able to now under-stand how Heart went off the rails when his wife had died, not knowing how I'd survive it.

We pull up outside the emergency room and I almost lay down my bike in my rush, remembering at the last moment to kick down the stand. Then I'm inside. The first person I see is Truck with a stitched-up wound on his forehead, and I run over. "Any news?"

He shakes his head. "Not yet, sorry, Peg. They won't tell me anything."

I leave him and walk over to the reception desk and, leaning over, I thunder, "Darcy Cavanaugh. I'm her fiancé. I need to know how she is." Then noticing the female flinching away from me, add, lowering my voice, "We're getting married tomorrow."

Her face softens. "I'm sorry, you'll have to wait for the doctor. They'll be doing everything they can. If you want to wait with the firefighters, we've given them a room. I'll tell the doctor where you are."

Truck's by my side, and leads me, followed by my brothers, into a waiting room. There's half a dozen firefighters here, but the only other person I recognise is Hammer, who has his arm in a sling. He nods and comes over.

"What the fuck happened?" I ask him and Truck. Prez, Rock, Mouse, Hyde, and Wraith gather around to listen.

"It looked like a normal warehouse fire. Checked the inventory and saw nothing explosive was being stored. We went inside. It was a big one, so several crews attended."

Truck takes over, his face red as he spits out. "It was a fucking meth lab. Fucking place exploded, beams came down… Flash was trapped, alongside Slade. Took us a while to get them out."

"What are her injuries? She gonna make it, Truck?" I'm surprised I managed to stammer the words out. In my head I have visions of her being burned, or even at this moment dying or dead. *She can't be gone.*

But it's Hammer who tells me, "She was unconscious, took a blow to her head. But apart from that we don't know. Sorry, Peg. Fuck, what a time for this to happen. You're supposed to getting married in the morning." As he shakes his head, he looks like he's in shock himself.

Right now, I can't give a fuck about getting married. I just need to know she's going to be okay.

"Any others hurt? And what about Slade?" Prez asks.

"A couple from another crew are suffering from smoke inhalation, but they should be alright. Slade was trapped by his leg, don't know if he broke it or not yet. Apart from Flash, everyone's conscious. Truck got struck on the head, but that will probably have done him good, and I wrenched my arm as I…"

As he got Flash out, I complete in my head.

"I'm so fucking sorry, Peg," Hammer stammers out as he ruefully rubs at his shoulder. But he's got nothing to be sorry about. He got my woman out and hurt himself in the process. I raise my chin to him.

A doctor stops by. "Firefighter Hammer?" I step up with Hammer alongside the medic. "You can go see Captain Slade now."

As the doctor turns to go, I touch his sleeve. "Darcy Cavanaugh? I'm her fiancé."

His kindly sympathetic eyes do nothing to reassure me, and neither do his words. "I'm sorry, they're still working on her. I'll get someone to come speak to you when we have any update on her condition."

Prez steers me to a chair and I sit down clumsily, dropping my face into my hands. Wraith sits beside me, his hand on my back. I hear quiet mumbled conversations from the other firefighters.

One comes over. "Firefighter Cavanaugh is one tough cookie. She's going to be fine." I nod automatically at the words while knowing there's no way he can promise that.

Snippets of various discussions going on around me reach my ears, *cancelled* and *wedding* and *poor fucker* come over loud and clear. A delay to the wedding is a small price to pay. Christ, I don't care if she never marries me, I just need her alive. Need to know Darcy will be coming home with me. I don't need that ring on her finger as long as she's back in my arms. *Darcy, don't leave me.* I bang my fist on my knee repetitively, barely able to keep my body still. My good leg bounces in time.

There's a clock on the wall, it's hands ticking round so slowly. I stare at it, convinced it's stopped, and then the second-hand flicks on. It's eleven-thirty at night. Almost my wedding day. I've already been here three tortuous hours, and there's still been no word. *If she's gone, I'd rather time stopped completely.* I don't want to know, don't want anyone to tell me. I wouldn't be able to handle it.

A nurse appears at the doorway. "Er, Peg?"

I stand, unusually for me having trouble getting my balance, Prez puts out his hand and stops me falling back, and then steps up alongside me as I go to the nurse.

She smiles. "You can come and see Ms Cavanaugh now."

The relief I feel almost has me falling again, my legs barely able to support me. *She's alive.* "How is she?"

"She took a while to come around, but we've done all the tests, and though she's inhaled some smoke, and possibly has a concussion, she's going to be fine. Come on, she's eager to see you." *She's going to be alright.*

Prez gives me a push to get moving. After everything I've been thinking over the past few hours, I can't let myself believe that she really is going to be okay. I send up a silent prayer as I follow the nurse down a maze of corridors and up in the elevator to the next floor. Then, at last, she stops in front of a door, opens it, and waves me inside.

I pause, taking it in, seeing the love of my life lying there, smiling at me. "You know, we've got to stop meetin' like this." But my breath catches as I make my joke, and then tension of the past few hours comes out, and suddenly I, sergeant-at-arms for a one percenter club, have tears running from my eyes and streaming down my face. As I wipe them away Darcy holds out her arms, and immediately I accept her invitation, going to her and holding her as though I'm never going to let her go, ever again.

CHAPTER 43

Darcy

Peg sobs, then hiccups, and I giggle. It sounds silly, but while I've got the mother of all headaches, I'm deliriously happy that I'm alive *and* tomorrow is my wedding day. If I needed any reassurance that this big, strong man loves me, it's seeing him like this, in pieces because I was hurt. I'd rather not have given him more need to worry, but knowing how much he cares for me is just one more sign, should I need one, that he's the man I've been waiting for all my life. It's so right we're going to be legally joined. Husband and wife. I like the sound of those words.

He reaches for a tissue from the box by the bed, then turns his head and blows his nose noisily. When he looks back, his eyes are clearer, and they narrow, and he winces as he gets a look at my face.

"Is it bad?" I ask, cautiously.

He reaches out his fingers, touching my cheek just below the place where I've had stitches. "You're still beautiful."

"You're biased."

"That I may be." He smiles, that gorgeous smile, the one I notice he reserves just for me.

"They think I may have concussion, so they're keeping me in overnight." I cover my face as I cough.

He nods. "Rather have you with me, but if that's what they're advisin', then it's best for you to stay here." He straightens. "I'll make sure to cancel the arrangements."

"What?"

He tilts his head to one side and says slowly and carefully, "The weddin'?"

Does he think I don't remember? "What about the wedding?"

"Well, it can't go ahead now."

"Of course it can," I scoff. "I might not look as pretty…" breaking off, I flutter my eyelids, "as I do normally, but I'll be fine."

His eyes narrow again, and his brow creases. "Are you sure?"

"Of course I'm sure." I lay my hand over his. "Not taking the risk of you changing your mind."

"Change my fuckin' mind? You must have had one fuck of a hard bang on your head if you're thinkin' there's any fear of that, darlin'. Ain't no fuckin' chance. You're mine, and I'm tyin' you to me."

My fingers entwine with his. "This wasn't how I envisioned my last night of freedom."

"You weren't gonna stay with me anyway, darlin'." He pouts.

"It's bad luck to see the groom on your wedding day."

He barks a laugh. "Think you've already had yer bad luck, Flash. And we've broken that rule anyway now."

"What do you mean?"

He takes out his phone. "It's already twelve-thirty." Leaning forward, he places a kiss to my mouth. "Happy Weddin' Day, Flash."

Now it's my eyes that fill with tears. *My wedding day.* Peg wipes an escaping droplet from my cheek. "That bad, eh?"

Covering his hand with mine, I shake my head. "That good," I correct.

"Get some sleep, Darcy. I'll be here in that chair."

"You're not staying," I say emphatically, then put up my hand to pre-empt any protest. "I mean it, Peg. And you're not coming to collect me in the morning."

"The fuck I'm not." He rears back.

"Listen…" I keep my voice calm. Oh, I learned how to handle this man of mine. "Can you ask Sam to bring my… clothes in the morning. And I'll meet you at city hall."

"Babe."

"No, Peg. I'll be fine here. Let's both get some rest so we can enjoy tomorrow. I can't wait to be your wife." Though what sleep I'll get I'm not sure, not with the nurse waking me up every two hours to check on my head and this persistent cough I can't shake. I gaze at him, this man that I love, hoping we've already dealt with enough bad luck to last a lifetime, but unwilling to tempt fate any more than I already have. "Please, Peg. I want to do this right."

He stares back at me. Eventually he runs his hands through his hair, and then shakes his head. "You promise me you'll be at city hall? And let me know if you're not feelin' up to it?"

"Try keeping me away. You're not getting free from me now, Peg."

Leaning over, his lips meet mine, a soft, loving caress. One I suspiciously don't think I should be indulging in on what is officially my wedding day. But I give into his touch and enjoy it.

"Still want me to leave?" he whispers as he pulls away.

"Nice try, Peg. But, yes." I smile into his eyes.

"Ring on your finger or not, Flash, you're mine already. And don't you forget it. Okay, I'll let you do it your way." He stands with one last long look, as though he's imprinting my face on his mind before he leaves.

Quashing my feelings of regret that I've got what I asked for and am now alone, I close my eyes and try to get some rest. But half of me is still burned up with excitement about the day ahead. By the time I've managed to switch off my mind and drop off, a nurse wakes me up.

Morning comes, and I don't feel at all rested, but the medical staff are pleased with my progress, and happy to start the discharge process. Sam has good timing, arriving just as I'm ready to leave, and bringing with her exactly what I need.

"You're going to blow Peg's mind, you know?" Reverently she opens the large bag she's carried in over her arm. "He's not expecting this at all, is he?"

I giggle. "Well I did sort of lead him to believe I'd just be wearing jeans."

"Well, this is a bit nicer than jeans." She carefully slides my wedding dress out of the bag. It's a traditional white, an A-line style that leaves my shoulders bare, and has a lace overlay covered in sparkling diamante. I'd splashed out on it. I might only be getting married at city hall, but I'm determined to make the most of it, as I'm only doing this once.

The nurse comes in with my discharge papers. "Oh my." She laughs as she sees what I'm putting on. "You look beautiful."

"Not yet, but she will do." Carmen steps in, her hairdressing bag in her hand.

The nurse thinks for a moment. "It's going to take a bit longer to get your discharge completed after all." She grins. "You can stay here and get dressed up. Give me a shout when you're ready to leave. I'd like to see the finished product."

It takes an hour, and when I look in the mirror in the bathroom I'm amazed at what Carmen has achieved. Some of my long hair is up on top of my head, the rest curled and hanging over one shoulder. She's worked wonders with my makeup too —the scar I picked up yesterday, while not completely disguised, is not so red or noticeable, and some of my hair is tastefully arranged to hide it. Looking at my reflection, I can't believe that it's me.

Sam puts her arm around my waist. "You look beautiful, Darcy. I can't wait to see Peg's reaction."

Neither can I.

When we'd planned the wedding, it was just going to be Peg and I quietly sneaking away to get married, but when Ma and Peg's brothers got involved, it turned into something different. The long line of Harleys parked up therefore doesn't surprise me, but it still takes me aback to see them all waiting for me. I falter, my wedding dress fluttering around me in the breeze, and the men I've come to view as friends point and good-naturedly laugh.

"Darcy, stay here. I'm going to get these douchebags inside and make sure Peg's ready. We don't want to spoil his first view of you, do we? Wait here until I come for you."

So I stand outside, feeling all eyes upon me, and suddenly feeling nervous. Not about marrying my man, but standing up in front of everyone. *Buck up, Darcy. You can do this.* Cigarette s smoked, watches and phones consulted, one by one the brothers disappear into city hall.

When at last Sam returns, and she's got Drummer with her. He pauses by me and holds out his arm. "Thought you might appreciate some company walking up the aisle."

He's giving me away? Eagerly nodding, I rapidly blink to keep back the tears and link my arms through his, more than appreciating his thoughtfulness. Then it's time, and Drummer and I walk in with Sam and Carmen following, meeting Sophie, Ella, Marcia, and Sandy just inside. My personal escort into the room that's jampacked with bikers and firefighters, and there, in front of the table behind which sits the judge, is my man. Peg.

He turns his head and sees me, and his jaw drops to the floor. His mouth opens and shuts in amazement, and pride shines from his eyes. I focus on him and on no one else, and during the short ceremony barely hear the words that will bind us together.

When the officiant pronounces us man and wife, Peg picks me up and swings me around him, cementing his mouth to mine. All our audience is hooting and hollering. When Peg puts me down he takes my hand, and we walk through the throng. Once outside, Mouse starts waving us into position, and we wait while people around pose for the photographs.

Before the camera clicks the first one, I pull on Peg's hand to get his attention. As he lowers his head, I speak into his ear. "The doctor told me something this morning."

His eyes open wide in concern. "Fuck, Darcy, are you okay? Should you even be here?"

"More than okay, Peg." As his brow creases, I put him out of his misery. "Appears I'm pregnant."

Mouse snaps the first picture as Peg roars, lifting me once again into his arms and swinging me around.

Well, my intention had been to quietly let him know the news I was having difficulty containing, but Peg's so delighted he can't keep it to himself. "My wife's knocked up!"

So pleased myself, I can't admonish him. I only know we've got strange wedding photos to come, with everyone smiling and laughing and me being twirled in the air.

When finally Mouse says he's got enough, I realise there's something I've not properly thought through, when Peg hands me my property cut and leads me to his bike.

"Er, Peg?" I gesture at my dress.

"My woman, my bike." He's grinning. He sits astride, then waits for me to slide my cut on, then holds out his hand. Pulling up my dress as best I can, I sit with it bunched in my lap, making sure it's well away from the wheels, laughing as I expose my bare legs, and hanging on tight to my *husband*. He's right, there's no other way I, as his bride, should be returning to the compound.

Drum waves Peg into pole position, and that's how we go home, at the head of the procession of bikers.

Ma and Sarah have stayed behind to put the finishing touches on the reception I hadn't thought I wanted. But as we walk into the clubroom that's been transformed with decorations, streamers, and banners, I know it's the best I could have had. The other old ladies disappear into the kitchen and start bringing out a huge buffet.

"Eh!" Peg gets to his feet and shouts at Beef. "My wedding. My reception. My fuckin' choice of music."

"Give me a chance, Peg." Beef waves him down. "This one's for you and you're ol' lady."

Peg sharpens his eyes, but I place my hand on his arm.

The music starts to play, and then the whole room is in uproar as Bruce Springsteen starts to sing about the virtues of a Red Headed Woman. Peg glances down, and his mouth quirks, then he cups his hand to his mouth and yells out, "The Boss has got it right!"

I feel myself blushing at some of the lyrics, especially when his brothers start singing along. With my hands over my face, I glance over to where Hammer and Slade are sitting, both with wide grins on their faces. Truck, doing his prospecting duties, is walking around and collecting empty bottles.

When that track, thankfully, finishes, Peg puts something else on, and soon I'm dancing in his arms, gently swaying, so happy, so thankful that in the end I made the right choice.

"You're going to be the death of me, Darcy." Peg gazes into my eyes, his arms tight around me. "Yesterday I thought I'd lost you for good, and today you tell me you're pregnant." I see him wipe moisture away from his cheeks. "You're all I ever wanted, and now you're going to give me the family I was startin' to think I'd never have. You can't imagine what this means to me."

"And to me, too, Peg." I don't have words to express how much he's changed my life, and for the better.

"Hey, you'll have to stop workin'."

"For a while, Peg."

I can see future discussions about that. But won't let it spoil my day.

The song ends. Mindful I'm still recovering from my head injury, Peg sits me down and goes to the bar to get a drink.

Taking the opportunity of seeing me alone, Ma wheels herself over. "Hitched and knocked up." The words might be harsh, but her eyes are twinkling. "You'll be good for him. Peg deserves a good woman by his side."

I wave at the room. "Can't thank you enough, Ma. I know all this was your doing." I notice she looks tired, and wonder whether she's overdone it, feeling guilty all her work was on my behalf. "You okay, Ma?"

"Fit as a fiddle," she replies, and puts her scrawny hand over mine. "I can't tell you how much I've appreciated being part of these boys' world. They've given me months I'd never had had."

"And a lot more to come." She might not have been here long, but already I can't imagine the clubhouse without her.

"Here, Flash. Get some food into you. Need to look after yourself and the babe." Peg sits down beside me. I've already eaten, and now Peg's giving me more? But it looks so delicious I won't be objecting to another plate.

"You look after her, you hear me?" Ma looks him straight in the eye, and then turns her attention to me. "And you look after him. I've got a feeling you two are going to be good for each other."

Peg grins, then looks inside the sandwich he's just taken a bite out of. "Your recipe, Ma?"

"Of course."

"Fuckin' good."

"Well what did you expect. Now, I'm going to leave you young folks to party. It's time for my bed."

Without pause, Peg shouts, "Prospect!" Truck runs up, understands what Peg's asking, and takes the handles of Ma's wheelchair. At her instruction, he takes her around the club-house, and my eyes follow her as she says goodbye to everyone, seeming to pause and have a quiet word with each as she accepts their thanks for arranging tonight's party.

The rest of the evening passes quickly, Peg and I getting separated as so many people want to talk to us and offer their best wishes. When I catch up with Slade and Hammer, our conversation is punctuated by coughs, the only remaining outward sign of the yesterday's incident, as luckily Slade's leg was badly bruised but not broken. When Slade puts his arms around me to give me a hug, I return it.

"So, you're going to keep working after you've had the baby?"

"Of course I am."

"No she's not."

I bat Peg's arm and roll my eyes. "This we'll be talking about later." Then, as he leads me away from my laughing teammates, I add softly, "But I think we've got better things to do tonight."

I'm not surprised when Peg drags me up to the suite not long after.

CHAPTER 44

Peg

I don't know what I did to deserve her. If I was a praying man I'd be sending up thanks. My arm tightens around her as she sleeps, her head resting on my chest. I'm wide awake, trying to process that this is my family beside me.

When I'd watched my brothers finding their old ladies, I'd hoped, but never expected, I'd find my own. I certainly couldn't have predicted coming across my woman, my *one*, as I had, by the side of the road.

We've been through some shit together, and if that didn't break us, nothing will. I'll dedicate the rest of my life to making her happy. Both her and the babe.

She's pregnant. Not planned, though not entirely avoided. It will mean some changes to her job, and some discussion.

But I wouldn't change her, impose my thoughts on her. I'll trust her to do what's best.

I must have eventually dropped off, as it's daylight when I awake to hear a banging on the door to the suite.

Flash is still sleeping, probably still tired after a lack of sleep in the hospital, coupled with the busy day yesterday and our numerous couplings when we got back to my bed, so quietly I ease myself out, strap on my prosthesis, and pull on my jeans.

Truck's at the door looking sombre. I raise my finger to my lips and tell him, "Flash is still asleep."

"Need you to come with, Peg."

"Let me get my boots on."

I'm back in a flash and asking. "What is it Truck?" I start to turn towards the clubhouse, but he's pointing in the opposite direction.

I change course and walk alongside him. "What's going on, man?"

"It's Ma," he replies, and carries on walking.

"Ma?" But by the time I've asked my question, we're arriving at the house we did up for the old woman and her great-granddaughter.

Pushing inside, I hear subdued voices and follow them, finding Drum and Wraith standing around Ma's bed, Sarah sitting by her side holding a frail, bony hand, and Hyde behind her with a supporting hand on her shoulder.

Fearing the worst, I look at Ma's face. She looks like she's sleeping, a small smile playing at her lips. Her face is relaxed but already paling. I look for signs of her chest falling and rising, but she's not breathing. She's left us. *Oh fuck.*

I rest my hand on Sarah's other shoulder and lightly press in my fingers. "I'm so sorry, darlin'."

Sarah looks up at me. "She knew, Peg. She had a long chat with me yesterday. Told me she loved me, which is something she never says. Oh, I knew that she did, it was just something she never vocalised."

It makes me remember how she left Flash and I yesterday, words that could be interpreted as a goodbye and how she made time to speak with everyone. *She knew.*

"And, look." Sarah's still speaking. "She's left this out. I've never seen it before. Didn't realise she'd brought it with her."

She holds out a well-worn book, and as I take it a note flutters out. I catch it before it falls, snatching it up and try to read the scrawling writing. "To the Satan's Devils' women. May you make good use of this and keep feeding my boys." Opening the book, I find it's handwritten, hundreds of recipes Ma must have devised during her long life.

"She's laid out her will." Drum gets my attention, and I see he's holding some papers in his hand. "She's left the land where her house stood to Hyde and Sarah, along with enough cash for rebuilding. And the rest of her money comes to us."

My eyes widen, and I don't know where to look. At Drum, or… "What the fuck, Hyde?"

Hyde sinks down, and crouching, pulls Sarah into his arms. "Ma must have seen this coming."

"You and Sarah?" Wraith questions.

"We haven't talked about it yet," Hyde replies. "But yeah, I was thinking of making her my ol' lady."

Sarah sniffles, chokes back a sob, and then lays her hand over his. "Do I get a choice in this?"

Hyde grins. "Not accordin' to Ma."

It's a private moment we're watching, so I keep quiet and wait for her to respond.

"Gramma was a wise woman."

Then I turn away as Hyde takes her in his arms.

"Well fuck me. That's another vote comin' up." Drum sounds resigned.

"Fallin' like skittles," Wraith observes.

I step back and go stand next to the prez and VP. "Better get a doctor here. Especially if she's made us beneficiaries. Just how much we talkin' here, Prez?"

He points the document he's still holding toward the woman and man who are still clasped together. "Whatever's left after the estate's settled and Sarah and that fucker Hyde get their share. Might be nothing."

But she thought of us. Wanted to repay us for taking her in. She didn't need to do that. I turn and look at the woman on the bed, and then at her great-granddaughter in Hyde's arms. "Old woman's still jerkin' the strings." I smile for the first time since Truck got me up. "She had a good life, and we helped her live it."

"That she did, Peg. That she did." Drummer slaps my back and starts to walk out. "I'll go get a doctor. Mouse will find the one she was seein'. As you say, we've got to take care to get this buttoned up right."

By the time the news has filtered through to everyone, the clubhouse is a muted place. There's no one wheeling themselves over and berating us for infractions real or imagined. No sarcastic comments coming our way. The doctor's been and gone, satisfied it was simply her time. The funeral director's removed her body, and Hyde still hasn't let Sarah out of his sight.

Drummer walks in with Matt Gore beside him. I nod across, knowing Drummer wanted a quick word before formally introducing the new prospect. Personally, I think he'll be a good fit. As I go to the bar to get a drink, Prez brings him up beside me and nods at Truck. "New prospect for you. Show him the ropes?"

Truck's eyes light up, and Fergus gives a nod. It's hard work prospecting, and the more hands the merrier. As Matt goes past me, I say in my sergeant-at-arms voice, "Beer and a soda. Jump to it, man."

With one hand on the bar, Matt jumps over the top, and soon I have two drinks in front of me. I turn away and wink at the Prez.

He grins, then frowns. "Bad shit, Ma going like that."

I've had a while to think about it. "You see that look on her face, Drum? She went happy, can't dispute that. And a couple of months ago it could have been a very different story had Dollar not reminded us she was our neighbour."

"There is that." He orders a whisky, then resumes our conversation. "I was just getting used to having her around."

"Won't get told off for trackin' oil in anymore."

At that moment Sam walks in. "Drum, you clean your boots before you came in?" she throws at him as she walks past.

I spit out the mouthful of beer I've just unfortunately taken and start choking on the little that had gone down the wrong way. Prez slaps my back. "Fuck, Prez," I start when I can speak again. "Think she might still be around."

Drum's staring after Sam with narrowed eyes. "Left a legacy, that's for certain."

"Yeah, about that. We gonna take her money?"

"Mouse has done some investigatin, and Dollar's done some sums. They think it will be around two hundred thou. I suggest we should take it and invest in a new business."

That's a great idea. The more we have coming in legit, the less inclined we'll be to slip back into old habits. "Any ideas?"

Drum shakes his head. "We'll discuss it at the table. Now, I think your *wife* wants you."

Throwing a glance her way, I see Prez is right. She's motioning with her hand, showing she's thirsty.

"Pussy-whipped." Drum chuckles.

"Too right," I agree, and start walking then turn back. "Fuckin' love it."

I leave him chortling, then go over to my *wife* and, as I pass, I hear Hyde and Sarah starting to make plans to rebuild Ma's house. Looking to the future that she's handed to them.

After I've given Flash her drink, and have just raised mine to my lips, Sandy comes over to join us. "Have you seen this, Peg?"

This being the recipe book Ma left behind, I nod.

Sandy's eyes gleam. "It's incredible. I'm going to try some of these at the Wheel Inn. There's stuff here I'd never have thought of. Will certainly bring the customers in. My mouth's already watering just reading about it."

Sophie's looking over her shoulder. "Oh, I fancy that. It looks bloody delicious."

"We got the makings?"

"I believe we have."

"Com'on Soph, let's give it a try." The two women disappear into the kitchen.

Grunt bounces in accompanied by Marcia, Heart, and the babies. Wraith appears and is throwing Olivia up and down in the air, making the toddler giggle and laugh. Jayden arrives with Amy, who immediately runs over and throws her arms around the dog. The arrival of the children lightens the atmosphere some more.

Joker comes in, holding hands with Lady. It's become such a common sight recently no one says anything. He throws a chin lift with me, which I return. Since getting everything out in the open, Joker seems far more relaxed, and sees it as being me who forced the issue.

Prez is heading toward his office, then hearing a shrill shriek spins around and crouches. Eli lets go of Sam's arm and runs to Drum, throwing himself trustingly into his arms.

I look around the room at my brothers, their old ladies, all the children, and not forgetting the fucking dog, coming together and being what I've always called them, a mismatched family.

Remembering not so long ago I used to be on the sidelines, looking at what my brothers had, never thinking I'd be so lucky that it would come to me. I hitch a breath, then reach out my hand and place it on Darcy's flat stomach. She looks down at my arm, then up at my eyes, a slight questioning look on her face as I gaze at her.

Just one word escapes my lips, one word which carries so much meaning. "Mine."

She smiles, and it's like the sun rising on a dark morning as she lays her fingers over my hand, squeezing gently. "Mine."

She'll get no argument from me.

ROCK Bottom

SATAN'S DEVILS #7

Rock

*I've committed the ultimate crime, I've stolen from my MC.
Now, I'm out in bad standing.*

*Cast adrift from all men I called Brother, I join a rival MC.
They have welcomed me and want me to help them take out
the Satan's Devils.*

*Having to start from the bottom as a prospect is a shit job,
but I'm grateful they've given me a new home in exchange
for information about my old club.*

*The Chaos Riders are a completely different type of club,
and as I betray the Devils, I slowly learn the Riders' secrets.
Including what they keep in the basement.*

Becca

I've been kidnapped. Kept chained in this filthy place which reeks of blood. I can't remember the last time I showered or had a change of clothes, and I'm fed only enough to keep me alive.

As time passes, my hope of rescue fades. But then a new man appears bringing me my food and emptying that disgusting bucket I'm forced to use. Could he be my ticket to escape? Or is being a member of this hateful motorcycle club more important than saving me?

SATAN'S DEVILS #7: Rock Bottom

As the youngest sister of the ruling sheikhs of Amahad my life has no significance except what I can bring to the country. A political marriage. To avoid my fate, I've stayed away from the country of my birth, and remained forgotten until it appears someone is looking too closely into my life.

To ensure my protection I reluctantly return to Amahad ignorant that my fate would fall into the hands of a terrorist, nor that I'd meet three men who equally attract me. One I know immediately is submissive, perhaps a yin to my yang as I'm a Domme. Another a Dom and while life with him would be fun, it would be a constant battle for control. The third, a man who doesn't label himself, but dominance pours out of every pore.

Three men who want me. Three men who vow to protect me. Three men who I want. Three men who each want to fulfil all my erotic fantasies.

Spoilt for choice as I'm thrown into a world of violence and terror, each will demonstrate why they are the man for me.

OTHER WORKS BY MANDA MELLETT

All books can be read as a standalone.

Blood Brothers

A series about sexy dominant sheikhs and their bodyguards

- *Stolen Lives* (#1 – Nijad & Cara)

- *Close Protection* (#2 – Jon & Mia)

- *Second Chances* (#3 – Kadar & Zoe)

- *Identity Crisis* (#4 – Sean & Vanessa)

- *Dark Horses* (#5 – Jasim & Janna)

Coming soon:
- *Hard Choices* (#6 – Aiza)

SATAN'S DEVILS MC

- *Turning Wheels* (Blood Brothers #3.5, Satan's Devils #1 – Wraith & Sophie)

- *Drummer's Beat* (# 2 – Drummer & Sam)

- *Slick Running* (#3 – Slick & Ella)

- *Targeting Dart* (#4 – Dart & Alex)

- *Heart Broken* (#5 – Heart & Marc)

- *Peg's Stand* (#6 – Peg & Darcy)

Coming soon:
- *Rock Bottom* (#7 – Rock & Becca)

Sign up for my newsletter to hear about new releases in the Blood Brothers and Satan's Devils series:
http://eepurl.com/b1PXO5

ACKNOWLEDGEMENTS

I visited Tucson a year after the Aspen fire, and went to Summerhaven. Still got a wind chime I bought in the rebuilt gift shop. While I never expected to write about a wildfire, the memories must have stuck in my mind. Some years later, my brother was living in Escondido, California, and was evacuated due to fire. It came pretty close, but luckily didn't reach their house. I was in regular communication with him, as, at the time, it seemed very likely it would take his home. It was pretty scary stuff, even watching from across the other side of the Atlantic.

Gradually it dawned on me that I could have the Satan's Devils up against not a human enemy, but a natural one. But what do I know about firefighting, and particularly in America?

I have to stress this is a work of fiction, and isn't meant to be a factual account of a real fire, and some things I've added which are pure fiction just to make the story flow. I've had some help from firefighters, and in particular, need to extend my thanks to the Tucson Fire Department. Anything I've got right is down to them, what I've got wrong is entirely down to me. Some things are accurate and local to Tucson, like the shift patterns firefighters work, and the fact urban teams are trained to support wildland firefighting.

I again had amazing help from my team of beta readers, and am so grateful to all of them. Mary, Danena, Colleen, Sheri, Terra, and Zoe, and of course, not forgetting Nicole, who not only beta read, but had won a competition to be featured in one of my books. So please, stand and take a bow, beta team.

Steve, my wonderful husband needs a mention. He not only read an early version of Peg's Stand, but he's always been supportive, and understands if he's talking to me, and I don't reply, I'm listening to those voices in my head.

Thanks once again to Brian Tedesco, my editor, who wants me to explain any typos left in the book are apparently down to his three-legged cat who likes jumping on his keyboard while he's proofreading. Must be the best excuse I've ever heard. It's important to me I've an editor who I can relate to and share a laugh with, and Brian's certainly that. Always enjoy working with you, Brian.

Lia Rees. What can I say? Lia's inspiration has taken my limited suggestion of 'can we see more of the models?', and turned it into an amazing revamp of the Satan's Devils covers. I'm so happy with them, and it's given each book greater individuality. So thank you, again, Lia, and for the great work you do on formatting.

Then there's Deb Carroll, who keeps me on the right track, always there to give advice and pimp me. Love working with you, Deb.

Thank you Sara Parr for last minute proofreading.

But the greatest thanks of all go to each and everyone of you who've bought or read my books on Kindle Unlimited. I know many are still taking a chance on a relatively new writer, and I love hearing what you think, and particularly if you take the time to write a review. I can't express how important reviews are to a writer.

I'm asked many times if this series is ending, and like to assure you it's not. I've got plenty of ideas to keep going for a while.

So it's goodbye, but only for now, but there'll be another Devil coming soon.

STAY IN TOUCH

Email: manda@mandamellett.com
Website: www.mandamellett.com

Connect with me on Facebook:
https://www.facebook.com/mandamellett

Sign up for my newsletter to hear about new releases in the
Blood Brothers and Satan's Devils series:

http://eepurl.com/b1PXO5

ABOUT THE AUTHOR

After commuting for too many years to London working in various senior management roles, Manda Mellett left the rat race and now fulfils her dream and writes full time. She draws on her background in psychology, the experience of working in different disciplines and personal life experiences in her books.

Manda lives in the beautiful countryside of North Essex with her husband and two slightly nutty Irish Setters. Walking her dogs gives her the thinking time to come up with plots for her novels, and she often dictates ideas onto her phone on the move, while looking over her shoulder hoping no one is around to listen to her. Manda's other main hobby is reading, and she devours as many books as she can.

Her biggest fan is her gay son (every mother should have one!). Her favourite pastime when he is home is the late night chatting sessions they enjoy, where no topic is taboo, and usually accompanied by a bottle of wine or two.

Photo by Carmel Jane Photography